STAFF
PICKS
PRESS

Kateri

Lily of the Mohawks

Kateri

Lily of the Mohawks

JACK CASEY

STAFF PICKS PRESS
ALBANY, NY

First Edition

Cover design by Jenny Kemp and Jenn Peyser
Book design by Jessika Hazelton

Published by Staff Picks Press
The Book House of Stuyvesant Plaza
1475 Western Ave. Albany, NY 12203

To order additional copies of this title,
contact your favorite local bookstore or visit www.staffpickspress.com

ISBN: 978-1-935680-031

For Anne,
whose help with this was heavensent

Acknowledgements

I wish to thank my children who accompanied me into the fortress of solitude last Christmas when I reopened this story and encountered once again a deep and lonely heart of darkness. Watching them grow and learn to love and to seek justice – Molly in the law and John in literature – confirms me in my faith, and gives me great hope for our future.

I wish to thank Anne Malaney, to whom I dedicate this book. Her conversion this spring inspired me as I imagined Kateri first embracing "the Prayer." Anne generously shared her time and her unique sensibility in helping me frame this story, craft dialogue and weave in source material to widen points of view. Her patience and diligence as editor has resulted in its readability and freedom from many of my idiosyncracies. For those that remain we'll hold her harmless.

Thanks are due to Dawn Weinraub for her painstaking translation of Claude Chauchetière's impenetrable French prose. While it was a great thrill to find his unpublished handwritten autobiography in the Jesuit archives in Montreal, it was only Dawn's quick turnaround that allowed me to explore Father Claude's deep spiritual doubt in order to explain his sublime and rapturous devotion to Kateri after her death.

Jennifer Peyser has designed covers for three of my novels and her instinct in creating the "feel" I wish to communicate in prose has always been infallible, but never so deeply as here. Jenn created the haunting image that appears on the cover of this work, communicating, I think, the solitude, the humility, the integrity and the holiness of Kateri as she looks out over the river valley of her native land.

As for influences, let me pause to thank my grandmother, Molly Costello Casey, a humble immigrant from Tipperary who took time to hold a little boy in her lap and tell him stories about the magic times, about giants and gnomes and billy goats gruff, and stories from the bible

– Adam and Eve, David and Goliath, Jonah and the whale, the plagues of Egypt – and, of course, the lives of the saints.

Thanks to her son, my father, Justice John T. Casey, who imparted to me many of the more difficult lessons about the spirit and the letter of the law. Thanks as well to my mother, Dorothy Carroll Casey, who used to sigh watching the Sisters of Charity playing badminton in their winged bonnets as she raised her five rowdy sons and her lone precious daughter. She is with Kateri now.

Let me acknowledge also the many spiritual women and men who have guided me for six decades, some of whom are still with us: the Sisters of Mercy at St. Paul the Apostle, particularly Sister Edna and Sister Cecilia; the Christian brothers of La Salle Institute, especially Brother James Romond, who lived always in a remarkably saintly aura; the priests of my parishes and spiritual advisors, Monsignor Daniel Horan and Father Joseph Barker of St. Paul's, Rev. William Sloane Coffin at Yale, Father Donald Ophals at St. Francis de Sales, Father John Prevost at St. Henry's and now Father Mario F. Julian, O.F.M., of St. Anthony of Padua in Troy.

Let me thank our current spiritual leaders, too, Bishop Howard Hubbard who has steadily piloted our Albany Diocese—Kateri's own—through some stormy seas, and Timothy Cardinal Dolan, elevated recently to lead us in our faith. Their task is so very lonely and often so unappreciated. Now they can look for guidance and strength and comfort to our resident saint, our own pure Lily of the Mohawks.

And finally, let me thank you, the reader, for your curiosity, your belief, your faith. We all live and work and grow in each other's sight and your selecting this volume completes my act of authorship, a role I consider my sacred calling. May Kateri's canonization comfort us all in our individual journeys wheresoever we are called, and bring us all collectively to ever higher plateaus of peace and enlightenment.

Contents

Book III: Father Claude Chauchetière

Foreword

As you open this version of Kateri's story, let me share some thoughts on how and why I am offering it.

I first heard of Kateri Tekakwitha in the hoarse whisperings of an old nun who lingered long on the gnawing of fingers and the amputation of Isaac Jogues's thumb. I was born and raised where the waters of the Mohawk flow into the Hudson, and Kateri, Isaac Jogues, René Goupil and Jean de le Lande were figures of our misty local folklore. As children, we took field trips to Kateri's birthplace, and the nuns taught us to pray to her for guidance and grace.

After Kateri's beatification three decades ago, I researched her life and published *Lily of the Mohawks*. To make the novel work dramatically, I took liberties with facts and blended historical figures into composites, filling with imagination and authorial license many of the empty spaces my research left. I was in my thirties, and encountering so deeply this shy, half-blind orphan as I was becoming a father and entering the practice of law, I was struck how her inner resolve transmuted Mohawk stoicism into Christian virtue.

Father Claude Chauchetière, one of her biographers, celebrated her spiritual strengths. He personally witnessed her piety, her quiet, humble devotion, her unyielding integrity while she lived, and her transfiguration as she passed from this life into the next. Father Claude's encounter with Kateri healed a deep spiritual wound that had crippled him and so, wishing to share her gifts with others, he began using her relics to effect cures. He wrote her biography and painted her portrait—the portrait that appears in sepia on the back cover of this book—to give permanent testimony to her holiness.

In her own short life Kateri found inner peace and achieved, by the accounts of both Chauchetière and Father Pierre Cholonec, a mystical union with God. Neither the cruelties of nature nor the brutalities of her

culture ever broke her, or even deterred her, and her holy life still shines
with a pure and steady light out of the darkness.

In the years after publishing the novel, I visited Kateri's shrine at
Kanawaka many times. I often turned to her to strengthen my resolve and
to meet life, not as it appears or as I want it to be, but as it truly is. Kateri
answered my prayers in quiet, subtle ways.

The news last December that Pope Benedict XVI would elevate this
humble Iroquois maiden into the pantheon of Catholic saints encouraged
me to revisit her story. Since my earlier book appeared, anthropological
work had expanded our knowledge about the great Iroquois League, about
Kateri's Mohawks, easternmost of the league's five nations, and about her
sanctity. I avidly read these new works. They showed me with greater
clarity what I'd seen before, and their diligent footnotes helped me locate
primary source material, Father Claude Chauchetière's handwritten
autobiography in the Jesuit archives at Montreal, for example. My recent
completion of some life tasks sent me back to the gospels and the rituals
of my youth, and I knew I must paint her portrait, as Father Claude did
so long ago, using fresh colors and new points of view.

Apart from her celebrated spiritual gifts, Kateri Tekakwitha appears
in history as a unique and pivotal character in the European imperialists'
systematic destruction of Native American cultures. Holland, England
and France all sought to penetrate her Iroquois homeland. Born in the
easternmost village of the great league, Tekakwitha felt the full brunt of
these European seductions and incursions, the lure of their trade and
liquor, the carnage of their plagues and bloody wars. Until she turned to
the Jesuit missionaries, Kateri lived a retiring, solitary life in her uncle's
cabin. After she converted, her path was inextricably bound to those
bold Jesuits who'd left the universities and cathedrals and seminaries
of post-Renaissance France to brave the stormy Atlantic and bring
the message of Christ to tribes living in the Stone Age. The struggles
of three European crowns to dominate this land brought bloodshed,
tragedy and death that tore open Kateri's life, and she responded by
embracing her conqueror's deity. Forgive them, Father, for they know
not what they do.

Today the politically correct may deny the harshness of America
during this epoch, but all contemporary records give it shape and voice.
The heroic Jesuits faced violent native practices not as we do, mere verbal
accounts to be believed or disbelieved, but as smoking war hatchets and

scalping knives and gauntlets to run and torture platforms and flaming holocaust offerings to Aireskou, the Iroquois god of sun and war.

Quite apart from the motives of their king and the military force of their governor, the Jesuits' gentle civilizing influence on the Iroquois calmed the violence and brutality, and channeled their energies into paths of virtue. Only the Jesuits saw these fierce natives as human beings, as God's children, with immortal souls, not to be conquered and run off their land, but to be loved and taught in order to cultivate their goodness and virtue and guide them into paths of peace and redemption.

Without the Jesuits, Kateri would have lived and died an anonymous Mohawk. To tell her story accurately, then, we must view her alongside the missionaries who influenced and converted her. This realization suggested a new way for me to present her drama. Last winter I imagined this story as a three-sided altarpiece, a triptych, like those painted in the Middle Ages to teach bible stories and lives of the saints to the unlettered. You can easily see my purpose if you imagine this work in such a form, a triptych, and it will help you understand why you won't meet Kateri until the story is far advanced. We must ready the earth before our lily can bloom.

Father Isaac Jogues occupies the first panel, Book I. Captured and tortured by the Iroquois, he displays unfailing courage and superhuman forgiveness as the Mohawks murder his companion and enslave him. We thrill at his daring escape, and we know when he returns as an emissary of peace that martyrdom is only a matter of time. Yet, we hope, even as the Mohawks tomahawk and behead him, that his gentleness and Christian forgiveness will not perish from this land.

Tekakwitha occupies the central panel, Book II. Born ten years after Jogues's murder, she copes with the ravages of the white man's smallpox which orphan, scar and nearly blind her. She lives quietly in her uncle's cabin, fleeing into the forests in terror when the French attack and burn her village in 1666, and then helping her warriors fight off the Mohican attack of 1669.

Three thousand miles away, another orphan, Claude Chauchetiére, fastens on the heroism of Jogues to lift himself out of a spiritual agony. He joins the Jesuits and, seeking obscurity and a personal union with God, volunteers for the missions. He sails to New France, then paddles upriver to St. Francis Xavier mission near Montreal where Kateri, likewise fleeing her homeland, soon arrives. These two spiritual refugees help each other achieve higher levels of enlightenment. Father Claude attends her during her final illness and carries the Eucharist to her deathbed. The miracle he witnesses at her dying gives him the spiritual solace he has searched for in books, in the wilderness of New France, and in his own shivering heart.

The final, smallest panel of the triptych, the denouement, portrays Father Claude after Kateri's death. He chronicles her return to this world in heavenly visions. He begins to effect healings and cures with her relics. He casts a jaundiced eye toward the continual warfare and the arrogance of his governor and bishop as he retires to a humble log rectory in Montreal. With unflagging devotion he writes Kateri's biography and paints her portrait and he continues to spread news about her miraculous cures until his death on the twenty-ninth anniversary of hers.

I believe this three-fold treatment, a classic trilogy, gives the story of Kateri Tekakwitha the perspective it deserves historically and thematically. I have carefully followed the ample source material and I have striven to be true to the many characters who populate this time and place, as well as to their value systems that clashed so violently. As a novel, this is a dramatization, yes, but it is not make-believe. If there is any doubt about the power of Kateri's intercession, read accounts of young Jake Finkbonner's cure which recently propelled her to sainthood. View online the pictures of his face before his family prayed to her. Modern doctors with all their sorceries can't explain his cure, but Father Claude can.

And so, as we approach Kateri's canonization, let me recede into the background and commend to you this new account of her life. Writing it has helped me explore once again who she was and what her short, often tragic, but always heroic life meant then, and means to us still. I hope this narrative will help you appreciate Kateri's continued presence in our world, and that her elevation to sainthood this October 21 will encourage us all to look forward with faith, as Father Claude did for twenty-nine solitary years, to encountering her in the next.

Troy, New York
July 14, 2012

– JACK CASEY

FATHER ISAAC JOGUES, S. J.

FOUNDER OF THE IROQUOIS MISSION,

Killed near Auriesville, N. Y., October 18, 1646.

Saint Isaac Jogues, S. J.

Martyred at Ossernenon in the Land of the People of Flint
October 18, 1646

Nautæ fuis infensum vitijs in deser=
tam Insulam expofituri, fubito vento re=
pelluntur, ac inuiti licet ad Cyprum uehunt.

25

Voyages Of Faith

From safe European havens, Jesuit missionaries embarked in small boats onto
stormy seas to carry the word of Jesus Christ into lands around the globe

Book I

Father Isaac Jogues
(1642 - 1646)

"I am the good shepherd.
I know mine and mine know me,
as the Father knows me and I know the Father;
I will lay down my life for my sheep."

— JOHN, 10:14-15

Chapter 1

Mohawks Ambush Father Jogues As He Returns To the Land Of the Hurons

ALL LAY READY FOR THE TRIP UPRIVER. Huron guides strapped luggage to the tholes and rib work of fifteen bark canoes. In those bundles the priest and his *donnes* packed a year's supply of wheat for hosts, wine for the chalice, vestments and beeswax candles for saying mass. Laymen packed goods for trade—hatchets, kettles, beads and cloth that purchased elk robes and beaver skins to bring a good price next year in Quebec. They carried, too, letters from loved ones in France, and books, precious books to read among the unlettered Hurons.

Darkly the river glided past the mud bank where the stockade of Trois-Rivières rose in the gloom. A light shone from a small log chapel on the verge of the forest. In the chapel, the missionary band of forty knelt in candlelight as Father Isaac Jogues held the host between his thumbs and forefingers: "*Hoc est enim corpus meam.* This is my body which is to be given up for you." Natives and Frenchman bowed reverently and prayed for safe passage through lands of the Iroquois.

Out they came, after the mass, in the soft ringing of the bell. The eastern sky was blushing and birds calling happily, beating alive the bosoms of maple and oak. It was the first of August in a full bloom of summer along the river.

Eustace Ahatsistari, a massive Huron chief, gave his signal and the other Huron guides slid the canoes down the mud, floating and balancing them in the water. All of the band, native and French alike, even little Theresa, hunkered down upon the grass for a word of farewell. Eustace spoke:

"We have been to the mass and we have prayed for safe journeying. I add only this: If I fall into the hands of the Iroquois, they will surely kill me because of the many war parties I led against them. As they torture and burn me, I shall remind them that Dutch palefaces give them only the gin that destroys from within. Our priests bring news of the one true God who made all things, of the fire beneath the earth made ready for the wicked, and of the holy place in heaven where our souls will rise at last, freed from all suffering. If they capture me, I will invite them to inflict their utmost cruelties upon my body, for they will never kill my soul."

Eustace turned to Steven, his second-in-command: "If I am captured and you escape, my brother, visit my kinsmen and tell them they must accept this faith, and become followers of God in Whom I wish to live and die."

"I will do this," Steven promised and waved his brawny arm, "and so will these others."

Nodding assent, the natives stood, large, strong men, hardened from life in the wilds. Beams of sunlight were penetrating through the trees, sparkling on the water as in they waded.

Father Jogues stood too. He was a small, slender man of great intellect and refinement, prematurely bald at thirty-five. He moved with grace and gentle confidence in the black soutane and he boarded the second canoe. His hazel eyes surveyed his expedition favorably. Six years he had served in the Huron missions, a thousand miles inland from Quebec. Earlier in the summer he'd brought old Father Raymbault down to die. With supplies and reinforcements, he was now returning to his Mission of Sainte

Marie, and also ferrying home three children from their study with the nuns. Favorable news preceded his journey. A fleet of French shallops carrying soldiers and engineers, they heard, was on its way from Quebec to raise a fort where the waters of Lake Champlain poured into the St. Lawrence. Reports that Iroquois had fled before this force encouraged Jogues to set out on this day—the day after the feast of Loyola—and slip through their ambushes.

Eustace gave the signal, "Hiii-yeee-hah! Hiii-ro!" and they started upriver.

All day they paddled against the current. They knelt on fur rugs set on the ribs of the canoes and threw their backs and shoulders into the work. Ahead lay three weeks of paddling twelve and fourteen hours a day, rain and sun alike, the rigor broken only by portages, hauling loaded canoes up steep paths while the river roared and thrashed on the boulders below.

"This first day has been favorable to us," Father Jogues announced that evening at the campfire as they were hunkered down, eating corn mush from the kettle. "We covered at least ten leagues."

"Let us now, Father, choose our course for tomorrow." Eustace drew with a stick in the dirt. "We may pass along the open waters in the center of the river, a longer but safer course, or we can move through the defiles on the north shore, a shorter and more direct route. These islands to either side of the channel, though, might conceal Iroquois."

In the firelight they debated the likelihood of an ambush, Father Jogues and Eustace and the stout, swarthy William Couture, a carpenter. Couture's opinion that the Iroquois had fled before the French shallops encouraged them. He had friends among the soldiers and engineers. "They will see the ships and hear the songs of the mariners, and vanish into the forest like mist."

"Can we be sure?" young René Goupil asked.

"Nothing is ever sure," Couture replied.

They decided to take the shorter, bolder way.

"We will advance tomorrow along the most direct route," Eustace concluded, "and will cover even more distance than today."

After this council, Father Jogues left the circle of firelight to walk along the sand. A crescent moon sparkled in the flowing water. He prayed. Six years before he had made this journey, a stranger into the wild heart of this land. So much had changed. Six years ago he was tender, apprehensive at carrying his faith to natives. He'd converted many since then. He'd seen many horrors and he knew well the customs and the land. He prayed tonight in thanksgiving for the chance to return to the Hurons and to win souls for heaven. He prayed, also, for those entrusted to his care, little Theresa, disconsolate at leaving the nuns, for her cousins Luke and Matthew, and the three old men, and the Huron warriors, too. They were such good and pious men when they turned from superstition and war. He prayed fervently for safe passage. Yet as he turned his mind to the future, he recalled a meditation from last Easter. Had it been a prophecy? He shivered, considering it might.

He was praying on Good Friday in the log chapel at the Mission of Sainte Marie. He was kneeling before the altar in adoration of Christ hanging crucified above the tabernacle. He knew now the sufferings of Christ for he had witnessed torture firsthand. The Hurons had captured an Iroquois chief, an Oneida, and "caressed" him in their manner of welcoming prisoners. Father Jogues baptized the screaming, sweating chief while they burned him at the stake.

With the horrors of the Oneida chief's torture in mind last Easter, Father Jogues convulsed in the deepest chamber of his heart. He bowed his forehead until it touched the smooth wood of the prie dieu: "I offer You my body, O Lord, my soul and my will. Let me be Your sacrifice. Do with me as You please." He meant this pledge sincerely, yet he wondered—did he possess the courage to follow the crucified Christ Jesus? Perhaps his offer was just an empty vanity? Or the work of the devil? He felt a soft flutter of dove wings at his ear that day:

"Your prayer is heard," a voice whispered. "Be comforted and strong of heart. It will be done as you ask."

Moonlight sparkled on the river and a gentle breeze sighed in the pine. Jogues knelt upon the sand and spread his arms to embrace the water and the forest in the moonlight. Tonight, his first again in the wild, he foresaw the agony, the numbing hardships of the journey ahead. And when he arrived? The squalor of the Huron villages, the lean winter months as Hurons slaughtered their dogs when the game vanished, and he could offer only his meager "bread of life," wheat hosts to starving natives. He murmured a prayer then:

"Help me understand the mystery of Your crucifixion, O Lord. I will endure all hardships to save these good people from the devils who now hold sway in this land. As You sweat blood in the garden the night You were betrayed, let me follow You through the portals of human endurance and glimpse what lies beyond as You did when You cried in Your agony: 'Father, Father, why have You forsaken me?' This is my prayer. Grant it or deny it, O Lord, but fortify me as I proceed and lead these people to You."

He sensed someone nearby.

"Father?" It was René Goupil, a slender young lay brother trained as a surgeon. Jogues stood up and went to him. René was trembling. "I know I need my rest for the journey, Father, but I cannot sleep. The forest seems filled with wild beasts tonight, and I worry they will devour me."

The priest put his arm about the young man's shoulder. "Pray as I do, René. Prayer will remove your fear."

Father Jogues led him back to the glowing embers of the campfire where the men were already snoring. They found their blankets and wrapped them against the flies and mosquitoes.

After a hasty breakfast, they embarked next morning, paddling with confidence. Soon the north side of the river closed in upon them. The sun rose and they glided into a shady narrow channel between the mainland and a long rocky island. They paddled steadily on. At midmorning, Eustace signaled for the flotilla to pull ashore. He had seen broken reeds, and tracks from moccasins in the mud. He pointed them out with his paddle.

"Iroquois?" Father Jogues asked, as they inspected the large footprints.

"Perhaps," Eustace said. His face betrayed little of his agitation.

"Shall we go on?" Steven asked.

"It seems to be a single canoe," Eustace said. "Three or four men at most. We should not be alarmed."

With such bold words and a fearless expression Eustace sought to instill courage in the others, yet when they returned to the river, they all paddled in quiet, alert for a sign of the Iroquois.

Then it came, a heart-stopping war cry—"Aiyeeeee!" Alive sprang the forest with arrows and musket explosions. "Aiyeeeee!" Ahead, three canoes blocked their passage. With quick back paddling, they spun, but four canoes to the rear closed off escape. In confusion their single file broke and they made for shore, paddling as furiously as birds from the hunter.

Loudly, wildly, triumphantly the Iroquois closed in. Their chilling cries and musket blasts scattered the missionary party. Atieronhonk, pilot of Jogues's canoe, held up a bleeding hand. "The bees are stinging, Father. I would like the baptism now." He'd been receiving instruction but was still months away from the sacrament.

"Do you accept the Prayer?" Father Jogues asked. More gunshots and war cries.

"I do." Atieronhonk bowed as the priest cupped his hand and drew up river water to dribble on his forehead. They both resumed paddling as the priest spoke:

"I baptize thee in the name of the Father and of the Son and of the Holy Spirit, Amen. From this moment forth you shall be called Bernard."

Another volley of shots barked from re-loaded guns. The Iroquois pursued, smacking the paddles against the sides of their canoes between strokes and screaming their high-pitched war whoop.

"The bay! Make for the bay!" Eustace cried, diagonally cutting to a tranquil landing place of reeds and willows. One by one the canoes ran aground, men young and old spilling over the gunwales, splashing up the bank, running and tumbling into the forest to hide. Jogues helped the old men from the canoes. He made sure little Theresa was protected by her uncle, and the boys, too. Since his holy vows forbade fighting, he waded into a marsh of long grass to wait.

As the others fled into the forest, the Huron warriors, Eustace and Joseph and Steven and Paul, drew a battle line upon the shore to repel the landing Iroquois. Yet behind them, out of the forest shadows, came faces hideous with war paint—red and black and yellow—Iroquois who'd run to meet them, a dozen big men with bulging muscles, arquebuses, hatchets and war clubs. They were dressed only in loincloths and moccasins. Their rooster combs of hair stood straight up from bald heads. Eustace attacked with his tomahawk and cut his way through the Iroquois line and fled into the forest. Joseph and Steven and Paul fell and the Iroquois pounced. René, too, flailing his arms, fell under the blows of their war clubs.

Peering through the reeds, Father Jogues murmured a prayer as the Iroquois carried René into the forest. He watched as the Iroquois attackers beat the Huron converts, hauled them up and pushed them into the shadows. If he remained motionless, he might escape, yet he could not abandon René or Couture or the un-baptized Hurons.

Father Jogues stood and called to the Iroquois who guarded René: "I am father to these you have taken." He spread his arms. "Because of my blackrobe they call me 'Ondessonk' (Bird of Prey)."

The warrior raised his spear as Father Jogues waded out of the reeds. He approached, grunted suspiciously, circled the priest expecting a trick.

"Please do not hurt him," Father Jogues held up his hands. He spoke in Huron, a variant of the root Iroquois language. "René is gentle and will do as you say."

The warrior sprang upon the priest. Other Iroquois came running back. They fell upon Jogues and beat him with fists and war clubs on the head and the shoulders. They knocked him down and stripped off his black robe and dragged him and René to where the others huddled at the base of a pine tree. One of the warriors produced leather thongs to tie his legs so he might not run.

"No. Please. You don't need to tie me." His quiet authority assured them of the truth of his words. "I will stay with my people as long as you hold them."

The Iroquois warriors scowled, grunted something and left to pursue others.

René's eyes were wide with fear: "O, Father! What will happen to us now?"

"Let us trust in Our Lord God who has allowed this to occur," Father Jogues said. He walked over to the Hurons who were securely tied hand and foot. "We cannot know His will, but we must accept it. What He has done must be good in His eyes. Blessed be His holy name!"

The converts nodded, but fear quickened in their eyes. The priest turned around to the noise of others. Out of the forest the Iroquois led a small band, two old men and little Theresa, dazed, and the two boys who wailed in terror as the Iroquois prodded them along. Then more loud shrieks and whoops. Out from the shadows more Iroquois marched, exultant as they led Eustace, bloody and bound with leather straps.

"It is Ahatsistari, the Huron!" one cried. "Ondessonk and

Ahatsistari! Our devil smiles upon us today!" As they showered kicks and blows upon Eustace, he walked with pride, undaunted, into the midst of the captives.

"Eustace!" René cried in despair, "They've caught you too?"

"Do your worst to me!" Eustace taunted to his captors. One hit him with the butt of his arquebus and opened up his eyebrow. "I laugh at you," he spit, "and I laugh at pain!" Another hit him on the head with a war club and staggered him.

"Please, Eustace," Father Jogues said, "don't insult them." He went to Eustace to show the Iroquois he controlled this chief.

"I have given you my oath, Father, and I will honor it."

Roughly the Iroquois hauled Father Jogues away from him, threw Eustace to the ground and bound him more securely.

Another rousing war cry and out of the forest the Iroquois led the muscular Couture. Jogues rushed to him, threw his arm around William's neck and kissed his forehead to show them he, too, was under his protection.

"I killed one of their chiefs," William said. As he spoke, four Iroquois were hauling their dead chief from the forest. "They will surely burn me now!"

"Have courage," Father Jogues said. "God has willed this. We must accept it."

"I will pray for His grace."

One of the captors, seeing Jogues kiss the murderer of his chief, pulled the priest from Couture and beat him. Jogues raised his arms to ward off the blows. Others joined in the beating, flailing at the priest with clubs and muskets about his head and his shoulders till he sank to the earth. They kicked him. Two of the younger Iroquois grabbed his hands and pulled out his fingernails with their teeth. They took his forefingers in their mouths and crushed them, too, mutilating his fingers to the bone so he could not untie his bonds.

"Father!" René cried nearby as they were doing the same to him. "They're chewing my fingers!"

"Pray, my son!"

"Why are they doing this?"

"It is God's will."

The leader of the Iroquois then arrived, a massive man whose face was painted in stripes of red and yellow and black. With short words and a few grunts he congratulated his warriors.

"For a year we have sought French prisoners to offer Aireskou. Now we have the brave Ahatsistari of the Hurons, and Ondessonk, the blackrobe. Well done!"

"We killed two Huron," one added.

"We have taken twenty-three as captives!" another called proudly.

"Fifteen escaped, Father!" René whispered, clenching his mangled hands.

"May they be safe," the priest said. His head and his hands were bleeding and, stripped of his black robe, he was dressed only in a linen shirt and drawers.

"Let us split their baggage," the chief said. "Let us lead them to our land and burn them as offerings to Aireskou, and as a warning to other French."

"I know him, the leader," Eustace whispered. "He is Huron. He was at the mission of Sainte Marie with us. You called him 'Mathurin's Man,' Father, because he assisted your laborer Mathurin."

"I remember him," Jogues said.

"That's how he knows you and knows me. The Mohawks captured him, adopted him and now he brings us to them as war trophies."

"Surely he will be merciful," Jogues whispered.

"Surely he will not," Eustace said. "He must show them how fiercely he hates us."

The Iroquois were swaggering among the beached canoes and the subdued prisoners, pulling apart their packs. For days they'd been lying in wait for such a party, and now they ransacked the bundles stowed in the canoes and paraded about, wrapping themselves grandiosely in the bolts of cloth and the vestments. They ripped up precious missals and bibles and books and broke into casks of wine and drank with hilarity, throwing out their arrogant chests and calling attention to their bravery.

Eustace and Steven and the others sat quietly, refusing to show fear. One of the old men, though, was annoyed and he called out:

"Your Lord blesses us indeed, Ondessonk. Praise be to His glory! He chooses for us the best captors a man could wish." It was irony from the old Huron. "These are Mohawks, the fiercest of the five Iroquois nations. No one tortures and kills with greater skill than the Mohawks. How lucky we are! How blessed! They know how to wring a death song from a dying man, and roast him and eat him with the appetites of wolves."

"Silence, old one," his guard growled. "Silence, or I'll split your skull." The guard brandished one of the shiny new hatchets he'd retrieved from the luggage.

"Do your worst to me," the old man spat at him. "The priest tells me of a happy land that awaits. Better I go there now than burn in your land."

"Silence!" The guard held him by the throat and waved the hatchet high.

"Speak to the old man, Father," René urged. "His sharp tongue will enrage them against us."

"Please," Father Jogues gently stepped between the old man and the guard. "You cannot enter heaven until I baptize you. Are you ready to accept God?"

"I'll accept anyone who will save me from the Mohawks!"

"Bow your head, then." Father Jogues stooped to a puddle of standing water. With his cupped hand he dripped water on the old man's head. "I baptize thee in the name of the Father, and of the Son, and of the Holy Spirit, Amen."

The man nodded, then returned to his taunts:

"Now I am assured of great reward, so do your worst."

The Mohawk guard grunted and lifted him to his feet.

"Easy there, idiot," the old man complained. "I am old and frail and of use to no one. Leave me here. Do you think I wish to go visiting new lands?"

The Mohawk called to another for help. They were now readying the prisoners for transport. Father Jogues whispered: "Do as they say. It's your only chance."

"No, no, no," the old man laughed. "Don't you know what awaits you? Far better is it to die here than be dragged along for days, beaten to catch up, then prodded to ascend the scaffold and tortured and burned all night. Death is the only certainty, and better that it come now." He turned to his captors and he spat on them. "Leave me here, you cowards! I am too old. Kill me now and finish it!"

The second Mohawk drew his hatchet and buried it in the old man's skull. The old man's eyes rolled back into his head and he sank to the ground. Deftly the Mohawk scalped him, muttering, "Rare is the man who gets what he asks for."

Jogues was beside the corpse praying. Brusquely the two Mohawks lifted him and carried him toward the water. "Come, Ondessonk, counsel your companions. This one is beyond your help. Tell the others not to resist."

The Mohawks lifted the other captives, too, hands bound with leather thongs, and shoved them down the bank. The Frenchmen and the children strove not to look at the bloody corpse of the old one, but the Huron warriors looked at it and laughed with scorn. "He was old!" one said. "Weak and filled with complaints."

Down the bank they were pushed and then lifted into the canoes. When all were aboard, Mathurin's Man gave a signal and the canoes glided out of the bay, across the channel between two islands, then out onto the sunny, broad expanse of the St. Lawrence.

The Mohawks paddled strongly for six hours, twenty canoes in all, overloaded with prisoners and baggage, until they reached the confluence of rivers the French called Sorel, a site for their fort. The ships Couture spoke about had not yet arrived with engineers and soldiers. Boasting and arrogant, the Mohawks beached their canoes and shoved the prisoners up a steep hill. Once there, they lit their fires and slung their kettles.

As they were preparing the evening meal, one of the Mohawks stripped a great sheet of bark from a tree and he and two others painted heads upon it, twenty-two faces in red for those captured, Eustace, Steven, Paul, and in smaller heads, Theresa and the boys. They painted three heads in black for those killed, the two in battle and the old man. They held up this great cartoon to the laughter and applause of those around the fire, then they hung the sheet of bark from a branch, a defiant boast to anyone passing that intrusions into this land would be severely punished.

After their meal, the Mohawks lay upon the ground and soon were snoring. Father Jogues crept near to René who was weeping with fear.

"What will happen to us, Father?" He had curled his mangled fingers together.

"We are in the hands of God now. Trust in Him."

"I'm trying, Father."

Beside him was little Theresa and the two Huron lads. Their faces were stoic. Unable to penetrate their feelings, the priest crept back to his resting place. He gazed up through the great pines, into the impenetrable stars. He breathed easily and implored God, "Deliver us, O Lord," but accepting how things stood, he ended his prayer with, "Thy will and not mine be done."

13

Chapter 2

✣

The Mohawks Bring Father Jogues
and His Followers Into Their Land Of Flint

Onward the Mohawks drove their captives, up the path, above the foaming rapids. Starved and beaten, the prisoners' untreated head wounds and gnawed fingers were infested with flies and mosquitoes. When the water leveled off at the top, they slid their canoes into the river and paddled upstream until the next set of rapids where they disembarked, and hauled the canoes in portage uphill once more.

Prevented by illness from taking his vows the previous year, the frail René trained as a surgeon. On the second night in the camp, he administered to Father Jogues and then he went among the Hurons to dress their wounds. One of the Mohawks lay groaning from wounds he had suffered during the capture, and René approached him timidly. Mathurin's Man signaled that he might treat the wounded Mohawk. Using a sharpened stick, René opened his vein to bleed him and relieve the pressure. René then dressed the wound and sat with the warrior until he slept. Observing this charity, in the canoe the next day, Father Jogues asked if there was anything he might do for René's benefit.

"Yes, Father, there is. I have long wished to consecrate myself, body, heart and soul, to Almighty God. I should like to make my vows, Father, if you consider me worthy."

Tears welled up in Jogues's eyes. "Your vow will be most pleasing to God, and to me as well. But we have no book."

"I know the vows by heart." Now René's eyes welled up with tears. So long had he dreamed of this moment. Now it had arrived in the most unexpected manner. He bit his lip, fought to control his emotion and then whispered to the priest ahead of him in the canoe:

"Hear me, O Lord. I, René Goupil, unworthy in Thy Divine Sight, vow before the most sacred Virgin Mary, the whole court of heaven and Thy Divine Majesty, perpetual Poverty, Chastity and Obedience, in the Society of Jesus. I humbly beseech Thee to vouchsafe to admit this holocaust in an odor of sweetness, and that as Thou hast already given me grace to desire and offer it, so Thou wilt bestow plentiful grace on me to fulfill it. Amen."

Father Jogues turned: "Your vows are accepted, Brother René. God bless you."

"I am your servant, Father."

His vow had strengthened him.

As they witnessed the courage of Ondessonk, the Hurons' respect for him grew. No longer set apart by his black cassock, they saw he was only a man, half naked, bruised and bloodied, fingers mutilated by their captors' teeth. They'd been puzzled before by his gentleness, his ethereal meekness, but they witnessed now the strength his faith gave him in the face of doom.

Steven, the defiant Huron chief, refused to subjugate himself to his captors. Constantly he boasted to them about the Iroquois he had killed, and how he would get revenge once freed. The Mohawks in turn taunted him with the tortures they would inflict, how they would roast him and eat him. Hearing this back-and-forth, Father Jogues took Steven aside as they camped for the night and sought to baptize him. Steven declined.

"Your great chief tells you to forgive your enemies," he said. "I do not forgive these Mohawks. An eternal hatred between our people heats my blood against them. Given the chance, I would visit upon them all the sufferings they promise to me. Look how they beat you, Father. Look how they haul you into their strongholds to torture and kill you as a warning to other French."

"Yet we bring only the good news of the gospel," Father Jogues said.

"That is not how they see it," Steven said. "We Hurons live far in the fastness of the lakes and the forests. The Iroquois live in the lowlands where many whites penetrate and ruin them. Disease, rum, firearms, they see what the white man brings. They will oppose you. They will burn you as a sacrifice to Aireskou and eat your heart to obtain valor and strength to oppose your people and discourage your brothers who arrive in greater numbers every summer."

"I have witnessed the torture among your Hurons, too," Jogues said. "At Teanaustayae four summers ago, your people captured an Oneida chief and eleven of his companions. Just before he was to be killed, the Oneida converted and I baptized him 'Peter.' Your people scalped and mutilated him, and as they scorched his flesh and he did not stop resisting and attacking them till they had severed his feet and crushed him with a tree trunk. Still he crawled after them on his elbows and his knees, until one of your warriors, struck him down and cut off his head."

"I have heard of this," Steven said. "I will be as brave as this Oneida, and I will vex them and never surrender."

"Yet the eternal fires and torment surely await if you die without baptism."

"I have listened often enough to this."

"Then I will attend you and place the saving water upon your brow." Steven nodded with interest. Jogues continued. "On the scaffold, if you wish to accept baptism, point your finger heavenward and lift up your eyes. No matter in what extremity you are, I will come to you and administer the sacrament."

"It shall be done, Ondessonk." The chief embraced the priest and the look that passed between them sealed their bond.

As the trees parted, a lake lay before them, shimmering. Father Jogues gazed upon the water with hope for deliverance until his Mohawks shoved him roughly toward a canoe. Carefully he cleaned his feet—natives hated sand in the canoe—and they thrust him down into a kneeling posture. When the other canoes were floated and loaded and balanced, they set off upon the smooth water. The boats lay low, heavy with prisoners and baggage so the flotilla hugged the western shore where the water was calm.

Ceaselessly they paddled in the swelter and glare, and camped on an island in a shower of stars. Their supply of corn meal was nearly exhausted, so the Mohawks let the prisoners scavenge. Father Jogues and René and Couture learned from the Hurons to forage for roots, grubs, frogs and snails. Eustace snared a squirrel, and ate it raw. So hungry were they, they ate what they could catch whole and gulped it down with water from the lake.

About midmorning of the third day a canoe appeared with a single scout. The Mohawks held a hasty conference and mumbled loudly and pointed in the distance. Columns of smoke rose from an island along the southern shore. Instantly the Mohawks sprang to life and paddled, beating time in the off-stroke with their paddles against the canoe.

"What is it, Father?" René turned, his eyes wide with fear.

"A war party is assembled," the priest said.

"This cannot be good."

As they rounded the southern tip of the large island, thirty or forty canoes lay inverted on the beach and dozens of wigwams were pitched in the great pines. About two hundred men, naked but for loincloths, moved down the bank to welcome them. Mauthurin's Man gave a deep-bellied shout and those in the canoes clenched and raised their fists and roared a triumphant greeting. Some on the shore fired arquebuses into the air. The Mohawks ordered the Huron captives to stand on display in the canoes. From shore a great shout of triumph sounded at the prizes. Over the intervening water the canoes skimmed and men from shore came wading into the water, clamoring for the prisoners.

As they reached shore, the Mohawks shoved the prisoners out of the canoes and into a swarm of fists and angry shouting. Eustace screamed with defiance, and Steven too, and the other Hurons joined them insulting the Mohawks who beat and kicked and screamed and laughed. Now the festivities began. Half a dozen hauled Father Jogues and René Goupil and William Couture to shore. The three children were placed off to the side for possible adoption as the great mob of Mohawks fell upon the captives, stripped them naked and beat them to the ground.

Soon the clamoring mob separated into facing lines. As leader, Mauthurin's Man roughly set the order for his prisoners to run the gauntlet. They were required to run uphill to the encampment. First would go the old men to slow the pace. Weaker Hurons would be interspersed with the stronger to do the same. Mauthurin's Man ordered the French to pass by rank—first, the thick peasant Couture, then the slender *donne* Goupil and, finally, the dignified Jogues.

Into the gauntlet they shoved the first Huron, an old man. A scream of rage went up. He spun and stumbled and groped uphill as they beat him with war clubs and spears and branches. The old man tried to ward off the blows with his forearms. He screamed and ducked as the Mohawks laughed and rained down blows. Another Huron and then another passed in. Couture went in fourth, screaming at his captors who set upon him with fury as he danced and whirled to escape the sticks and cudgels. The Mohawks shoved two more Hurons in and then René was screaming, "Help me, Father!" as they grabbed him and threw him between the lines of men. René was quick on his feet, but they lashed him with switches and thorns and clubbed him and stuck out their feet to trip him. Three strong Mohawks then seized Father Jogues.

"Ondessonk," one said, his face painted hideously red with war paint, "we save you for last."

Into the gauntlet they shoved him and the blows came faster, the crowd in a frenzy. He stumbled and sprawled onto the pine needles. As he lay curled up, they rained down blows from their clubs until he lost consciousness. Then they dragged him up the hill and threw him off to the side.

The war party had erected a scaffold half the height of a man, and onto this they drove the prisoners. When Father Jogues awakened, they were lifting him onto the platform, standing him up, goading him with burning brands. One young Mohawk burned his right hand with a live coal. All around him they dug their fingernails into his flesh. He passed out again.

When he came around, rather than abate, the blood fury of the Mohawks was in full sway. All of the Hurons and René and Couture were tied to stakes and the mob was slashing at them with knives. When the wounds bled too freely, they cauterized them with burning sticks and hot stones.

A Huron whom Father Jogues had baptized "Paul" was standing over him, protecting him from the mob. He screamed at the Mohawks,

"Leave Ondessonk alone! Torture me instead!"

"Ah-ha! But we will caress all of you," one promised. However, seeing that the whites were not defiant, and realizing their hostage value, the Mohawks cast the whites off the platform and focused on the Hurons.

Eustace was tied to a stake with a dozen Mohawks about him. He laughed, taunting them, "Do your worst! You do not hurt me!"

They slashed his flesh with knives, then closed the wounds

with burning torches. They lifted his arms and cut off both thumbs. One Mohawk stripped a stick of its bark, carved a point on it then rammed the stick into Eustace's thumb socket and forced the stick up until it pierced the skin of his elbow. Eustace showed no pain. He stood up higher with pride and arrogance and laughed at them.

Seeing this, Father Jogues rose unsteadily up and limped in his nakedness to the edge of the platform.

"Remember God!" Father Jogues called, his arms spread out. "Remember the suffering of Jesus Christ. I love you, Eustace, and Jesus loves you!" The priest was weeping at the sight of his converts pinioned to the stakes, writhing in agony. Seeing him shed tears, the Mohawks ridiculed him, called him a coward, and began to strike his bald head.

"Stop!" Eustace called, his arm muscles bulging against the bonds. "Do not beat Ondessonk!"

The Mohawks turned to Eustace. "But he weeps like a child!"

"Those are not the tears of a coward," Eustace chided them. "Ondessonk sheds tears of courage, for he pities me. He does not weep for himself. He endured your caresses without a tear."

"Remember," Jogues called to Eustace, "eternal life is coming, and God Who sees all knows how to reward us who suffer for His sake."

"I will be firm, Father!"

Two warriors jumped to the ground and hauled Father Jogues away. One took out a long knife, pinched the priest's nose and made a move to slice it off. Ondessonk looked evenly at him; the Mohawk studied his face. Sensing the priest's acceptance of death— if he mutilated the priest so badly, death would necessarily follow— he lowered his knife and walked off. Father Jogues collapsed and blacked out.

The torture raged all afternoon. Finally the sun set in flaming orange behind the tall pine of the mainland. Night was full as the torture slackened. The bloodlust of the Mohawks was sated with the flames and blood and shrieks of pain for it affirmed their courage. Torturing these French, they no longer feared them. Now the main war party would proceed north to raid and murder and drive the French from this land, while the smaller party would drag its prisoners home to the three Mohawk villages along the river.

Father Jogues lay in cool dirt beneath the moon. He lay between his countrymen and the Hurons. All were smeared and caked with blood, their skin festering with sores, darkened with ashes, blistered from the burns. Flies and mosquitoes fed mercilessly upon the wounds.

"Father?" It was René, gentle René. He was softly weeping, like a child.

"Yes, my son?"

"What will they do with us now?"

"We must trust in the Lord."

"I do, Father, but even so . . ."

"Trust in God and that will be sufficient."

The moon and stars seemed heartless, distant tonight. Father Jogues's heart cried in desolation, and he recalled his Savior's agony in the Garden of Gethsemane. If he could, like Christ, take upon himself the sufferings of these others, he would. The Mohawks, too, if he could exorcize their fear and open for them the path for salvation, then his suffering and this temptation to doubt and despair—work surely of the Evil One—would dissolve.

Morning came, overcast and muggy. Smoke hung in the air with a stink of burning flesh. Charred stones and sticks lay scattered about, the platform broken under the strain of the torture. Near Father Jogues, René and Couture and the Hurons lay sleeping, dreaming, perhaps, of happier times.

He heard men talking. Down by the waterside the Mohawks were swaggering, parading boastfully, sated from yesterday's long ordeal. Father Jogues nudged his comrades awake to form a circle about him for prayer as the Iroquois held a hasty council before departing north and south.

The Mohawk captors came for them, threw some clothing at them, lifted them to their feet, shoved and mocked them. Down to the lake they dragged them and let them scavenge and don what other clothes they might find. Soon they were in the canoes again upon the water, paddling toward the southern tip of the lake that narrowed between mountains, and was choked with swamps.

At landfall on the southernmost shore, a great outcropping of flint spilled with swelling winter frosts countless thin, pointed chips. The Mohawks believed that spirits, helpful *okies*, caused these chips to fall upon the beach to give them tips for their arrows and spears. To pay tribute and assure the squalls that beset this part of the lake would not capsize their canoes, they left offerings of tobacco for the *okies*.

They unloaded the canoes on the grass and rested through the swelter of the afternoon sun. As the sunset, Mauthurin's Man ordered his prisoners to stand and loaded them with all the baggage. Father Jogues's captor loaded bundles upon the priest, but Father Jogues was so weak from hunger and torture he could not move. He threw down the bundles, and the Mohawk seeing the futility of loading any more upon him, relented and gave him a lighter pack.

Into the dim forest they passed. It was a foot trail, and the Mohawks loped in a half-walk-half-trot, interspersing the Hurons and the French amongst them. The path ran thirty French leagues—about ninety miles—through shade and dappled sunlight, a journey of three or four days. By now the entire food supply had run out, so they sought as quickly as possible to reach the first of the Mohawk villages.

The next day, at a shallow ford, the swift current threatened to carry away the unsteady priest. His captors relented and led him to a deeper crossing. As Father Jogues began to wade through the water, he slipped and went under, but he soon rose and swam for the opposite shore where René came to his assistance and helped him out of the water.

"Are you all right, Father?"

"I'm just winded. I will be fine."

The Mohawk guard stood over the two who were now soaking wet and heavily breathing on the rocks. "We must reach Ossernenon soon or we will be food for the crows, yet you linger. I will not starve just to keep you moving." So saying, he trotted off, leaving them behind.

"Now," Father Jogues urged René, "make your escape. The trail is well-marked and it is only a day's journey back to the canoes. When you get to the broad St. Lawrence, just go right and you will be back in Quebec within a week. This may be your only chance to escape. If you proceed onward you surely will be killed."

"I will go if you come with me."

"I cannot leave the others," the priest said. "They will need the last rites when the Mohawks burn them. Half the Hurons still must be baptized."

"Then I will stay," Goupil said, helping the priest to his feet. "Come. I am a brother in the order. Let us make the best time we can."

They stumbled along, down defiles between the mountains and along churning rivers. The mountains gave way to sandy foothills and pine forests. The priest and his *donne* staggered into camp as the sun was setting. A kettle hung above the fire in the midst of the Mohawks. Thinking it held food, they went over, but it was only hot water. The Mohawks taunted them.

"You think we have food? We would if we roasted and ate you. It is only hot water to take away the pangs of hunger. We are saving you for the whole village." And they laughed. With kicks and cuffs they drove the priest and the *donne* away from the fire to sleep on the ground.

The next day the party dispatched a runner to announce their advance. As they paused for this last night on the trail, women came out from the village to meet them with food. The Mohawks squat and ate ravenously. They beat the French and the Hurons who, in their hunger, tried to share the corn meal and dried fish. At last some scraps of food were shared with the captives and they fed themselves with their bloody, crushed fingers.

On the following morning, August 14, the eve of the Feast of the Assumption, Father Jogues prayed with great feeling. René was on his knees, dry-heaving with fear. Father Jogues went to him. "Bear up, my son. Trust in God."

"I'm trying, Father." Tears streamed down his face.

Since there was nothing more to eat, they set off. Along the trail, groups of Mohawks were lined up, curious villagers who'd come out to see the prisoners, and to hurl rocks and insults at them as they trotted along.

Chapter 3

❧

Mohawk Warriors Display Their Captives
In Villages Of the Turtle, Bear and Wolf Clans

ABOUT THE THIRD HOUR, they came into a clearing, a meadow of long grass. They climbed a mud trail to the crest of the hill where the long grass swayed, and below, a river flowed through a wide valley between forested banks. As the river curled gently eastward, dozens of bark canoes lay inverted on the bank, and up from the bank on the facing hill ran four trails to the gates of the fortress. Breastworks of stout gray logs were set in the earth. This was Ossernenon, village of the Turtle Clan of the nation of Canienga, People of the Land of Flint. Smoke of the cooking fires darkened the sky, and cries of anticipation echoed from the gates.

Up the trail from the river, crowds were forming—women, children and old men—lining up to welcome the prisoners. They beat skin drums and shook gourd rattles in happy anticipation.

The leader, Mauthurin's Man, stepped to the edge of the hill and raised a conch shell high and blew a note that rose and rose, then fell and echoed down the valley. The crowd roared and drummed and rattled louder, blew their conch shells in answer. Their Mohawk escorts shoved them forward and downhill the prisoners stumbled. The crowd on the facing bank yelled and danced in delight.

At the ford they waded across the river, chest deep, pushed

and shoved by their captors through the water, and then they emerged as the crowd's anticipation exploded and they beat drums and screamed "Aiiii-yeee!" Aiiii-yeee!" The captors stripped their prisoners naked, but allowed Goupil and Jogues to keep a cloth tied about their loins. In an ascending order of importance the Mohawks released their prisoners to run the gauntlet.

They put Couture first in line because he shot a chief; then came the Hurons, Eustace, Joseph, Paul and others. In the middle they placed René Goupil, then the remaining Hurons. Saving Ondessonk for last, they fed the prisoners into the gauntlet one by one and up the hill they ran.

Now the crowd surged forward, beat the prisoners with clubs and branches and briars, slashed them with knives. Small boys and girls whacked at their shins and ankles with sticks. Up the mud of the path the prisoners ran. They held up their forearms as long as they could to ward off the blows, and when they dropped their arms in exhaustion, the blows rained upon their heads and faces. The men and women screamed and hissed at them, beat them, taunting: "We will burn you! We will eat you!" Hating the sight of Jogues baldness, they rained blows until he bled copiously.

When the captives reached the top of the hill the crowd's fury abated. Warriors with spread arms offered imprecations to Aireskou, god of sun and war. Through the open western gate appeared the rounded roofs of a dozen long houses. Now the drumming and rattling and shrieking began anew. A second gauntlet formed toward the village and the crowd fell upon them. Women took Father Jogues's fingers in their mouths and ground them between their teeth, pulling out his two remaining fingernails.

"This," one orator cried, "this is the notorious blackrobe, Ondessonk!"

The crowd responded with glee and into the gauntlet he was hurled, branches and briars and rods and knives lashing out at him.

One warrior swung an iron turnbuckle on a leather thong and hit him above the hip. He rose up off the ground in pain and he fell. The crowd surged forward, beating and cutting him until he pushed himself to his feet and stumbled on.

Inside the gates of the village the prisoners huddled. René had received the worst of the punishment, his face was a bloody pulp, his eyes nearly closed. The crowd ceased its beating, but continued its taunts and threats.

They had built a sturdy platform in the center of the village and here they led the prisoners. Up they hauled them, and placed the three naked Frenchmen in the center. A chief with all the calm and dignity of his office, stepped forward and raised his arms for quiet.

"Our brothers, the Hurons are our enemies because they follow the palefaces, but the palefaces are our sworn enemies above all others." With an iron rod he hit Father Jogues three times on the back, staggering him forward. Then he hit Couture and René Goupil. "The whites enter our land and build their forts to force us from our fishing streams, our hunting grounds. But the blackrobe is the worst of all, for he discourages us from making war. Bring him out!"

Two women led an Algonquin woman forward. The chief held up Father Jogues's left arm. He gave the Algonquin woman a knife. "Cut off his thumb!"

The woman took the knife that was thrust at her, but she backed away and shook her head.

"I cannot . . . I am Christian . . . he is a priest."

"I will strike you down if you refuse!" The chief pulled a hatchet from his belt and brandished it above her head.

She put the knife upon Jogues's thumb. She was weeping. She looked up into his eyes. "I'm sorry, Father! I have received the Prayer, but I cannot defy them! They will kill me!"

Father Jogues lifted up his eyes to the sky and prayed as she hacked at the joint of his thumb. She was trembling and unsteady as she cut. The priest bore the pain and when she had severed the tendon and held up the bleeding thumb, the crowd went wild with shrieks and more drumming. She threw the thumb down in horror and as she backed off, other women led her away. Father Jogues stooped down, picked up his thumb and held it up to the sky as an offering.

"My God!" he groaned. "This is the price of their conversion?"

"Throw it away!" Couture cried. "Throw it away or they'll force you to eat it!"

Father Jogues threw his thumb into the street where a dog pounced upon it.

Now they led René forward. They forced another woman to cut off his right thumb with an oyster shell. She was cutting at the wrist and blood spurted from his artery, pumping upon the scaffold until one of the men brought a hot iron and cauterized the wound. René turned his bleeding, unrecognizable face to the priest.

"Oh, my God, Father! When will they stop?"

Now the Mohawks moved to the doughty Couture, forcing him to sing and dance. They stabbed him with hot iron awls and pointed sticks. They carved off pieces of his flesh and burned him with hot irons and smoldering sticks until he fell lifeless upon the floor. They then turned to "caress" the Hurons and left the French alone.

The next day and the next the prisoners were paraded out and tied to the posts upon the scaffold, fit objects for torture for any of the villagers. On the third day, with the next village upriver, Andagaron, village of the Bear Clan, demanding the prisoners be exhibited there, the merry captors led them tied by the neck from Ossernenon, down a path along the river. After four or five miles, women and children from the next village appeared, dancing and taunting them, leading them to the village.

Across a meadow and then up a steep pathway, they led the

naked prisoners. This headland was higher than at Ossernenon, and the stockade of logs was set at an angle outward above ditches of the breastworks.

A squirming line of villagers prepared for their entrance as a chief in an antlered bonnet stood upon the hill:

"Let us show these whites the love we bear for them!" He raised his spear and shook it against the sky. The crowd responded lustily and through the gauntlet the crippled French and Hurons staggered. Again they stumbled and fell, rose and blundered on under the blows and the screams of insults, the fists and the kicks and the spitting. Again they were placed upon a scaffold in the center of the village. The chief, inspecting the victims, was shocked when he noticed two of Couture's fingers remained uninjured.

"How can this be?" he cried, and he seized a clam shell and began to saw at his right index finger. Couture screamed and tried to pull his hand away. The chief pressed but could not cut the tendon or finger joint, so he gripped the finger and tore it until he ripped the tendon back from the wrist and held it up, bleeding, to the cheering throng. Couture swooned. His arm swelled up immediately. Fearing they would lose him, they lifted him off the scaffold and carried him into a long house to nurse him back to consciousness.

As before, the torture continued all day. Father Jogues continually exhorted René and the Hurons: "Do not lose confidence in our God. Only through great tribulation can we hope to enter heaven. We are like a woman who goes into labor and sweats and strains, but when she brings forth the child she forgets her anguish. Only through such suffering is a man is born into the world. Trust in the Lord for in a few days, at the hour of our death, we will exchange these momentary sorrows for eternal joy."

At night the warriors staked them to the earth floor of a long house and children were let loose to sprinkle live coals upon them.

The following day the muggy August heat spell broke. A cold rain slashed from the sky and dark clouds rolled down the valley, thunder shaking the earth, lightning cleaving the sky, cold sheets of rain falling. Again they were forced onto the scaffold for torture and they were left exposed when the rain became too intense for the villagers. Out in the rain, hair pasted to their faces and necks, the Hurons endured the storm and the chill winds that blew. When taken down at the end of the day, Jogues and Goupil were brought before an assembly and forced to sing and dance. They sang *De Canticis Domini in Terra Aliena*, "Songs of the Lord in a Foreign Land."

The following day they were hauled along the river path to the third Mohawk village, Tionontoguen, village of the Wolf clan.

"I beg of you," Father Jogues asked his guard, "give me something to wear to cover my nakedness."

The man found gave him moccasins and a discarded old Dutch jacket of heavy wool. The priest put it on but the wool irritated his blisters and scraped off the scabs that were forming, so he threw the jacket aside and went on naked. Two hours they marched until they reached a hill. Above a wide plateau a long rectangular stockade rose. The gauntlet here was half-hearted, but once upon the platform, the torture resumed in full fury. After the weeks of torture and starvation, the prisoners hung lifelessly from the cords. The blows and cuts elicited only muted groans. At dark, members of the Wolf Clan cut them down and carried them into a cabin to stake them to the ground for the children's enjoyment, but they selected Ondessonk for special treatment.

Three men lifted him high into the rib work of the long house and with vines they bound his arms above the elbow onto the crosspiece. High above the dirt floor where the others were staked Father Jogues hung as if crucified, his breath labored, nearly stopped up from the position of his arms. His pain mounted and he grew dizzy.

Below him a mob with upraised fists urged the torturers on,

stamping and screaming for his death. So intense was the pain that Jogues cried out, "Please! I beg of you! Loosen the bonds!" but they tightened them instead, the mob howling in approbation. Alone, crucified, the object of contempt, Father Jogues raised his eyes heavenward, "O, my God!" he screamed as if summoning his last breath. "As your only begotten son cried from the cross, 'Father, my Father, why have You forsaken me?'"

As he was blacking out from the unendurable pain, suddenly someone cut the bonds and he fell into the waiting arms of a woman. The crowd raged at the man who cut him down, but he stood against them, his knife drawn, and he guarded Jogues's removal to another cabin where they lay him beneath a deerskin infested with lice.

In the morning, the Wolf Clan came for him and hauled him with the others again to the torture platform, but as they began to torture the lifeless French and Hurons, a conch shell blew and the crowd ran to the western gate. Father Jogues slumped down from the platform and staggered after the crowd. Warriors back from the western reaches were escorting four new Huron prisoners.

Pushed, whipped and beaten, the four Hurons stumbled into the village and the howling mob replaced Jogues and his companions on the scaffold with these fresh prisoners. Father Jogues recognized these Hurons from his mission of Sainte Marie. They were not Christian, though, and so he desired to baptize them before they were killed.

The council of elders met and decided two of the new prisoners would be burned that night. All afternoon and into the evening the crowd tormented the four, but especially the two who were condemned. Father Jogues stayed with them and urged them in their own language to accept baptism, promising them eternal life in paradise if they but consented to have water sprinkled upon their heads and the words spoken.

As the torture increased, finally one and then the other agreed to be baptized. The Mohawks had tossed raw corn at the prisoners and the corn husks were wet from the fields. Father Jogues gathered droplets of water from the husks and dripped it upon the foreheads of the two, reciting over them, "*In nomine Patris, et Filii, et Spiritu Sancti, Amen.*" Seeing that he was attempting to give solace to the victims, the Mohawks unleashed their rage upon him anew, beating him to the edge of the platform and threatening to murder him along with the Hurons. Jogues retreated to his companions.

That night they burned and ate the two Hurons. The council of the village met and with the blood lust slaked and uncertain about the palefaces, they voted to send the Hurons and Europeans back to the village of the Bear Clan, Andagaron, where the council for the entire Mohawk nation might decide their fate. And so on the following day, all of the party with Jogues as well as the two Hurons recently captured were led back to the Bear Clan.

Along the way, naked except for a cast-off piece of cotton, Father Jogues walked close by the newest prisoners, comforting them, promising them that if they accepted baptism they would enter heaven. When at last the two Hurons acceded, the priest waited until they were crossing a small stream and he dipped his hand into it as if he were taking a drink and trickled the water upon their foreheads, murmuring the baptismal words.

The chiefs of the Mohawk council sat that night, passing the calumet as they considered the weighty question of what to do with the French captives. The chief who housed Jogues returned to his long house late in the night and summoned the prisoners about him.

"We have met, Ondessonk, and deliberated long and hard upon the question of what to do with you. I argued that we should keep you as hostages to use as barter for a lasting peace. Yet the warriors, whose blood is young and hot, want to make you an example to your countrymen, and with your deaths assure that no more of your people will intrude into our lands. You are to be burned in the morning."

Father Jogues accepted the news with resignation. "I thank you for urging our cause," he said to the chief, and he related the news to René and Couture. They knelt together with the Hurons and prayed for courage. Knowing what awaited them, they hardly slept. As the rays of the sun lanced into the cabin the next morning, they awoke to women preparing the kettle for breakfast. The friendly chief returned at midday.

"Ondessonk," he said, "some of the elders want a reconsideration of the vote."

"On what basis?"

"They argue that we can make peace with your people and turn them against the Hurons and Algonquins if we give you back. Burning you and your friends will end that possibility. If we can keep you alive, our options are open for we can always kill you."

"We will do what we can to help negotiate peace," the priest said.

"Our assembly wishes to hear from you." The chief then instructed the women to find clothes for the Frenchmen. Soon, dressed in old buckskin, Jogues and the others were led through the village to the council chamber.

It was an ordinary long house, looking inside like an upturned canoe, the twenty-foot-high frame covered with large bark shingles. The cabin was smoky and dim. On fur rugs the elders sat, some wearing their ceremonial antlered bonnets. They smoked and nodded and grunted and gave a respectful heed to the speaker in the center who was talking in deep oratorical tones with many hand gestures.

The chief seated the three Frenchmen near the doorway. After they talked and deliberated, they motioned for the Frenchmen to stand.

"It is the wish of the chieftains that this paleface," he pointed to Couture, "be returned to Tionontoguen to take the place of the chief he slew when our warriors ambushed you. It is the wish of the chieftains that you and the other paleface," he indicated René, "be returned to Ossernenon where you will be indentured to the chief who captured you, to serve as a slave."

Father Jogues nodded, accepting the verdict of the council.

"As for the Hurons, the young girl and the two boys will be accepted into the Wolf Clan at Tionontoguen. The one called Paul will be led with you back to the Turtle Clan where he will be burned tonight. The one called Steven will be burned in this village tonight, and the one called Eustace will be led back to the village of the Wolf Clan where he will likewise be burned tonight. This will appease our god and the remaining Hurons will be fostered to families in Ossernenon. You whites will be held as hostages so we might broker a peace with your people."

All the chiefs were nodding assent. Father Jogues then translated the verdict to René and Couture who received the news with hearts grateful for themselves, but in sorrow for the impending and unavoidable fate of Paul and Steven and Eustace.

Back in the cabin, Father Jogues related the verdict to the Hurons. The three sacrificial victims received the news stoically.

"As you are about to die," the priest asked Steven, "will you receive the saving waters?"

"I will, Ondessonk, and I will spit in their eyes as they torture me."

Father Jogues brought a dipper of water. Solemnly, with the other prisoners watching in the dim recesses of the long house, he baptized Steven. Steven closed his eyes and composed within his heart the death song he would sing.

Now the priest gave them absolution for their sins. As they knelt, he assured them that a heavenly reward would be theirs this very night. With tears in his eyes, Father Jogues embraced Eustace who faced his fate with unflinching courage. He embraced Steven. He bid goodbye to little Theresa and the two boys who were to be adopted into the Wolf Clan. Soon he and René and Paul and the other Hurons were led along the river to Ossernenon.

They entered the village of the Turtle Clan that afternoon by the western gate. With the verdict announced, and Ondessonk and René accepted as slaves, and Paul condemned to die in the fires, there was no gauntlet to welcome them.

Warriors of the Turtle Clan had repaired the sturdy platform. They collected brush and firewood. A pyre was ready for the holocaust. The Mohawks escorted Paul to the platform. Women brought water and bowls of venison and fish and sagamite for his final meal. As the sun set beyond the treetops, they ordered Paul to sing and dance.

Paul, the brave Huron who'd repeatedly protected Father Jogues during the captivity, prayed for courage to face his death.

Father Jogues watched the torture from below the scaffold. Courageously Paul sang to his persecutors as they burned him with fiery brands and sliced him with their knives. They led him to the center pole and tied him fast. Still he sang defiantly, demonstrating his unflagging courage in the face of death. They heaped burning brush and wood about his legs and as the flames reached up, he sang of a better life to come. Finally he looked over at Father Jogues and raised his eyes to heaven. This was the signal, and the priest gave him final absolution, sending his soul to heaven. At that moment, a Mohawk came up from behind and split Paul's head open with a tomahawk. Blood spurt out and hissed into the flames. He slumped over and the flames licked about him. The Mohawks danced in triumph, the ire of their war god sated.

Far to the west that night, along the dark river that meandered through the hills, two other fires burned, one in the center of Andagaron and one in Tionontoguen where Steven and Eustace were likewise burned. Ever the Christian—as William Couture later related to Father Jogues—Eustace called out from the midst of the flames:

"As Christ forgave the Romans, I forgive you! You know not what you do! Heed the words of the blackrobe! Accept the Prayer! I charge you, William, to tell all my relatives that they should accept the Prayer. They should not seek vengeance, but forgive these Iroquois and seek together to find a lasting peace."

Chapter 4

❦

Father Jogues Is Enslaved
To a Mohawk Woman

For three weeks Father Jogues and René lay recuperating in a long house. The council put them in the care of an elderly woman whom they were to call "aunt." She fed them each day from the common kettle. Slowly their festering wounds healed. When they went outside even to the privy ditch they were scorned and shunned and even threatened with imminent death, so they spent their days and nights inside.

Soon the war party they'd met on the island returned. Despite their warlike spirit outbound, they'd been rebuffed by the French. The ships of soldiers and engineers had finally reached the Richelieu and the men were building a fort when the Iroquois attacked. With the assurance of their sorcerers and excited by the torture of Jogues and his party, they'd considered themselves invincible, but they soon lost heart when a French squadron of bluecoats sallied out from behind the stockade to attack them with muskets and bayonets. Three of their chiefs fell. With the food supplies running low, they turned around in defeat.

"Why should these French be permitted to live when their brothers killed three of our chiefs?" they asked about the captives. "Convene the council again! Ondessonk, whose evil magic robbed us of victory, must be tortured and killed or we will do it without permission."

Before the Mohawk women's council could convene and decide this question, however, a Dutchman, Arendt Van Corlaer, appeared at Ossernenon on horseback. He'd heard from traders at Rensselaerwyck that the Mohawks held captive a French priest and two other Frenchmen. He set out from his settlement to ransom them. The clan mothers told Van Corlaer that permission was necessary from the central Mohawk council, and so after speaking at length with Father Jogues, Van Corlaer went west to Tionontoguen.

But the council there indicated it could not order the release. Since this was a matter of peace between the Iroquois and the French, he would need permission from all five nations of the League when next they convened at Onondaga. They were able to assure Van Corlaer, though, that the French would not be further harmed.

Postponed by violent thunderstorms, the council for the five nations met during the final week of September at Onondaga. They sent word down to Andagaron and when the prisoners were produced there, René and Father Jogues from Ossernenon and Couture from Tionontoguen, they were held in a pen outside the council chamber. The Wolf and Turtle Clans urged releasing René and Father Jogues. The Bear Clan adamantly refused, bragging that they were not afraid of the French. With furious howling, they threatened to kill the prisoners pre-emptively.

Jogues and Goupil and Couture listened and when the talk grew violent and threats filled the air that the Wolf Clan would murder the French that very night, Father Jogues urged them up:

"Come, René and good William! We must hide ourselves tonight or we won't live to see the morning." He led them to a lean-to out in the cornfield and they hid under the corn husks until the sun rose.

As they entered through the village gate the next morning, their aunt saw them and hastened over: "Be on your guard! A gang of young warriors from the Bear Clan sought you last night, threatening to kill you with a tomahawk in the skull. No one could restrain them. They accused you of casting an evil spell that caused them defeat on the attack to the north. They say you are demons with potent magic. Our clan and the clan of the Wolf consider that peace is possible, but the Bears refuse to think of it and want you dead. Be on your guard!"

The Mohawk council declined to accept any Dutch ransom for the three Frenchmen. It directed Couture to return to Tionontoguen, and gave Jogues and René Goupil back to their aunt to return to Ossernenon.

The beatings and torture had permanently scarred René. As a surgeon, he developed a gentle, sensitive nature, and seeing this, the Mohawk hunters and warriors considered him cowardly. They came to hate him more than they hated Ondessonk who moved with a refined dignity. They watched René closely and thought him deranged: He murmured when he prayed. He bowed his head in reverence or he looked up to heaven for guidance. He beat his breast to show humility.

René loved children and they loved him. He played with them, bounced them on his knee. One day, he picked up the baby son of a warrior who'd been recently killed, and he took the infant's hand and taught him to make the sign of the cross. Seeing this, the child's grandfather cried out and leapt across the cabin to wrest the child from his evil spell. Loudly the grandfather screamed at René and beat him on the head and on the shoulders till he ran from the long house, out into the cold. Father Jogues was carrying a load of firewood and saw him race out and he went over.

"How have you angered the chief, my brother?"

"I was teaching his grandson how to make the sign of the cross. The chief began to shout and pulled the child out of my arms."

Jogues looked about. "Come with me at once!" He led René

outside the stockade and across a meadow to the privacy of a grove of fir trees. "You cannot flaunt our faith, René!"

"I wasn't flaunting it, Father, I was practicing it."

"They consider any sign we make an evil spell."

"Well, that's not true."

"They will harm you, brother."

"I don't fear them so long as I am in a state of grace."

"But I don't want to lose you. We are in danger every second. Be vigilant. If they attack either one of us, pledge to me that 'Jesus' will be the last word we utter."

"Yes, Father. I pledge it will."

"Let us pray then," and Father Jogues knelt on the pine needles and spread his arms toward the rays of sunlight which were piercing through the forest canopy. "We offer You our lives, dear Lord," he murmured as the wind played with the leaves and the songs of birds sweetened the air. "Receive our lives and our blood, if it is Thy will to take us as an offering for the salvation of these poor people whom we forgive."

René followed the priest, repeating his words, and when the sun was setting they started back, saying the rosary as they walked. As they turned a bend of the path, two Mohawks approached. One was from René's cabin, brother to the chief slain at Fort Richelieu and son of the old man who protested the baptism. He was the tallest warrior of the entire Mohawk nation. He and his companion wore woolen blankets, their arms folded within.

"Ondessonk," the tall one commanded and cocked his head. "Return to the village."

Father Jogues reached for René's arm and urged him along, and they started walking together past the warriors. "They have an evil design," the priest whispered. "Let us commend ourselves to God and the most Blessed Virgin."

"They've turned, Father. They're following us."

"Hail Mary, full of grace, the Lord is with thee, blessed are thou . . ."

"Ondessonk," the tall one called, "walk on ahead. You," he stopped René, "wait behind. Go, Ondessonk!"

Father Jogues turned to walk on, but after three steps he turned back and saw the tall warrior throw open his blanket, raise a tomahawk in the air and swing it with all his strength into René's skull.

"Jesus! Jesus and Mary! Jesus!" René cried out, and he staggered forward and fell.

"Into Thy hands I commend his spirit," Father Jogues called out, and he fell to his knees. "Will you give me a moment?" he asked them, and he took off his cap to show them he would not resist. He recited the act of contrition and then looked up. "Do whatever you please. I do not fear death." He bowed his head in submission.

"Get up, Ondessonk," the towering warrior said to him. "I would kill you if I could but you belong to another family and you have not given cause so I cannot kill you."

Father Jogues stood and rushed to René who was still breathing. "My brother!"

The two warriors saw that he still lived. They hauled Father Jogues away from him and sank their hatchets again into René's head.

At the gate to the stockade a dozen or so villagers had watched the murder. They came running down the hill, some to deplore the violence, some to applaud. Father Jogues was trying to wrest the body away from them when a man of his cabin grabbed him, pulled him off, "Get back to the cabin! Now! They will hurt you for interfering!"

"I must bury him! René!"

They struggled. A crowd of villagers was screaming. The tall warrior watched the commotion with a sneer, the bloody axe ready in his hand. Dozens of villagers came pouring through the gate and the clamor rose. Father Jogues was choked up, tears streaming from his eyes.

"René!" he sobbed, and he reached out and struggled to go to him.

"Go at once!" the man said. "You are not safe here." He pushed the priest up the hill. "Go back to the cabin and wait! Stay inside! Do not leave!"

Reluctantly Father Jogues turned and started up the hill. He went through the gate and into the village. Dogs were snapping at each other over discarded bones, and children ran naked in the warm September sun. Father Jogues hastened to his long house and opened the heavy flap of bearskin and went inside. His aunt looked up as she stirred the kettle, and she muttered: "Be careful, Ondessonk." She stirred her kettle silently. The chief of his long house arose from his mat. Children had just told him about René's murder.

"Come here, Ondessonk," the chief said. He placed his hand upon the priest's heart to feel his agitation. Feeling none, he called to others to witness Father Jogues's calm. "He has no fear," the chief concluded, then he spoke to the priest: "Do not go out alone, Ondessonk. If you are accompanied by a member of our family, they can't kill you, but if you are alone, you will die."

Father Jogues went to his pallet of twigs and skins and he lay staring at the poles of the ceiling.

The noise of crowds ebbed and flowed for the next few hours. Having witnessed René's violent murder, Father Jogues accepted the certainty of his own. When three warriors came for him at sunset, he was resigned and followed them to another long house. A shout went up as he entered and the inhabitants glowered at him.

"You are a dead man, Ondessonk," the shaman taunted him. Others called menacingly. He did not react, but took the insults with a stoic indifference. The guard who had given him the moccasins he wore approached.

"I want the moccasins again," he said. "Soon you will not need them. To prevent someone from stealing them, why don't you give them to me now?"

Father Jogues removed his shoes and gave them back. He lay down on the pallet they shoved him toward. With sunset, the tumult of the village lessened and certain of his approaching death, he slept only fitfully.

As a gray light stole through chinks in the plates of bark next morning, Father Jogues tiptoed from of the long house in his bare feet. Indistinct shapes loomed out of the mist, rising from the warm river into the cooling September air. He heard muffled speech and as he drew closer and the others saw him, they expressed surprise that he still lived, and that he showed his face when the Bear Clan wanted him dead. Father Jogues ignored the comments and as he reached the south gate, an old man sat on a tree stump: "Where do you go in such a hurry?"

"I must bury my friend. They killed him yesterday."

"You have no sense. They will kill you, too, if they meet you. You would risk your own death to bury a stinking corpse, fit only for dogs?"

"I must pray over him and commit him to the earth. Where is he?"

"The children tied a rope to him and dragged him all about, then they rolled his body into the ravine where we throw our refuse. By now he stinks and the dogs have been at him."

"I must bury him."

"Do not go to the ravine alone. You'll never return."

"I do not care for my safety. It would be a mercy to kill me now."

"I do not understand the paleface," the old man said, shaking his head in disbelief, but he called an Algonquin slave he'd adopted and ordered him to follow the priest and watch over him.

They walked to the edge of the cornfield and peered down the ravine. Crows circled above and some on the ground cried from below. The Algonquin followed the birds and spied a hand among the fallen leaves. Together they slid seventy feet down the embankment to where the body lay. The feasting birds gave up and reluctantly took to wing. René's body was smeared with earth and blood, the loins chewed off and the eyes pecked out. Weeping inconsolably, Father Jogues cradled the body in his arms and rocked it back and forth, "Oh, my God! My God!"

Lacking a shovel, he could not bury René then, so he rolled the corpse down the hill to the bank of a rivulet, then he rolled him over the bank and into the water. Stepping into the water himself, he piled stones upon René's body to keep it from floating away, and to prevent animals from eating it any further. Climbing out of the water he asked the Algonquin if he would return the next day and help dig René a proper grave. The man nodded assent.

For two days he watched, but he had no opportunity to leave the village. On the third day a thunderstorm lashed the river valley. He awoke on the fourth day and slipped out of the cabin. Rather than arouse curiosity, he did not ask the Algonquin to accompany him. He borrowed a spade from the field and he ran across the field to the ravine, then half-stumbled and half-fell the down the embankment to the stream below. The little rivulet was now swollen with water from the storm. Father Jogues walked to the place where he had piled the stones upon René. He entered the stream. The water was chest-high and cold. He felt the outline of the mound beneath his feet, but submerging his face and looking all about he could not see the body.

"René!" he cried in anguish. "René! Where have they taken you?" Despairing, he looked on the bank in the damp grass, and he went back into the stream and groped about in the cold water. He splashed downstream, followed both forks, the one to the river and the one that flowed past the village, but he could not find the body.

At last, soaked and cold and utterly demoralized, he trudge up the hill to the village. No longer did life hold any value for him. He knew his days were numbered and they would kill him as easily as they killed René, but it concerned him no longer.

To everyone he met he asked the same question: "Do you know what they've done with the body of my brother?" The villagers laughed at him, mimicked him and ridiculed him. One Algonquin woman, though, told him that the young warriors had found the body where he hid it and taken it a mile hence and thrown it in another stream.

"The body has already washed away," she told him, though he suspected she lied. "It is useless for you to go there."

At last he gave up the effort to bury René, and he made up his mind to wait as a condemned man to be struck down.

Two weeks after René's death, Father Jogues had a dream:

He proceeded out of the village to the forest to lament and pray for René. When he returned, the village had become a great stone fortress with shining towers and bulwarks and walls of startling beauty. It was an old city, grandly constructed. As he approached the gate, on the post was carved the figure of a slaughtered lamb with a Latin phrase, "Let them praise Thy name, O Lamb of God." He saw, as though a light shone outward from deep within his soul, that all the citizens of this city praised the name of him who imitated Him who was led like a lamb to the slaughter. As he entered, he passed a guardhouse, but he failed to heed a soldier who told him to halt. At the second warning, the soldier advanced in a wrath, seized him and hauled him into the gilded hallways and chambers of the palace.

Crowds were milling about at the door to the inner courts, and within a room of magnificent beauty he saw an old man, venerable and majestic, clothed in a dazzling robe of royal purple. The man walked about quietly, rendering justice to people who knelt beyond a railing. Father Jogues recognized some people from Quebec who surely knew him to be innocent.

47

When the judge—for so the old man was—heard the charge from the sentinel, he drew a rod from a bundle and he beat Father Jogues long and severely on the shoulders, then on the neck and finally on the head. The pain was every bit as intense as his first entry into Ossernenon, yet despite the beating, he did not utter a single cry.

When the judge finished the punishment, he clasped his arms about the priest's neck in an embrace and soothed him and comforted him, imparting a feeling of happiness divine and completely inexplicable. Moved by this heavenly consolation, Father Jogues kissed the hand that had beaten him, exclaiming: "Thy rod, O, God, my King, and Thy staff, have comforted me." With that, the sentinel escorted him back to the palace gate. He began to follow after his dear companion René, who was accepted now into eternal happiness, but while he was following him along a twisting road, he visited churches, one-by-one, that stood along the roadway in order to pray. In doing so, he lost sight of his companion.

Awakening, Father Jogues understood this dream to signify that he would be worthy to enter the mansion of the Blessed but only if he persisted in patience and faithfulness. Despite the constant threats of his captors, his death was far off, and so he must persevere. The vision gave him great comfort.

As the autumn faded and dead leaves spun in the wind, Father Jogues immersed himself in learning the Iroquois language so he might instruct them in the Faith. No longer were they his captors or murderers. Now he saw them as his brothers and sisters whom he might lead to God.

Soon winter was upon the land and the cold winds blew incessantly. The light of day shortened and the nights grew. Ponds and the river froze into brittle sheets of ice and blizzards filled the air with pelting snow. The stores of corn were unable to support the village during the winter, so the Turtle Clan separated into bands of hunters, six, seven, ten, and strapped packs on their backs and snowshoes on their feet and hiked off into the mountains to hunt.

High in the mountains the snow was deep. On snowshoes of lashed racquetwork they trudged. Men carried their weapons, arquebuses and spears and bows and arrows. The women carried babies on papoose boards and cooking implements in bundles strapped to their foreheads or on sleds they pulled. His aunt had assigned Father Jogues to one such party, and with only a piece of cloth girded about his hips and a castoff red cape, he went north into the mountains. He was light and agile, to be sure, but without the protection of snowshoes, and loaded down with bundles, he broke repeatedly through the ice crust and had to climb painfully out. In eight days they covered ninety miles, arriving at a place where they would camp for the winter. The women set up the tripod for the kettle and stitched the skins for the hut while the men put up the teepee frame.

At first the hunting was good. The men brought back deer in abundance and everyone ate well. However, when Father Jogues realized they were consecrating the venison each night to Aireskou, he refused to eat. With no other food, his scruples cost him dearly. The family denied him the comfort of a sleeping robe and he lay shivering on the ground. They ridiculed him for not eating the plentiful meat, and when, unexpectedly, the game became less plentiful, and then altogether ceased, they blamed him for bringing bad luck upon them by not eating. Cruelly they insulted him, humiliated him and punished him.

After a month of hunting, two of the old men and a pregnant mother indicated they would return to Ossernenon, and the others sent Ondessonk, considered an unlucky omen, down with them. The priest interpreted this as being his death sentence. He expected upon entering Ossernenon that he would be killed.

Down they hiked, Father Jogues nearly naked, his skin split and scaled from frostbite.

Into a gorge they went, a fallen tree providing the bridge over the gushing river, its banks icy and steep. Loaded with bundles and an infant in a wicker pack, the woman started across, but she lost her footing and plunged into the stream. She was weighted down by the baggage and by the babe in her womb, and she sank to the bottom. Instantly Father Jogues jumped into the water and strongly swimming, he reached her, pulled her to the surface, handed the child up to waiting arms of the old men, and then pushed the pregnant woman up out of the stream as they pulled.

On the bank they kindled a fire. In view of his heroic rescue they allowed the priest to warm himself. Rubbing her hands and feet, Father Jogues brought the woman back to life. Secretly he had baptized the infant but the baby died from exposure a few hours later. On they tramped the following day.

As they descended into the foothills, they stopped at other hunting camps, and in the second one they stayed, Jogues met the chief who had ordered René's death. When told about Father Jogues's heroic rescue of the woman, the chief gave him a bark plate of steaming meat. As he blessed the dish of meat, the chief stopped him:

"Do not do that, Ondessonk."

"I am thanking my God for providing this food to me."

"That is the hated sign our Dutch brothers warned us about. It is the means by which you exert your magic over us."

"This is not magic," Father Jogues countered. "I am calling down the blessing of the one true God upon this food, and upon us all so that He will protect us." He continued with his blessing.

"It is that very sign which caused the death of the young paleface," the chief said.

Curious, Father Jogues asked the chief to explain.

"I saw the young paleface make that sign with the hand of my daughter's child. He was casting a spell over him, and I stopped him. Yet the young paleface would not cease in this practice, and so I ordered him killed."

Father Jogues turned to his daughter. "René loved your child," he reached out to touch the lad who was in her lap, but she pulled him away. "He wasn't hurting him."

"It was the very spell the Dutch warned us of," she said, caressing her child's hair. "They tell us it is how you obtain control over us."

"I will continue to do this," Father Jogues said evenly and the chief, in view of his rescue of the pregnant woman, just grunted and puffed on his pipe.

Upon reaching Ossernenon, the village was nearly deserted. Father Jogues's aunt had tramped off to another hunting camp. The journey, the plunge into the cold stream, the nakedness in the snow and ice had severely debilitated the priest, and he lay for two days upon his pallet.

Learning that he had returned, the chiefs put him to use. Another hunting camp was having difficulty with game and had sent a runner back to the village asking that bags of corn meal be carried out so they would not starve. Women packed four big sacks with corn and they summoned Father Jogues, still clothed only in a thin piece of cloth and the red cape, and they loaded him down with the sacks and set him on the trail. Uncomplaining he began, but so weakened was he from the starvation and the cold, he collapsed just beyond the stockade. They sent the corn out by another slave and confined the priest to his aunt's cabin.

Two weeks later, his protectress returned. Having lost a son just after René's murder, she adopted Father Jogues formally, and she gave him two deerskins, one to fashion clothes out of and the other to sleep under at night.

Father Jogues disappeared each day into a grove where he had stripped the bark off a tree and carved a cross. In this small chapel he opened his heart in prayer, reliving his six years at the mission of Sainte Marie, his journeys on the raging rivers, the fellowship of the Hurons and the other Frenchmen as they set out only a few months before, and then the horrific tortures and burnings he had witnessed, saving prisoners from the fires of hell by baptizing them just before they expired.

As spring at last breathed upon the hills, bands of hunters returned to the village and prepared their nets and weirs for fishing. Father Jogues had another errand in mind.

A half-breed lad with blue eyes name Togoniron whom some called "Kryn" indicated that René's body had been removed from the stream and hidden in the ravine. Gossip though it was, Father Jogues asked questions of everyone as to where René's corpse could be. Searching every day as soon as the snow melted, he found at last the yellowed skull and ribs among dead leaves beneath a tree. Reverently he kissed the three tomahawk wounds in the skull, and the other bones, the ribs and the arms and the hands, the teeth marks from coyotes and fox. He raked through the loam, collecting the bones into a pile.

Murdered for making the sign of the cross, René was surely a martyr to the cause of Christianity, and so a saint. Father Jogues wished to transport the relics back to Quebec and possibly to France. With an eye to accomplishing this, he deposited the bones in a hollow tree and intoned funeral hymns.

The burial of René closed a chapter for him. Gone was any need to remain among the Mohawks. The constant threat of death, causing him to prepare so often for the end, would continue until he lay, too, in the leaves, a collection of bones gnawed by dogs. Understanding this, he committed himself to his survival and either his ransom or escape.

Chapter 5

✠

Father Jogues Attempts an Escape

Toward the end of April, ambassadors from the Sokoki nation appeared at Ossernenon. The Mohawks lodged and fed them, and gave them tobacco pipes to smoke after the meal. Their leader asked if they might meet in council. The council was held in the long house where Father Jogues resided.

"Like you," the Sokoki chief said gravely to the assembled, "we hold the Algonquin as our enemies, never to be trusted. Last fall, they captured a great chief from among us and tortured him and paraded him on a leash among the French at Trois-Rivières and at Quebec. Recognizing him, Onontio, the great chief of the French, begged the Algonquins to release our chief and offered a great ransom. The Algonquins agreed to his release, and the French sent him back among us, loaded with gifts. Onontio made one request in return, that we ask you, the great Mohawk nation, to release Ondessonk, the blackrobe. Therefore we ask that you lead Ondessonk and Ihandich (Couture) back among their people and we will add much precious wampum to offers of the French goodwill."

The Mohawk chiefs deliberated privately. They accepted the wampum belts and promised to return the two Frenchmen. The Sokoki departed, satisfied with their mission, yet in the days following, the Mohawks spoke more of Father Jogues's death than his release. Indeed, a warrior of the Bear Clan, hearing of the ransom plan and hateful toward Jogues, rushed into the long house brandishing a club and knocked the priest unconscious. With this, Father Jogues saw the course he must pursue.

As the weather warmed, his aunt and the people of her *ohwahchira*, her matriarchal family, packed up their canoes to visit Fort Orange. They invited Father Jogues along. A flotilla of a dozen canoes from Tionontoguen arrived at Ossernenon, and three from the Turtle Clan joined to transport the winter's furs to Fort Orange. Together the flotilla proceeded eastward. Moving with the current, the paddling was effortless and the twists in the river, new vistas of sky gladdened Father Jogues's heart. Gone was the confining long house and palisade, the enmity and spite of the people, the constant fear that a wrong word or movement would visit death upon him. William Couture was among those from Tionontoguen and their reunion was warm and happy.

After a long portage at the Cohoes Falls, the river of the Mohawks flowed into a broader stream named by the English for Henry Hudson, which the natives call the "River That Flows Both Ways," for the Atlantic tide reverses its direction every six hours. Through islands on the swift current, and then into the open water they paddled. The lowlands opened to blue mountains in the distance. Around a wide gentle curve they paddled with the current toward the bastions and walls of the Dutch fort and the fur trading outpost, Rensselaerwyck. A cluster of log and plank buildings surrounded it. A three-masted ship lay at anchor in the middle of the channel, a rowboat filled with furs from the winter trapping plying the water toward it.

The flotilla made for shore and tied up at a small dock. The dock was attached at the bank to a warehouse and, facing toward the street, a shop. Father Jogues helped unload furs from the canoes. Afterward, he was allowed to walk in the streets and mingle with the Dutch. When Arendt Van Corlaer heard that Father Jogues was visiting, he called at the Dutch Reformed Church to collect the minister, Dominie Johannes Megapolensis, and together they found Jogues and brought him to a tavern for a meal. Speaking through a Huguenot interpreter, Jan Labatie, who had accompanied Van Corlaer to Ossernenon the previous fall, they greeted each other warmly. The Dutch Reformed minister carried a bundle, and when they sat at the table, he spoke through the interpreter:

"I have something to give you," he said and handed the wrapped bundle to Father Jogues. The priest opened it and looked up at the minister, tears welling in his eyes.

"My breviary? Where did you find it?"

"The Mohawks who captured you brought it to us last autumn."

"I have nothing with which to pay . . ."

The minister clasped his hand warmly. "Back home, in France and in Holland our religions direct us to be enemies. But here, in this new land, we may be true Christians with each other."

Father Jogues was sobbing as he turned the pages of his prayer book with his mutilated hands.

Van Corlaer returned with Jogues to the Mohawk camp and he made an offer of three hundred florins to the elder of the expedition who sat on an elk skin robe smoking.

"Without authority of our great council," the chief said, "we cannot let this man go free. I will pursue this when we return to our homeland, and perhaps we will deliver him to Trois-Rivières this summer."

Van Corlaer communicated this to Father Jogues. He bowed his head. "They have promised the Sokoki likewise that they would deliver me home, but nothing has come of that."

"Do not give up hope," Van Corlaer said. He lowered his voice.

"If they won't agree to ransom you, then we will help you escape. The domine and I have made up our minds."

Jogues looked at him with penetrating eyes. "If you try that, they will massacre you in your beds."

"Much of what they say is swagger," Van Corlaer said. "If we let them take you back, your life will be upon our heads."

The offer of ransom had a negative effect since the Mohawks, realizing how valuable Ondessonk was to the Dutch, guarded him more closely. After three days, the flotilla set out southward to the mouth of a tributary stream where they could rig their weirs to catch spawning steelheads and to spear and net trout and striped bass in the river.

They pitched their tents on the riverbank. The women set up their weirs in the stream. The men fished in the placid river as the tide flowed in and then out. At night they set up tripods in the canoes and lit fires of pine knots. The effect was pleasing as the boats, carrying the low braziers, drifted back and forth across the river in the moonlight.

The pace of this life pleased Father Jogues: the slow, peaceful current of the river, the easy wind from the west, the enormous stripers that the men pulled from the river and then cleaned and gave to the women and to Jogues to hang on frames for smoking. The cycles of sun and moon and the deep quiet of the stars restored him, banished memories of the village with its fleas and lice, rodents and prowling dogs, wailing children, the pervasive smells of urine and excrement, the scenes of copulation rarely concealed. He grew contemplative and even philosophic.

In camp, the Mohawks relaxed as well. They wove the weirs and repaired their nets and sharpened spears and gaffs for the striped bass. They sat by the outdoor fires at night talking low, re-telling the tales and legends of Sky Woman and Deganawida and Hiawatha founding the Houdesaunee, the League of the Great Long House, and of the stone giants in the north.

Couture talked about returning to Quebec, but the priest locked away in his heart his yearning to escape which Van Corlaer and Megapolensis had placed there. Soon the fishing party broke camp and paddled home, passing by the fort and trading post.

Father Jogues returned with his breviary to Ossernenon. The book, onion skin paper and bound in leather, connected him to his days in Rouen and prompted memories of his seminary days. The village, the Mohawk nation and, it seemed, the entire confederacy were suddenly enraged against the French. War parties danced in the firelight to the beat of a drum. They buried their hatchets in the war pole and prayed to Aireskou, then left the dwindling fires for the war path north. Because of his prowess, Mathurin's Man led new war parties to capture French and Hurons.

When a Mohawk asked him to write a letter as a ruse to open the gates at Fort Richelieu, Father Jogues did so. In the letter to the French commander, he indicated he had given up hope of being ransomed and vowed to remain in Ossernenon as long as the Lord required.

An embassy of Mohawks set out to visit other nations which they held in thrall to collect their yearly tribute. They took Father Jogues to display as their captive. The priest did not enjoy the attention and spent his time ministering to the sick, particularly infants, baptizing those he could and comforting all the others in their infirmities. At the third or fourth village, he heard his name called from the shadows of a long house:

"Ondessonk! Don't you recall me?"

He went to the pallet and saw an emaciated man struggling to breathe.

"I do not recall you, sir," he said.

"Do you remember being delivered from death?"

"It has happened so many times."

"At the third village of the Mohawks, they tied you to a cross rail, above the ground. You were swooning with the pain. Someone cut your bonds and helped you down?"

"I remember. Who was he so I might thank him?"

"It was myself. I took pity on you. I ignored their criticisms and I cut you down."

"May God bless you! It is so troubling to see you in this condition." Father Jogues spoke to him about salvation, and the man opened his heart and asked to be baptized. So weak was the man that Father Jogues remained by his pallet until he expired some hours later.

Back they went, finally, to Ossernenon, loaded with furs from the other nations.

On the feast of St. Ignatius, July 31, the eve of the anniversary he had first set out from Trois-Rivières, Father Jogues again knelt paddling in a canoe toward Rensselaerwyck. Furs captured from the Hurons and other nations accepted in tribute were to be traded for implements of Dutch iron. Resigned to remain among the Mohawks, Father Jogues looked forward to speaking to the Dutch Reformed minister about theology and metaphysics.

The minister lived in the second-finest house in the place. Around the little log fort with its four or five Breteuil cannon and half dozen swivel guns, there had been erected twenty-five or thirty plank houses with thatched roofs, and these housed the traders and farmers of the settlement. Cows grazed on the common pasture in the midst of the houses, chickens ran about pecking in the gravel and pigs wallowed in the mud and slops. Summer was fully in bloom, and balmy, sunny days were followed by lashing thunderstorms. Flies and mosquitoes swarmed both inside and out.

Compared to the homes of the burghers, the parsonage was large and commodious. The minister gave Father Jogues a chamber on the second story, and the first night Van Corlaer dined with them.

"I approached your captors once more to purchase your freedom," he said.

"They will not grant that favor," Father Jogues said. "It must be God's will that I administer to the new captives they will seize in the north. I am resigned to my fate."

"No, Father," Van Corlaer said. "It is not right that a man so learned serve as a slave to these savages."

"Christ bathed the feet of his apostles at the last supper," Father Jogues said.

Van Corlaer, a man of the world, brushed aside that comment with annoyance. "They are worse than animals the way they torture and eat each other. They accepted some gifts I gave them in return for a promise they would not torture the new French captives, but I cannot get them to release you."

"Help him see, then," Jogues sought the assistance of the minister, "that it is God's will."

"I do not agree," the domine said. "The lord helps those who help themselves. We will afford you the opportunity of escape, and you must take it."

"No," the priest said, shaking his head, "that would bring a calamity down upon your heads. I will not be the cause of mayhem and murder."

Staying with the domine, Father Jogues took up a quill and wrote a thirty-page account of his life in the fourteen months since he'd left the Huron mission. He gave the letter to Van Corlaer to post it back to France, and then he departed with his aunt to fish the shallows down river.

Father Jogues walked along the river in the stars that night, recalling his prayer on the St. Lawrence a year ago, and finding

René observing him. He prayed now for guidance. The sign came the next day as they stretched their nets and fixed weirs in the current. A canoe straight from Ossernenon hailed his aunt as he stood knee-deep in the river. Warriors boasted loudly enough so he might hear every word:

"A war party returned to our village, victorious over the French. They carried six scalps, one the color of corn silk. They escorted four prisoners. We caressed them well, and then we burned two. The other two are being held until we return, when they will sing their death songs."

Father Jogues felt he was needed at the village to baptize the prisoners, or if they were French, to hear their confessions and give them the last rites. He approached his aunt when the warriors were at the campsite eating from the kettle.

"I must return to our village. Could you spare me, Aunt?"

"Of course. Go back with these who arrived today. Take food with you. It is a journey of three or four days."

"Thank you," the priest said humbly. He walked up the bank and to the fire pit where the bragging warriors were eating grilled fish. He told them of his desire to return. They nodded and grunted and agreed to take him back.

Soon they were paddling on the river. The tide was running in and so they were with the current all the way up to Rensselaerwyck. As the fort and the thatched cottages came into view, they paddled for shore and put in just below the dock of the principal fur trader. They climbed out of the canoe and walked into a compound where other Mohawks were standing about. When these warriors saw the priest, they all rushed to him and began beating him and cursing him, calling him a dead man. Only then did he realize the appearance of the warriors had been a ruse to get him away from his aunt.

"Dog," they said, "traitor, sorcerer, worker of evil spells, we shall kill you!"

"What is the reason?" he asked, and one of them cried:

"The paper you gave us with marks upon it, when we delivered it to the French garrison to trick them and get inside, they fired their cannon upon us!"

"We lost a canoe, three muskets and other valuable baggage!" another said.

"We returned empty-handed from the campaign because of your treachery."

"You must be returned to Ossernenon and burned."

As it was afternoon and the Mohawks were desirous of drinking Holland gin that evening, they placed Ondessonk under guard and locked him in a barn.

Word of Father Jogues's return reached Van Corlaer and he walked down to the Mohawk camp and found the priest.

"Death is certain if you return, Father. Remember my offer, which I will honor tonight. See that vessel at anchor? It is sailing to Virginia and then to Bordeaux or La Rochelle, and it will carry you home to France."

"I thank you for your concern, but I believe it is God's plan that I return even if it is to die."

"God's plan is what we do with the opportunities He sends us. Had you been in Ossernenon when the warriors from the failed campaign returned, you would be food for crows by now. As it is, the means for your escape is readily at hand. Heed me. You won't get another chance."

"Monsieur, this matter is of such importance. Tomorrow morning I will have an answer for you."

"Delay causes the bird to slip from the net."

That night the Mohawks slept in the barn, a dozen of them stretched about him on the ground. Father Jogues, though, lay awake with indecision. He weighed the alternatives. René was dead. Since Couture was adopted, he did not need the priest as his protector. Many of the Hurons had escaped and those left were unconverted shunned him, believing he was destined for the fires.

At daybreak, before the Mohawks stirred, Father Jogues stole off to Van Corlaer's house. The agent summoned Domine Megapolensis and they formed a plan to get his captors drunk that night and leave a small rowboat for him to take out to the ship. During the day they called upon the ship's captain. He agreed to stow the priest away and take him eventually to France.

During the day of anxiety and inner turmoil, Father Jogues reconnoitered the farm to remember in the dark the easiest way to get through the fences to the river. Again he retired in the August heat and insects with the Mohawks who snored and groaned drunkenly in their sleep. Around one in the morning, he arose and stealthily crept over their sleeping forms to the door. The door creaked as he opened it, but no one awakened. He slipped through the opening and started across the yard but a chilling bark announced he'd been discovered and a pack of dogs attacked him. A mastiff bit his naked leg.

The Dutchman came out cursing, and with a club he beat the dogs away from the priest and brought him inside the house. Red-faced and cursing, he lit candles. To guard against rabies, the Dutchman placed a hair of the dog in each wound, then tied rags about Jogues's legs and sent him back into the barn. The Mohawks whom he awakened from their hungover sleep, slapped him, sent him to the ground and locked the door against the dogs who were still barking and lunging outside. Soon the Mohawks were snoring again.

Father Jogues lay in despair. Trying to read the word of God, he kept getting mixed signals. Because of the dogs, he despaired of deliverance, but when a servant opened a door from the house, he got onto his hands and knees and crawled over the sleeping Mohawks. He whispered that the servant should tie up the dogs, and he waited a moment, then went out into the misty morning.

Ignoring the pain in his leg, he ran for the riverbank. Through reeds and thorn bushes he ran, and beyond the houses of the settlement and their gardens and fields, he arrived at the fort. He spied the rowboat Van Corlaer promised, but the tide had receded and it was stranded in the mud. He pulled at the boat this way and that. He rolled it from side to side. He tried to lift it. It did not budge. He went to the water and called to the captain. No one heard him.

Nearby were the huts of Mohawks. They would soon awaken. Praying from the depths of his soul, he grasped the boat and pushed with all his strength. It moved! He tried from the other direction, and it moved that way. Slowly he worked it down to the water and he swung the bow around and pushed the boat into the water. He was floating!

As he rowed, the sun streaked the sky pink and crimson. He rowed happily to the ship, bumped into it, tied the boat and climbed up the rope ladder. The blustery captain came out.

"You made it, lad! Good! It was certain murder to leave you ashore with those savages! They're man-eaters, you know. Now, so they don't discover you, down in the hold you go. Can't be very pleasant for you, but you can come up just as soon as we're under sail tonight."

He opened a trap door. Father Jogues descended into the dark fetid hold that smelled like a sewer. Above him the captain closed the trap door, extinguishing light, closing in the damp and nauseating air. To hide the trap door, the captain moved a heavy chest over it.

When they discovered their prisoner gone, the Mohawks exploded. Straight to Van Corlaer's house they stormed and beat upon his door until he opened it to a cluster of war clubs and hatchets.

"Give us Ondessonk or we will fire your town!"

"I don't have him," Van Corlaer said.

"We will slaughter your cattle and scalp you and all who live here!" another threatened.

"I do not know where he is," Van Corlaer said, "but if it will help you swallow his loss, I will offer again the three hundred gilders."

"What is your gold to us?" one asked. "Can we eat it?"

"We have no authority to set him free," another said. "We must answer to the council, and when it hears what you have done, we will return and level your fort, and your village will be a heap of ashes and bones."

"Look for him," Van Corlaer invited them. "Perhaps he is walking about."

"Don't trifle with us," one of the warriors wielded his axe at the agent.

"I wouldn't do that."

"You produce him today, or all of you die!"

When they left, Van Corlaer visited Domine Megapolensis.

"We should keep him close by," Van Corlaer said, "in case they begin to make good on their threats."

"I will go out and fetch him a boat," the minister said. "He will return when he hears what danger we are in."

Early the following morning the minister and the commandant of the fort slipped out in a rowboat to the ship still anchored in the channel. A doctor summoned by the captain had attended to the priest's dog bites, but he put on an ointment that exacerbated the pain and made his leg swell up. Father Jogues was in horrible pain and could barely walk.

"We will not give you back to the Mohawks," the minister told the priest, "but we should like to show you to them if they believe you are gone. It may quiet them and prevent them from destroying our homes."

The ship captain listened to the minister and the commandant and then he exploded: "If you take this priest back to shore he will die! I'm no lover of Catholics, but that is certain death. I will not allow him to leave my ship! Both of you cowards, get off my ship!"

Now Father Jogues spoke: "I am greatly moved, Captain, by your loyalty and your fear for my safety. My desire is not so much to survive as it is to do God's will. I sensed it was His will to return with my captors, even to certain death in the fires, but these Dutch, out of the kindness of their hearts, sought to rescue me. Now, before the fury of the Mohawks bursts about their heads I will surrender to the Mohawks and accompany them back to Ossernenon."

As he finished this speech, he fell to the deck in a swoon. The captain sent for a jug of brandy and they gave him a good drink of it and revived him.

"Very well, gentlemen, let us go."

At midnight, as the Mohawks slept, they rowed the priest back to shore. He met with Van Corlaer and the principal men of the settlement who apologized profusely, but indicated that their survival might require them to produce him.

They housed him now in the commandant's house. The surgeon of the settlement was called and found that the ointment and filth from the hold of the ship had caused the wound to become gangrenous. He feared he might have to amputate the priest's leg.

Two days later, under cover of night, they moved Father Jogues to the sutler's house. The miserly old sutler stored and sold provisions to the settlement. He hid Father Jogues behind a corner partition up under the eaves. Unbearably hot by night and by day, he crouched behind barrels and casks even as the sutler invited the Mohawks up to the attic to carry their furs for storage, or to fetch articles they bought from him. He crouched there in apprehension for two weeks while the sutler and his wife stole most of the food sent to him. The old sutler even gave him drinking water out of a tub he used to make lye and this poisoned the priest and wracked him with cramps.

Only Domine Megapolensis visited him. He reported the Mohawks were constantly searching everywhere for him. The Bear Clan was furious that their victim had been stolen. By mid-September, when the priest had been a month in hiding, the Mohawks threatened Van Corlaer to destroy the settlement if Ondessonk were not produced.

"You have said this many times before. I cannot understand your mind," Van Corlaer said courageously. "I rescued Ondessonk for his own safety, and I offered you three hundred guilders for him. You refused the gold, and I refused to turn him over, knowing you would torture and murder him, a man who has not harmed you in the least. Now you threaten me with a massacre? I will return the threat. If you don't relinquish your claim to Ondessonk, we will cease trading with you and you will get no more gunpowder or muskets or knives from us."

This quieted the Mohawks. The passage of time also had mollified them. They saw that they might live down the insult of having a hostage stolen. They launched into their oratory and announced that they would accept the presents at last. Since his aunt had already conceded that he was gone and not coming back, they would be consoled over the loss of Ondessonk.

Van Corlaer gave them the gold, but he also suspected treachery. He waited another week before spiriting Father Jogues out of the sutler's garret in the dead of night and aboard a rowboat to another waiting ship. Once again, Father Jogues walked the deck of a ship in the middle of the river, and in the cool wind of a late September evening, he offered prayers to God for his deliverance. The next morning the sloop weighed anchor and set sail down the river with a contingent from the settlement going to meet with the governor in Nieu Nederland. The ship gracefully tacked from shore to shore in the crisp westerly breeze.

Chapter 6

Returning To Civilization, Father Jogues Rejects Its Many Pomps

THEY ANCHORED NEAR the fishing ground in the shallows. They'd dropped down river from Albany to avoid the Iroquois. Dressed now in an ill-fitting costume of a Dutch burgher, Father Jogues joined in the celebration, the drinking, the cheer. He did not want to seem ungrateful, but the attention embarrassed him. Domine Megapolensis sat with him on the deck of the sloop on his first night of freedom, opening wine bottles and offering grandiose toasts, even christening an island, "the island of Jesuit Jogues." Trying to think best of the festivities and of the Dutchmen with their flushed faces, Father Jogues concluded: "Each man shows love in his own way."

On the deck of the sloop the plump Dutchmen in their wide-brimmed hats, their long-skirted coats, knickerbockers and buckled shoes proudly displayed the prosperity brought by the fur trade. They smoked clay pipes and drank tankards of ale or the domine's wine or Holland gin. This trip was a junket of sorts, for Director-General William Kieft had summoned them to bring the priest to New Amsterdam in order to discuss the French, the Iroquois and the fate of the Dutch colony. Leaves were changing, brilliant red and yellows, on either side of the broad blue river, and a soft wind wafted of freedom as the sun set ever so gently and stars uncovered themselves.

Next morning the sailors hauled up the anchor and continued down river. Behind was the cramped, narrow, twisting river of the Mohawks. This North River of the Dutch opened spectacularly into glittering bays as wide as a lake in the embrace of purple mountains near the Tappan Zee. Behind him in the midnight forests Jogues had left the ritualized torture and burnings, the dream feasts and mayhem of the natives, and now on the broad afternoon of his life—he was only thirty-six years of age—God had saved him from a certain and painful death, granting him another chance to live and do good work.

On the fifth day, great rusted cliffs rose upon their right, and the island of Manhattan appeared on the left, a low hump of forested land. Around the foot of this island they sailed breezily. A salt-laden wind from the sea was in their sails. A windmill spun and stone walls of Fort Amsterdam rose up on the shore. Back they tacked toward the sunny current, and then once more toward the rows of gabled brick houses and the wharf and strip of rock of Schreyers' Hoek.

Domine Megapolensis led. Father Jogues along the cobbled street and through the gates of the Dutch fort. Soldiers lounged by the barracks. In front of the new church stood the massive red brick mansion of the colony's Director-General.

They were ushered into the wide, low-ceilinged hallway and living room by a servant and out the door to greet them burst Director-General Kieft himself, a squat, pudgy man with bushy white hair who threw a manly embrace around Father Jogues.

"Welcome, Father!" he said. "We heretics are not used to having holy Jesuits as our guests." Domine Megapolensis feigned shock at Kieft's self-deprecation. Jan Labatie provided a serviceable translation. "I see the generous souls of Rensselaerwyck gave you the finest garments money could buy," he said with merry sarcasm. "Dirk! Dirk!" His servant responded with a tray of tankards of ale.

"Call Van Schoonhoven to measure our guest for a new suit of clothes. A cloak and hat as well. And a walking stick!" He winked at the priest. "One needs a walking stick for the dogs, eh, Father? Best tailor in the colony though. We've made up a room for you here in the mansion."

"I could not possibly impose . . ."

"Nonsense! I won't hear of your going elsewhere. I have called for a state dinner Tuesday next, too, to celebrate your deliverance from those barbarians."

"I cannot put you through the trouble." Self-consciously he looked at his mangled fingers.

The governor handed the priest a tankard of ale. "Here's to your health!" They clinked and drank.

Father Jogues's room was above the courtyard where the soldiers drilled in the morning. Pretty milkmaids congregated with their milk pails to watch, all too briefly, the manly parade. Horses, too—until Van Corlaer's visit Jogues hadn't seen horses since leaving France seven years before—horses drew coaches of the wealthier merchants.

Each day Father Jogues dressed in his fine newly tailored clothes and he walked out of the gate, along the streets and down along the waterfront with Megapolensis. New Amsterdam was a bustling place, as busy as the port of La Rochelle. Eighteen different languages were spoken here, the domine told him. His keen eye observed vices of drunkenness in the taverns and he noticed prostitutes where the sailors put in. The good domine revealed harsh criticisms of Kieft, his temper and his irascibility which had earned him the nickname "William the Testy." Just now there was unrest with the Algonquins who had murdered forty Dutch, slaughtered their cattle and burned their homes, and the Dutch farmers had fled to the fort for protection.

At the state dinner, the Dutch burghers questioned Jogues about his time among the Mohawks. They asked him to explain, good

Calvinists all, what rewards he might expect from the Messieurs of the Company of France for his sacrifice. He told them:

"I have not come to this land for riches or any other worldly benefit. I have come to preach the Gospel and to win souls for Jesus Christ."

They shook their heads, some in disbelief, others surprised by his naivete.

Unfortunately, being October, Father Jogues had arrived in New Amsterdam after the last vessel left the colony for Europe. He made it known that he was willing to board a coastal trader if bound for Quebec. When Megapolensis and the Rensselaerwyck burghers returned north, he feared he would be stranded in the Protestant colony all winter.

Finally, in late October a small bark sailed into the harbor, a collier. So desperate were the Dutch for reinforcements to fight the Algonquins, Kieft convened the Council of Eight and they voted to memorialize the company and sent the ship back to Holland for soldiers with a request:

> We were here pursued by these wild heathens and barbarous savages with fire and sword; daily in our houses and fields they have cruelly murdered men and women; and with hatchets and tomahawks struck little children dead in their parents' arms or before their doors; or carried them away into bondage. . . . We turn, then, in a body, to you, Noble, High and Mighty Lords . . . that your High Mightinesses would take pity on us . . . to forward us, by the earliest opportunity, such assistance as Your High Mightinesses will deem most proper in order that we, poor, forlorn people, may not be left all at once a prey, with wives and children, to these cruel heathens.

Kieft generously offered Father Jogues passage aboard the coal ship:

"The ship is small to brave the sea this time of year, Father, but you are welcome to a berth if you wish."

"I am eternally grateful for all you and those up the river have done to rescue me," Father Jogues told him. "This gift of passage home will far outshine everything together, and I am humbled. I sense the workings of Providence here."

"We will give you a coat and a blanket and a six weeks' supply of food. Along with our good wishes, we send you home to your loved ones."

Father Jogues pressed his hand in both his own and a tear filled his eye. Kieft gave him a letter of passage identifying him and asking that others, in view of his captivity and torture, treat him with kindness.

On November 5, well beyond the usual end of navigation, the little ship cast off from Schreyers' Hoek and ventured into the stormy North Atlantic.

So small was the boat, Father Jogues was assigned to sleep on deck among coils of rope and rigging. There he was splashed and soaked by waves that roared up over the railing as the ship lumbered through the late autumn seas. When he descended into the hold for shelter, a horde of cats fouled his blanket and his clothing. The craft tossed about ceaselessly, and not without irony did Jogues consider himself the marked prophet Jonah on his way to Nineveh.

Forty-eight days the crossing took. As the ship made for the English channel, a gale blew it off course. The captain sought shelter in Falmouth, and as Cornwall came into view, two vessels rose out of the mist and gave chase, letting loose with volleys of cannon when they were in range. The little boat drew in between the hills that sheltered the Bay of Falmouth and the two ships faded into the mist.

Falmouth was now held by Royalists supporting Charles I in putting down the rebellion. The two ships had belonged to the Parliamentarians, and so Father Jogues narrowly escaped death at the hands of Oliver Cromwell and his Roundheads who had executed four Jesuits the year before. At long last, on the morning of Christmas

Eve, Father Isaac Jogues landed in Brittany. He wore a seaman's cap now, and a ragged overcoat. He heard mass at a small church on the coast and made his way to the Jesuit house in Rennes. At five in the morning on January 5, 1644, he knocked upon the spiked wooden door to the Jesuit College of Rennes. The brother porter, who was ringing the bell for morning mass, heard the pounding and opened the door. Outside stood an emaciated man in an old overcoat, a scarf about his neck and a sailor's hat on his head.

"What can I do for you?"

"I should like to see Father Rector if possible."

"We are about to hear mass, sir. You may come in and wait."

"If at all possible, I should like to see Father Rector immediately. Even before mass. I bring news from Canada, from the fathers there."

"I will ask him." The brother went to the sacristy where Father Rector was in his alb and stole getting ready to say mass. "A poor man has arrived," he said, "with news from the fathers in Canada."

"We are ready for the mass," Father Rector said, then he mused, "perhaps the man is in a hurry or needs help?" He removed his alb and stole and went downstairs to the parlor. The man handed him a letter which Father Rector did not read. "You have come from Canada?"

"Yes, Father."

"Do you know Father Vimont?"

"Yes, Father."

"Father Brebeuf?"

"Extremely well."

"Father Jogues? Did you know him?"

"I know him very well indeed."

"We understand he was captured by the Mohawks. Do you know if he is dead or still a captive?"

"He is at liberty, Father," and he knelt at the Rector's feet. "It is he who speaks to you." He kissed the Rector's hand and begged his blessing.

Father Rector lifted Jogues from his knees, threw his arms around him and kissed him on both cheeks. In a loud voice that echoed through the vaults and corridors of the monastery, he welcomed Father Jogues home, and other brothers and priests, hearing the commotion, hastened into the room, hugging and blessing him and weeping for joy at his return. Half an hour late, they celebrated mass with Father Jogues in attendance, and he received communion among his fellow Jesuits in the sweet chanting of the choir for the first time in over a year.

News of Isaac Jogues's return flew through France. Each year the populace devoured the *Relations*, letters of the Jesuit priests from New France which detailed progress made in the missions. These first-person epistolary accounts read like exciting adventure stories. Now a true hero of these accounts had returned, seemingly from the dead. People clamored to see him, to touch him, to revere and flatter him for the great faith he had shown in the face of martyrdom. Though Father Jogues did not want to discuss his captivity, the Jesuits at Rennes pestered him for more and more details about his capture, his servitude and his escape. He wrote to his mother to assure her he was yet alive, contrary to the surmise of this year's *Relation*.

Despite his joy to be delivered, Father Jogues abhorred the notoriety. Constantly gaped at, questioned, revered and flattered, he withdrew and avoided his fellow priests. He informed the rector that he wanted only to return to New France and to journey again among the Hurons. The rector relayed this request to the provincial superior observing, "He is as cheerful as if he had suffered nothing. And he is as zealous to return to the Hurons with all those dangers facing him as if they were safe harbors. He expects to cross the sea once more to assist those poor people, and to finish the sacrifice already begun."

The road to Paris ran through Orleans, the city of his birth and early years. He spent January 16-17 at his old house. Madame Jogues wept over her son, over his mutilated hands. He kept accounts of the pain and the horrors minimal and expressed happiness to his mother for the mission God had given him. She held his hands— eight of his ten nails were torn out, the tips of his fingers mangled, the left thumb amputated and the index finger barely a stump. She scolded him for being so underweight, urged him to take care of his health and pleaded with him not return to those barbarous lands.

With his family calling him a canonized saint, he shied from the adulation that bordered on adoration, and he escaped as soon as he could to Paris. Yet there he discovered that an addendum, "Deliverance and Arrival" had just been added to the published *Relation of 1642 and 1643* detailing his return. All of Paris was reading the story of his suffering and his escape, how Father Vimont called him "this living martyr, this suffering confessor, this man rich in extreme poverty, joyful and contented in the land of pain and sadness—in a word, this Jesuit clothed like a savage, or rather, like St. John the Baptist."

Again, Father Jogues chaffed under the notoriety. He constantly expressed his desire to return to New France. The two thousand students at Clermont College where he was housed craned to see him in the mess hall. Some begged him for details, untested fledglings who had little courage to move beyond the cloisters and the classrooms. Everywhere he went, people announced his presence. News callers cried out his story in the Gardens of the Palais Royal and the Luxembourg. This silly fame, he felt, was like North Atlantic seas rising above the taffrail and drenching him, awakening him to the artificiality of monarchs, of hierarchies, of bishops and cardinals and even, sacrilege upon sacrilege, the pope. In those horrific times of torture and fire and screaming and blood, of murder and dismemberment and cannibalism, Jogues had penetrated into the very essence of things, the horrible things civilization hid behind its taboos. What significance did the fine fabrics, the ermine robes, the gowns of the ladies, the marks of rank and office hold when within we are all nothing more than pitiable, shivering souls in a blizzard? What significance was there to the sumptuous banquets and collations, the viands of beef and pork and fowl, the bouquet and sparkle of wines, the chocolate, when we might survive on raw frog and rotting meat or a handful of dry corn meal? What significance attended the palaces and cathedrals, the cloisters and rectories and elegant country chateaux if we could curl into a snowbank and shiver until the sun appeared again?

Jogues had seen the uselessness of wealth and comfort and status. The essence of life might only be glimpsed and sought and to any degree attained through self-sacrifice, suffering and forgiveness. He took Jesus Christ literally now: "If you want to be complete, go, sell your possessions and give to the poor, and you will have treasure in heaven. Then come, follow me."

Still his eyes and his mind and his heart were filled with scenes of the great rivers and mountains and forests. Still his flesh felt the burning brand, the knife, the teeth of his captors. Still he witnessed the fiery dances, the screaming pain as the Hurons and Mohawks tortured victims to the war god. What did rank and privilege—military or political or ecclesiastical—mean if pain and unimaginable violence was the true foundation of civilization? That's what war taught, even though the military arts disguised all this to civilians with rank and uniform and polished boots. Rare was leader who boasted about the corpses strewn on battlefields, the stench of decay, the carrion birds. But that's what coups and revolutions and mutinies taught and, darker than all else, the Inquisition. Joan d'Arc was no less a torture victim than Eustace. These were not aberrant occurrences. This was normal. The peace and prosperity were exceptions to the rule.

Everywhere he looked this European world seemed constructed of *papier-mâché*, fragile, transitory. The great stone cathedrals with their massive bells gave no sense of permanence since within it the pagan heart seethed with bloodlust. The logical refinements of dogma, the endless debates about creed and doctrine—the virgin birth, transubstantiation, the resurrection—no longer held any fascination or even curiosity now that he had witnessed the fiery, bloody, raw and palpitating heart of darkness. The heat and the pressure of his year among the Mohawks had fused Jogues's experience with his reason and he saw the uselessness of all pomp and ritual and the endless debates. Even the architecture, the traceries and the stained glass, the gothic vaults and elegance of La Chappell, the sheer size of Chartres and Reims and Notre Dame— testimony in stone to the fervor and permanence of Catholicism— all seemed vain in comparison to the majesty of the forests and mountains God Himself had created. Yes, he wanted only to return.

In the midst of these ruminations, his Father Confessor relayed that an invitation arrived for Father Jogues to appear at court and for an audience with the Queen Mother, Anne of Austria.

"But I am so unworthy!" Father Jogues protested. "These courts and rituals, their robes and gowns of office, their coats of arms, their palaces, their crowns—these mean less than nothing to me. Why should I go to her and pretend they do?"

"It is not a request," Father Confessor stated, "it is a royal command."

For days Father Jogues avoided any talk about the invitation or acceptance of it. When a second more strongly worded invitation arrived, Father Confessor told him he must respond and attend to her. In a new black soutane he appeared at Court and was received. The Queen Regent paid him direct tribute:

"Our tragedians have to invent adventures and stories to touch our imagination, but here is a true story of colossal adventure and heroism," she said. She motioned for the hands which Father Jogues held within his cassock so as not to offend. He produced his mangled hands and the Queen dropped to her knees and kissed them. All of her ladies in waiting did likewise and Father Jogues, mortified and shamed, wanted only to vanish.

And so he made up his mind, however he might, to get back to the Huron mission as soon as possible. When he petitioned his superiors at first they scoffed mildly and told him to take some time to consider the rashness of this decision. Surely if he went back into the wilds he would die there. That did not matter, he assured them, for God, the missions and New France already owned his life whatever they might do with it. He could not remain here when so much work remained to be done "at home" in New France. So insistent were his entreaties and so compelling his logic that his superior finally relented and ordered him to leave on the first transport for New France in the spring of 1644.

As overjoyed as a lover granted his ultimate wish, Jogues went happily about his preparations. Because of his audience with the Queen Regent, Cardinal Mazarin and the Directors of the Company of New France met with him and listened to his request for more soldiers to guard the waterway between Quebec and the Huron missions. Mazarin ordered troops to sail that spring and to serve the colony by holding the Iroquois in check.

Father Jogues wrote to Arendt Van Corlaer and arranged to pay back his ransom of three hundred gold florins. He wrote to Domine Megapolensis as well and urged him to return to the fold of the one true religion. He spoke with his superiors, Fathers Filleau and Charles Lalemant, requesting that more missionaries be sent to the field. Finally, because his crippled, mutilated thumb and forefinger prevented him from saying mass, he drew up a petition for special dispensation and forwarded it along with letters from Queen Anne and her Council to Father Mutius Vitelleschi, the General of the Society of Jesus in Rome who submitted the petition to Pope Urban VIII.

The pope responded: "It would be shameful that a martyr of Christ not be allowed to drink the blood of Christ," and he granted the petition. The pope's ruling reached Paris in March and Father Jogues felt as if he had entered paradise. The last mass he had celebrated was August 1, 1642, the day he had set out for the Huron mission. Now, twenty months later, he again raised the host and pronounced the words *Hoc est enim corpus meum*, and lifted the chalice to change the wine into the blood of Christ.

In April, Father Jogues learned that the first ship would depart for Quebec in six weeks. He made his way to La Rochelle. The journey took him again through Orleans. He stopped to bid farewell to his mother and the rest of his family. His mother knew she was seeing her beloved Isaac for the last time. She held his hands and wept over them, touched the scars on his face and neck and arms. She knew he would suffer again, perhaps lose his life for the greater glory of God, and she resigned herself with a flood of tears to be the mother of a martyr.

When he arrived in La Rochelle, there was both good news and bad news. Soldiers assigned by Cardinal Mazarin would sail on the same vessel with Father Jogues to augment forces in New France. The bad news—the vessel was a old leaky tub hardly fit for a transatlantic crossing. Though the soldiers—either rough-and-tumble young men from the poorer sections of Paris or hayseeds and bumpkins from the provincial towns—cursed Cardinal Mazarin and the queen as well for the condition of the ship, Father Jogues believed that providence dictated his return, and so the ship would transport him safely back to New France.

Chapter 7

Father Jogues Returns
To New France

TIPPING AND SHAKING, the leaky little vessel climbed each forty-foot wave, tottered a moment on the crest like an uncertain bird, then ran swiftly down the trough only to face the next wall of water. The decks and companionways stank of vomit from the soldiers' sea sickness. Battle-hardened infantrymen screamed in despair at every wave, "*Mon dieu!* We're lost! We'll perish for our sins!" Father Jogues went about the ship comforting them, urging that they trust in God and all would be well.

Seven weeks they were at sea. They reached the Gulf of St. Lawrence and Tadoussac and Saguenay in late June. As he walked down the ramp with his seabag, Father Jogues paused to smell again the charmed air of the New World. Back it all came in that one whiff, the smell of wet pine needles, the sweet decaying smell of last year's leaves, the smell of hickory smoke and roasting meat from chimneys among the clusters of log cabins and bark huts.

At the trading post in Saguenay, Father Jogues saw again—and smelled, too—the bronze-skinned natives wrapped in their blankets and skins. He observed again the long greased braids of the women and the small square of hair upon the men's plucked-bald heads. As they traded their furs from the winter, they were grunting assent with dour, expressionless faces. Jogues went through the stalls of the marketplace, avoiding the fat merchants, to the chapel where he greeted two reed-thin Jesuits and they prayed in thanksgiving for his return.

Father Jogues proceeded on to Quebec in a shallop. The shaggy magnificence of the forest, the shimmering breadth of the river as they tacked against the current, the call of gulls urging on the sailboat, the fresh, new dawning of his life—rescued from slavery and execution, now returning, his mission here sanctioned by the highest earthly authority—his joy and his ambition knew no limit. He would help bring peace at last to this land! Exuberant and lively, he disembarked at Quebec and he climbed the great rock to the provincial house and presented himself to his Jesuit brothers.

Exultation filled the Jesuit house that day. They'd known little of his fate. Rumors had reached them that he had escaped and was now living with the Dutch in New Netherland. Since he had left for France late in the year, then crossed the North Atlantic on the first ship back, no news of his rescue or return preceded him. To them he was a sudden "gift from God," a modern Lazarus, or perhaps even Jesus Christ, risen from the dead. How they embraced him, wept for joy over him, asked him questions! And he answered them now for these men, unlike the cloistered priests of France, knew firsthand the humility of their effort with no romantic glow, and so did not annoy or insult him by calling him "saint" or "martyr."

Father Jogues learned that the Iroquois had captured an Italian Jesuit, Father Francesco-Gioseppe Bressani, just above Trois-Rivières where they had surprised Jogues' party two years before. Father Bressani with six Hurons and a French lad were trying to get through the Iroquois ambushes in order to bring much-needed supplies to the Huron missions which had not seen any shipment since 1641. The familiar story had been told by an escaping *donne*. Father Vimont related it to Jogues.

As they paddled quietly through the islands, ice just barely off the river, one of the Hurons foolishly shot a buzzard. This shot alerted the Iroquois who pounced on them. They tortured the blackrobe, cut and burned him as a sacrificial victim in their villages. All five nations of the Iroquois were on the warpath against the French now, as well as against the Neutrals and the Petuns. With Dutch muskets and war hatchet they prowled the St. Lawrence and the Ottawa, the forests of Montreal, and all around the Lake of St. Peter.

Father Vimont added: "The Hurons and the Algonquins are disappearing. Famines and plagues kill them each year in great number. The loss is dramatic, even over the past two years. The Iroquois slaughter them, and with the raiding parties lurking always in the forest, they cannot hunt or fish. Where just eight years ago you would see a hundred cabins, now there are hardly five or six. Where you would see eight hundred warriors in a campaign, now there are hardly fifty. Flotillas of canoes used to number three and four hundred. Now there are scarcely twenty or thirty. Most of the men are gone. The women and children live on, starving in their miserable lives."

Jogues thought deeply on it. If the Huron settlements were so decimated, his return there would be a meaningless gesture. His efforts would be better spent seeking to melt the heart of the Iroquois League so peace might reign everywhere. Father Vimont assigned him to the new outpost, Ville Marie, a fort erected on the island of Montreal. In late July he sailed up the St. Lawrence to Trois-Rivières. Only two years had elapsed since his August 1, 1642 farewell mass.

Onward he proceeded, through Lake of St. Peter to Fort Richelieu, built on the high ground where the Mohawks had led him and mutilated his fingers that first night of his captivity. Now a bulky fort stood guard over the confluence of two rivers. The shallop tacked along the wide bend and up the broad straight path to the island of Montreal.

It was a religious village primarily, not for traders. Only men and women bound to the apostolate of the Society of Notre Dame were allowed to settle at Ville Marie. The three founders, De la Dauversière and Maisonneuve and Madamoiselle Jeanne Mance, had dedicated the settlement two years before to converting and civilizing the natives, administering to both their physical and spiritual needs. In addition to the high principles of the settlement, Father Jogues rejoiced that his dear friend and spiritual adviser from Clermont College days, Father Jacques Buteux, would share his cabin. Father Buteux was a worldly man of peasant stock and had a great practical sense of how a spiritual impulse might express itself and work effectively in the world.

As Father Jogues made his annual retreat, he confessed to Father Buteux his sins and serious temptations, but he withheld, with his deep humility, occasions of his virtue. Learning of Father Jogues's visions, Father Buteux asked him to commit them to paper. Jogues balked. He professed unworthiness. He declined to elaborate except to write about the voice on Good Friday years before which had indicated he would become a sacrifice, and also the dream of Ossernenon becoming a walled City of God.

Father Buteux expressed astonishment to his superiors about the depth of Father Jogues's humility. Jogues disagreed. Never, Jogues told him, had the Society of Jesus accepted a man less fit than he was to serve the Lord. Never had he known anyone so ungrateful to God and so little responsive to God's many graces. When Father Jogues spoke about the graces God allowed him during his torture and servitude, he wept inconsolably, and he confessed that his greatest sin was a desire for death when he was in the extremity of the pain and despair. He would not elaborate about the consoling visions that came to him in his dreams, but Father Buteux imagined them to be like the dreams of Joseph, son of Israel, wearer of the many-colored coat.

The two men spent the winter of 1644-1645 in prayer and meditation. Father Jogues told Buteux that he sensed God preparing him for a greater calling and would soon lead him to a far greater sacrifice, and that this winter in contemplation with his adviser and confessor was preparatory to the next stage of God's plan. Father Buteux mused that like the purest marble, ordinary limestone pressed and cooked by intense forces below the earth's crust, the sufferings of Father Jogues had changed him deeply, purified him. The sufferings forged in him a penetrating vision into the nature of things—the workings of fate and destiny, the purpose of his life—and perhaps of all human life—as the eternal war between good and evil raged.

It was at this time that propitious developments among the natives placed a lasting peace within their grasp. An Algonquin chief, a Christian, delivered two Iroquois prisoners to Governor Montmagny, the new Onontio, to broker peace. One of the prisoners who was returned, a Mohawk, was a grandson of Father Jogues's aunt. The other gave thanks with a great oratorical flourish:

"I hail you, Onontio! You have given me my life and I thank you for it. My nation will thank you for it and all the earth will be beautiful, the river will flow smoothly from our land to yours. Peace will make us friends. No longer will the shadows of hate cloud my eyes. The souls of my ancestors, killed by the Algonquins, have found their rest. Our anger has fled."

The warrior then launched into a violent dance, seized a hatchet and slashed it back and forth, up and down, then threw it into the fire. "There is my anger cast away. Farewell to war. I lay down my arms. I am your friend forever."

With his forces strengthened by the new detachment of soldiers, Montmagny was in a position to negotiate peace. He sent the two Iroquois up to Trois-Rivières, ordered the release of another hostage to return to the Iroquois and to thank them for releasing Fathers

Jogues and Bressani. Onontio promised the release of two others if the Iroquois wished to embrace a universal peace.

The Iroquois soon responded that they, too, wanted peace. They sent ambassadors to Trois-Rivières. Hundreds of Algonquins and Hurons came as well. Father Jogues paddled down river from Montreal in great anticipation.

"Bonjour, Father! You look well!" It was the booming voice of William Couture.

"Good William!" Father Jogues embraced him. "You are nearly thin."

Couture laughed at the unusual turn of events. "Can you imagine? I am the Iroquois interpreter."

"Who have they sent to negotiate?"

"You will know them." Couture led Father Jogues to a hut on the riverbank where the three were housed, Kiotseaeton, the finest orator of the Mohawks, Aniwogan, the shrewdest diplomat, and the man the French had recently sent home, Tokhrahenehiaron. The three, of course, recognized Ondessonk and recalled how they had beaten and tortured him when his captor, Mauthurin's Man, paraded him through the three villages. They greeted him haltingly, guiltily, but Father Jogues was effusive and embraced them as brothers.

Father Jogues saved his warmest greeting, though, for Honattenitate, grandson of his aunt. Until he saw Jogues, the young man had sulked in his dungeon cell and rejected any kindness from the French or the Algonquins. After Jogues embraced him and thanked him and his aunt for all their kindnesses during his captivity, the young man laughed and danced and lost any arrogance in his bearing.

All sides, dressed ceremoniously for negotiations, met in council July 12, 1645. The French pitched a tent in the courtyard of the fort at Trois-Rivières. Dressed in a cloak and a coat of red brocade,

Governor Montmagny entered with the fort's commandant, Sieur de Champflour in a gleaming breastplate. Fathers Jogues and Vimont and LeJeune in black cassocks followed with other dignitaries and soldiers. Montmagny sat in a large armchair propped against the wall of the fort and his priests and officials sat next to him.

Opposite the French sat Algonquins, faces and bodies streaked with white paint, their hair adorned with bright feathers. The Mohawks insisted on sitting directly in front of the French on hemlock mats since, they said, they loved the French so much they were now inseparable. The Mohawks, too, had painted their faces yellow and black and white, and they wore headdresses of bright feathers, buckskin jackets embroidered with porcupine quills and beads, and wampum belts hanging about their necks and arms.

Silence fell. The peace pipe was lit and passed among the assembled, then Kiotseaeton, the Mohawk ambassador, a towering figure, bellowed out a song. Four other Mohawks joined him in a pantomime dance, swaying, beating their bare heels upon the ground, crouching, leaping, moving back and forth. Then Kiotseaeton opened his elk skin pack and pulled out fourteen wampum belts. The ceremonial belts each held a meaning woven into the patterns of black and white shells. Intoning deeply the significance, he presented them one by one to Onontio.

The first was in thanksgiving for the French governor rescuing his kinsman from the Algonquins, and sending him back to his village. He thanked Onontio.

The next belt signified the return of William Couture whom they brought now, after three years, to seal the treaty. "Did we send him home alone?" the orator asked. "Did we risk that his canoe would capsize or that he would be eaten by wolves? No! We brought him to you personally."

A few wampum belts were offered to signify that the waterways between the two lands were now safe and the path between the

Iroquois lands and the lands of the French joined by a broad and level road. "We can see the smoke of your villages, from Quebec unto the farthest reaches of our Seneca. All obstacles have been removed."

With the tenth belt he linked arms with a Frenchman and danced him across the middle ground to link arms with an Algonquin, and then brought this threesome before the governor.

"Here is the knot that will bind us forever, even if lightning strikes, even if we lose an arm, we will link together with the other. Come unto our villages as guests and friends. We have elk and deer and beaver, the skins you cherish, and we have plenty of fish and venison for you to eat. Stop eating those stinking hogs that run in your streets and eat only filth. Come eat good meat with us."

The twelfth belt signified the sun bursting through the clouds to illuminate the hearts of the Iroquois and to show the French there was no malice or treachery so they must not be shy.

The thirteenth collar was offered to save face. With it, the Mohawks claimed they always intended to deliver Ondessonk and Bressani safely home, but simply would not allow them to risk the dangers of the journey alone. They claimed, also, to regret that the Dutch stole Father Jogues from them for they had intended to escort him home themselves.

At this, Jogues whispered to Father Le Jeune, "Many times they had the stake prepared to burn me. A hundred times they would have killed me had not God Almighty intervened. This man twists the truth with remarkable skill."

"Ah," Father Le Jeune observed, "but isn't that how diplomacy works?"

The final belt was offered on behalf of Jogues's aunt who thanked Onontio for saving her grandson and sending him home. "She rejoices, too, that her 'nephew' Ondessonk is among his people safe and well. She loved him and was good to him and treated him as a member of her family. She will welcome him once more if he journeys to Ossernenon."

Kiotseaeton concluded by promising to spend the summer in feasting and dancing, not on the path of war. He reached out for the arms of his new brothers, the Algonquins and the Hurons, and they formed a long colorful line and danced around the courtyard.

That night, in council with his advisors and priests, Montmagny praised the oratorical skill of Kiotseaeton, but expressed grave doubts about his sincerity.

"I wouldn't trust that man to bring me snow in a blizzard."

"I have been invited into their country," Father Jogues ventured. As one who knew the village and the people and the language, he had been asked to attend the council. "Let me go and put his promises to the test."

Montmagny thanked him. "Father Jogues, you are most courageous, and your reputation precedes you, but we must refuse."

"I won't risk losing him again," Father Vimont said.

Montmagny gave his reason: "Let the Iroquois prove they have put aside their treachery before we send any ambassadors into their midst."

Two days later, the governor presented fourteen gifts to the Iroquois. He promised peace and protection to those who ventured into his land, but insisted upon one non-negotiable condition. The Iroquois might enjoy peace with the French so long as they committed no hostile act against any other nation. The truce must be universal. The Iroquois assented and accept the gifts to seal the agreement.

Back to their council at Onondaga the Iroquois traveled to obtain ratification of the treaty. Even though he was allowed to remain among the French, William Couture returned with the Iroquois to help broker the peace among the fifty sachems.

Disappointed in his bid to serve as an ambassador, Father Jogues went home to Montreal for a month until the Huron flotilla, returning with an acceptance of the peace, stopped at Montreal. Father Jogues joined and paddled down river with them.

What a celebration now! So long suspicious and warring, all nations convened in the courtyard of the fort at Trois Rivières on Monday, September 18. The Mohawk chief announced that his nation accepted the terms, but was careful to indicate he did not speak for the other four nations of Iroquois. He promised, in view of the universal peace, even to return little Theresa who was now married and living in Tionontoguen.

Before he returned to Quebec, the governor met with his advisors, Jogues among them, to sound out the likelihood that the peace might be maintained. When he was called upon, Father Jogues observed:

"Respectfully, Governor, when they were my captors, the Mohawks promised again and again to release me, even accepted tribute from the Sokoki for my release, but they did what they wanted regardless of their promises. I feel our problem is with the Bear Clan. The Turtle and Wolf Clans want peace and a re-established trade, but the Bear Clan, so closely allied to the Dutch, carries deep resentment toward us, and will never be satisfied."

"You know whereof you speak," the governor said.

"I should like to return among the Mohawks," Father Jogues said. "I think I might be of service in sewing this pact together."

"We will consider your request further," the governor promised, and he nodded at Father Jogues's superior Father Limont, "but for the time being we shall see how they honor the agreement."

Graciously Father Jogues bowed to the civil and ecclesiastical authority, and the following day he departed in his canoe to return and wait in Montreal.

Chapter 8

Father Jogues Travels
As An Ambassador To The Mohawk Nation

A SENTRY SOUNDED THE ALARM one snowy morning at the fort of Ville Marie. Troops hastened from barracks and climbed rickety ladders to the scaffold along the palisade. Father Jogues heard the alarm and came from his small log rectory in a woolen shawl. He climbed upon the platform to observe.

A dozen or so dark forms were moving slowly against the dead white of the landscape.

"Hold your fire," the commander called. "They signal friendship."

The soldiers opened the gate and a delegation of three went out across the spiked ditches, then turned and waved. All the men returned together to the barking of the dogs. The soldiers and the priest went to the gate to greet the visitors.

"Bonjour, Father," William Couture called, and he clasped Father Jogues in a great bear hug. The Mohawk orator Kiotseaeton accompanied him with six other Iroquois and two Huron hostages. They had traveled far on snowshoes and their coats were crusted with ice.

"We come to announce the terms of peace are accepted," Kiotseaeton cried. "Come, let us warm ourselves and eat, and we will relate to you wondrous things."

The commander fired cannon to celebrate, and villagers clustered around the delegation in welcome. While soldiers took the others into the barracks, Couture, Kiotseaeton and Jogues accompanied Commandant Sieur d'Ailleboust into his house, knocking the snow from their boots. Before his ample hearth the four sat on benches. A subaltern served them stew in wooden bowls.

"The Mohawk nation enthusiastically embraces peace with the French," Couture related, "though the four upper nations have not yet agreed."

"We are willing to undertake peaceful relations with the Hurons and the Algonquins as well," Kiotseaeton added. "Someone must come to our council and persuade the other four nations about the advantages of peace."

Another alarm sounded just then and the men threw on their coats and blankets and ventured into the cold. They ascended the scaffold once more and observed over the snow a dozen forms. With the gates open, dogs ran down the roadway barking.

One of the soldiers went out, parleyed with the group, and then returned with them. As they came through the gate, William Couture whispered to Father Jogues, "Sokoki."

The commandant greeted the leader and invited him inside while his men were directed to the barracks. They stacked their snowshoes and tromped in and sat before the commandant's fieldstone hearth. The leader carried a leather satchel with him. As his companions ate greedily, the leader of the Sokoki spoke:

"You Mohawks have always said that the Algonquins were your mortal enemies, that you would pursue and kill them even in the next world after you die. We are your friends. Two years ago we came to your village to ransom Ondessonk," he nodded at Father Jogues, "so that peace might be achieved between you and the French. Now that has happened." He lifted the bag, opened it and shook out on the table five human scalps. Father Jogues bowed and made the sign of the cross. The commandant grumbled. "Here are the scalps of Algonquins," the Sokoki leader said. "Christian Algonquins we have slain as they celebrated the birth of their peacemaker in Sillery."

Kiotseaeton rose up in a wrath. He hammered his fist on the table, rattling the wooden bowls and the pewter tankards. "I will not sit here and listen to your arrogant boasts!" He bent and glared at the Sokoki leader. "How can I explain this deed to Onontio? I will say, 'We Mohawks have not killed these Christians and broken the peace,' and he will say to me, 'No, but your arm and your hatchet, the Sokoi, have.' If Algonquins observe the scalps of their kinsmen in our cabins, they will scalp us." He pushed the Sokoki. "No! We will not have these dark deeds affect our treaty. Hide those scalps! Take them away!" He turned to the commandant. "I ask you, owner of this place, tell these Sokoki to depart at once."

The commandant stood up, called for soldiers and soon the room was filled with shouting, the soldiers wrestling the Sokoki out of the house, onto their snowshoes and then out through the gates to the dancing and barking of the dogs. Quickly the gate was slammed and fastened, and sentries observed the Sokoki until they disappeared in the white-gray of the landscape.

In the commandant's kitchen Kiotseaeton was snorting and fuming to calm himself.

"The Sokoki don't see this is a different time!"

Father Jogues took William Couture aside. "I am pleased to see the chief so intent on establishing peace. How has this happened?"

"The sorcerers warn that their war god turns away from them. The deer and elk and moose they hunt have becomes scarce. They now want to hunt unmolested in the lands of the Algonquins. Also, with French muskets in Algonquin hands, the advantage they had held from their Dutch weaponry has been neutralized. All lines up," Couture concluded, "to favor peace."

Kiotseaeton, calmer than before, spoke: "Ondessonk."

Father Jogues turned. "Yes, chief?"

"We wish that you return among us. Your aunt holds open your place at her hearth fire still. Our people recall how kind you were to everyone when you were among us even though we treated you as a slave. We love you and trust you and if you were to come as an emissary, it would go far in sealing the peace with all five nations of the Houdesaunee."

"I want nothing more," Father Jogues said. "It was good you dismissed the Sokoki."

"And yet I wanted to strike them down as they did the Algonquins."

"Anger and violence beget more anger and violence," Jogues said. "A rash deed will shatter this fragile peace. The Oneida, Onondaga, Cayuga and Seneca need to hear our plan. If my superior allows, I will gladly return to Ossernenon."

As the meeting was breaking up, William Couture approached Father Jogues and asked if they might speak in private. They bundled up and Jogues led him along the lane to the humble log cabin, thatched roof, earth floor, small fieldstone hearth and two rough bunks, which he now shared with Father LeJeune. They sat in chairs and the priest put chips of firewood upon the coals and then logs and it soon blazed up casting a warm glow upon their discussion.

"You and I have lived through what few men can claim, Father," Couture began. "In the backwards logic of the Mohawks' thinking, I killed one of their chiefs on the day we were attacked, and so they adopted me into the dead chief's clan. They tortured and killed and ate our Huron brothers, Eustace, Steven and Paul, but allowed me to live. Then, as I learned their language, they called upon me—a carpenter—to negotiate peace."

"Jesus was a carpenter."

Couture gave a laugh. "But he was also God, Father, and I am far from that. I don't have the head for intrigue. I am too direct. I lack the skills that you possess, the intelligence, subtlety, persuasion, and so I make a poor ambassador. But I wish to share my thinking with you. Long have I ventured among the Mohawks and much have I seen of their superstitions and their violence and their debauchery, especially when the whites bring casks of liquor to help in the trading. I want to leave this life now."

"But you are so effective, William!"

"I grow weary of the duties, Father, the constant paddling here and there, the negotiations and arguments in councils, the empty parade of fools whether in elk robes and antler bonnets or in brocade and periwigs. Half the time the brokered peace agreements are breached immediately, and then the whole cycle of warfare, prisoners, burning and murder begins again—how will that ever stop?"

"I have hope that it will. I see a great value in working for peace. We serve the greater glory of God. We serve the Queen Regent. We serve the Iroquois, too, by helping them see how men should live in this world, not murdering each other, but as brothers. Once they see that, there will be peace, and so I want nothing more than to go again into their land as a missionary."

"It will never happen, Father."

"And yet their hearts are open to the message. You heard Kiotseaeton today. The Mohawks seem to understand my kindnesses. I will write a letter to Father Lalemant, ask for this assignment, and you will deliver my letter into his hands when you reach Quebec."

"Of course, Father, of course. It is good you go there for no one else can speak with the force you carry having suffered at their hands, escaped and returned." William thought deeply for a moment on how best to unburden himself. "I need your guidance, too, Father, about another matter."

"Anything, William."

"Eight years ago I pledged myself to serve God as a *donne* for the Society of Jesus. I vowed poverty, chastity and obedience. I must now renounce those vows, Father. A hunger works within me for a wife and a family and the quiet security of a farm. I want to leave behind my life among the Mohawks and settle as a *habitant* near Quebec."

Father Jogues reached over and touched his former *donne* on the shoulder. Affectionately he looked into his eyes. "So, we exchange places, my friend. You take up this sedentary life I wish to leave, and I go back, God willing, into the land of the Mohawks to bring peace and save their souls."

"Be careful, Father. You above all others know their treachery." Couture then knelt, opening wide his arms to receive Father Jogues's blessing, and Father Jogues made the mark of the cross upon his forehead.

Carefully scratching a feathered quill upon paper with his mutilated hand, Father Jogues wrote a letter imploring Father Lalemant to dispatch him as an emissary to the Iroquois confederacy in order to seal the peace. He knew the language, he knew many of the chiefs, he had their respect and he might argue the wisdom of such a treaty forcefully and credibly. He revealed to his superior— no secret—that wanted above all to open the Iroquois confederacy to missionaries, and he saw that his year of slavery in their midst now gave him the credibility to seek such permission.

Down in the provincial house in Quebec, Father Lalemant conferred with four other Jesuits and they voted unanimously to recommend that the governor send Jogues on this mission for peace. They also approved Couture's petition to withdraw his vows and marry.

Before his answer arrived, Father Jogues entered upon his yearly Spiritual Exercises. He retreated from his compatriots and his parish duties so he could refine his understanding as to the purpose of his life. He recalled his sins in general and he meditated upon the Kingdom of Christ. He offered himself as a Soldier of Christ in God's conquest of evil in the world. As he was finishing his ten days of retreat, Father LeJeune handed him a letter just brought by courier. Jogues's hands trembled as he broke the seal, and he read with great joy the few lines that Father Lalemant wrote—he was assigned as a missionary to the Iroquois and ordered to be ready to leave as soon as possible if the governor would employ him as an envoy to return with the Mohawks after the council at Trois-Rivières.

Governor Montmagny held his council May 7, 1646 at Trois-Rivières with the French, the Mohawks, the Algonquins, the Montagnais and the Hurons all present. The council proceeded so well, Father Lalemant sent immediately for Jogues and on Sunday, May 13, the governor offered to employ Father Jogues as his envoy, along with a young French settler Jean Bourdon, a map maker, to survey the route and prepare a map. The Mohawks welcomed the men and two young Mohawks were assigned to transport the baggage.

Seizing the opportunity to prepare a mission in Mohawk country, Father Jogues had packed vestments, a small chalice, a missal, candles, hosts and a bottle of wine into a small black trunk. In a larger case he packed clothes and glass beads for wampum and iron hatchets he would use as presents. An old Algonquin offered him advice: "Ondessonk, listen to me. There is nothing so repulsive to us as what you preach for it goes against all that men seek to do, and your blackrobe preaches as much as your words. You should wear the clothes of a French emissary on this mission."

Father Jogues agreed his role had changed, and so he obtained high-topped boots, pantaloons, coat and cloak and a broad-brimmed hat. He packed his soutane in the box as well. He planned to leave the box with his aunt while he attended the Mohawk council fire at Tionontoguen until he returned to Ossernenon for the winter and settled in as a priest.

They departed Wednesday, May 16, to the cheering of the entire settlement of Trois-Rivières. Canon fired from the ramparts. White flags snapped in the morning breeze and the two canoes, one with

Father Jogues and Bourdon, with the two Mohawks guides, the other with two Algonquin ambassadors and the other two Mohawks, moved onto the broad St. Lawrence. Upriver they went to the ruins of Fort Richelieu, then they paddled and portaged into Lake Champlain.

Father Jogues came again upon the island where the Iroquois war party had first tortured him.

Farther on the Mohawks stopped to burn tobacco as an offering at the place where the *okies* left them flint arrowheads. At the end of the lake they took a different direction than the overland route through the Sacandaga valley, and they reached a new lake which Father Jogues, on May 30, the feast of Corpus Christi, named the Lake of the Blessed Sacrament.

Down that lake they paddled and then hiked overland, carrying the small black trunk and a dozen elk skins as offerings of peace. They arrived at a fishing ground where clusters of Mohawks came out in a throng to welcome the envoys. Among them was Theresa, now a young woman of seventeen, married to a Mohawk from Tionontoguen. Father Jogues spent as much time as he could with her, hearing her confession, indicating that he brought presents to purchase her freedom. She implored him to do so for she wanted to return to her people.

When they reached Ossernenon, all the villagers came to greet Ondessonk and escort him in triumph up the path. It was the same path where they had mercilessly beat him and knocked him unconscious as he ran the gauntlet four years before. Now he was no naked slave. He was dressed as an envoy and animated by confidence and good will that he might achieve a negotiated peace, and the people stood in awe of the change. His kind old aunt hugged and kissed him and thanked him for saving her grandson. He asked a simple favor of her. Would she store and guard his trunk while he went as an ambassador to the other villages?

"As you wish," she said, and put it under a sleeping shelf.

The chiefs sent runners westward to summon leaders for a council at Tionontoguen. Before leaving, though, Father Jogues visited the ravine. He found the cross he had carved upon the tree where he had buried René, and he knelt there and prayed in celebration of René as a martyr. He considered a number of coincidences as he prayed: the two young Mohawks who had murdered René were now dead; the woman who had sawed off his thumb was dead, and the warriors who had captured him, Mathurin's Man and the others, had been killed in the last Algonquin attack.

Father Jogues and Bourdon soon departed for Tionontoguen. Along the river, from the cornfields and the fishing shallows and the village of Andagaron, natives greeted them, came close to welcome them and, recognizing Father Jogues as Ondessonk, now arrayed in the garb of a French ambassador, to express respect and even awe at the transformation. At Tionontoguen the Mohawks called a council to discuss Onontio's peace proposal. The chiefs wore their headdresses of colorful feathers and antlers. In the largest long house of the village they held a feast of corn porridge and fish, and then lighting their pipes and filling the air with tobacco smoke, they settled back to hear and deliberate and make up their minds.

When they called Ondessonk to speak, the chiefs fell silent. Warriors and the women in the shadows sat down and children were ushered out of the room. Ondessonk stood and walked into their midst. He produced a wampum belt and held it high.

"I bear this gift on behalf of Onontio to my brothers the Mohawks, first family of the Houdesaunee, People of the Great Long House." He hung the long wampum belt upon the cross rail for all to see. "This belt tells you that the council fire burns always at Trois-Rivières, and it welcomes you to journey there, along with your allies, and to sit there as our brothers."

Jogues used the stern inflections of voice and the dramatic pantomime of Iroquois orators as he spoke. He produced another wampum belt. "Here is a second belt to console this village for the departure of Theresa, the Huron, so that you will allow her to return to her people after four years amongst you."

He pulled another from his leather pack: "Onontio offers a third belt in deepest gratitude to you for rejecting the gift of scalps offered by the Sokoki."

He pulled another belt and displayed it. "Finally, here is a belt of three thousand beads offered to the Wolf Clan, an ancient and powerful family among the People of the Great Long House. The Wolf Clan has always sought closer ties with the French, and thus the French look upon the Wolf Clan as their brothers. May the Wolf Clan always keep the council fires burning in the Mohawk villages with much wood stacked beside it."

He looked about at the assembled, and he called, "Hiro!" or "I have spoken!"

The chiefs were nodding, smoking their pipes, gravely and favorably considering Jogues's offer of peace. How different Ondessonk seemed now. The authority with which he spoke, his refusal to refer to his torture or enslavement, or to seek retaliation or punishment for the pain and indignities they inflicted upon him—his speech was most pleasing.

The Algonquin emissary stood and announced that because he did not know the Iroquois language, Ondessonk would be their mouthpiece too.

Again Father Jogues rose: "So great is the love the Algonquins bear that they loaded their canoe with twenty-four elk skins and carried them along the lakes. Reaching the shore, though, the skins proved too heavy to transport, and so they were only able to bring a dozen. For this they feel shame and embarrassment.

"The Algonquin do wish the Mohawks to know, though, that they have hurled the war hatchet so far into the sky that it cannot be found. They pledge always to keep a fire burning in their cabins where the Mohawks might rest and eat, and that their lands, teeming with deer and elk and beaver, their rivers filled with fish, are open and waiting for Mohawk hunters and fishermen who may now take game and fish without fear of attack."

The Mohawk leaders met in private the following day to consider the pledges of peace. Summoning the others later that night, they announced that peace with France had been agreed to, and they gave a wampum belt ten feet long to memorialize it. Although Theresa was married to a Mohawk and presently away in the fishing grounds, she would be given her freedom upon her return, the young man to go with her or not as he chose. They answered the Algonquins and the Hurons with reserve, but assured both nations that because it was Onontio's wish, they would keep the peace.

His mission completed, Father Jogues went among the people baptizing the elderly who were approaching death, and also some infants who were ailing.

With the council over, they walked back along the river to Ossernenon, but oddly enough the reception there was not warm and happy. Father Jogues's black box, locked and hidden in his aunt's cabin, caused alarm because the suspicious shaman could not open it and look inside. He feared that Jogues had left a demon there who lived within. Stoked with suspicion by a young man named Iowerano, they suspected that Jogues's friendly demeanor, in view of the torture and starvation they had inflicted upon him before, was simply a ruse to put them off guard so the demon in his box could destroy them.

Father Jogues smiled at their childish superstition, and he produced what few of them had ever seen before—a key. He opened the box and took out his vestments, the chalice, the beeswax candles, the wheat hosts and wine for saying mass. He emptied the trunk so they might lift it and hold and it look inside. He locked it and opened it and locked it again, and allowed them to lock and unlock it, open and close the lid. Iowerano, though, shook his head, unconvinced.

As he was calming their fears about the box, runners entered the village from Tionontoguen. A war party from one of the western Iroquois nations had left for the Ottawa River in order to attack the Hurons as they descended the river for the summer's trading.

"Make haste, Ondessonk," the chief of the Turtle Clan said. "While we don't believe they will be hostile to you, we cannot speak about your Algonquin companions."

Father Jogues, in an uncharacteristic display, reacted angrily: "How does this happen? We have all worked so long and so hard to achieve the peace. How can another nation be permitted to break it so easily?"

The chief replied that only the Mohawks negotiated peace and no other nation felt bound by the pact.

"Do you not understand?" Jogues insisted "Onontio will hold you responsible even though it is a rogue group who threatens us?"

The Mohawk chief assured him the council would consider it, but he should leave at once. Entrusting his small trunk to his aunt, Father Jogues collected Bourdon and the Algonquins and departed. They took the trail through the pine barrens to the long river that reached north, and within days they were at the shore of the Lake of the Blessed Sacrament. Their canoes were gone. From bark and vines and pine pitch they quickly made new ones and they paddled north along the lakes and rivers, then eastward down the St. Lawrence to Trois-Rivières, and then to Quebec. As they reached Quebec, the cannons blasted the joy at their arrival and the peace that it portended.

Chapter 9

A Warrior Of The Bear Clan
Martyrs Father Jogues

IMMEDIATELY UPON RETURNING to Montreal, Father Jogues sought permission to go again among the Mohawks as a missionary. Father Lalemant demurred. The peace with the Mohawks was still new and tender, the history of their duplicity abundant. Father Lalemant wrote he would consider sending Jogues back only if "an excellent opportunity" to insure the truce presented itself.

In August, sixty Huron chiefs met with Governor Montmagny at Trois-Rivières, expressing their desire to accept the Mohawk offer of peace. Father Jogues was restless. All seemed favorable to his return to Ossernenon, yet the Huron council might oppose this final suit for peace. In mid-September he wrote a Jesuit friend back in France:

> *Alas, my dearest Father, when shall I begin at length to serve Him and to love Him, whose love for us has been without any beginning? When shall I begin to give myself entirely to Him who has given Himself wholly to me and without reserve? Although I am the most miserable of creatures, and though I have made poor use of the graces which our Lord has bestowed upon me in this country, and have responded to these so wretchedly, nevertheless, I do not despair in my soul; for I see that He takes care to offer*

me new opportunities through which I may die to myself and by which I may unite myself to Him inseparably. . . .

Peace has already been established, to the great joy of the French and it will last as long as pleases the will of God. It seemed necessary, to maintain the peace, and unobtrusively to see what might be done in the matter of instructing the Iroquois, to send some one of our Fathers there. I have reason to believe that I shall be employed there, for I have some knowledge of the language of that nation and country. . . ..

And so, if I shall be employed in this mission, my heart tells me: "Ibo et no redibo—I shall go, but I shall not return." In very truth, it will be well for me, it will be a happiness for me, if God will be pleased to complete the sacrifice there where He began it, if the little blood which I shed there in that land will be accepted by Him as a pledge that I would willingly shed all the blood which I bear in the veins of my body and of my heart.

Montmagny and Lalemant summoned Father Jogues to Trois-Rivières. He arrived September 19 as the council between the Huron chiefs and Montmagny was concluding. The Hurons wanted peace, but they did not trust the Mohawks and saw little purpose in the truce unless the other four Iroquois nations opted for it as well. The Hurons, Jogues's original converts, formally requested that Ondessonk accompany the delegation.

Montmagny and Lalemant called Father Jogues in to a private conference.

"All impediments to your return have been removed," the governor told him. "Do you still wish to go?"

"More than anything else, Your Excellency."

"You understand," Father Lalemant said, "that although you will help the Huron emissaries in their suit for peace, you go this time as a missionary?"

"I will wear the black robe," he said. "There will be no confusion."

"And you know that the Mohawks are unresponsive to the Word of God?"

"With abject humility, Father, no one knows or regrets that more deeply than I."

To assist him on his mission, Father Lalemant assigned Jogues a *donne*, Jean de la Lande. After Father Jogues described the privations of a Mohawk winter, the slender young man accepted. Upon questioning by Father Jogues he said:

"I had a revelation, Father. This is God's will. I know I will go, but I will not return." This did not surprise the priest; indeed, it pleased him very much. "I know it is, and I will not shy from it." The priest nodded, but did not tell him he'd had the same premonition.

On the morning of September 24, three canoes glided out from Trois-Rivières and began to ascend the St. Lawrence. At the confluence of the Richelieu, they camped the night. Father Jogues spoke with the Hurons who seemed edgy, fearful. While they could point to nothing specific, their intuition told them not to trust the Mohawks; indeed, told them to abandon the journey to Mohawk country.

"If you're unwilling," the priest said, "you cannot be forced."

Next morning, all but one of the Hurons departed for their own country. Alarmingly, the Mohawks who were acting as guides also departed.

After consulting with Jean de le Lande and the remaining Huron, who had a pledge of safe passage from the Mohawks, Father Jogues decided to proceed, the three of them in a single canoe.

Up the river they paddled through the quiet wood. Encountering rapids and waterfalls, they disembarked and portaged up the trails, the calling of birds only making the quiet seem deeper and more lonesome.

On his first passage along this route, Father Jogues had lingered behind and had begged René Goupil and William Couture to escape. Now he encouraged Jean to hurry along with him for he felt he was returning home.

As they approached Ossernenon, Father Jogues saw a file of Mohawks coming toward them up the trail. He called out. Ominously the natives melted into the forest. He looked everywhere, but he saw nothing. The forest was quiet and still. Then it erupted. On all sides the Mohawks attacked. They screamed out their war cries and brandished their tomahawks and muskets and long knives and they danced about the three menacingly.

"I am Ondessonk," Father Jogues explained, his palms held out imploringly. "We have come to secure the peace we discussed this summer."

The Mohawks pounced on him and upon the Huron and Jean de le Lande as well, beating them and tearing off their clothes.

"What is this, Father?" the youth asked.

"They repudiate the peace," the priest said. His soul was sick with the knowledge of what awaited the innocent Jean and the Huron. Perhaps he might somehow secure Jean's release?

As if in a repeating nightmare, the Mohawks forced Jogues along the path as he had been forced along four years before. Up a hill and quickly down to the mud bank and the ford they went. The villagers did not form a gauntlet this time. In a clamorous crowd they argued, some urging the customary welcome, others fighting to receive Ondessonk without violence, even to protect him. As his captors pushed him through the crowd, some raised their fists and war clubs to strike, but others warded off the blows. Three or four good Samaritans grabbed the emissaries, hauled them up the hill and through the gates to the village and into a cabin.

Father Jogues's aunt appeared with food and pieces of cloth for them to cover their nakedness. She was quite concerned. "The Bear Clan has taken to the war path," she told him. "The Turtle and the

Wolf Clans wish to receive you as emissaries and to maintain the peace, but the Bears want to kill you. You are in a Wolf cabin now, and they will not enter, but you must remain here."

"This is so sudden!" Father Jogues complained. "What happened?"

"When you were last here, the Bears were seeking support for their opposition to the peace among the other four nations of our people. They succeeded. The Wolf and Turtle Clans have failed to gain any support for you among the other nations. Soon after you left, many people fell sick. The disease progressed from cabin to cabin. The sorcerer read dreams and offered sacrifices and danced and chanted and brought the afflicted into the sweat lodge. Nothing worked. Some of the adopted Hurons then explained how this came to be. The blackrobes, they told everyone, were evil sorcerers, and Ondessonk the worst of all. The blackrobes wish to destroy us, the Hurons said, in order to take our land. This explanation gained much support.

"Then," his aunt continued, "the corn near the river began to wither just as it should have been fattening for harvest. The stalks shriveled and we saw worms attacking. There will be no corn this winter. They consulted the sorcerer again, who recalled that you had left your black box in my cabin. The box contained an evil spirit, they told everyone. They marched to my cabin and demanded I give it over. I refused. I reminded them how you opened it and showed them what it contained. They pushed me aside and ransacked my cabin to find it. When they seized it, they dared not open it for they feared the evil spirit would escape. They took it down to the river and paddled it out in a canoe. Where the river was deepest, they dropped it over the side. This took care of the demon, but Ondessonk, they said, still lived. And so they set out to capture you. They plan to take your life." She dropped her eyes.

"It has always been so," he said.

"It will be different this time," she said.

A throng of angry warriors of the Bear Clan entered. Though it was against their law to injure anyone in the sanctuary of another's home, they clustered about the priest shouting menacingly: "You will die tomorrow! We will not burn you or torture you, but we will bury our hatchet in your skull and impale your head on the pikes of the stockade as a greeting for your brothers."

"You mistake me," he told them. "I have come to your country to preserve the peace and to show you the road to heaven, and you treat me like a dog. One true God rules the French and the Mohawks alike and He knows well how to punish you!"

"Our god Aireskou is stronger and smarter than yours. We will show you tomorrow!"

All night a riot raged between the Bear Clan on one side and the Turtle and Wolf Clans on the other about what to do with the emissaries. Morning dawned and the village was quiet. Father Jogues's aunt returned from gathering news.

"The clans are battling over your fate," she said, and she handed him and Jean back some of their clothing. "To settle the dispute, they will hold a council tonight. Though you can go outside the cabin, you must not leave the village before your fate is decided. To disregard this prohibition will mean certain death."

"Ask the chiefs if I may address them," he said.

"You are a prisoner," she said.

"I am also an emissary from Onontio."

She left and returned an hour later. "They wish to see you now," she said gravely and led him out of the cabin and to a large chamber where again the Turtle Clan chieftains sat in council smoking their pipes and listening to the drone of the oratory. The gathering grew more animated when Father Jogues entered the room. After some preliminary matters, the head chief invited him to state his case:

"I have come among you to seal the peace we agreed upon three months ago." Father Jogues was animated, as close to anger as he could get. "With treachery you have betrayed us and violated the peace without warning. You will incur the wrath of Onontio and he will march upon your villages and burn them and turn you into the forests to hunt like the bark eaters."

"We do not fear Onontio," someone called. A general hubbub arose.

Jogues paused, collected himself. "You now state that the black box is the source of your illness and the failure of the crop. I opened the box before you. I showed you what it contained. Your sorcerers are wrong and their conclusions absurd. I am sorry . . . we are all sorry for these events, but I did not cause them. I have nothing but warm feelings for the Mohawks. I have come to correct your thinking, to allow you to see without the mists of superstition clouding your eyes."

Some grunted assent; others fixed their faces with suspicion and hatred. After Jogues finished, the chiefs set forth on the trail up the river to confer with fathers of the Bear and the Wolf Clans. For two days there was no news, but the lanes of the village were quiet and no one molested Father Jogues or Jean de le Lande.

At sundown on the second day, as they awaited for the verdict, a young warrior came to invite Ondessonk to eat with his family. Father Jogues recognized him as being a member of the Bear Clan. He consulted with his aunt and friends of her family.

"Turning down an invitation is an insult, not easily forgiven," she said.

"But I recognize the man who was hostile to me previously."

"You had better go. I will send Honatteniate, whom you rescued, as your guard. You saved his life and now, if necessary, he will save yours." The two followed the young warrior to a long house. He stood aside and nodded for the priest to enter.

Father Jogues placed his hand against the bearskin curtain and pushed it aside. Down the length of the long house, families were sitting about their fire pits. The unmistakable smells of cooking meat and tobacco smoke met his nostrils.

Suddenly, from behind the doorway, a young warrior sprang

out. Honatteniate saw him, jumped forward to save Father Jogues
from the hatchet swiftly descending, a massive warrior's full
strength behind it. The hatchet cut Honatteniate's arm open, but
he did not deflect it sufficiently. It dashed against the priest's skull
and sent him reeling. In like manner, the blow to his arm threw
Honatteniate to the ground.

The warrior then sprang upon Father Jogues and buried his
hatchet in the priest's skull. He pulled the hatchet out, then looked
at his bloody blade in disbelief. He then looked upon the priest.
Many of the others in the long house arose from their meal and
came to the door and looked down at the body of the priest, slowly
shaking their heads. So many times had Ondessonk escaped death,
they could scarcely believe he was at last gone.

Suddenly the bearskin flap opened and Father Jogues's aunt burst
into the cabin. She screamed, "What have you done? Murderers!
You have violated the ancient law! You have killed a part of me! He
was my adopted kinsman! He was of my family!"

Roughly they pushed the woman aside. The warriors scalped the
priest and, wielding their long knives, decapitated him. They held
up Ondessonk's head, his blood flowing over all, and they paraded
it down the dark, chilly lanes of the village. In the torchlight, the
murdering warrior climbed onto the scaffold that ran along the
palisade and lifted up the head of Ondessonk. He hurled a defiant
war cry at the moon, and then he jammed Jogues's had down upon
the sharpened point of a pole, and he turned the face of Father Jogues
toward the valley and the forests and the mountains of the north.

Jean de le Lande heard of this from the priest's aunt. "Do not stir
from this cabin," she warned after telling him what had become of
Jogues; yet the youth was drawn to visit his mentor's corpse that still
lay in the lanes of the village, food for the dogs. He wanted to recover
some of the objects Father Jogues carried and to keep them as relics.
After midnight, considering everyone was asleep, le Lande stole out of

the cabin. Quietly three of the Bear Clan warriors, though, had been waiting for this moment. They rose before him and hacked open his skull with a blow from their tomahawks. They scalped him, too, and severed his head and carried it to the stockade where, climbing upon the scaffold, they impaled it next to the priest's.

The next morning a deputation arrived from the council at Tionontoguen with the decision. The great Mohawk chiefs had decreed that Ondessonk and his young French brother were to be set free. No harm must be done to them. They were to be escorted safely back to Trois-Rivières.

When the messengers heard of the double murder, they turned abruptly back. So horrified and shamed were the chiefs at what the warriors of the Bear Clan had done before receiving the decree that they commanded the deed be kept secret. Soon, though, news of the murders reached Rensselaerwyck. Father Jogues's aunt appeared to tell the Dutch what had become of the priest, and to deliver into their hands what possessions she kept of his—a pair of pantaloons, a missal, his breviary and a few trinkets.

While the heads remained on the pikes, young warriors led by Iowerano dragged the bodies of Father Jogues and Jean de la Lande down the hill and across the flats to the river where they were released to the current. All through that winter the bleached skull of Father Jogues, picked clean by crows, stared empty-eyed and grinning towards New France as a warning to all who might seek to follow him.

Catherine Tegahkoüita Iroquoise

Kateri Tekakwitha

Lily of the Mohawks
from a painting by Father Claude Chauchetiére

on bâtit la première chapelle

Building The First Chapel

Father Claude Chauchetiére's pen and ink drawing depicts the building of the first chapel at Kanawaka when he arrived at the Mission of St. Francis Xavier in 1677. The Jesuit in the lower right is thought to be Father Claude speaking with the French carpenters. The three figures near the crucifix in the background anticipate Kateri, Marie-Thérèse Tegaiaguenta and Marie Skarichions planning to form a convent

Book II ~
Kateri Tekakwitha
(1660 - 1680)

She dwelt among the untrodden ways
Beside the springs of Dove,
A Maid whom there were none to praise
And very few to love:

A violet by a mossy stone
Half hidden from the eye!
—Fair as a star, when only one
Is shining in the sky.

—William Wordsworth

Chapter 10

Anastasia, a Christian Algonquin, Attempts To Foster a Mohawk Orphan

Sᴍᴏᴋᴇ, ᴄʜᴏᴋɪɴɢ ʏᴇʟʟᴏᴡ sᴍᴏᴋᴇ, hung in the lanes of the village from untended fires. The wailing of children rose and fell over the steady drone of old men moaning, and a young mother wept inconsolably at her dead infant who would not suckle. Hunters and warriors lay on their mats struggling to breathe.

An epidemic of white man's smallpox swept through Ossernenon. The virus came in woolen blankets the English traded for beaver, deer and otter skins. Men and women who still had strength crawled on all fours outside to fetch wood and water. Within, through the heavy bearskin curtain, in the smoke and stench and flies and mosquitoes, those in advanced stages lay groaning on their mats, skin peeling off in bloody shreds when they strove to turn.

Tegonhat-siongo, a handsome young woman with a long black braid, entered the dim long house to locate her friend. Born as an Algonquin and baptized "Anastasia" when she became a Christian, the Mohawks abducted her from Trois-Rivières six years ago along with Kahontake (Meadow) who was now the wife of Tsaniton-gowa (Great Beaver). Anastasia walked among the corpses and the almost-dead who raised up hands, groaning for a drink of water. She'd just returned from the fishing grounds and was spared the contagion. Seeking news of Meadow, Anastasia proceeded to the third fire pit where the family cooked and ate and slept. The fire pit was cold with the charred remains of their bark plates and bowls and spoons, burned because they lacked firewood.

Swarms of flies buzzed around the elkskin robes. Anastasia pulled a robe aside and gagged to hold down her morning meal. The great chief's face, blistered and matted with bloody sores, was now a home for maggots. Next to him, wrapped in a deerskin robe, the beautiful Meadow lay in a like condition. In her arms she held a bundle. Anastasia unwrapped it and the corpse of a baby boy fell out. She cried out in pity. Meadow, christened Irené in the same mission class, had died without the last rites. Anastasia picked up the baby covered with pustules and placed him upon his mother. He had died without baptism.

"Where is Ioragode (Ray of the Sun)? Has she perished too?" Anastasia asked out loud. In a shaft of light from the chimney hole she searched among the skins and sleeping pallets. "Perhaps she escaped, or went into the forest to die."

Light from the doorway lanced through the smoky gloom as four young warriors opened the curtain and entered. They came to fetch the dead and bury them in a mass grave beyond the stockade. Two of them lifted corpses from the second fire pit, a mother and two babies, and the other two came toward Anastasia.

"They are dead," she said. One lifted the chief, and the other took up the wife and baby boy. Stirred up, fleas began leaping about. Anastasia paused for one last look, and she observed a slight movement in a tangle of deerskin. She stepped over, reached down and pulled back the skin. A little girl lay back, naked, gasping, covered in her own filth, her eyes half-closed, her skin encrusted with red scabs and a thick white film was oozing from her eyes. Anastasia cried out, picked her up and the child moved. "You live, little one! Come, let us leave this house of death."

Down to the river she carried the child, away from the lines of men dragging corpses to the common grave, away from the thick, foul smoke from the bonfire where they burned the louse-infested skins and wicker work. Two dozen bark canoes lay inverted on the mud bank, and weirs and nets were drying unused in the sun. The river ran sparkling and quiet by the ford and landing place. Gently Anastasia wiped the white discharge from the little girl's eyes, then dipped the naked child in the river. The cold shock of the water brought screams of fear and pain from the little girl, attesting to her will to live. In the summer morning sun, the child's skin was blistered and scaly and oozing. Anastasia held her, rocked her for comfort and then carried the dripping child to a tree trunk where she wiped off the filth with handfuls of moss and sawdust. Back in the water she rinsed her clean.

Anastasia carried the naked child to a shack beyond the plantation where the corn and squash and bean stalks were ripening. The shack was where women stayed during their flow of blood, away from their men and families. Anastasia lived there and administered to them. In the shack she found a soft deerskin and she wrapped the child in it and rocked her to sleep. "I will be your mama now," she said, trying to put aside her sorrow at the death of her girlhood friend Irené Kahontake.

A month passed. With clean air and water and food, the child of four summers revived. Blinded as she was from the smallpox, soon she was trying to stand and trying to walk. Pitiable was her appearance as the sores healed into scabs, encrusting her face and her arms and her body. She squinted to see, her eyes nearly closed, but she bore her afflictions like a little stoic.

"Where's my mama?" she asked Anastasia one morning.

"Mama's gone away, Ray of the Sun." The woman embraced the child.

"Where did she go?"

"She went to heaven."

"Where is heaven?"

"Far, far away."

"When will she come back?"

"She won't be coming back."

"Why not?"

Anastasia held her. "Mama loves you more than anything in this life, but she can't be with us anymore."

"Why not?" the child raised up her scabbed face and Anastasia's heart overflowed at the measure of pain this little one needed to endure.

"Because . . . because . . . well, because she's with God in heaven and He needs her to be with Him." Anastasia was sobbing. "I'm sorry."

"And Papa?"

"He's gone away too."

"Hunting?"

"No. He's gone away with Mama and little Aronsen. They all love you and miss you, but they all had to go away."

"Why didn't they take me with them?"

"So you could be my little girl."

"Oh." She reclined her head upon Anastasia's breast and rested it there as she considered all of this. "It's so dark now," she murmured. "I hear the birds. When will it be morning?"

"Soon, my little Sunshine. Soon."

Barren of womb from the white man's diseases, and divorced by two men, Anastasia had given up village life. She rejoiced now, as the days passed, for the gift of this little girl. The child's infirmities did not diminish her curiosity, and Anastasia told her stories and taught her songs and they laughed and played together all day. Anastasia made her a doll from corn husks that she cherished and held through the night as she slept.

Anastasia kept Ray of the Sun outside the palisade all during the Strawberry Moon when the village children usually run into the fields and pick strawberries. There was no festival this year. Soon she considered the child her own, and so it was most upsetting when a messenger summoned Anastasia before the Women's Council.

It was a time to make plans. The Women's Council made all important decisions in the nations of the Iroquois. The Women's Council had recently voted to move the village upriver to a prominent hill on the north side of the river in order to leave the contamination behind. They sent men to prepare the site, and until it might be ready for occupation, the sorcerer went through the old long houses burning torches of tobacco weed to clean and bless the air.

Recognizing the difference between men of the mind and men of action, the Women's Council appointed some men as clan chiefs to carry out its directives, and others as war chiefs to fight its battles. The Women's Council likewise ruled on issues of marriage, divorce and the custody and care of children. The young woman who summoned Anastasia one morning informed her that the Women's Council wished to foster Ray of the Sun to the family of a chief:

"The Council wishes that the child be given to Moneta, wife to Iowerano (Cold Wind)."

"Moneta has no greater claim to the child than I."

Anastasia bent and pushed from the sunshine through a flap of moose skin into the great long house. Dim and smoky, the air was filled with cooking and far less pleasant smells. In the center, the matriarchs sat cross-legged on mats, their wide faces, high cheekbones and greased long black braids were lit by the low red glow of the fires.

Anastasia waited until her matter was called, and then she stood and walked to the mat directly opposite the three women who issued decisions. One said to her, motioning, "Please sit."

Anastasia sat down.

"It is true that you rescued the daughter of the great Tsaniton-gowa?"

"It is so. Yes." Anastasia acted with respect. She wanted to keep the child. "Meadow, the child's mother, was my companion when People of the Land of Flint welcomed us to this village six summers ago."

"You are Christian too?"

"I was. Since no blackrobe is among us, I no longer practice my faith."

"But you keep your detested Christian name?"

"I do."

"Iowerano (Cold Wind), brother to Tsaniton-gowa, has no children. His wife, Moneta, is barren. Ordinarily our blood lines proceed from mother to child, but this child's mother was Algonquin, not of our blood. Iowerano is a blood relative, and so it is our decree that you turn the child over to Iowerano so she may be raised in the *ohwahchira* of her blood and be one of our people."

"Please hear me," Anastasia said. "I know I am not Mohawk. I am Algonquin and I have practiced the Christian faith, but I saved the little girl's life and under my care she has returned to health. She sees light and shadows now where before she was blind. I am teaching her the bead work and embroidery and she sees well enough now to be useful in that occupation. I can care for her in my cabin. I ask you to reconsider your ruling and let her stay with me."

"Impossible," one of the old women growled. She was thick-faced and her eyelids drooped. "She must learn the lessons of our people, all the lessons. This can only happen in the village among many of our people, not outside the stockade with an Algonquin."

"I could bring her within the walls," Anastasia said. "I am happy to move."

"Ray of the Sun will be raised Mohawk, not Christian." The

ancient matriarch, her lined face and long gray hair lit in shadows by the fire, motioned with her finger. "Bring Moneta to us."

A young messenger left on the errand. Soon a haughty young woman stood before them, arms folded. She and Anastasia exchanged nods of annoyance. They detested each other.

"It is the decree of this council that you will be mother to Ray of the Sun," the ancient matriarch said hoarsely.

"I have no children," Moneta said, "and I have no wish for any, especially one who's blind."

"Iowerano is her father's brother."

"I cannot help that."

"We decree that Anastasia turn the child over to you by sunset today."

"I have no spare sleeping mat. I don't need another mouth to feed. I have seen the girl. She is horribly scarred. She will never be marriageable, a burden always to anyone who takes her in."

"Summon Iowerano," the old woman said impatiently. The young messenger left once more.

A few moments later, the chief himself entered. It was no wonder, as he entered, how he obtained his name "Cold Wind." He was a large, imposing man, his height increased by the tall rooster comb greased straight up from his otherwise bald head. He was dressed in leggings and a buckskin shirt embroidered with porcupine quills. He moved with arrogant confidence.

"You asked me to appear?"

"Your brother's daughter has lived," the matriarch whispered. "The Christian here rescued her and keeps her in a cabin near the ravine. It is the wish and mandate of the Women's Council that she be brought back within the village and fostered to you."

The chief centered himself, breathed deeply, threw out his hands and spoke in a deep, oratorical voice: "Women of the Turtle Clan. I hear your decree. Let me answer thus. The white man's disease has killed many. The mass grave outside our walls, hardly covered with earth to this day, bears witness to the evil he spreads. Those whom he cannot kill, he sends the blackrobes to corrupt in order to get our lands. We must be strong in our resistance. I thank you for summoning me. This child deserves to learn and to live our way of life."

"I have told them . . ." Moneta stood to speak.

"Silence, wife. We will accept this youngster into our home as we are also giving shelter to your cousin and her daughter, and we will raise them both Mohawk."

"But I told them . . ."

"Silence," Cold Wind bowed. "I submit to your wishes and I accept my niece to my hearth with open arms."

"Very well," said the old matriarch. She nodded at Anastasia. "Make her ready to come back within the village, and see that it is accomplished before nightfall."

Anastasia bowed in defeat. "I will bring her here by sundown." She turned and glanced at Moneta who smirked, but was not herself happy with the decree. Iowerano nodded, satisfied by his display of oratory and magnanimity, and he turned and walked out through the flap that Anastasia held open for him.

Out of the village gate and through the humps and burnt stumps of the corn plantation Anastasia walked, disconsolate with the thought of losing the child. Moneta's temper was notorious in the village and she used Cold Wind's status as chief to shield herself from criticism.

Anastasia felt deep sympathy for the child who was sitting now in the sunlight, face up, turning her cheeks this way and that to bask in its warmth, her eyes closed against the hurtful glare.

"Little Ray of the Sun!" she called happily. "I have such good news for you."

"Tell me, aunt." She turned toward Anastasia, but her eyes were closed against the pain of the glare.

"You have recovered so well, the villagers want you to go home."

"But I like it here. I will remain with you."

"I want you to stay as well . . ."

"Good. Then it's settled."

Anastasia went to her and gathered her up in her arms. She held the poor scarred little child close, and the child inclined her head upon Anastasia's breast.

"You must go back, my little Ray of the Sun." She said this with great cheer, hoping the child would not react adversely.

"Why?"

"The clan mothers have decreed it."

"But why? We live here."

"Yes, we do. Of course."

"Then it's settled."

"I'm afraid not," Anastasia said. "Let us pack up your things."

"Where will I be living?"

"With your uncle Iowerano and his wife Moneta."

"I didn't think they liked me," she observed without any rancor. "Do they want me to live with them now?"

"They do. They have agreed to foster you, and the clan mothers have decreed it so. I must deliver you to them before the sun goes down."

"Very well," the child said and she started to walk toward the cabin with her hands out to encounter anything that might obstruct her way.

A crimson sun hung above the trees as the woman and child walked, holding hands. The woman carried a bundle of bedding, and the child her pack and the cornhusk doll. They walked back through the stockade gate. They passed through the lanes where dogs glowered at them, and proceeded to the long house in the middle of the village where the great chief made his home. There was a spread of moose antlers above the door. Through the heavy curtain they pushed.

At the first fire pit Cold Wind was sitting cross legged, smoking the calumet with three other men. He nodded and grunted at Anastasia and the little pock-marked girl. Anastasia led the child to the next fire pit where Moneta was stirring a kettle of corn porridge flavored with bear fat and chunks of dried trout. She saw them and nodded a greeting, then wiped her hands upon her apron and stood.

"So, this is the girl?"

"We call her Ray of the Sun for the light and the joy she has brought to us—her mother and me—since she was born."

Anastasia dropped her hand and the little girl began to reach into the air to find her bearings in the strange place.

"In addition to being scarred, she is blind?"

"Her sight continues to improve. She can differentiate light from dark."

The child was moving forward, waving her hands in empty space to encounter and guide herself about obstacles in the strange new place.

"This girl is no Ray of the Sun," Moneta said in derision. "She is clumsy, and so I shall call her 'Tekakwitha'— She Who Gropes Her Way."

"She was the most delightful child before the disease."

"She is disfigured and blind now and will always require more care than she is worth."

"Be kind to her," Anastasia said. "She is so docile and sweet."

Moneta put her hand on her hip and watched the child critically. "There is no room for sweetness in my long house, and as for docile, well, docile can sleep over there in the corner. Make her up a pallet and then leave us."

Anastasia led the little girl to a corner where the lashed shelves that stored baskets and bark utensils met the curved rib work of the wall. Anastasia gathered some discarded pine boughs and she spread the girl's fur blanket over the bed. "You'll be comfortable here," Anastasia said.

"But why can't I live with you?"

"The Women's Council considers that you will be safer here with your uncle the chief, and that you will learn the ways of the Mohawks."

"My aunt doesn't like me."

"Yes, yes, she does. She loves you. And it was your uncle who petitioned the Women's Council so you would join his family."

"He never spoke to me. I don't know him at all."

Anastasia sought to hide her sorrow; yet the child felt her sobbing.

"Why are you crying, Aunt?"

"You have suffered so already. This is needless."

"But you may visit me, and maybe they will let me visit you?"

"Do what your aunt tells you to do," Anastasia advised. "I'll come to visit you in the morning."

"Tekakwitha!" Moneta called. "Come over here and eat your supper."

"Good-bye," the girl said and reached up into the open air between them for the woman to embrace her.

"Tekakwitha!" Moneta commanded.

"Good-bye, my darling girl."

"Come along. We don't have all night."

"Apparently I'm not invited," Anastasia said.

"We don't have enough for you," Moneta said. "I scarcely have enough for this one." She rapped the spoon upon the kettle. "Come! Eat!"

"Thank you, Aunt," the little girl said.

They embraced a last time and Tekakwitha, her hands in the air and her eyes gazing upward, started toward the family circle while Anastasia slunk through the doorway and out into the night.

Chapter 11

The Half-Breed Kryn
Returns With Prisoners Of War

W ITH THE PASSING OF FOUR SUMMERS, Tekakwitha's eyesight improved markedly. Although she wore a shawl outside in the daylight to shield her eyes from the sun, in the dim long house she went bare-headed. The Turtle Clan had moved its village upriver to the north shore to a place called Kanawaka (At the Rapids), leaving behind the death and contamination of Ossernenon.

Tekakwitha now worked indoors all day stringing wampum beads and embroidering tunics and ceremonial robes with dyed porcupine quills. Chief Iowerano had taken under his care a second wife, Moneta's cousin, a widow with a daughter named Rainbow who tried all day to lure Tekakwitha out to play. The orphan, however, preferred solitude. She worked near her pallet in the chief's long house in the new village. Moneta, her stepmother, saw repeatedly how valuable was the work the scarred little girl produced as she bartered it with others, yet she resented her and nagged her and refused to excuse her from the usual errands of fetching wood and water.

"If she thinks the robe she embroidered for the chief's appearance at the Onondaga Council will excuse her from her chores, she is sadly mistaken."

What galled the woman most, though, was her cheerful attitude.

Tekakwitha never complained and seemed always to be smiling. She kept to herself, creating designs that drew attention and admiration from all. With the completion of each new work, she held it up, gazed upon it and then set it aside so she might start another. The girl's cheerfulness offended Moneta for she was a constant reminder of Moneta's inability to bear a child of her own, and the girl grew even more cheerful around Kryn the half-breed.

Four summers ago, the Women's Council had elevated Iowerano up as a governing chief of the Turtle Clan to succeed his brother who died from the smallpox. At that same council, the women named Kryn a warrior chief. Although his Mohawk name was Togoniron, everyone called him "Kryn" after a Dutch fur-trader believed to be his father. Massive in size, but proportioned and well-defined of muscle, Kryn had light skin and, unique in all of the great league, blue eyes. He refrained from using war paint or marking his flesh with tattoos. He wore his hair in a high Mohawk style, the rooster comb from the forehead back, ending in a rattail tied with a red ribbon of eel skin that swung when he walked. In summer he dressed in a buckskin loincloth and moccasins; in winter in leggings and a tunic of deerskin.

His pale skin was a cause of shame to him. In the matriarchal culture, he was Mohawk, a member of his mother's *ohwahchira*, and on its behalf he hunted and fished and built long houses and canoes, but the notion that his father may have come from a degenerate race of farmers who drank spirits and beer, smoked their pipes each evening and ate the filthy swine that rooted amongst their sewage gave him a humility rare among the Mohawks.

Kryn often visited Iowerano to discuss weighty matters, particularly the likelihood of war with the Algonquins, the Mohicans or the whites, and Tekakwitha was thrilled by his presence. She waited on him as he sat at the fire smoking the calumet, and his twinkling blue eyes, which she could discern with her own dim vision, charmed her when he looked her way. His wisdom and good sense were legendary, his fidelity and courage unmatched. Indeed, he represented for her all the attributes of the mighty Deganawida of legend. And so it was with great dismay she learned one day that Kryn was returning with Algonquin prisoners seized while hunting in the forest, and he was bringing them back for the torture and sacrifice that upset her so.

Quite a stir accompanied the announcement as a crier went from long house to long house. The women brought out iron rods and knives and the children swung sticks and switches to practice for the gauntlet. It was a chilly October afternoon, the reds and oranges of hardwoods flaming among the deep green of the pine. In a rush the villagers poured out of the gate and formed a line down to the ford at the riverbank. White Adder, the albino sorcerer, chanted and danced and shook his tortoise rattles as drummers beat a tempo to incite the villagers.

Suddenly, on the facing hill, Kryn appeared. Despite the chill, his torso was naked. He wore a loincloth and leggings and moccasins. He raised his arms and bellowed out a war cry that sent the villagers into spasms of joy, "Aiiii-yeee!" They danced. They waved high their spears and rods and birches in anticipation. Kryn reached behind him and produced a tall Algonquin, his hands tied behind his back, fear and defiance mixed in the expression that peered from under his matted hair. The villagers went wild. Kryn shoved him forward, then pulled up another prisoner, a pregnant young woman. This brought shrieks of laughter from the women waiting to beat her, and the terrified prisoner shrank from the impending violence. Next he brought forth an old man with a cloth about his skinny buttocks. He was thin and stooped and haggard and his hair was limp and fell about his face. He wore a look of great sorrow and resignation. The villagers howled in derision at his age and infirmity. Kryn again raised his hands in triumph and brought forth a well-proportioned young man, naked, his hands tied in front of him. The women shrieked with laughter at his nakedness. Kryn pushed him down the hill.

"Come, Tekakwitha," Spotted Fawn urged. Rainbow, her adopted sister, ran forward to join the gauntlet, "Let us welcome these prisoners."

"No," Tekakwitha said. "I hate to hear their screams of pain."

"It's fun to watch them dance as the torches burn them and the knives open them up. How can you not enjoy it?"

"I imagine how I would feel if it were being done to me."

"But it isn't being done to you!" Spotted Fawn said. They laughed. "You're doing it to them." The two girls ran forth to join the gauntlet, and Tekakwitha turned back, alone, to her long house.

Dinner was postponed that night as all the village welcomed Kryn's prisoners. Iowerano returned to his fire pit to don his headdress of horned elk with eagle feathers. He did not notice the young maid in the shadows quietly stitching.

As the chief was readying to leave, Kryn came in: "Great Chief, may I have your ear a moment?"

"Of course, Great Warrior."

"The villagers are escorting a young warrior to the platform in order to offer as a holocaust to Aireskou."

"The pole and the platform are ready, and Aireskou thirsts for his blood. It will bring us good hunting and will aid us in keeping the French away."

"I come to you to seek his release."

"But you brought him here as a prisoner!" Iowerano said.

"You speak often, Great Chief, of the need to build up our nation. This warrior showed courage and resourcefulness in battle and was captured only with great difficulty since he wished to fight to the death. He is worthy of the name 'Canienga,' the People of the Land of Flint."

"As worthy as you?"

Kryn ignored the gibe. "Burning him upon the platform will bring us only a temporary benefit, witnessing his courage as he dies; but adopting him into an *ohwahchira* will bring lasting benefits since he will hunt to feed his family, and fight both in attack and in defense, and he will breed strong sons like himself. We have welcomed him and caressed him sufficiently. His face has not yet been painted black. Let us cut him down and adopt him."

"It has been a year and more since we have sacrificed a prisoner to Aireskou."

"Has the god asked for this?"

"The gods do not speak to men except by signs. The sorcerer and the people require this sacrifice, and so I must deny your request."

"Hold him there a day. Convene the council and let's put it to a vote."

"We only do that when there is some question as to the prisoner's value as a hostage. An Algonquin has no political value, and so there is no need."

"My words fall, then, upon closed ears?"

"I have spoken. We are grateful to you for capturing these prisoners. Let us put this one to good use."

Kryn glared at Iowerano. He turned away, and then he saw Tekakwitha in the corner.

"Who is this?" Kryn asked.

"My foster daughter," Iowerano said.

"She is not out welcoming the prisoners?"

Tekakwitha tried to hide in the shadows.

"What is it that occupies her?" Kryn asked, walking toward her. She looked up and saw Kryn's smile, and she looked at her step-father to see if she might speak with the great warrior.

"She's always working on something or other," Iowerano said with annoyance. "Let us go out and watch how well these prisoners die."

Kryn ignored him. He squat down on his haunches and reached

out for the robe she embroidered. She handed it up to him, then dropped her eyes and turned her face away.

Kryn ran his thumb over the small pictograph she was sewing into the soft doeskin. A woman with wings hovered above the treetops. "Who do you picture here?"

"Sky Woman." Haltingly she looked at him and his eyes were warm and blue as summer.

"So it is." He noticed another pictograph. An eagle with a wide wingspan soared over pine trees that towered over a lake. "And this?"

"The eagle who is vigilant to keep the peace of Deganawida and Hiawatha."

"Your work is exceptional," Kryn said. "What is your name?"

"They call me 'Tekakwitha.'"

"Well, then, Tekakwitha, will you embroider a robe for me?"

She smiled and dropped her eyes. "Yes," she said meekly.

"Speak to Moneta," the chief said impatiently. "She deals in these trifles."

Just then a loud scream startled them, a scream of sudden pain, ending on a note of defiance and rage.

"Come," said Iowerano, "they have placed one on the platform. Let us watch how heroically he will die."

"Will you embroider a ceremonial robe for me?" Kryn asked.

"I will," she said with modesty. "Gladly."

Kryn and Iowerano then left to witness the ceremony. Tekakwitha remained behind, and as she began a new scene, she selected red quills and sewed flames to surround the warrior who was even now being tortured and burned at the stake as an offering to Aireskou.

All night she listened to the warrior's song of death. By the dim light of dying embers in the fire pit she worked the porcupine quills into the soft doeskin as the hoarse song, ripped from the soul of the Algonquin with knives and hot irons and flames, rose in a crescendo of defiance, edging now and then to despair. She had no words to describe the horror of what came to her ear, but alone in the cabin she imagined a young man, a brave man as Kryn described him, roasted alive. Why did they kill the deer and hare and fish they cooked for food so mercifully, but burned a man to listen to him suffer? It made no sense. She bore his pain with empathy, each scream, each defiant howl of, "Is that the worst you can do?" followed by an agonized scream, and other than the embroidery in her hands, she moved not a muscle.

Morning light seeped into the cabin. Forms of sleeping people lay sprawled throughout the long house. One by one they had drifted in and fallen upon their pallets to sleep, spent from the night of agony and torture. Tekakwitha spread out the embroidery she had completed. Kryn had admired her work last night, and his praise lifted her spirits for she loved Kryn from afar, his fierce independence, his courage, his defiance of Iowerano. She stood and went outside to visit the privy ditch. In the center of the village stood the remnants of the platform and the pole where the Algonquin had died. Crows were strutting on the platform searching for morsels of meat. All was charred and wet with the dew and a sweet, sickening aroma of burned flesh hung low like a mist. Death had visited this place in the deepest hour of the night. Summoning death from the darkness and parading it in flames and the screaming hostage, the villagers would now be sullen for a day or two, not out of reverence, but out of satiation.

Through the village gate she went and to the ditch. Crows in the branches above seemed to laugh at the folly of the human sacrifice. When she adjusted her tunic and was starting back to the village, she heard her name called, her former name, "Ray of the Sun!" It was Anastasia. "You're stirring while others sleep?"

"The night is over. It is morning."

"I tried not to listen, yet even in my far cabin with the wind blowing across the maize I heard the screams."

"May I visit you?" the girl asked.

"Come along, yes. I will feed you."

The woman and the child walked through the waist-high corn together, and beneath the girdled trees with their gray, barren branches where crows ominously cawed. Beyond lay the blue ribbon of river between green folds of the hills. Burdened no longer by the blood offering in the night, and happy to be with Anastasia, Tekakwitha skipped along and greeted Coon-Hunter, Anastasia's mutt, who came to meet them. The girl played with him and nuzzled him and kissed him on his wet nose.

In the cabin, Anastasia gave her a bark bowl of porridge upon which she generously ladled maple syrup and sprinkled some strawberries. They sat cross-legged by the fire.

"My aunt never gives me strawberries."

"Then you must visit me more often."

"Kryn came to see my uncle last night," the girl said. "He asked that the prisoner be spared, but my uncle turned him down. Kryn captured the prisoner. Why did he need my uncle's permission?"

"Iowerano is a powerful chief. Kryn is only a warrior. The prisoner was a prize from the attack Kryn made, and Iowerano determines how the spoils of war are to be distributed."

"But Kryn made so much sense."

"Ah, little one, you will soon see that sense has little effect on people's actions. People act out of fear and envy and hatred far more than they act out of good sense."

"Kryn praised my work. I showed him Sky Woman and the eagle of peace and Hiawatha, and he asked my uncle if I would embroider a ceremonial robe for him."

"Kryn will surely be an ambassador if we sue for peace."

The girl pulled her knees up to her chin and folded her arms around her legs. "Tell me again the story of Deganawida and Hiawatha and the Great Peace."

"You will be a wise matriarch someday, for you never tire of the old legends."

"They are from a better time before the whites came here."

"But those times were less good in many ways, too," Anastasia said. "The five nations of our league fought constantly with each other. There was much envy and aggression and no one spoke the truth. Atotarho, the most powerful chief, lived in the land of the Onondaga. His hair was a writhing mass of snakes. He lied, he cheated, he stole the wives of other men. He gave his word on treaties and then broke it."

"And Deganawida?"

"Ah, the Peacemaker! A young Huron woman who never knew a man with her body bore a child and named him 'Deganawida.' He practiced oratory on the banks of the river and soon became a gifted speaker, wise and deep-thinking and able to touch people's hearts with his words.

"Deganawida saw the war and burned villages and scalpings and death brought by men's passions and it saddened him greatly. One night he dreamed of 'The Great Peace,' and when he awoke he dedicated his life to achieving it. He saw a way. He journeyed to the land of the rising sun, everywhere encountering hunters, urging them to return to their hearth fires with his message of peace.

"He came at last to Onondaga. There Deganawida, who called himself the Peacemaker, met Hiawatha. He converted Hiawatha from eating human flesh. He charged Hiawatha with combing the snakes out of Atotarho's hair. The Peacemaker then continued his journey east through the land of the Oneida, and then through the land of the Mohawk, coming at last the great falls at Cohoes. He climbed a tree and sat and waited. The Mohawks saw him, though, and cut down the tree and it fell into the river and was swept away. They considered him dead, but the next morning the Great Peacemaker was sitting by his fire. The Mohawks saw that if he were killed, he would come back from the dead, and that this power opened their ears to his message of peace. In this way, our nation, the Canienga, became the founder of the league.

"Hiawatha's efforts to comb the snakes from Atotarho's hair proved dangerous and unsuccessful, though. Atotarho summoned the Thunderbird, and with lightning leaping from his talons, the Thunderbird swooped down, picked up Hiawatha's daughter and carried her away. Hiawatha was grief-stricken. He left Onondaga and paddled east.

"He came to a lake. A great flock of ducks flew up and drew the water of the lake with them. Hiawatha walked across the lake bottom with dry feet. He gathered shells into his leather pouch. When he came to the Peacemaker's camp, the Peacemaker took the shells and made strings of wampum from them, uttering the words of the Requickening Address. With each string of wampum he drew grief from Hiawatha's heart. They sang the Peace Hymn together.

"Together, then, Deganawida and Hiawatha came here to the Clan of the Turtle and taught this nation of Mohawks the rite of peace. Then they journeyed to the land of the Oneida who joined immediately into the league of peace. They bypassed the Onondaga for Atotarho still ruled there, and they went to the Cayuga who immediately accepted the peace. With three nations in the League, they went to the Onondaga at last. All embraced the peace except Atotarho. Now, with the strength of four nations, they went to the Seneca who joined and completed the League.

"The final step was to comb out the snakes. With the five nations unified into the Great League, the Peacemaker promised Atotarho that the council fire would always be at Onondaga if he embraced the peace and he could be the most powerful chief. Atotarho then accepted the peace for the benefit he would glean. The snakes crawled from his hair and he rose up to be first among the fifty-one chiefs. The Peacemaker placed antlered crowns upon all their heads as a sign of their authority, and they met in the first great council where Deganawida taught them The Great Law. And that, little one, is how we lived, in peace and happiness, until the white man came."

"Why has he come here, the white man?" the girl asked.

"He comes to drive us from the Land From Which All Rivers Flow, and occupy it for himself. That is why we wage war upon him, capture him and strike fear into his heart as to the consequences of invading our land." She stroked the little girl's braid. "Without his disease, your mother and father would still walk the earth. Your little brother would be alive to play with you. Instead, they are under the earth and you are nearly blind, and even your aunt taunts you by calling you 'One Who Gropes Her Way Along.'"

"Please tell me of the symbol of the Great Peace, Mother." She dropped her head, embarrassed that the word slipped from her lips.

"Mother?" Anastasia jostled her affectionately.

"I think of you as my mother. You were her friend."

"I loved your mother as my sister. Let me try to take her place." She hugged the child and the child hugged her in response. "Hiawatha and Deganawida established a great pine tree with five strong roots to fasten the peace in the earth. The five roots are the five nations of the league, and upon the very top of the pine tree he set an eagle, ever vigilant to spy and attack any enemy of the peace."

"Can I share with you a secret?"

Anastasia held Tekakwitha close to her breast. "If I am to be your mother, you can tell me anything in your heart and I will hold it fast in mine."

"I see my uncle, Iowerano, as Atotarho, the chief with the snakes in his hair."

Anastasia laughed with her. "That is fitting."

"And I see Kryn as the great peacemaker. When he looks at me I know he wishes for everyone to live in peace."

"We could, except for the white man who knocks at the eastern gate. Kryn sees this more than anyone else. His blood is mixed. His eyes of blue are an accident of his breeding. He cannot deny his parentage, and so he works ever harder to prove himself worthy to be 'Canienga.'"

"He is a true hero," Tekakwitha said, "strong and brave, but he is also kind."

"Yes," Anastasia rocked the diminutive girl in her lap, "and you must work harder, too, at being Mohawk since half of you is Algonquin, like me."

"I shall watch Kryn," she said, "and imitate him."

"You make me laugh," Anastasia said. "As if you could be as great as the great warrior himself!"

"I know what I know," the girl answered. "And I will be what I am."

Chapter 12

Claude Chauchetière Becomes a Jesuit and Volunteers For the Canadian Missions

THE JUDGE'S HOUSEHOLD, recently so busy with physicians and important visitors and servants on errands of dire importance, now grew ominously quiet. The judge was dying. The Jesuit rector of the boys' school had heard Jehan's last confession and given him the last rites, and he opened the chamber door and invited the judges sons in for the final moments.

Father first called Jean, the oldest, forward. As he whispered to him and clasped his forearm, Claude, the middle son, looked about at the candles, the bed curtains, the crucifix, and out the latticed window to the steeples and weathervanes of Poitiers.

"Claude?" The sound of his name in his father's voice, the summons, startled him. He stepped forward and placed his hand in his father's. It was cold as clay. "You are my sensitive one," the judge whispered. "You will struggle with your sensitive heart and it will appear be your weakness. But be strong of will, and find your purpose and your sensitive heart will become your strength."

"Oh, Father!" the boy moaned.

"You must be strong, Claude." He placed his cold hand upon the boy's forehead, and Claude, overcome with sorrow, bowed for the benediction, then turned and as Jacques the youngest was called, he fled. Out of the chamber and down the hall he passed, a great sob pressing up in his throat. He pulled open the door to his own chamber and hurled himself upon his bed. Waves of despair passed through him. The world he knew was coming to an end.

"Dear God," he cried in despair, "I am an orphan now. I throw myself into Uour arms. Make of me what You will."

In time he stopped his weeping. He listened for an answer, the beating of the wings of the Holy Ghost, perhaps. No answer came.

The flames of twelve candles surrounded the bier in Cathédrale Saint-Pierre de Poitiers where *procureur au siege presidial* Jehan Chauchetière lay in state. Gothic vaults from the twelfth century receded into shadows and the chanting of monks ebbed into silence. The stern lines of the judge's face found no repose even in death. In his black judicial robe and the four-cornered hat limned with scarlet, he was as severe, inscrutable and unyielding as he had been on the bench. His fellow judges, solemn in their robes of office, paid their respects, but whispered over his remains about who would succeed him.

In a pew sat the three slender, pale lads, orphans now, Jean the eldest, Jacques the youngest and Claude, the middle son. At sixteen, his delicate face with almond eyes, high cheekbones and full lips framed by long curls might have been a daughter's. When Jean the cynic whispered, "He died well, didn't he, our father?"

Claude answered, "He believed in justice."

"And he dispensed it well," Jean smiled, "to the highest bidder."

The remark wounded Claude, more for its truth than its cruelty. The funeral mass began, the choir intoning the Requiem. Claude folded his hands and prayed for the soul of his father that seemed to glow dully like marsh gas from the casket. Claude feared that the patriarch had too long neglected his soul in favor of ambition, and so finding its way into heaven might be difficult.

His father's appetite for public office troubled Claude, the endless plotting, the service to moneyed nobles and deference to ecclesiastics, the harsh rulings that sent poor thieves who stole bread to support their children off to an oar in the king's galley ships. The patriarch's reputation was not for wisdom or compassion, but for severity. And yet with the lords and their households! Anything he might do to ease the harshness of the law. This hypocrisy offended Claude.

Unceremoniously the household was disbanded. Relatives came for furniture and paintings and draperies, the servants packed and left, the notary auctioned the empty structure. All three sons took up residence at the Jesuit college in Poitiers where they'd been day students. They looked no farther to find their life's work. Far-flung realms where the Jesuits held influence opened glorious vistas to them. Each boy in his own way had a bit of Jehan's grandiosity. Far nobler was the idea of going forth as a soldier of Christ than practicing law in the pettifogging hierarchy of this provincial capital.

From the Jesuits in classrooms and in chapel they learned egalitarian principles: no matter what his rank or intelligence, every man was equal in the eyes of the Lord and possessed an equal opportunity for sin and redemption. The passionate teachers sparked a desire for seeking truth and finding God in this world, a transcendent path away from filthy lucre and the clashing cymbals of prestige. All three young men turned one by one to the order to receive them as seminarians.

In the great library Claude thrilled reading the *Relations* about New France. Since he was a small child the word "Canada" had conjured images forests and mountains, wild natives and brave soldiers and heroic blackrobes who went among the natives to preach the gospel with nothing but a crucifix. Claude attended at the death of an old priest who personally knew the holy Jogues as a seminarian. His lifelong wish, unfulfilled, was to journey as Jogues had, a missionary to New France. "Go out, live your life," the old priest directed him in his raspy voice. "Don't dream about it! Act! Don't let this happen to you."

And so, two years after his father's death, on his eighteenth birthday, Claude bowed his head and took his initial vows to serve the greater glory of God as a Jesuit. Handy with chalk and oil paint in drawing and painting illustrations, he put aside his other ambition, which was to travel to Paris and live as an artist. He asked that God reveal His purpose in his life. He bowed his adolescent will to the rigorous training of Loyola. He strove in the Jesuit way to forge a unique and individuated "self," both to fight pitched battles with the demon, and to assist others along their roads to enlightenment.

To prepare himself for such a life, Claude Chauchetière was inducted by the *Spiritual Exercises*, a series of visualizations conducted under strict discipline of a sponsor. He meditated upon a perfect union with Jesus Christ, the splendor of the virgin birth, the wily resourcefulness of the devil. He fasted, deprived himself of sleep and occasionally mortified his errant flesh with a cat-o-nine-tails, praying to be released from temptation—

"Who art thou, O man, that darest to measure thyself against God? Thou art but flesh and full of impurities. Behold the corruption of thy nature: as dried grass ready to fall beneath the scythe. Behold thy weakness: a leaf the sport of the wind. Behold the inconstancy of thy heart: a vapor scarce formed, and already dissipated in the air—this is thy life. A little dust and ashes; behold thy origin and thy end upon earth: 'Dust and ashes.'"

During his two-year probationary period at Bordeaux, Claude Chauchetière scribbled in a journal constant assessments of his unworthiness. He sketched pictures of his fellows and constantly noted how weak and vacillating was his vocation, how he feared that he might at any moment be ejected and then have nowhere in the world to go. He even worried that his ambition to purge all his worldly cravings might itself be the work of the devil. To correct this error, he practiced humility. He volunteered for the lowest jobs; he prayed for the success of his fellows; and he kept secret the one burning desire of his heart—to stand in the presence of God and fill his soul with light and love and purity.

At the age of twenty, Claude returned to Poitiers only to be assigned to teach elementary Latin to boys in a college at Tulle while he pursued a three-year course in philosophy. He hated Tulle, its cramped provincialism, the deadening ignorance of the students, the absence of any inspiration or path for transcendence. He edged close to despair.

"Not only did I seek to detach myself from the world," he wrote of this time, "I wanted to detach myself from myself. For a long time, I was like an animal that thinks of nothing."

Still, he persevered in his studies, he received the sacraments, he conquered the cravings of his young flesh, and even ignored the comfort of affection in family and friends, seeking to purge from himself all that stood in the way of a perfect union with God. Then, unexpectedly, he was rewarded. God, he believed, touched him.

"On Christmas Eve in the year 1668, about nine or ten at night, I heard the bells softly tolling. I listened and enjoyed this contemplative sound until suddenly—I cannot say how—my soul was transported, swept up, higher and higher. I wept in joyous thanksgiving as the Lord drew me upward, and I followed wheresoever He led."

As if in clouds he floated. The warm sky a golden, liquid blue, reverberated with a holy drone, a single musical note as bright as a river of white light, containing all music in its sweet tone as white light holds all the rainbow colors.

"An odor of sanctity emanated from my body," he wrote. "I spent the night in a holy state of rapture so deeply pleasurable, I nearly missed mass on Christmas morning where I was to serve on the altar. I went through the motions dazed and distracted until it was time for communion. When the priest placed the host upon my tongue, the tingling spread through me and as I swallowed it, I felt a sharp pain in my chest. I thought I would suffocate and pass out. I followed the priest with the lamp as he gave out communion, and I stumbled through the rest of the mass. I then struggled back to my cell. As I removed my surplice, I was in a swoon, caressed by God both within and without. I knew at last God's love for me, a humble wretch. It was a love of such intensity and purity that I was ravished. My will merged in love with that of God so that no temptation or thought of disobedience seemed possible. All desire was gone. I had reached complete indifference to self, an annihilation of any portion of me that could be separate from God, and I saw at last the opening of my path."

The path led him out of the limestone cloisters of ritual and routine unto the missions of New France. Since boyhood he'd been enthralled by tales of the wilds of New France, the privations and horrors of the Jesuit heroes Jogues and Brebeuf and Garnier and Chabanel. He had imagined the frozen lakes, the blizzards, the brawny natives dressed in fur chanting in their smoky superstition, erupting in violence at a wrong word. Yet cowardice soon followed upon the heels of his rapture and he feared abandoning everything familiar to him.

From the height of mystical ecstasy, Claude Chauchetière immediately plunged into confusion and despair. He could not repeat the religious ecstasy of Christmas Eve at will, nor could he hasten his escape from the long course of study necessary before he might make his final vows:

"I found myself so full of disorder as to become insupportable to myself. I was insensitive to God. I had stumbled into a labyrinth and could find no way out. Backward and forward I went sighing for a hidden life, experiencing an alteration of consolation and desolation." He carried his desolation everywhere. It attached even to his devotions and corroded them like lye. He understood that his despair arose because "I had not wanted to do the will of God, so He didn't want to do mine either."

He returned from Tulle to Poitiers, and then he taught at Saintes and finally he was sent to teach in the Atlantic port town of La Rochelle. Fervently prayed to experience again the deep communion with God, and finally his prayers were answered. His second spiritual awakening occurred on the feast of St. Francis Xavier:

On December 3, 1671, God gradually dispersed all my clouds. I was kneeling at the statue of St. Francis Xavier as I had since childhood and again I felt at one with God. For days this time the sensation lasted. Now and then I felt a feverish heat and I stopped breathing. I had the distinct sense that I was floating. When I awoke in the middle of the night, I felt God present at the end of my bed. I was so elevated in prayer, I knew not the passage of time. I hungered and I thirst, but the thought of ordinary food disgusted me. I desired only the host and the wine transubstantiated into the body and blood of Jesus Christ. In those few days of spiritual transport, God gave me such deep knowledge of His mysteries that all of my faith seemed completely new and glistening in the light of a new morning sun. I saw then that I must at last and finally abandon myself to Him, to give myself completely to God. He spoke to me and I heeded his message, 'Come to the missions.'

When Father Joseph-François Le Mercier, former superior of the Canadian missions, returned from New France the following year, Claude's seven-year course was nearing completion. Ordination grew closer and his choice must be made. He attended Father Le Mercier's lecture about the missions of New France. As he listened to the haggard priest, aged and weathered by the privations of the colony, Claude knew where he would do God's will:

I selected Canada because it was the less civilized, the more obscure place. The sacrifices were vast and the rewards small indeed. Father Le Mercier confirmed the accounts of the Relations that not much might be done there, the natives so decimated by disease and warfare, and so suspicious of our motives that I would not be hungering for martyrdom or fame. There I might better serve the greater glory of God with no expectation of any reward in the regard of other men.

With the choice made, Claude now burned with happiness, certainty and impatience.

I had to flee from the close and heated corridors of the college to the gardens where I might cool from the fire of zeal that burned within me. I sought out Father Le Mercier for a private audience, and he was gracious enough to meet with me the day before he departed for Paris.

Father La Mercier welcomed the young man into the guest apartment at the college.

"Come in, my son, come in," the elder priest took Claude's hands in both of his. His skin was bronzed and weathered, and the sinews showed. The lines of his face, too, were pronounced, the nose long, the jaw sharp, and his eyes burned with zeal. "The prefect indicates you have volunteered for the missions of New France and you seek some information."

"That is correct, Father."

"A noble calling! Come in, please! Sit down. I shall ring for tea."

"Please, Father, make no fuss . . ."

"We shall be comfortable, eh? Been so long without them, I find the amenities pleasing. Indulge me." He smiled at the younger man and directed him to a chair. It was a small, simple apartment, whitewashed walls and leaded glass windows that overlooked a quadrangle of clipped grass and a sundial on the facing tower. The May sun had the birds singing and a bell tolled the quarter hour. Tea was served shortly and they sat together relaxed.

"The *Relations* may have been accurate in their time," the priest began, "but the colony is all changed."

"For the better, I hope?"

"It is the curse of civilization, I suppose, that vanquishing of the great forces in both man and nature reduces everything to the commonplace." He shook his head. "A Jogues in this day and age would be impossible."

"Is it because the savages are so tamed?"

"Let us speak about the Iroquois. They are not savages. True, they are more primitive than we, but they have a surpassing intelligence and a deep integrity that once turned toward the Lord rarely wavers or backslides. They have an enormous capacity for work. They can paddle their canoes fourteen and sixteen hours a day without complaint. They can erect a hut for sleeping in less than an hour, and can fashion a canoe from the bark of an elm or birch in half a day. They are far more courageous in battle than our finest soldiers, and they accept the privations of their world like the stoics of old. Once instructed in rudimentary precepts of faith, they evolve far beyond what our peasants here at home or our *habitants* or our *couriers de bois* of New France."

"And so the natives accept civilization?"

"After a fashion. Not often by choice."

"It is forced on them?"

"This is what has happened, my son." Father Mercier sipped his tea. "A new era commenced in 1665 when Marquis de Tracy landed at Quebec. The lookouts hailed the fleet as it passed Isle de Orleans, and we lined the high rock to watch the ships approach. Such great pomp was never seen before in that land. The Chevalier de Chaumont and a hundred young nobles embarked from the ships in a long line, their lace and ribbons fluttering in the wind, their great lion's mane wigs beneath plumed hats. They marched along the narrow streets to the tap of a drum, escorted by the regiment Carignan-Salières, lately returned from the Turkish wars. These were battle-hardened soldiers and they marched in slouched hats and nodding plumes, bandoliers across their chests, fire-lock muskets over their shoulders.

"Then came the great de Tracy himself. He's one of the largest men I have ever seen, yellow and sallow from his illness in the fields of Turkey, yet vigorous in step, accompanied by four pages and six valets. All in all it was a glittering pageant such as Quebec had never witnessed. As the Frenchmen shouted and the natives stared in disbelief, they threaded through the streets of the Lower Town, and then climbed the steep pathway to the cliff above.

"Breathing hard, but still vigorously walking, the Marquis looked askance at the dilapidated fortifications, the humble shed we called with mounting irony 'Castle of St. Louis.' He passed Bishop Laval's new seminary, and reached the square between our Jesuit college and the cathedral. How the bells rang to welcome him! Bishop Laval in his crimson pontificals, surrounded by priests, and our Jesuits, offered him holy water and a *prie-dieu* to kneel and pray, but the old general declined, even declined the offer of a pillow and knelt instead on the bare pavement. He spread his arms and began the *Te Deum*, and we all sang with him as he bellowed out the hymn."

"How I long to see this place!" Claude Chauchetière said.

The elderly priest smiled at his enthusiasm. "The cliff of Quebec is twice again as high as our cliffs of Brittany. Imagine our great admiration for Marquis de Tracy in all his grandeur, bringing with him soldiers, settlers, women to be wives, horses, sheep, cattle to populate the colony. A few days later, Monsieur de Courcelle, new governor to the province, and Monsieur Talon, the intendant, landed with their trains of valets and followers. In all, five hundred troops from the regiment of Carignan-Salières were soon quartered. This new force was de Tracy's cocked crossbow aimed at the Mohawks to stop the raids and the scalpings and bring peace at last. You have read the *Relations*?"

"I have."

"Then you know how Courcelle set out in the dead of winter down to chastize the Iroquois, but stumbled into a colony no longer Dutch, but recently taken by the English under the Duke of York and Albany. Even though Courcelle retreated without firing a shot, the Mohawks saw what the future held and came that summer to sue for peace. On their way back home, though, a Mohawk killed François Chazy, the Marquis's nephew, who had been out hunting. That was the end of his patience. The marquis sent three hundred men to attack the Mohawks, but they met a Mohawk called 'the Flemish Bastard,' or 'Kryn' who, seeking peace himself, was returning the captured French officers and offering payment for the death of Chazy." The priest smiled. "In wampum," Claude was assured.

"On the final day of August, de Tracy invited this Flemish Bastard and his lieutenant Agariata to dine. The sight of these natives dressed in their buckskin and feathers, and our noblemen and priests and the bishop himself dressed in scarlet and lace was most pleasing. It seemed as though terms of peace still might be reached. But during dinner, de Tracy offered them wine. The Flemish Bastard declined to drink, but Agariata swallowed two or three glasses, and when the discussion turned to the murder of the Chazy, Agariata thrust out his arm and bragged: 'This is the hand that split the head of that young man!'

"Immediately soldiers pounced upon him. Kryn rose, thinking at first he was to be seized, but he made no protest in view of Agariata's guilt and the force of arms. The soldiers hauled Agariata into the square and threw a rope up over the limb of a tree. Calling all the Mohawks to witness, as Agariata sang his death song, they kicked the barrel out from under his feet and he sang no more."

"But this did not end it?"

"No. De Tracy spoke no more about peace. He sent the Flemish Bastard home but kept two dozen hostages. He told this Kryn to tell his countrymen that their nation would soon be destroyed. During the month of September, Quebec and Fort St. Anne on the Isle La Motte in Lake Champlain, were scenes of busy preparation. We set out from Quebec on the day of the exaltation of the Cross, September 14, with an army of six hundred French regulars, six hundred Canadians and a hundred Algonquin and Huron guides, all loaded down with supplies and ammunition.

"We paddled in boats upriver and portaged up the Richelieu and into Champlain. Imagine a paradise of color—the crimson and gold and evergreen and orange of the trees receding into blue and violet of the mountains, the great rocks lapped by the lakes—a heroic vista to our heroic enterprise.

"On our leaders urged us, but de Tracy had the gout and had to be carried. Once, crossing a stream, his bearer stumbled and fell into the water, and the two had to be rescued by a Huron. Courcelle suffered from stomach cramps and needed to be carried as well. After ten days our food gave out. Onward we plunged through the forest. A grove of chestnut trees gave us food for a sort of soup and greedily the men ate.

"On October 1, St. Theresa's Day, as we approached the first Mohawk castle, a sweeping, soaking rain set in. To keep the advantage of surprise we kept marching through the night. The wind moaned and the cold rain pelted. By the early morning light we saw their stockade rising up behind the rolling hills of bleached cornstalks, already harvested. Marquis de Tracy ordered a charge *coup-de-main* and our drums beat a furious tattoo. The soldiers rushed the gates and burst into the town with a battering ram to discover all the inhabitants had fled. The marquis ordered us onward in pursuit.

"High on the hills we saw here and there a Mohawk scout and heard them firing a signal to their fellows, but they were out of range, and they disappeared as we advanced. Up the river we marched, thirteen hundred strong, and into the next village we swept. This was taken as easily as the first. We heard the Mohawks yelling in the distance as they fled to the next village. 'Onward!' again was the order, and to the third and then fourth town. Finding no resistance in the fourth town, the men rested, but an Algonquin woman, a slave who was being held prisoner, told of a final stronghold. She led the way, a pistol in hand, to seek her revenge.

"To the fifth village we marched, the largest of all. The fortification was laid out as a quadrangle with a triple palisade, one inside the other, twenty feet high. We entered with no resistance. Bark tanks on scaffolds along the walls had been set up to douse fires from our attack. Within the stockade the houses were built of wood, far more solid than the bark huts of Jogues's time, some a hundred and twenty feet long with fire pits for eight or nine families. We found two old women, a small boy and an old man who was hiding under a canoe. He told us the Mohawks had assembled in this fort, determined to fight to the death, but when they saw our battalions marching, they exclaimed, 'The whole world is coming against us! Let us save ourselves!' and they fled.

"Marquis de Tracy ordered a cross be erected and the royal arms set forth. He drew up all the troops—we lost in this campaign only one man who drowned in the lake—and Jean-Baptiste du Bois, appointed by Tracy, advanced to the cross wielding his sword proclaiming: 'We take possession of these lands in the name of King Louis XIV!' and all the men waved their plumed hats and cried three times, 'Vive le Roi!'

"That evening we posted sentries and encamped, feasting on the stores of corn we found in underground vaults, and the smoked fish and meat hanging in their long houses. As the sunset on the 17th of October, our men set fire to the town. Two Mohawk women, distraught, threw themselves into the conflagration. Higher and higher rolled the flames against the dark sky and sparks exploded and smoke billowed into the clouds. By morning the town was a smoldering heap of ash and cinders. The men lined up before the cross and the royal standard and I said mass on a field altar. After mass, we sang *Te Deum*, that hymn echoing for the first time in this heathen land.

"Back down the valley we marched and we put the other villages and the massive stores of corn to the torch. The way back to Quebec was fraught with difficulties, swollen streams, canoes capsizing, but we had plenty of corn from the Mohawk stores and we reached the forts on the Richelieu before the snow flew."

"It was that campaign which brought peace at last?" Claude asked.

"Ah, yes, but the English were highly insulted at our march into lands they claimed. Throughout their colonies of New England they sought to muster forces to attack us and thereby win all of Canada for their crown, but so ill-prepared were they for war, nothing came of it. The advantage, though, was that the lesson learned by the Mohawks was also learned by the other four nations of the league. After a winter spent as nomads on the hunt, they listened when Marquis de Tracy sent word: sue for peace or risk another massive raid. In April the half-breed Kryn appeared again in Quebec along with representatives of the other four nations. Terms were negotiated. The Iroquois capitulated, and among the provisions of peace, they asked de Tracy to send them carpenters, blacksmiths, surgeons and Jesuits. The death of young Chazy was avenged. The insolent Iroquois were humbled in their own country and peace was bought by the blood of young Chazy. But most importantly for us, the land where Jogues and Goupil were martyred now offers fertile ground for our faith."

"Nearly ten years have passed. The Mohawk villages are rebuilt and we have missions there?"

"The natives' minds still vacillate. As you have read, no doubt, we have priests living among them, but there is much backsliding and a hankering after the old ways. Our fathers, while not clothed with authority by the crown, nevertheless serve as eyes and ears, vigilantly monitoring the peace to avoid further raids or abductions."

"My ship sails this spring, Father. I pray I will be assigned, like dear Father Jogues, to minister to these Mohawks."

"The other peoples of New France receive the Word more easily, however. The Iroquois, and the Mohawks in particular, pose the greatest challenge of all." Father Mercier raised his hand and the younger priest knelt to receive his blessing. "May the Lord be with you and shine every favor upon your journey in that savage land."

"Thank you, Father."

Chapter 13

De Tracy's Attack Sends
Tekakwitha Into the Forests As a Refugee

Wʜᴇɴ Kʀʏɴ ʀᴇᴛᴜʀɴᴇᴅ ꜰʀᴏᴍ ᴛʜᴇ ᴘᴇᴀᴄᴇ ᴛᴀʟᴋꜱ at Quebec, a cloud hung over his brow. He sat at Iowerano's fire. Tekakwitha ladled the porridge into his dish, and he ate quietly, chewing his food with his massive jaw. He would say nothing until the plates were cleared and the calumet was lit. The girl sensed something momentous, and so she retreated to her corner to work and listen.

As Iowerano stuffed the pipe with tobacco and lit it, he complained:

"Such a rash act in hanging Agariata! Do they not see the retribution this will bring?"

"The rashness was ours," Kryn said. "We should no longer be surprised if they respond to our provocation." He accepted the pipe and drew in a long pull of the smoke. "We fashioned a treaty in good faith that would provide for mutual benefit as to hunting grounds and the fur trade. Onontio wanted also to send the blackrobes again into our midst. Agariata recalled the box left by Ondessonk that brought the illness again and infected our crop with worms. He spoke against receiving the blackrobes, but he was out-voted. He could not bury that grievance.

"As we paddled through the great lake to bring news of the peace and have it ratified, we heard shots. Agariata paddled hard beyond a spit of land. We heard another shot. The French were only hunting. There was no menace to us at all, but Agariata attacked and killed one of the young men, Onontio's nephew. He captured the other six whites and was all for transporting them home to be caressed in a way that would persuade the French not to look anymore with such fond hope at our lands, but knowing what would happen to our hostages, I fought Agariata and won. I was escorting the French prisoners back toward Quebec when we encountered soldiers Onontio sent to chastize us. I turned our prisoners over, but they arrested me as well, hauled me back to Quebec and threw me into a cell. Only when one of the whites told the great chief how I had rescued him did de Tracy summon myself and Agariata forth. He laid out a great feast for us, but Agariata drank wine and insulted Onontio in his own hall by bragging that he had killed his nephew. How is this not sufficient provocation?

"Immediately the great chief brought the hostages from the dungeons and arrayed us all in the square to watch his men hang Agariata. As the body swung in the wind, Tracy released us and told us to return to tell you he is now marching upon us and will destroy everything in his path. He returned the hostages to their captivity."

"An idle boast. We will resist them."

Kryn took a puff of the pipe and let it out slowly, then spoke: "I have seen their armies, Great Chief, hundreds upon hundreds of soldiers armed with muskets and ready to march. Our retribution will be like a small flame in a thunderstorm."

"This is our home and we will defend it." Iowerano took a long pull of smoke and closed his eyes, defiant, arrogant, masking his fear with pride. "Let them come!"

"They will. They will burn our villages and put us to flight. We must prepare to winter in the forest on what we can hunt, for that will be our only option. I begin packing tomorrow."

"You will desert your people in its time of need?"

"I will tell anyone who asks me what the proper course will be."

"Where is your courage?"

"It is not a matter of courage. It is a matter of survival."

In her corner, quietly, unobtrusively, the girl of ten summers was stringing wampum beads. Kryn's words caused her concern. As Kryn rose to depart, he noticed her and he stepped over to her and reached down and hefted the wampum belt she was making.

"You put so much meaning into your designs."

She looked up at Kryn, courageous, wise, always certain of the right course. She yearned to ask him to take her along, to adopt her into his family.

"You do me great honor," she said. He put his hand on her head and she raised up her face and squinted at the chief.

"Speak to your uncle, little one. With your clouded vision you see more than he can. It is wise to stand and fight only when you can win."

As he left she went back to her work. She watched Iowerano smoking and considering and rejecting alternatives with a toss of his head. He spiraled downward in his thinking until he burned with deep resentment. Moneta made a movement to go to bed. As Iowerano went out of the cabin to the privy and then returned, the girl stood and went to him.

"I heard, Uncle, what Kryn our war chief has said."

"Yes?"

"May I go with his family on the winter hunt?"

"No."

The tone of his voice indicated to her further inquiry would be useless, but as she lay her head down to sleep, she envisioned all the marvels Kryn has spoke about, the city upon the rock in the north, the hundreds upon hundreds of soldiers, and the retribution this army would now bring upon the Mohawks, causing the Canienga to flee like a flock of birds.

The weather grew mellow after the rains let up. With news of the impending attack, many families were packing hunting and fishing gear and a supply of food. In the next few days dozens of families left through the village gates and wended down to the riverbank to paddle upstream into the lake country.

A week passed. Another. Up and down the valley the leaves were turning, red and orange and golden, and the blue river flowed through the hills clean and shimmering. Geese were on the wing in long V formations and the nights left frost upon the squash when suddenly, through the gate came a scout who called all to rally around him.

"I saw the army of the French," he cried with wild gestures, his eyes opened wide. "A hundred boats they row down the lake, not canoes, but great flat boats bristling with men and arms, coming to burn us in our homes. This is no army that will turn back. It will seize our land and make us captives."

Panic swept the lanes of the village. Tekakwitha listened as Iowerano received the news and tried to remain calm and counsel others not to panic. First he denied the report, and summoned the young man to him in person. Two strong warriors hauled him before the chief.

"Tell me what you have said is not so or I will have you bound and burned at the stake."

"I saw it! I can't deny what I saw!" The young man's eyes lurched in panic. "We cannot defend our village against them, Great Chief! We must flee!"

Iowerano exploded: "How can there be that many French?"

"In great boats they come! My cousin who lives near the whites has told me. The boats are bigger than our entire village! They arrive and march through their city, each soldier with a musket, hundreds upon hundreds of them."

"How can they march that many against us?"

"They did it in winter when the blizzards were blowing, and they can do it now as the weather is favorable. I have seen their flat boats loaded with men. Flee, I tell you! We must all flee!"

"Surely they will accept terms?"

"That time has passed! When Agariata struck down the great chief's kinsman, he sealed our fate." The young man looked at the warriors who had escorted him here, and since they made no move to restrain him, he said, "I must depart," and he left.

"Anything else, chief?" the warriors asked.

"Tell the other long houses we will retreat to Andagaron and there we will make our stand with the brave Bear Clan."

It was then Iowerano's obstinacy broke. He struggled to his feet and called to his wives. "Moneta! Garahonto! Begin packing. You, there, Tekakwitha, roll up your blankets and pack your things. Rainbow, you do the same. We're leaving!"

Hastily she complied. She carefully folded the beadwork and the embroidery and placed it in a doeskin pack. She rolled her sleeping skins up, and was soon ready to depart.

Moneta dished a final meal from the kettle and took it off the fire to cool. She folded the sleeping skins and bound them with a piece of rawhide. Iowerano took down his antlered bonnet which denoted his office and he placed it upon his head. He grabbed his musket impatiently and he pushed aside the curtain and squinted out into the bright sunlight.

Tekakwitha pulled her shawl down to shade her eyes. She adjusted the eel skin strap to her forehead, lifted her bundle, and went outside. The villagers in various stages of agitation assembled in the center, and Iowerano called out: "We will journey to Andagaron and there we will make a stand against the French."

Half-hearted cheers met his bravado. They turned westward and passed single-file through the gate and down the pathway to the river trail.

Tekakwitha bowed her head away from the bright sunlight and set her moccasins upon the path. This move unsettled her. No longer might she seek shelter in the corner of the long house with her work. No longer would she know the familiar fire pit and her sleeping pallet. As uncomfortable as Moneta made her feel, she'd know the domesticity of this family no longer.

In three hours they came to Andagaron, but rather than offer them sanctuary, the Bear Clan was in turmoil likewise preparing to flee.

"Runners have brought the news," Mountain Cat, chief of the Bear Clan, revealed in a hasty conference. "We cannot defend this place."

"We will pass the smaller villages and journey all the way to Tionontoguen," Iowerano said. "Tionontoguen has a triple stockade and will give us proper defenses where we can make our stand."

And so they continued along the river trail, refugees. They paused for the night at a small fishing village on the riverbank, and early in the morning, as mists rose from the warmer water into the cold snap of autumn air, they continued on. The small girl walked uncomplaining. She ate only three strips of dried venison which Moneta doled out. It was the farthest she had ever ventured from her village. As the sun was at its highest, they rounded a corner and high on a hill rose Tionontoguen. The great squared sides were topped with bastions. Hammer blows everywhere were heard as the Mohawks readied the fort to repel the French attack. Women carrying buckets from the river filled the bark tanks hanging from the inside walls to be used to douse fires that attackers might set. Their effort was helped by a cloudburst that broke as the Turtle and Bear Clans trudged up the trail.

Tekakwitha entered the busy village of Tionontoguen behind Iowerano. Everywhere men and women were working to reinforce the stockade. The heavy rain drove everyone who could find shelter indoors. Children wailed and dogs barked and as they passed through the high gates they went directly to the center of the village where women assigned them lodging.

With such a large influx of refugees, the long houses were filled beyond capacity. Iowerano and his family were taken in by Gray Stag, chief of Wolf Clan, and Moneta and Tekakwitha slung the kettle above a crowded fire pit. Garahonto and Rainbow went to the next fire pit. The village was mass confusion, and the worried chiefs closeted themselves in a disused sweat lodge with their bonnets and their pipes to deliberate.

The common areas of the place were swarming with angry warriors and distraught women. Babies wailed, children argued and the heavy smoke, driven back down the chimney holes, intensified the unpleasantness. In a state of excited anticipation they spent the night, and in the morning scouts ran into the village announcing:

"The whole world marches against us! There is no use to make a stand! We must flee!"

Iowerano, vain as ever, grabbed the messenger. "Tell me how many are they?"

"More than all our village of men, women and children. They march to the drum and they have passed Ossernenon and now are nearing Andagaron. They will be here tonight."

This news sent the whole village into an uproar.

"Make haste!" Iowerano cried. "We must flee into the forest!"

"Kryn warned you of this!" Moneta reminded him. "You should have listened to him!"

"Silence, woman!"

Tekakwitha thrilled to hear the name of her hero. Indeed, he had predicted this for he was all-wise, and he advised how to avoid it, but her uncle's stubbornness denied it all. Quickly she packed up her bundle, adjusted the eel skin strap on her forehead and they were ready to escape within the hour. Out through the western gate of the village the line of refugees wended. Having no destination, they fled upriver and then fanned out into the hills.

Iowerano fumed and raged as he marched along. The incursion of the hated French! Since the time of Jogues when the priest left the black box behind and worms infected the corn and he and his brother had sunk it into the river, these whites had brought such difficulty into their lives.

The fleeing bands climbed into the foothills and camped. Two nights after they had departed, the eastern sky blushed a deep and lurid red.

"They burn our villages," Iowerano spat in disgust.

"Now we must hunt like the bark-eaters," Moneta remarked, "starving so in winter they eat their dogs and tree bark and their elderly."

"We shall punish this outrage," Iowerano promised, impotently shaking his fist at the sky.

"That I doubt," Moneta grumbled to Garahonto.

All night the fires burned against the eastern sky. In the morning they took stock of their situation. Very little food remained. Two boys with the family threw up a weir in a small stream and caught brook trout which they cooked over the fire.

"Let us go back to the village," Iowerano announced on the following day.

"The village is destroyed," Moneta said. "There is no reason to visit it."

"Perhaps there will be food or tools we can use this winter."

"All that remains there is your foolish pride," she scoffed.

Garahonto, his lesser wife, was more humble. This was her opportunity to comfort him. She urged him to remain as well, but the next morning, Iowerano and two youths and Tekakwitha returned to Tionontoguen. Other refugees had come out of the hills and were combing the heap of ash that once was the proud village

Tionontoguen, strongest of the Mohawk towns. When Iowerano saw the great cross erected, he called to others to help him, and they pulled it down, claiming again this land for Aireskou.

Into the mountains the small band wended. The mellow weather turned biting. The soft blue skies, alive with migrating geese, soon darkened and snarled into gray storms and the snow flew. Along a plunging stream they built a hut of bark and skins, large enough for a fire pit and nine sleeping pallets. Iowerano, wisely, conscripted two young hunters, White Moon and Little Wolf, and two young women, Blossom and Fawn. Day by day the sun fell farther in the west and the cold night lengthened with its howling wind. The girls Blossom and Fawn were fourteen and sixteen summers and they giggled and flirted with the young hunters while Moneta heaped jealous criticism upon them to Garahonto who said only, "Leave them alone. We were girls once and behaved so."

Never a good hunter, Iowerano delegated the capture of meat to the young men, but they stayed in the hut until the sun was up and returned each night empty-handed. Fawn and Blossom knew how to set rabbit snares and the group subsisted upon hare for a dozen nights, waiting for a deer or an elk. Tekakwitha remained in the corner of the hut idly working her crafts, careful not to eat much and to avoid setting off Iowerano's smoldering wrath.

As the dark and the cold deepened and the prospect of game lessened and hunger and Moneta's jealousy increased, the mood in the hut became intolerable. Iowerano, afraid of failure in the hunt, did not venture outside, and the young men went out each day on snowshoes but returned with nothing. In dire straights, as the rabbit population gave out, they butchered one of their skinny dogs, and then the other.

A fortnight after pulling down the cross and leaving the smoldering heap of ashes that had been the proud village of

Tionontoguen, the group lay groaning with hunger, scarcely able to get out each morning for firewood and water. Moneta boiled bark and roots and hickory nuts to make a soup and they began chewing the rawhide and the skins of their clothing. Garahonto huddled with Rainbow who wept herself softly to sleep. At night Blossom and Fawn shared their favors with the young hunters, and occasionally Garahonto coupled with Iowerano, to the stern indignation of Moneta.

One night, as the wind howled and the snow blew, hunger pains seized Tekakwitha. Iowerano was busy with Garahonto, and Fawn and White Moon were groaning with pleasure. Tekakwitha could not tolerate the sounds of their intimacy, and she arose and pulled wide the flap.

"Where are you going?" Moneta, half-asleep, asked.

"Outside."

A stiff wind blew and the moon, nearly full, lorded over creation in a soft blue majesty. Tekakwitha took her snowshoes that leaned against the hut, fastened them to her feet, bundled herself up against the wind and trudged off, uncertain of where she was going, only certain her troubled heart needed to get away.

Chapter 14

❧

Kryn Begins And Ends An Eat-All Feast

THE MOON LIT HER WAY. High in the sky it cast a silvery blue light upon the mountain peaks, its soft glow out-shining the pinpoint stars. Wolves and coyotes howled and their wild calling struck fear into her heart. Rarely did Tekakwitha venture out of her cabin, and never had she gone this far alone. The work of snowshoeing warmed her, but without a path she was moving aimlessly away with no destination, and this confused her. In the hush of blue moonlight she pulled back her shawl and looked out.

Before her the landscape was desolate. Great masses of earth and rock, covered with snow, undulated to the horizon. Forests reached up toward the bald peaks and the courses of streams wended in fissures below. She followed the trail they'd made climbing up to this place fifteen days before. With regular breathing of the cold air and the exertion dulling her hunger, she was soon yawning, deeply fatigued. So quiet, so still, so lovely was the moonlight it seemed like a dream, and she longed to lay upon the soft snow and sleep.

Onward she trudged. With no way to measure time or distance, she became disoriented, lost in the wide, bright moonscape. Down a path through the forest she went, and in the shelter of a great pine she rested. She knew well the seduction of sleep in the cold, how the temptation of sleep lulled many to a frozen death. She wanted to keep moving until the sun rose, but the shadow of the pines and the softness of the snow beckoned her to rest. She sat upon the trunk of a fallen tree, and then, feeling wearier, she wrapped her cloak and shawl about her and curled up against the massive trunk.

"I'll just sleep a few moments," she told herself, and she surrendered.

She woke with a start. Someone was shaking her. She did not know where she was, but she was bone weary and chattering with the cold. Her insides ached with hunger.

"Tekakwitha!" she heard, and she peered up. A rosy glow was in the east and it lit a chapped face which was wrapped in a shawl and looming above her.

"Anastasia!"

"Why did you leave the hut?"

"I heard them groaning. I couldn't sleep."

"You might have frozen!"

"I hate the sound of their groaning. They grunt like animals."

"Little one!" Anastasia embraced her.

"How did you find me?"

"The night was clear and the moon strong. I followed your tracks."

"Why are you here?"

"Kryn and I trailed a moose for a day and a half, ran it into a ravine and killed it. As we were transporting meat back to our lodge last night, we saw smoke from Iowerano's hut. Kryn gave the meat we carried to Moneta, and he led Iowerano and the two lads off to get the rest of the carcass. When I heard you had departed, I set out to bring you back."

"I will not go back there."

"You must. You'll freeze out here on your own."

"But they won't stop. Blossom and Fawn."

"We will spend the night with you and tomorrow you can return to our lodge with us."

"I will do that. Either you or Kryn must speak to my uncle, though. He will not grant the permission if I seek it myself."

"It will be done. Let me help you up." Anastasia pulled her to her feet and they trudged back on the snowshoes as the sun rose.

Great billows of fragrant cooking smoke rolled up from the hut. The snow before the entrance was red with blood from the butchering. Down the path came Iowerano and Little Wolf and White Moon loaded with slabs of meat. Behind them came Kryn with the antlered head. Anastasia called out to Kryn, "I found her!"

Kryn walked down the path. His buckskin leggings and fur coat were stained with the blood of the moose. His face, too, was smeared with blood, but his blue eyes danced.

"Don't go wandering away like that," he said. "We don't want to lose you."

"Enough about that," Iowerano said, all business, as if he were suddenly the great hunter who had saved the expedition. "Moneta has meat cooked. Let us begin the Eat-All feast."

"I have six people waiting for my return with this meat," Kryn said. "I cannot celebrate the Eat-All feast with you."

"Nonsense. Go get your people and bring them here."

"I will give you a hindquarter and the head if you want it. We can bury half of the meat in the snow where it will keep until we need it."

"No!" Iowerano said with an air of command. "We will host an Eat-All Feast. Go get your people and bring them here. We will eat until nothing remains of your kill."

"I know the way back," Anastasia said. "I will get the others."

Moneta opened the flap to the hut and a great fragrant cloud escaped. "I have meat cooked and ready. Come in."

"I will begin the feast," Kryn said, "but after I eat my fill, I will be off to my hunting lodge."

"You cannot dishonor the ancient custom," Iowerano said, putting his arm over Kryn's shoulders and leading him into the hut. He knew better than to press this any farther.

Indeed, Moneta had roasted a large cut of the hindquarter, and the savory aroma of it caused their mouths to water. They all sat about the fire as Iowerano passed around large pieces of meat.

"Before we eat," he said, "I will offer this first piece to our great god Aireskou who helped Kryn run this moose into a ravine." He cut off a piece of meat and tossed it into the fire where it sizzled and burned. "May Kryn's success bring us success in the hunt as well," and he bit into the meat and cut off a chunk with his hunting knife.

All ate. The boys ate greedily. Kryn savored his meat. Tekakwitha bit into the meat and the delicious flavor flooded her mouth, awakening her sense of taste and she cut the piece with her knife and chewed it well.

"Now let us cook the back strap," said Iowerano with ceremony. He produced the two long red muscles severed from the forequarters and handed them to his wife who placed them on the fire where they smoked and soon were charred. Around the fire there was little speech as the Mohawks ate hungrily. Iowerano then dished out portions of the back strap.

Again the delicious meat flooded her mouth with flavor and warm nourishment after so many days without food. The rich hot meat filled her stomach, she bit and chewed until she could eat no more. The thick forms around the fire eating, grunting, belching receded into shadows as her eyelids drooped and nearly closed, and she felt the happy, sated warmth of meat within her, belly-full like a woman with child. She lay back against a bundle of skins.

"Have some more!" Moneta lay another slab of meat upon her bark plate.

"No, Mother. I've had enough."

Iowerano was laughing, happy in the good fortune Kryn had

brought. "Eat, Tekakwitha! Have some more. We cannot stop until we finish."

"I've had my fill," she insisted and she groaned and turned away to sleep.

"The poor child," Anastasia said. "I found her sleeping on the snow. Let her sleep now."

"No," Iowerano insisted. "Sit up and help us finish this meat."

"I cannot," she said.

"But you must," he pulled her to a sitting position.

"We're not going to force her to eat," Kryn said. "Let the child rest."

"Tekakwitha defies me at every turn. When there is no meat, she leaves the hut and starts back to Kanawaka. Now that we have good fortune she refuses to share in it."

"She has shared in it enough," Anastasia said.

"I have eaten all I can," Tekakwitha groaned. "Please! Eat what you want, but let me be."

"No!" Iowerano said. "Everyone eats until this is finished." Iowerano suddenly jerked at her coat and she sat up. She thrust out her arms and opened her eyes and tried to focus. Her mouth opened and closed, opened and closed, and she scrambled on all fours to the door and then out into the sunny morning where she vomited on the bloody snow. In great surges the bloody meat came up and blood poured through her nose and the sour, bitter taste of the digesting meat sickened her further and caused her to heave and retch. Tears of shame pressed at her eyes. Within the wigwam she heard them laughing at her.

Anastasia was at her side. "It's all right, little one. We've had enough and we will take you with us."

"My uncle won't allow that."

"Kryn doesn't bow to him. Even now he's explaining why you will be leaving with us to spend the rest of the winter in our lodge. Do you have anything to pack?"

"My work and my bedding."

"Get it now before they finish talking."

"I don't want to go in there."

"But you must."

She pushed back through the flap and was again in the dim, smoky confines that smelled of cooked meat and heated fur and strong bodily odors of the people at the fire. She held down her gorge that threatened again to erupt, and without looking at Iowerano or Moneta or Garahonto, she packed her embroidery in a doeskin bag.

"You're leaving with Kryn?" Iowerano asked.

"If it pleases you, Father."

"It doesn't please me. The Eat-All Feast has hardly begun . . ."

"Far better is it to freeze the meat," Kryn suggested. "Then you will have it in times of scarcity when you need it."

". . . and you defy custom and you defy me," Iowerano told the girl. Nothing requires that I take you back into my household when we return to Kanawaka."

"We will discuss that later," Kryn said, and with his arm he guided the girl out of the hut.

Anastasia was smiling and the sun was streaming in the blue morning sky. Kryn shouldered a hindquarter of the moose. Anastasia wrapped some heavy cuts in her bag and put the strap about her forehead and began to move up the trail on snowshoes. Tekakwitha fixed her forehead strap as well and fell in behind her. The three walked up the ridge, high above the hills and the river valleys and passed along it until midday. They then descended into a sheltered valley where Kryn had made his hunting camp. Kryn's family came out at their approach and they congratulated him on his success. Karitha welcomed Tekakwitha into their midst.

Karitha stoked the cooking fire and soon had cuts of the moose meat grilling. She directed Tekakwitha to a pallet against the wall, and the girl lay down and soon was sleeping as the others quietly ate with none of the anger or hostility of Iowerano.

In the following days as blizzards shut them in, Tekakwitha worked upon her embroidery. Such striking pictographs did she stitch with the colored porcupine quills that Kryn asked her to describe them. She closed her eyes and spoke as if in a trance:

"Cold is moonlight on the snow. The wolf screams in hunger, and the stars echo with his fear."

"And this one?"

"The moose, running from the hunters, plunges into the ravine and the hunters cheer and dance for now there will be meat."

"And this one?"

"The chief laughs as his women eat until their bellies grow fat and they give birth to wild little boys."

"This is the finest work I have ever seen," Kryn observed. "I requested from Iowerano that you prepare a ceremonial robe, but we never discussed it further."

"I remember," she said.

"With the burning of our villages, we will soon need to make peace with the French," Kryn said. "Their great chief Onontio will offer us terms. They have been doing that since the days of Ondessonk," he threw his arm affectionately about Tekakwitha. "As a display of goodwill, I will give him a ceremonial robe, and so you will embroider it."

"It will be a great honor."

"I think it should be of elk skin," he rummaged among the skins that Karitha had cleaned and he held up the skin of a large elk. "This one. You can begin work on this one now while we hunt. Begin to sew your pictures."

"What would Kryn like to see?"

"Our three sisters—corn, squash and beans—growing in the

field. Perhaps the seasons of the moon, too—the Fishing Moon, the Planting Moon, the Strawberry Moon, the Green Corn Moon. I should like to see along the bottom, the symbol of the People of the Great Long House, five nations with the council fire in the center, and over all the tree of peace and its five roots while the eagle watches vigilantly."

Quietly and with a deep sense of purpose Tekakwitha took the soft skin from his hands.

"I will begin today," she said.

Kryn nodded and he took out his pipe and filled it with tobacco and lit it with a twig from the fire. The flame lit up his features as he pulled at the pipe to light the tobacco. Tekakwitha watched, feeling a deep gratitude for this man who had rescued her and now entrusted to her such an important task. Yes, she knew with a deep sense of purpose, she would embroider the robe for the great chief of the French. It would be more beautiful than any robe had ever been in order seal the peace between the two nations, and together they would bury the war hatchet and live as brothers.

Chapter 15

Kryn Carries A Message Of Peace
To The French Of Quebec

Down to the river valley the hunting parties came with their bundles of fur for trading. The Mohawk villages were mounds of ash. After a hurried council, the Turtle Clan mothers selected another site nearby for erecting a new village to be called, again, Kanawaka (At the Rapids). From the forests the men dragged stout logs they had felled with their hatchets. They stripped the logs, and set them in the ground to form a stockade. Within the large rectangle, they set tall saplings and bent them together and lashed them into the arching frameworks then covered the frames with bark.

Around the new village where they'd cut the trees, the women grubbed the ground with wooden hoes and in humps they planted corn and squash and beans from seeds they had taken upon their flight in the fall.

Marquis de Tracy sent word that unless the Iroquois league appeared soon at Quebec, he'd hang the hostages. Hurried preparations were made at Onondaga to assemble a delegation from the Oneida, the Cayuga and the Seneca as well. The Mohawks, however, were not disposed to sue for peace. Iowerano held a warlike resentment for all the French, now intensified by de Tracy's attack, and the Bear Clan, too, wanted to keep the war kettle bubbling. Kryn met with Iowerano:

"Our brothers are being held in the north. Unless we appear as summoned, they will be hanged."

"I cannot think of peace presently. I must supervise the building of our village and the recovery from their treacherous raid last fall. If we don't get crops in the ground we will starve this winter."

"Someone must negotiate this peace. All nations but the Mohawk have sent their delegations."

"Go if you wish and ask their pardon. I have a far dimmer view of the white man and his purposes here."

"If we could all live in peace, Cold Wind."

"Unfortunately it is always on the white man's terms." Iowerano spat in disgust. "You go and open the talks and we'll resolve the matter this summer."

And so Kryn journeyed to Quebec in April to open peace talks. Tekakwitha remained behind embroidering the ceremonial robe that the Mohawks would give Onontio to seal the terms of the treaty.

Week by week the new village swelled as families came back from the forests. By the Strawberry Moon (June), Kryn had returned from Quebec, assuring all that the hostages would be released during the Blueberry Moon (July). By then the Turtle Clan was living in its new village and ready to send a deputation to the Onondaga council fire to discuss the terms of peace.

Again the bitter Iowerano deferred to Kryn and deputized him to go. Kryn first paddled to Onondaga to discuss terms of the peace with the other nations, and by the time he returned, Tekakwitha had completed the robe. She had embroidered the borders with a geometric design. In the corners she had stitched pictographs to represent the four nations and then a large central depiction of the council fire at Onondaga. When she held it up to show it to him, he nodded with approval: "It is magnificent, little one!" He gathered her up in his arms and held her. Unused to anyone holding her, Tekakwitha went limp in his arms. He hugged her to himself and she felt him laugh. That was Kryn's reaction and she was moved by it.

Everyone else who saw the ceremonial robe paused in wonder, but the attention embarrassed her. She had also strung a long wampum belt out of white and purple shells to seal the peace, and Kryn handled the belt and rehearsed a speech he would make when he presented this "gift."

In a few days, with much fanfare, Kryn set out again for Quebec with a party of twelve. They walked single file overland to the lakes and reaching the shore they found three canoes and fashioned another one from elm bark. Soon they glided north on the lake, then portaged and set out on Lake Champlain, thence down the Richelieu River to the St. Lawrence Valley. Finally embarking on the broad river, the passage was easy as they moved with the current.

Before and behind them flotillas of canoes were descending as other nations, Algonquins and Abenaki and the Cat Nations sent their emissaries to the French to establish a universal peace.

High out of the water rose the great rock of Quebec. Here the river narrowed and ran more swiftly. Low along the river bank at the base of the cliff a village of tents was pitched, canoes with feathers flying in the wind were tied to piers, and in booths the natives and Europeans alike traded their wares. Three shallops and a brig were anchored in the basin. High upon the rock rose the walls of the fort encircling the homes of the governor and the intendant.

Kryn and his party steered to shore and claimed a plot along the river for their tents and sleeping rolls. The Mohawk delegation was the final nation to appear. They rested that evening and walked along the river, visiting the booths and the habitations, passing by the stone warehouses built for the fur trade. They slept soundly that night and next morning, as the sun rose in glorious streams of light over the river—a harbinger of the peace—they started up the path to the great peace council.

The fort rose above them, a strong stockade of massive logs, and here and there loopholes through which black cannon extended. The gate was open during this time of peace, and Kryn and his Mohawks in loincloths and leggings and deerskin tunics and the thin, high ridges of hair, entered with the Oneidas and the Onondagas and the Cayugas and the Senecas.

Wooden benches were set out in the stone square before the governor's mansion and the chancery. From bastions long pennants of blue and white and gold flew in the brisk summer wind above snapping blue flags with golden *fleur d'lis*. The Five Nations were arrayed along the south of the square and the Hurons and the Algonquins along the west. A military band marched out from the guardhouse and behind, with a large entourage, walked Marquis de Tracy, Governor Courcelle and Bishop Laval.

Protocol dictated that the Iroquois speak first in order to present their suit for peace. Garacontie, the ancient Onondaga, rose and stepped into the center:

"Great chief! We thank you for welcoming us to your fortress. Calling upon the sun and the moon and the stars, upon the four winds, upon the trees of our country and the grasses and the crops we plant, upon the bear and the moose and the deer of the forest and the fish in the lakes and streams, we salute you."

Marquis de Tracy, elegant in scarlet brocade and a silver ceremonial breastplate and buckler, nodded and motioned for him to continue.

"I speak for the five nations of the People of the Great Long House when I say that we wish now to live in peace with our white brothers. We ask that you return our brethren whom you have held as hostages for a year. In turn we will fling the war club as far from our hand as we can and we will bury the war hatchet in the earth once and for all."

The marquis nodded in satisfaction.

"We ask, O Great Chief, that you grant us favors."

"Name them!"

"Seeing how well your houses and fortifications stand, we have need of builders in wood and stone and blacksmiths to work in iron. We need surgeons to teach our people how to heal the body to do what our shaman cannot. Finally, we ask you to send among us your blackrobes to teach us the Prayer."

All the bonneted heads of the Iroquois delegation nodded in agreement. Marquis de Tracy bowed to Bishop Laval who in turn bowed to Father de Mercier, superior of the Jesuits.

When Garacontie finished, Marquis de Tracy announced: "It will be done as you wish, Great Chief. With the bonds of brotherhood we will knit our peoples together."

When his turn to speak came, Kryn carried the robe directly up to the marquis, and he unrolled it to cries of pleasure from those who viewed it. Kryn then produced the wampum belt.

"In condolence for the loss of your nephew last year, we wish to make amends," Kryn said. "I come bearing these gifts to demonstrate our clean heart in fashioning a lasting peace between our peoples where there will be no more warfare and no more bloodshed. May the People of the Great Long House live as brothers with you in this land."

Marquis de Tracy graciously accepted the robe and the belt of wampum. He clapped his hands and the twenty-four hostages were produced. They had been washed and dressed in homespun robes, and they were ushered out from the dim recesses of the government offices. They blinked uncertainly as they came into the sunlight. The Iroquois cried out with approval and stamped their applause upon the ground.

"I return your brothers to you in good faith," de Tracy said. "May there be no further cause for us to raise the musket or the war hatchet against one another."

As he concluded the peace talks, a detail of solders fired half a dozen musket blasts and then a great booming canon shot and the ringing of every church bell in Quebec sealed the peace for all the assembled.

Together the canoes moved upriver, those of the Iroquois and those of the blackrobes. At the Richelieu River, four of the Iroquois nations continued westward, while the Mohawks and the canoe with three blackrobes went south. Up the rocky course of the river they portaged, Kryn and his companions and the four Mohawk hostages. Together they worked to climb around the falls, and at night, reaching Lake Champlain, they camped and shared the food given them from the stores of corn at Quebec.

Kryn watched how the three blackrobes conducted themselves, polite, reserved, quiet men. They showed no aggression, but rather a stoicism and indifference to fatigue and pain unusual among whites. They traveled in their own canoe and slept close by each other. Upon rising they read from their breviaries, walking back and forth, praying to their God, as the others prepared the morning meal. Kryn knew Iowerano would be less than happy with the missionaries. He'd already announced they were not welcome to open a mission at Kanawaka.

Down through the lakes they paddled, past wooded isles, under the brow of shaggy mountains. They paddled the canoes in the sunshine and in the rain and in a furious summer hailstorm. A rainbow arced across the sky, and they took this as a sign of the covenant of God with man manifested in nature. At the end of the lake they paused to gather flints for arrows and spears and then they pressed on, down through the deep glacial valley of the Sacandaga, the course where Father Jogues first journeyed into this land.

They finally emerged from the woods upon the river of the Mohawks and they followed the river to the new village of Kanawaka. Women were planting the fields and no one really took note of their arrival. There was no hysterical display of violence, no speeches, no gauntlet to "welcome" them. Karitha greeted the delegation at the gate to the new village and she took Kryn aside.

"The English merchants passed through on horses three days ago with barrels of brandy. They were seeking our winter pelts at low prices. Iowerano led them to Tionontoguen where they will drink the brandy and trade . . ."

"That is not good," Kryn said. "The blackrobes should not see what becomes of a village when we drink the white man's liquor, how the English cheat us, how no one eats, how the children cry."

"Iowerano left instructions. He does not want the blackrobes to interrupt the drinking at Tionontoguen, so he instructed Garahonto and Tekakwitha to provide lodging and food until his return."

"Let us take them to Iowerano's cabin then."

The families of the hostages, who had been away a year, ran out of their long houses to welcome them home. Kryn escorted the three blackrobes, Fathers Bruyas, Frémin and Pierron, to the chief's long house. Tending the fire where a kettle of sagamite simmered was Tekakwitha.

"Welcome, young maiden," Father Frémin greeted her in passable Iroquois. His voice was sweet and musical. She turned from stirring the sagamite and squinted at him. The priests saw her smallpox scars. She was grateful they showed no disgust.

"How do they call you?" asked Father Bruyas.

"I am called Tekakwitha. My stepmother gave me that name, 'She who gropes her way.'"

"But it is not a good name because you don't grope your way."

"A name attaches and then it is difficult to shake off."

"You are wise beyond your years, young maid," Father Frémin observed.

"Please sit," she said and she dished out the sagamite and handed each priest a plate.

"This is the girl who embroidered the ceremonial robe I gave to Onontio," Kryn said with pride. "And she strung the wampum beads as well. She is most skilled."

"We thank you for allowing us to lodge with you," Father Pierron said.

Before they ate, all three of the blackrobes knelt down and in unison made the sign of the cross and said grace. They then sat cross-legged then and quietly ate the food she dipped from the kettle. As they were eating, the flap to the long house opened and Anastasia entered. She saw the priests and cautiously approached.

"Good afternoon, Fathers," she said. "Welcome to our village."

"Hello, kind woman," Father Frémin said. "We appreciate your hospitality."

"Will you be with us long?"

"We are told," Father Bruyas said, "that your chief does not want a mission at this village, and so as soon as we are permitted to journey west, we will set up a mission at Tionontoguen, Father Frémin and I. Father Pierron is journeying farther west to the Oneidas."

"I was baptized at Trois-Rivières and raised Christian," Anastasia said. "Do you say the rosary?"

"Yes, of course." Father Frémin went into the satchel they carried with them and took out a set of rosary beads. He handed them to Anastasia. She looked quizzically to determine if he was giving the beads to her, and he nodded. She took them and held them close to her heart and she seemed about to sob.

"I used to say the rosary with my mother," she explained to Tekakwitha.

"What is the rosary?"

"It is a way of praying to God the Father, to Jesus," she held up the crucifix at the bottom of the chain of beads, "and to our Mother Mary. It is like a chant." Anastasia turned back to the priest. "Can we say the rosary?"

He smiled and looked at the others. "In a little while. We began our journey today so early we haven't had time to read our breviary, so we'd like to do that now."

"Of course, Father."

They each went into their traveling bags and produced small black books which they leafed through, and they stood as one.

"With your kind permission, we will go down to the river." Father Bruyas addressed this to Tekakwitha since she had prepared his meal. She nodded in agreement.

They left the hearth and the long house to pray. The girl turned to the older woman. "What manner of men are these?"

"They are blackrobes. You have heard Iowerano talk about Ondessonk. They have journeyed over the great salt sea to come among us and teach us about Jesus Christ."

"Who is Jesus Christ?"

"A torture victim. He died upon the cross."

"Why do they teach us about a torture victim? We have had many, even here among the Turtle Clan."

"This man was God, and like Deganawida, born of a woman who did not know man. He taught all peoples to love and to seek peace."

"How can a man be both a man and a god? And what do you mean, he taught mankind how to love? Surely there were husbands and wives and families then."

"The love he taught is a different sort of love. It's a love expressed for everyone, and as a part of that, forgiveness. Instead of revenge, this Jesus Christ taught mankind to offer the other cheek to someone who slaps you."

Tekakwitha scowled. "Won't the attacker just slap the other cheek as well?"

"Of course, but then you can forgive that one as well."

"I don't understand," the girl said. "What are those things they took from these bags?"

"Prayer books. Missals."

The girl scowled. "What are they?"

Anastasia looked toward the door where the men had vanished, and she opened one of the bags. She took out another book and opened it.

"On these pages are markings. See? These markings set forth their prayers. They review the markings as we do designs in the wampum belts, and so recite prayers each day to their God."

Tekakwitha took the book and ran her hand over the smooth printed page. "How do they understand what these marking say?"

"They are trained. They call it 'reading.' They can recall from those markings what is printed there exactly."

"Can we ever understand what is there?"

"I have known natives who have learned to read, but it takes a very long time and requires much effort."

The woman and the girl put the book back into the satchel and they went outside. Down along the riverbank the three blackrobes walked, reciting their daily office.

"These men," Tekakwitha said, "are so very gentle, almost like women."

"Their religion does not allow them to argue or fight or make war, and so they become friendly and docile and considerate."

"And these are the men my uncle wants to keep from our village?"

"Yes," Anastasia said, and she rolled her eyes.

When the blackrobes finished saying their office, they walked up the hill to the gate and met Anastasia and Tekakwitha. Together they passed into the stockade and then to Iowerano's cabin. Once inside they gave the girl rosary beads as well, and they all knelt at the fire pit and recited the rosary.

The blackrobes remained at Iowerano's cabin for three days. In that time they spoke with the young woman and watched her work diligently on embroidery and wampum. She seemed happy to be hidden away in the smoky long house even while the days were long and sunny.

On the fourth day of their stay, Iowerano returned. He was moving more slowly than usual. He seemed depleted and humbled by the drunkenness. Moneta, too, was sluggish and irritable. The blackrobes presented the chief with a gift of peace from Marquis de Tracy, a silver peace pipe from Quebec's most skilled silversmith.

"Our chief," Father Bruyas spoke, "hopes that you will consider the great peace we have established whenever you smoke from this pipe."

"The Wolf and the Bear Clans will welcome you," Iowerano said dismissively. "You should leave this village as soon as you can."

The priests packed their belongings. Tekakwitha watched them with a sinking heart. The cruel and unpredictable Iowerano was back, and she was losing the influence of these calm and peaceful men of God.

"Let me walk you to our village gate," she offered.

"They can find their way," Moneta said.

"Prepare me some breakfast," Iowerano ordered her.

The priests thanked her for her hospitality and spoke to Iowerano: "You have a very intelligent and personable daughter in Tekakwitha."

"I'm glad you think so," he said. "Have a nice journey." And he turned away, ignoring them. The look that passed between the priests and the young woman was one of fondness and gratitude and, on her part, hope.

Chapter 16

Kryn Defends His Village
From A Mohican Attack

THREE YEARS PASSED. With peace in the valley, the cycles of the moon and the seasons spun in the sky. The women planted their crops in mounds, and the corn and squash and beans grew in the spring rain and the summer sun, ripened, were harvested and stored in underground pits. Hunters ranged over the hills and into the mountains after bear and deer and elk and moose. Fishermen caught the spawning salmon and trout and shad and pike with nets and weirs. When winter clamped down with the ice and blizzards, old men sat by the fire smoking tobacco, their lined faces flickering in the light, telling stories of ancient wars and hunting expeditions, and young women nursed their babies wrapped in fur against the cold.

As Tekakwitha began her fourteenth year, her body began to change and the subject of a husband arose. Moneta approached her one morning with uncharacteristic familiarity. "You are a child no longer, Tekakwitha. Now that you are ready to take a husband, your father and I have a match for you, Distant Thunder."

"But I do not wish to marry, Mother."

"Nonsense! What idle talk. Your fear of men will soon pass when you gain experience, and you will learn to be a wife and a mother."

"But I will never submit to a man."

Uncharacteristically Moneta sat next to the girl. "There are ways, little one, for you to manipulate men. Their wants are simple and when you learn how to supply them you know how to get what you want and need."

"That seems deceptive."

"It is the way men and women relate." She put her arm around the young woman and Tekakwitha shuddered at her touch. She did not like to be touched, and this new intimacy raised her suspicions.

"I choose not to do that, though."

"Nonsense! How could you support yourself?"

"My needs are simple. I can work with my embroidery and my beads. I can provide for myself."

"What talk!" Moneta laughed, treated the young woman's profound declaration as a misguided whim. "A hunter will bring our cabin the meat we need. My husband is too fond of sitting by the fire with his pipe, and so we might once again enjoy a steady supply of venison. You will be happy in the night when he shares your pallet, and perhaps you will enjoy what was deprived in my life by the white man's disease, children."

"Look at my face, Aunt. Look at these scars. What would Distant Thunder see in me when there are so many beautiful, happy girls who dress up and flirt and go to the dances? Let him court Rainbow."

"He has been approached. He thinks you're fine. Surely he is not the fastest runner or the cunningest hunter or the bravest warrior in the village. He has a tendency to brood and keep his resentments alive."

"And so that makes him more attractive to me?"

"You indicated yourself, yours are not the qualities the young men seek. They want beauty and gaiety and flirtation, not a woman who's so serious all the time."

"And so I should lower my expectations?"

"In order to marry, yes." Moneta was getting impatient. Her flattery and wiles were not getting her what she wanted. "Be realistic!"

"I am realistic. I choose not to marry and that's an end to it."

Moneta stood up, angry and shouting, "Why don't you think of someone else for a change? Your lazy uncle sits at the fire all day and won't bestir himself to bring us fresh meat. Everything we get he has to wheedle out of other men from what they kill for their families. We need a hunter for our cabin and you're of eligible age now. It's your duty to marry and Distant Thunder would make a good match for you."

"I will not do it, Aunt. Let there be no further talk about it."

Tekakwitha retreated to her small corner where the light was dim and her handiwork kept her occupied and she might ignore the chill that came over the family around the fire pit.

Five days later, Tekakwitha went to the forest spring with earthenware jugs to bring back water for washing and cooking. As she walked back into the cabin Iowerano and Moneta and the young man Distant Thunder were seated about to have their supper.

"Here, daughter," Moneta handed Tekakwitha a bowl of sagamite, "sit with us and give this bowl to him," and she nodded at Distant Thunder.

Tekakwitha immediately saw the trickery. When a young woman sat with a young man and served him food, it was a signal they were married. Tekakwitha shook her head and refused.

"I tell you, defiant daughter," Iowerano spoke up, "give this to the young man, or depart from our hearth fire and shift for yourself."

Tekakwitha said nothing. She turned and walked to the flap and opened it and went out into the bright sunshine. She adjusted her shawl and walked through the lanes of the village.

"Tekakwitha!" she heard Moneta's voice behind her. "Come back! Have supper with us!"

But she did not stop. She walked out through the eastern gate of the village and down through the plantation where the stalks of corn were high and waving in the gentle breeze. She entered a great stand of pine at the end of the corn brake. Here is where she felt happy. Here, away from all the gossip and chatter of the women, the braying of the men at their gambling or their bragging or, worse, their drinking, away from the whining and wailing of the children, here, alone in the forest she might sit and ponder and be alone and hear the voices within her that told her of what life was and why she was alive.

How pathetic was their trickery! Imagine! Setting up this purported marriage proposal and expecting it to result in a new family. How could the custom, the ritual ever mean more than what it was supposed to symbolize? She did not love Distant Thunder. She did not love anyone except perhaps for Kryn, and she loved him from afar. She could support herself with her work and not assume responsibilities for a man or for children. What did she need? A bowl of porridge and a bit of meat or fish every day? She made the clothes and the moccasins she wore. And as for a sleeping pallet, there were other families in the village that would take her in if Iowerano did not poison everyone toward her.

Such a pleasant place she had found here. The sun slanted through the pine and a clean wind blew from the west. Rarely did she venture outside her cabin and almost never outside the stockade, but this place with its vista charmed her and soothed her, and she vowed to return here early each morning to get away from Moneta's criticisms and the thick smells of the long house, and to start her day by watching the sun rise. As long as she returned with a load of wood, who would be the wiser?

And so, early each morning as everyone slept she left her cabin and slipped through the eastern gate and came here. On the sixth or seventh morning as the darkness receded and the first rays of sunlight pinkened the sky, she lay upon the pine needles listening to the jays. When she had thought about many things, she rose and climbed a rock and she looked eastward, out over the valley. Below her the river flowed in a broad sweep, and as she looked down she saw a large band of warriors wending along the river trail. Curious, she looked at them more closely, struggling to focus her eyes. Her ear told her they were not speaking Mohawk, or any language from any of the nations of the Iroquois league.

"Mohicans!" she said out loud. Fear seized her. She turned and ran back through the forest, over the great backs of rock, and down along the stream lined with fern, out into the open air of the corn fields, and up the hill, breathlessly, hardly able to cry, "Mohicans!"

The eastern gate was open and she raced inside, directly to Kryn's longhouse.

"Awaken, Great Chief!"

Karitha sat up and shook him. "What is it?"

"Mohicans!" she cried. "They are attacking."

Instantly Kryn was in battle mode. He pulled on his moccasins, took his musket and his war hatchet from where they hung and was out the through the door with an instruction to the young woman. "Go to your family and help us defend."

A great war cry went up and just as the Mohicans attacked, Kryn reached and closed and locked the eastern gate. Other Mohawks awoke and were running out to repel the attackers.

Tekakwitha stopped to watch. High on the ramparts Kryn was deploying young men here and there to take positions on the scaffold where they might repel the attack. He was talking loudly to the fastest runner of the village: "Race to Andagaron and Tionontoguen and summon our warriors from the Wolf and Bear clans!"

The young man leapt to the ground from the scaffold, and as the guards opened the western gate, he darted out and flew across the cornfields.

Another shrill war cry sent shivers of fear through the village. Kryn called out in response: "Steady. Let us be steady at our posts and we will repel the attack."

The cry came again, a wild, forlorn wail, and flaming arrows suddenly rained out of the sky, hundreds of them. They landed on the roofs of the bark long houses and they stuck to the logs of the stockade. Treated with pine pitch, they spilled fire on the dry bark and the wood.

Kryn had assembled two dozen archers on the scaffold along the eastern wall, and with the Mohicans within range, he raised his arm and cried, "Now!" The arrows flew from the bows and screams from outside the walls indicated the arrows had found their mark. The archers pulled new arrows from their quivers while another shower of flaming arrows fell from the sky.

"Help me!" Tekakwitha heard. It was Anastasia with a bark pail of water. She was proceeding from house to house, pulling out the arrows and extinguishing the flames. When they got to Iowerano's long house, Moneta rushed out.

"Your uncle's drunk. He's trying to load the musket."

"The fool!" Anastasia said. Tekakwitha followed her in. Iowerano was sitting cross-legged on his sleeping pallet with a musket in his lap. He had the ramrod down the barrel with the ball and the charge, but his eyes were heavy and he lost his grip.

"Give me that!" Anastasia said, and she snatched the musket away. "We need every hand and every gun!" She took the powder horn and musket balls and left the cabin.

"Tekawitha! Tekakwitha!" Moneta called. "Stay here with us."

"I must help," she answered and she left the cabin.

Outside, Kryn was on the ramparts in full view of the enemy, ordering men here and there to fire upon the Mohicans and to douse flaming arrows that stuck in the walls. Defying musket fire, he walked along the scaffold to the eastern wall where a battering ram was forcing the gate open. He helped three young men lift a pot of pine pitch up a ladder and, pulling a flaming arrow from the palisade, he lit the pitch on fire and poured it on the Mohicans below. The men screamed with burning pine pitch and the battering ceased.

Anastasia led the girl to a ladder and they climbed the fifteen steps to the scaffold and looked down upon the swarms of Mohicans in chest plates and war paint. Anastasia fired and hit one of the Mohican chiefs. Muskets barked from the ground below and here and there warriors fell.

Kryn saw the young woman and as another volley of flaming arrows came up and over the wall, he called Tekakwitha over, gave her a gourd dipper and led her to a mossy tank of water.

"Put out the fires, little one. Save our homes."

She looked up into his eyes and saw, to her surprise, joy. She tilted her head quizzically. He smiled, and she suddenly knew that Kryn was happiest in battle.

"You, there!" he cried and hastened to deploy a pair of warriors to the northern wall. The flaming arrows kept flying. Anastasia reloaded and fired and reloaded and fired.

More battlecries from outside the walls, the roar of musket fire, and now the battering ram began again. Kryn called to young warriors who had another kettle of pine pitch ready. Again they hoisted it up, lit it and poured it over the wall. The Mohicans below screamed in pain and the battering stopped.

Directly opposite, at the western gate, a battering ram began its deadly work. Kryn called to his warriors and climbed down the ladder and raced through the lanes of the village to stop the forcing of the western gate.

As Anastasia fired and reloaded, Tekakwitha moved along the southern wall which faced the river, pulling the shafts of burning arrows from the wood, dousing the flames with water. Now there was chopping as the Mohicans began hacking at the base of the stockade with their hatchets. Looking out over the cornfields the mob of Mohicans seemed endless, but then a wild war cry went up from the west.

"Our brothers!" Anastasia cried, and over the ridge from the west rose an army of warriors from the Bear and Wolf Clans. By now, she and the girl were on the southern wall. Across the shallow ford of the river came a hundred Mohawks screaming and brandishing their war clubs and hatchets. Some stopped, got down on one knee and fired at the Mohicans. Caught between the wall and the onslaught of the Bear and Wolf Clans, the Mohicans cried out and began a retreat.

Into the fray rushed the ferocious Mohawks, hacking and beating the enemy who turned, defensively, and tried to repel the attack. From the palisade above rained a steady stream of arrows and musket fire, and now, caught in a pincer move, the Mohicans fought to escape. The Mohawks were merciless, though, and they cut down the Mohicans as fast as they could move through the crowd.

A cry of retreat went up then. The Mohawk counterattack never eased, but the Mohicans turned north and fled across the corn plantation, and then eastward, away from Kanawaka.

Kryn leapt from the scaffold, ran to the gate, threw it open and led his men out. "After them!" he called with a wave of his brawny arm, and out they ran after the Mohicans, pausing here and there to shoot a musket or fire arrows at the stragglers.

Anastasia and Tekakwitha climbed down the ladder to help the wounded who lay groaning in the lanes of the village. Twenty or so warriors had been felled, and three women who, like Anastasia, seized weapons and fought to defend their home, and a young boy who caught an arrow in his left eye. The useless shaman was dancing about in a frightful mask and rattles, but everyone ignored him.

Kryn returned on the third day. His victorious band led prisoners tied with rawhide cords about the neck like leashes, and nineteen Mohican scalps hung from their belts. Rage at the insult of the attack filled the villagers and they formed a gauntlet to welcome the prisoners with rods and clubs and fire as the sun set in a bloody splendor.

Iowerano took command of the festivities. He had a stage erected with poles in the middle of the village, and he kindled the fires to torture the prisoners. Tekakwitha kept away from gauntlet and retreated to her corner to work upon a wampum belt in order to avoid the rush of the villagers' outrage. She averted her eyes and tried to close her ears to the incessant screaming of the captors and their prisoners. She thrilled, though, when Kryn entered the long house and sat with Iowerano. He was solemn and dignified and he accepted the pipe from the chief.

"You have distinguished yourself, Half-Breed," Iowerano said. "Tell me of your valor."

"True valor needs no boasting," Kryn said, drawing smoke from the pipe, then handing it back.

"Tell me then of the massacre."

The screaming outside, as darkness spread, grew louder and more desperate. The young woman listened closely to the warrior chief so she might understand.

"I sent Aronsen to Andagaron and Tionontoguen, and our brothers, the Bears and the Wolves, ran to our rescue. As we crushed the Mohicans between our two forces, many fled to their homeland Massachusetts. The English muskets they carried leave little doubt who sent them on this raid."

"But the English have been our friends," Iowerano protested. He took a long pull of the pipe. Outside, in the night, Mohican prisoners were singing their death songs.

"They resent the peace we have made with the French. They fear losing our trade."

"We shall visit them in Albany and display the scalps," Iowerano said. "They won't attack us any longer."

"If only they might only witness tonight's ceremony," Kryn said.

"Cowards!" Iowerano spat into the fire. Drunk during the attack, the chief knew something about cowardice. "Tell me how you reduced them."

"I ordered the Wolf and the Bear Clan to trail them, engaging their party from behind as it fled home, and I led our fierce Turtle Clan warriors along a parallel path down the falls at Cohoes and across the broad River That Flows Both Ways to the land they call called Hoosick (The Stony Place). I advanced to the narrow pass through which they needed to go in order to reach their homes. We waited in ambush.

"As they came into the pass, we held our fire until our brothers were behind at the entrance to the pass. As soon as they were trapped between our forces," Kryn suddenly drove his fist upon an earthenware jug, smashing it to pieces, "we struck! We left no doubter standing. The seven we bring back as trophies, three who are singing just now outside, and the four our brothers took home to Andagaron and Tionontoguen, are the only warriors left. Let the account of this reprisal dissuade others, including the whites, from attacking us."

"You have behaved nobly," Iowerano said. He handed Kryn the pipe of peace. "We shall hold a feast in your honor."

"I care not for feasts, great chief, I only want to go to my cabin and rest with my wife."

"You two shall produce great warriors to protect our people."

"I consider that she cannot bear a child."

"Alas, my Moneta was infected with the white man's illness and cannot give me sons." He spat again in disgust. The prisoners outside were screaming in the throes of their death agony. "Go home to her and rest. Know that I recognize your valor and from this day forward, all shall refer to you as 'The Great Mohawk.'"

"It is not a name that matters."

"Yes, but a name signifies those qualities within," Iowerano said and he gently touched his fist to his heart.

Kryn rose and dusted himself off. He walked to Tekakwitha. "You still work to produce the beautiful skins."

She looked up at him in admiration for his musket and tomahawk had killed so many to protect the village. Her eyes, unfocused, roamed until Kryn touched her on the cheek and tilted her face up. She shuddered.

"I will make whatever the Great Mohawk needs," she said.

"She will," Iowerano promised.

The screams from outside filled up the moment as her eyes focused on his and she marveled at how blue, like the sky, they were.

"We will not be suing for peace now, but I predict the English will approach us with more caution. Too much contact with the French makes them consider us weak."

"That is why I forbid their blackrobes from residing here," Iowerano said with satisfaction. "We will remain fierce," he struck at a pottery bowl with his fist in imitation of Kryn, but it did not break.

Kryn smiled kindly at the young woman, and she knew then that all the violence, the fire, the blood and even the screaming outside just now had protected her and the others of the village. She saw that it was necessary, but she wished it were not.

Chapter 17

Kryn Abandons His Newborn Son

Kᴿʏɴ'ꜱ ᴡɪꜰᴇ Kᴀʀɪᴛʜᴀ ʟᴏᴠᴇᴅ ʜɪᴍ for his strength and admired him for his bravery in fighting off the Mohican attack, and also for his wisdom in seeing what was out of Iowerano's reach. She desired to bear his son. She had watched the shaman try to cure the sick. She had watched as he shoved a stick the length of his arm down his throat and vomited all over a sick man, dancing and chanting and rattling to get him to stand and walk. She knew in her woman's heart that the shaman could not help, and so she turned to the blackrobe at Andagaron.

Along the river trail Karitha walked with Anastasia and five or six others once every seven days, returning in the evening with a deep peace and contentment. Though Iowerano railed against the blackrobe, Tekakwitha observed the effect upon Kryn's wife, and so after two years, when she announced she was with child, the blackrobe's magic seemed far more potent than the shaman's. Iowerano, of course, ignored this miracle. Although he wanted the village to thrive and return to the old ways, and so having children furthered his plan, the blackrobes threatened his authority and so any offspring attributable to them were not worth consideration.

Kryn, though, found a new happiness. Unlike many of the men who hunted and fished and ignored their pregnant women, Kryn was solicitous and kind to Karitha. As she grew great with his child, he carried her burdens and helped her with her work and brought her game and fish to augment the corn porridge and squash.

It was a cold, spitting winter morning when she came to term. She was scraping an elk skin when the labor pains grew severe, and Kryn went for the midwife to assist him in the delivery. Unlike many of the women who squat in the fields to deliver their children, then chewed the umbilical cord and wrapped the child in skins, continuing with their work, Karitha's delivery was difficult. Kryn and the midwife needed to reposition the child in order for it to descend the birth canal. Hour upon hour Karitha sweat and groaned and screamed in pain as life in the long house went on about her. About midday the baby appeared.

"All this for nothing," Kryn said when he saw the child. The midwife handed the baby boy to him, but he refused to hold it. She handed it to the mother then. "We must expose the child," he said to Karitha.

"No," she said, holding the baby to her breast. Perspiring in the firelight, her features seemed transcendent. She had just passed through the most horrible ordeal and had found an inner peace through the pain. She smiled at the baby boy. The midwife wiped the sweat from her face and lay her back to nurse the infant as she cleaned up the blood and the afterbirth.

"His right arm is withered," Kryn observed. "He will not be able to hold a bow or a tomahawk. We must expose him."

Karitha looked with defiance upon her husband. In the firelight, her eyes were ferocious. "I will not give him to you for that purpose. A man is more than good limbs. He shall be wise and become a great sachem." She stroked the baby's head as his mouth suckled at her breast. "Go now and leave us."

No one dared to look at the Great Mohawk for fear of his rage. He scowled mightily at mother and child, and then he pulled on his robe of elk skin and pushed through the flap and out into the weather.

A wet, blinding snow pelted the lanes of the village and smoke hung low over the huts. The river was frozen and men and boys had drilled holes in the ice to fish. Kryn did not know what to do or where to go, so he went to the chief's long house and sat with him and smoked.

". . . and the child has a withered right arm."

Tekakwitha listened. She had watched the progress of the pregnancy with great attention. "This is the blackrobe's magic," Iowerano concluded.

"Can you order her to surrender the child to me so that I may rid us of this disgrace?"

Iowerano smoked in silence. He considered the request. "Matters concerning the family are heard by the Women's Council. I cannot help you."

"Perhaps I can," Tekakwitha offered.

"You would speak to the Great Mohawk?" Iowerano thundered at the temerity of his niece. "Yes," Tekakwitha said evenly. She was embroidering the hem of a doeskin dress.

"What is it, child?" Kryn said kindly.

"I urge the Great Mohawk to find patience. Imperfections bring out our ability to overcome them. My eyes don't see well, so I have learned to listen more closely, to use my ears for eyes."

"You are wise," Kryn observed.

"She should learn her place and not eavesdrop on the talk of men."

"The chief, my uncle, forbids me to speak, and I respect him," she said. "But if I could speak to you, great chief, I would urge you to raise your baby son for despite his arm he might, too, become a great chief someday."

"I don't see how he will earn any respect. He can't hunt, he can't fish. He will never leave the company of women."

"But he can think, and he will learn to speak. Not being able to play lacrosse with the other boys or hunt of fish, he will grow wise."

"Like you, little one, wise beyond your years." His voice was weary.

"She should learn to keep quiet as we talk and not jump in at every crossroad." Iowerano turned the conversation back.

"I must leave," Kryn said. "I cannot dwell at that fire pit, or in that house, or in this village as long as she keeps the infant to remind me of its deformity."

"It is winter. Where will you go?"

"What does it matter, Cold Wind? I shall hunt and live alone in the forest until the spring and then I shall decide."

Kryn handed the chief back the pipe and rose to go. Tekakwitha turned away for she felt a tear pressing at her eye. There was a gentle touch upon her shoulder. She looked up to see the Great Mohawk towering over her.

"You shall marry a great warrior and become a great matriarch."

Iowerano spat into the fire. "That one? She will never marry. Look those scars. I have arranged two matches for her and each time they are not good enough for her. She will be like the vestals of old, women living apart from men."

"We all reach our destination when we do," Kryn said. "I leave, Great Chief, and ask that in my absence you watch over Karitha."

"She is descended from an ancient line in the Turtle Clan," Iowerano said. "Despite her consorting with the blackrobes, she is one of us and need not fear starvation."

Kryn turned and pushed through the door flap.

Tekakwitha felt Iowerano's eye of rebuke upon her, but she did not turn toward him and after awhile she gathered up her work and retired to her sleeping pallet.

The next day, as a howling blizzard blew from the west, Tekakwitha struggled through the lanes to Kryn's long house to visit the new mother. As she entered with a flurry of snow, she heard the joyful sounds of mother and infant, and around Karitha were the three women with whom she traveled to the mission in Andagaron.

Tekakwitha approached hesitantly, not wanting to disturb the gathering, but Karitha saw her and summoned her. "Come, Tekakwitha, look at little Martin."

Tekakwitha threw off her shawl and slowly her eyes grew accustomed to the dim light. The baby was nestled in fur, his little eyes still closed and his wet little lips looking for the nipple.

"Do you want to hold him?" Karitha asked, holding out the little bundle.

Tekakwitha took the baby and held him to her and the baby blindly searched about for the nipple. She laughed pleasantly at the sensation of holding something so small, like a puppy, yet it was human and vulnerable and required much attention.

"As I was saying," Karitha lay back and sighed as if from a great exertion, "Kryn's departure has cleared the way to take Martin to the blackrobe for baptism."

"We will bring him as soon as you are ready to walk."

"I will be ready this Sunday," Karitha said. "He is so fragile. I fear losing him and, wanting baptism, his not reaching heaven."

"Baptism?" the girl asked.

"The blackrobe drips water upon the baby's forehead," said the young woman now called Martha, "and he recites a prayer. Once he does this the baby can enter heaven."

"What is 'heaven'?"

"The place where the white man's God dwells, a place in the sky, above the clouds. If a baby dies before this baptism, he can never enter heaven."

The girl rocked the infant and he groped in the air. "And what about us?"

"We are baptized," Martha said.

"You should journey with us," Karitha said. "You could be baptized as well."

"My uncle would never allow it," Tekakwitha said.

"How can he prevent it?" the other young woman, Emily, asked. "He is the chief."

"The blackrobe teaches that we are responsible, each of us, for our own lives, and that no one can control another."

"If only that were true," Tekakwitha said and she handed the baby back to his mother. Then she reached into her tunic and pulled out a small embroidered fur blanket. "I made this for Martin." Karitha took the blanket and held it up. Tekakwitha had embroidered a small green turtle in the middle of the bottom edge.

"It is beautiful, little one."

"It is for the newest of our Turtle Clan."

"That was so very nice of you."

"When will Kryn return?" she asked as she put on her coat.

"Only he knows," Karitha said. She asked Martha for the baby back, and she wrapped him in the new blanket and placed him at her breast so he might nurse.

Chapter 18

⚜

Kryn Meets A Holy Woman
And Converts

ONWARD THROUGH THE BLIZZARD Kryn stumbled on snowshoes and his thoughts were filled with rage. Had he not survived fierce battles with smoking muskets and bloody tomahawks? Had he not spoken in the councils with the antlered bonnets of the fifty sachems nodding as smoke from the calumets hung in midair? Had he not hunted for elk and caribou while the crystal stars twinkled and wolves and coyotes complained to the indifferent peaks? In all these he thrived and emerged the victor, his courage and wisdom and cunning rewarded. But a woman's whim undid him now! What chance had a boy, a man with a withered arm? His right arm, no less! A cripple.

In everything, he—Togoniron, Kryn, the Great Mohawk—had triumphed but the simple act of fathering a child eluded him. To make matters worse, the woman, his wife, with her sentimental notions refused to allow him to correct the mistake. The ancient law required children so deformed to be exposed so the wolves and bobcats carried them off, yet the woman now suckled it and her Christian friends embraced and welcomed it.

Kryn plunged ahead into the teeth of the blizzard. When darkness came, he built a lean-to at the base of a great rock. He shaved wood chips with his knife for kindling, and he used his bow drill to start a fire to ward off the wolves and coyotes. He bundled himself in his skin robe and gazed into the fire as the snow blew. In his haste he packed only dried venison strips and he pulled these from his buckskin wallet and chewed pensively, looking into the flames.

As night deepened, his anger passed. He recalled his joy at learning Karitha was pregnant. He remembered their hope as she grew heavy with the child. The future seemed secure. Now? He fed a dried pine bough into the fire and settled into his robe. How different these Christians reacted. Calm, docile, happy, they accepted what came their way with little frustration or care, as if the unexpected, the unforseen was meant to be. A pale understanding glimmered on the horizon for a long moment like a rising sun, but no, he decided, he could not allow the impossible to go unchallenged.

Everything these days was flying apart. The order and ritual and certainty that held life together before was supplanted by upstart individuals making their own decisions, defying and rebelling against the old ways. This was the legacy of Christianity. Followers refused to work one day in seven. Grown men saw no value in war. Droves of people wended along the river bank to Andagaron so they might kneel in the little chapel and recite chants. What drew them there? The mystery was as dark and thick as this night's snowfall.

He awoke with light filtering through the pine boughs of his lean-to. The snow had stopped. A faint yellow light stole through the tree limbs furred with snow. He was alone and lost and empty, numbed by his flight from the village and uncertain where he might go or what he might do. He considered camping here, snaring a rabbit for food and then hunting for larger game, but he needed to keep moving, put distance and time between himself and the colossal disappointment the birth of his son had caused. Kryn readied his pack for transport, strapped on his snowshoes and set off once more heading north through the forest.

The vistas rolled out in white and blue, long views of hills and valleys and frozen lakes. The long winter night crept in early and the landscape seemed so empty and quiet and dead even as the hunger gnawed at him. He snared a rabbit and ate it. He shot a porcupine and ate it. He traveled on through the mountains. He even shot a skunk, and carefully butchering it, he ate the meat to keep himself going.

He had been away for a fortnight, and he had been without food for four days, when he spied a dozen columns of smoke rising far off in the valley by a wide expanse of snow that was a river. He made for the cabins and as he approached he saw that one of them had a cross upon it. He reached the small settlement as snow began again to fall, and he rapped upon the wooden door of the first cabin he reached. A woman answered.

"You are lost," she said. Her manner was knowing and she spoke the word "lost" as though it had more meanings than the usual.

"I am called 'Kryn' from the land of the People of Flint, eastern gatekeeper of the People of the Great Long House. May I warm myself at your fire?"

"Enter," she said and she stood aside.

Kryn entered the small, tidy cabin. It was made of logs and along the northern wall was a hearth of fieldstone where a kettle hung above a low fire. Above the mantel hung a large cross.

"You are Christian?" he asked.

"I am Gandeacteua, born Oneida and baptized Christian. Catherine is my name. Let me dip you up a bowl of stew."

She stirred the kettle with a ladle and dished a steaming portion into a wooden bowl. A savory aroma came from it, and she handed Kryn the bowl along with a spoon. The stew was hot and meaty, venison with bits of squash and beans and corn. So delicious was the unexpected food that he barely chewed it, and when he had finished the bowl, she gave him another along with a cup of water. Finishing that, too, she arranged a sleeping mat for him near the fire, and in a delirium of exhaustion he lay down and slept deeply.

Many dreams came to him. The woman, Catherine, appeared as a gatekeeper to a land of delicious quiet and peace. He dreamed of the birds and the fish speaking to him. A white stag with a ten-point rack of antlers grazed in moonlight, its muzzle steaming. He dreamed of the mountains reaching to the sun and the moon. He dreamed of the rivers flowing warm as water from a sweat lodge. When he awoke, Catherine was kneeling and passing beads on a thong through her fingers as her lips murmured prayers.

"What do you do with the beads?" Kryn asked.

Catherine continued to pray and did not respond to him. Kryn arose and pulled on his fur robe and went outside to the privy. The cabins here were built of logs, not bark, and the roofs were of thatch. Down upon the riverbank a dozen or so humps showed where canoes had been beached for the winter. A bell in the chapel rang and Catherine came outside, bundled into her coat and hood. She nodded to him and ambled along to the prayer service at the chapel. He declined to follow her, but he watched her recede down the lane and enter the chapel.

In the ensuing days, Kryn observed Catherine. So different from any woman he'd encountered, she was self-sufficient and direct and free from any coy suggestions. Her husband, Tonsanhoten, was back in Oneida for the winter visiting Father Bruyas and enlisting others to migrate to the mission. She and her husband had built this house, the first native residence at this site around which many others had recently settled at the request of Father Pierre Rafeix, and after his death, Father Frémin.

A week passed, and then another. Catherine made life comfortable for Kryn, but she also kept her distance. His curiosity about the service in the chapel led him, one morning, to inquire if he might attend.

"Of course," Catherine said and she led him with her to morning mass.

Kryn entered the dim chapel and saw, standing, a line of natives who intoned a sweet hymn. Father Frémin emerged from a small sacristy, and they knelt. Kryn knelt along with them. The priest spoke words in Latin, and the sacrifice of the mass proceeded through the *Kyrie*, the *Gloria*, the *Sanctus* and *Agnus Dei*. At the consecration, the altar boy rang bells and all bowed their heads. The choir sang in joy and triumph at the communion, and many of the natives rose and went to the altar rail to receive communion.

Kryn was moved by the singing and by the ceremony of the mass, and when they reached Catherine's cabin, he had questions.

"The mass recreates the sacrifice of Jesus Christ," she explained. "Although he was God, Jesus Christ allowed himself to become a victim of torture in order to save all mankind. He died and then rose from the dead. By re-enacting his death on the cross, we acknowledge his sacrifice. Because he was God, no other sacrifices are necessary."

"Christians are so quiet and calm," he observed.

"It is because we forgive."

"Who do you forgive?"

"Everyone. Everyone who wrongs us. Let me teach you something. Repeat after me." Kryn repeated while Catherine recited:

"Our Father, Who art in heaven, hallowed be Thy name. Thy kingdom come, Thy will be done, on earth as it is in heaven. Give us this day, our daily bread, and forgive us our trespasses as we forgive those who trespass against us, and lead us not into temptation, but deliver us from evil, for Thine is the kingdom and the power and the glory for ever and ever, Amen."

She nodded with satisfaction. He seemed to understand the Prayer.

"When you forgive others, you release yourself from bondage."

"What bondage?"

"Has anyone ever wronged you?"

"Of course."

"Have you forgiven him?"

"Her."

"Have you forgiven her?"

Kryn looked at Catherine and did not speak.

"Why have you not?"

"She acted contrary to custom."

"But did her action injure you?"

"Not directly. It has injured my reputation."

"Your reputation? How?"

"As a warrior. As a man."

"Did it help her, though?"

"She refused to expose our child who was born with a withered arm."

"So she refused to murder a baby?" Catherine's eyes bored into Kryn's. "A helpless infant."

"She did," he answered. He looked away.

"And you won't forgive her because she allowed your child to live?" Catherine shook her head as the misguided thinking became evident even to Kryn. "This is what Christians understand. Forgiveness liberates. It cancels a debt and allows us to live without anger or envy or recrimination. Was this woman your wife?"

"She was. She is. Yes."

"Once you forgive her, you will feel love for her again. A withered arm has no effect upon the ability to love. Your son will love you without reservation, and you must love him and raise him and protect him, for that is the natural order of things."

So simple and forceful was her reasoning and so direct her speech that Kryn was astonished. She had arrived in a very short time at the realization he had searched for during his many days of hunger and flight through the snow, and his long nights of doubt and despair. She had led him to this freedom and point of realization without magic or spells of any sort.

"This is what Christianity accomplishes," she said when she saw the recognition and joy light in his features.

In further talks, Catherine helped Kryn examine his motivations to measure the result against the impulse behind it, acquainting him with a process she called "right-thinking." This process required discarding the blind following of custom. Kryn came to see the value he sought to uphold by his every deed, and then honestly to measure how well it was done. Once possessed of this tool, he considered how well the Mohawks and the Iroquois had fared since the whites arrived and the debilitation from disease and drunkenness seemed irrevocable.

"We have a chief," he told her, "who urges returning to the old ways. Being only half Mohawk, I have sought to surpass those of full-blood by following him. I see now that is impossible. The only path I can follow must lead away from those ways much as villagers will leave their burning village."

"Consider," Catherine observed, "no longer do we look to the forests and the streams for our every need. The whites bring many things that are good—knives and cloth and kettles—and for these things we must trade with them. This dependency weakens us unless we find a new strength. The Prayer shows us this new path."

Catherine brought Kryn to meet the blackrobe, Father Frémin, and when Kryn held out his hand to clasp the other's, he recognized the priest as one of the three who had visited Kanawaka a few years ago. The greeting was very warm.

"You wish to receive instruction?" the priest asked him.

"I do," Kryn said.

"It is good you have come."

As the chilly weeks gave way to beaming sunlight and frost

steamed from the frozen ground, Kryn attended the blackrobe's instruction at the chapel. By Easter he was ready for baptism. As the sun sparkled upon the river outside, the choir sang the *Kyrie* and the *Gloria* and the *Sanctus* and the *Agnus Dei* in the soft candlelight with wild flowers around the altar.

Kryn had replaced his buckskin tunic with a robe of white cotton and by now his hair had grown in. Down the aisle he walked, solemn, dignified, filled with reverence, and he knelt while the priest dribbled holy water over his forehead: "In the name of the Father and of the Son and of the Holy Ghost, Amen."

"Amen."

"Do you renounce Satan?"

"I renounce Satan."

"And all his works."

"And all his works."

The priest asked his questions and Kryn gave his answers, and his sponsor, Catherine, told the priest, when he asked for the new convert's name, "Joseph."

"Welcome, Joseph Kryn," the priest said and urged him to stand in the lovely music and candlelight with the warm spring sun glancing in the door of the chapel.

Kryn was going home. With a hatchet and a knife he made himself a canoe of elm bark, lashing the rib work and the tholes, then smearing pine pitch along the seams. He whittled two long paddles out of ash, and one morning in May, after mass and communion, he walked down to the river bank with Catherine Gandeacteua and Father Frémin.

"May you have safe passage," the priest said, and he embraced the bigger man.

"I go but I shall soon return, and with me I shall bring such from our village who wish to live in the peace and tranquility, Father."

Catherine reached out to take his hand. "Bring your wife and your little son," she said. "We will care for them and soon you all may live in peace among us."

"I will return before the leaves are flaming, before the air fills with snow."

So saying, Kryn pushed the canoe into the water and jumped nimbly aboard as it glided into the broad current. He seized one of the paddles, waved to the priest and Catherine, and then threw his broad shoulders into the work, paddling down river toward the Richelieu.

Chapter 19

Kryn Returns To Bring His Wife
And Son To The Mission

ALONE JOSEPH KRYN CLIMBED the mud path to northern gate. The gate was open and no sentries stood guard. Entering the village, he heard loud laughter, and suddenly, around the side of a long house, a group of young warriors ran pell-mell into him. Abruptly they stopped and waited for him to speak for they recognized him and had considered him dead.

"You seem to be in a great hurry," said Joseph Kryn.

"We considered you . . . lost . . . and many thought you'd never return," one said.

"Why are there no women in the fields? Why no guards upon the walls?"

"It's the Festival of Dreams," one of the young warriors said with a snide laugh. "Yesterday we tore through the village to find a sacred wampum belt one old man dreamed about, and we found it. Quorenta, the old hag, dreamed Bobcat the Hunter came to her as a lover and so we roused him from his sleeping pallet and took him to her to comply. Iowerano dreamed the English had visited with a cask of rum, and so we raced down to Corlaer for a cask, and now everyone drinks of his dreamed-for rum."

"Yes," another laughed, "the dream feast becomes a celebration. Iowerano and Moneta host a Drink-All feast in their long house."

"And what of the girl Tekakwitha who lives with them?"

"She is sent on errands to fetch water and wood and even food from neighboring cabins."

Righteously indignant, Kryn turned from the young men and strode through the lane to Iowerano's cabin. He heard the beating of a drum inside, and as ripped open the bear skin flap the wild scene infuriated him. As a young warrior was drumming, a group of eight or so sat swaying on the ground, chanting, and in the midst of them White Adder, the shaman, danced wildly in a big face mask. All of the people at the gathering were screaming in laughter at White Adder's antics. Kryn looked into the direction of where Tekakwitha usually sat, and she was gone.

Joseph Kryn walked up to Iowerano, who sat like a king, arms folded, his antlered bonnet on his head. Iowerano turned drunkenly to him, tried to focus his eyes.

"Ah, the Great Mohawk!" he said through bleary eyes. "Where have you been?"

Kryn ignored the question. "Where is the girl who sits over there? The one who embroiders?"

"About here somewhere," Iowerano said. "What's it to you?"

Moneta, his wife, added: "She goes her own way."

"She has refused to marry," the chief said.

White Adder, shaking his rattles, danced up to Joseph Kryn and moved menacingly about him as if he were fending off an evil spirit. Kryn towered over the witch doctor.

"I sense the blackrobes' evil!" White Adder shook his rattles furiously.

"Is this, Great Chief," Kryn called over the shaman's head, "how you observe the old ways?"

"My magic is stronger!" White Adder hissed.

Joseph Kryn reached down and seized the shaman by the rawhide thong of his sun god amulet. "You are a fraud!" he said. "Your magic is nothing more than tricks!"

"So says the half-breed!"

"Let him go, Kryn!" Iowerano was laughing. "The fool entertains me!"

"He dupes you!" Joseph Kryn said. "He is no match for the power of the blackrobe."

With light from the doorway, Kryn looking over and he saw the girl Tekakwitha entering with an armload of firewood.

"You make this little one with the bad eyesight go out and fetch your wood and water? While you, able-bodied men and women, stay inside drinking whiskey?"

"Who are you to rebuke us?" Moneta spoke. "You abandoned your wife and child through this long, cold winter without provision."

"Come with me, little one," Kryn said to Tekakwitha. "Who knows what might happen as they lose their reason to the whiskey?"

"She stays!" Iowerano said, pounding his fist into his palm.

White Adder shook his rattles in Joseph Kryn's face, and he spun and leapt and shouted imprecations.

"Get your quills and needles," Kryn said to the girl, and he turned to her uncle. "I have some work for her to do," he said.

"Ah, take her away," Moneta said. "She annoys me with her long-suffering."

"Go!" Iowerano said.

Tekakwitha dropped her bundle of wood by the side of the fire pit and she collected a few scraps of doeskin and her basket of dyes and porcupine quills. Beside the great warrior she left the long house. She adjusted her shawl against the bright sunlight and walked along with Kryn toward his cabin.

"You have work for me?" she asked.

"Do you know the symbol of the blackrobes? The crossed sticks?"

"Yes," she said.

"You know my son?"

"Martin grows strong," she said. "He is a happy baby."

"He knows not yet how men will abuse him, but enough of that. I want you to stitch the cross of the blackrobes upon a skin for his mother to put around him on the papoose board."

"Gladly," she said.

He started to enter the long house where he had once lived.

"You are seeking Karitha and Martin?" she asked. "They now live with Anastasia."

"Lead me to them?"

She took his big, calloused hand in hers and led him through the cornfields to Anastasia's cabin. As they approached they heard the baby laughing inside.

"Shall we go in, little one, or do you think she will turn me away?"

"I have visited here through the dark winter months. Often she has prayed for your return."

Kryn pulled the great curtain aside. The girl followed him into the cabin. "Karitha?" he said. His wife turned, looked at him with surprise, then she stood, handed the baby to Anastasia and rushed to embrace him.

"You've come home!"

"I was a fool," he said, and he took her in his great brawny arms. After they had embraced, she handed him the baby.

"Hold your son."

Kryn's face lit up as he opened the soft deer hide wrapping and saw his baby. The baby's left arm was waving at him in the air. With his big fingers Kryn tickled the baby's chin and the baby laughed. The Great Mohawk cradled the infant against his chest and rocked him.

"Here," Anastasia said, "sit down on the mat. How long has it been long since you ate?"

Joseph Kryn gave a laugh. "I can't remember."

"You too, little one," Anastasia gathered Tekakwitha to her, "sit." She handed the warrior and the girl wooden bowls and she spooned up sagamite from the kettle.

"You seem changed," Karitha observed.

"I am," Joseph Kryn said. He looked at her with a penetrating light in his eye. "I am a Christian."

Anastasia dropped a bowl of the porridge and Karitha cried out, put her hands to her face and they both fell upon him, embracing him and crying out in thanksgiving. When the emotion subsided, Kryn explained:

"When I left this village, I traveled blindly for days and days. I had little food with me. I hardly cared whether I lived or died. My steps drew me into the mountains along the frozen lakes and then down to the great river of the north. Half-starved I stumbled toward a cabin and a Christian woman, Catherine, an Oneida, took me in and housed me. She met my arguments with such logic, it was as if she had been sent to me for that very purpose."

"The blackrobe calls such people 'guardian angels,'" Anastasia said.

Tekakwitha listened, moved at his change of heart.

"I was wrong-headed," he said, clasping the child to himself. "I learned from Catherine and from the priest the prayer they call the 'Pater Noster,' and in it they state 'forgive us our trespasses . . .'"

The women joined in, "'. . . as we forgive those who trespass against us, and lead us not into temptation but deliver us from evil.'"

Joseph Kryn put out his hand and touched Karitha's cheek. "Can you forgive me?"

"I did long ago," she said. "Let us have our supper, then." And she set about serving the porridge. Anastasia sat next to Tekakwitha and put her arm around the young woman's shoulder, welcoming her into this family.

Joseph Kryn was indeed a changed man. While the other warriors and hunters idled away their spring and summer smoking and gambling while their women worked the fields, Kryn doted on his wife and his son, even helping Anastasia in the garden and about her cabin where they all lived together. In the lanes of the village he might be spied carrying the boy on a cradle board, a decidedly unmasculine, un-Mohawk sight, and in the early afternoon he began a sort of academy for the young people, both boys and girls, to teach them about the Mission of St. Francis Xavier.

"There are a dozen cabins and in their midst is a chapel," he told the nine or ten young people who clustered about him near the swimming hole. "The chapel has the crossed sticks upon it, and a bell to ring for services, and there we go in the morning for mass and in the afternoon for a prayer service. When the workers are in the fields, or building new shelters, or down along the river repairing canoes and the bell rings for prayers, we kneel on the ground and we pray Matins or the Angelus. In such way, every few hours finds us thinking lofty thoughts, pausing and turning our minds and hearts heavenward in meditation and thanksgiving."

"Is there a stockade?" one of the young men asked.

"Yes, for defense," Joseph Kryn said. "Unfortunately war has not left this land forever. But at the mission there is nothing to fight for. There are no muskets or great bundles of furs to trade, no incentive to conquer. We grow what we need and we live humbly. Turn the other cheek to an aggressor and the aggression disappears."

"Do they marry?" another asked.

"Yes, but they take only one wife and they pledge to spend a lifetime together in work and in worship."

"I asked about the blackrobes," the youth said.

"Oh, no. We are allowed to marry, encouraged even in order to create families, but the blackrobes take no wife. They do not know women, and the women religious do not know men. They dedicate their lives, all of their effort to the mission."

"Do they work?"

"They do not till the field or build the cabins or cook the food. They do not trade or hunt or fish. They have another notion of work. They work to lead us into heaven. Toward this goal they direct all of their energies."

"Are all nations welcome there?"

"I have seen it with my eyes and heard it with my ears. Men and women from all nations live together in harmony: Hurons, Mohawks, Algonquins, Abenaki, Neutrals, Adirondacks, Mohicans. All our petty jealousies are left behind and we can devote all of our time to prayer and work in the field without nursing grudges or plotting revenge. It is a delightful way to live."

Each Sunday morning, Joseph Kryn and his family collected at the western gate and left the village in high spirits as the sun was clearing the hills. Along the river they walked, talking and laughing, Kryn carrying Martin. Tekakwitha heard them assembling, then watched them depart, happy and excited about attending mass and receiving communion. Her life was drudgery. Moneta, sensing her desire, ridiculed the Christians openly.

"Look at them! While the rest of us work to clean the skins and till the fields, they go off on a lark, laughing and skipping along the trail without a care."

And Iowerano chimed in: "Gone is any respect for the old traditions, for the Dream Feast or the Corn Planting dance or the Harvest Festival. Instead they worship the torture victim that Ondessonk spoke of who did not know women, who advised warriors not to fight."

These criticisms were meant for her ears, but the ridicule only intensified her desire to accompany the Christians.

As the summer mellowed, talk went around that Kryn was

departing from Kanawaka and inviting along any Christians who wanted to leave. All the cousins through his mother's line vowed to join him, and many others who had been baptized as well.

Hearing this, Iowerano complained bitterly that the half-breed was showing his allegiance to the white side of his parentage, and that true Mohawks needed to seal up their ears and not listen to him.

When the nights and the days were equal and a chill began to tinge the maple leaves, Kryn assembled his forty emigrants with their packs and their hunting gear.

"You must join us someday," Anastasia told the girl Tekakwitha, and she held her tightly in a hug.

"My uncle will never let me go."

"Our faith teaches that we are each responsible for our own decisions and so others cannot control us. Become a Christian, little one, and join us in the north."

She did not answer.

Bidding a fond farewell to their relatives, the Christians left in a merry band. Down the hill they wended and into the forest toward the trail that led to the lakes where they'd fashion canoes to bear them north to the great river.

Tekakwitha was deeply saddened, and as they went down the trail together, she stood alone at the gate to the village, wishing she might simply walk away with Kryn and the Christians.

Chapter 20

Father Claude Chauchetière,
Missionary To New France

For weeks, it seemed, Claude Chauchetière had gazed out his latticed window at the pelting rain. Clouds rolled and billowed in the western sky like smoke above a battlefield. On his hustling walks to the refectory or on those few days where, needing air, he paced in the cloister slowly, deliberately to quell the zeal that burned in his breast like a glowing iron bar, the wind played with his black soutane and his wide-brimmed chapeau, much as the brisk winds of change blew his life into the past, into the future.

In his small whitewashed cell, his pencils and paintbox lay idle, his quill and ink bottle unused, his output of letters fell as impatience worked him like the sinews in a young colt. The ship, *La Belle Yglantine*, a small, square-rigged transport from the Marseille shipyards, well-suited for Mediterranean work but not for an Atlantic crossing, sat at the quay like a roosting carrier pigeon until the sky would clear. And then, as if a clarion banished all dark and doubt, the sun beamed upon the sodden fields and the wet slates of the turrets and spires of La Rochelle. Bells rang the hours and his heart shivered in anticipation for he knew that soon these bell would regulate his life no more.

The ship was bringing three score *habitants* and their livestock—

sheep and swine and milch cows and half a dozen horses for the governor's stables—to the colony of New France. Barrels of salt pork and hard tack and water were stacked in the hold. The wind fluttered in a loose sail as he climbed the ramp, a large carpetbag over his shoulder with his belongings, and he looked up at the pennants flying from the fore and main and mizzen masts and his heart was streaming and glad. He was leaving behind the spiritual morass into which his soul had fallen as if into a fetid dungeon cell, and he was—dare he even breathe a comparison with the great Jogues?—striking out into a savage wilderness with only faith and zeal to guide him. Destiny awaited. Called thither across the sea to a great, misty, undefined consummation in the wilderness, he felt with uncharacteristic certainty a spiritual awakening awaited him in the primordial forests.

The sailors were yelling up and down the quay, casting off the hawsers that bound him to his home. He looked up. Gulls wheeled and cried above the twin turrets at the harbor's mouth, beckoning him on. Oarsmen in three pilot boats pulled at their oars to tow *La Belle Yglantine* into open water. Barefoot sailors danced aloft on the rigging, and as the ship cleared the towers and the breakwater, they unfurled the sails that dropped and filled with wind, making the masts creak with a happy groan to be moving at last.

In the bleating and mooing of cattle, the *habitants* nestled comfortably. They were simple peasants, small, thick, swarthy men with long filthy hair and knotted beards. They wore leather vests and homespun flannel shirts and canvas breeches and clogs. Their simplicity pleased the priest far more than his two Jesuit companions who seemed fastidious when sleeping on the lower deck or eating the first uncooked meal of salt pork and biscuit or seeking privacy where there was none. Yet he slept close to his fellows and he quietly observed the captain and the crew and the pulling of ropes and sail that caught the wind and propelled them into the future. He doodled and sketched and he daydreamed, looking at the blank pages of his drawing book, at what scenes might soon enliven those sheets.

The first storm hit four days out. The seas had been brisk and steady, large swells that lifted the gliding ship up and carried her along and then eased her down into a trough, but toward evening on the fourth day, Father Claude stood with his two fellows watching a thunderstorm sweep across the water like the hand of God.

"Trim the sails!" the first mate called through his speaking trumpet, and the crew sprang up the rope ladders and out the yardarms and hauled up the swelling canvas as the sky darkened and the rising seas tilted the masts. Then a flash of lightning and thunder crashed, the storm enveloping them. Up, up, up the ship rose, pointed at the sky, hung a moment on top before plunging down, down, down as if it would stab the bowsprit through the gates of hell. Sweet rain and salt spray lashed at them hanging onto the belaying pins and ropes. But for the leather thong beneath their chins the hats would have fluttered away. Father Claude looked out in mortal fear as the once-placid and shimmering ocean suddenly became an infinite succession of curling mountains of black water and deep troughs into which they plunged headlong, oblivion awaiting at the end of each free fall. His gorge rose and struggle as he might to lean over the bucking deck rail, he vomited on his clothes and his shoes and the deck.

"Below! Get him below!" someone cried, and Father René and Father Michel put their shoulders beneath his arms and carried him to the companionway.

Below all was mayhem. The floor of the lower deck rose and fell at impossible angels. The beasts bleated and screamed in fear. The *habitants* cried out in superstitious panic or else clasped their hands above their heads with rosaries and crosses screaming out in prayers of deliverance. The smell! Vomit, diarrhea, manure all mingled with the pervasive body odor of stale sweat and Father

René seized a bucket for Claude and he vomited and vomited and vomited until he felt as though his insides would rise up in convulsions and pour out through his mouth. Then Father Michel was sick. Then Father René. They shared the bucket, and between episodes of sickness they fell upon the heaving floorboards and tried not to slip backward and forward as the craft rose and fell.

In an eternity of screams and bellows and the slosh of fetid water somehow the night passed. In the gray light of morning, the storm petered out, yet the waves still dashed against the hull and sent great clouds of spray high across the deck where Claude and René and Michel struggled to breathe some fresh air.

"Gives one a new appreciation for the suffering of Jonah," René said. He was an irrepressible slip of a young man with a cowlick of red hair and bright blue eyes with pale eyelids that made his eyes always seem sleepy. "At times last night I would have preferred to be cast into the sea."

Indeed it seemed to Claude that the storm arose only to admonish him for his vanity. The block-shaped captain was passing at that moment. He had an evil look to him, as if he'd gazed too long into the abyss and viewed the mortals that he transported as cowering land-lubbers who could not possibly understand the magnitude of forces at work in his world.

"Aye, Fathers," he said in derision, "your God was asleep last night, eh?"

"He listens to our prayers," Michel said, "but he tests us."

The captain shook his head at the absurdity of these flimsy young men with their crosses and rosaries and breviaries, and he swaggered to the bridge to set a course with the helmsman.

"The scars of his many sins weigh him down," René said to comfort Claude who, in truth, seemed about to burst into tears. If last night were any indication, what horrors had the captain indeed witnessed? Abused as a cabin boy, cheated by wharfsmen and merchants, bested in tavern brawls, cast into prison for smuggling, the tale lay beyond Claude's imagination and with his stomach in revolution he wanted only to curl up and rest.

Father Claude never fully recovered for the six weeks they were at sea. Five more storms hit in the tempestuous spring in those trade latitudes of the Atlantic, and fear that the precarious craft would not make the climb of the next wave or pull out of its plummet into the following trough sickened him. He had ceased, even, to think of himself as a priest, and knew himself to be nothing more than a cowardly wretch, huddled in his own sweat and filth on stinking blankets. He watched the *habitants* and came to envy their simplicity, their stupidity. To be dull seemed a blessing for not only did the lack of imagination reduce the perception of fear, but the lack of intense memory reduced its duration and the apprehension of its return.

He wanted never to harbor a regret, yet his soul was lost at sea. Gone were the gothic arches of home that shielded him from the storms and the limitless depths of the stars. Gone were the rituals marked by the clappers of tolling bells which were pulled by priests and sextons and hooded monks all over the city in service to Him. Gone was the regularity of meals and digestion and even the clean, simple joy of voluntary fasting. Present only was the agony of a sick stomach, a vitamin depletion near to scurvy and the spiritual doubt that his ambition or devotion or faith, whatever robes and raiments he sought to dress it in, was nothing more than an adolescent vanity. In seeking to transcend his dissatisfaction with the narrowness of a clerical life by rebelling against it, he was only to find, upon awakening in a swinging hammock in a storm at sea, that his rampant willpower had nothing to feed or warm or comfort it.

This crisis of faith, which he hid as a shameful secret from his fellows, persisted long beyond the seasickness. On the forty-fifth day of the voyage they spied land, Anticosti Island, and they made landfall at Havre-St. Pierre. Briefly they stopped to take on fresh water, and then they sailed up the Gulf of St. Lawrence into the embrace of the estuary, and on to Ile d'Orleans. With the tide they floated upriver into the shadow of the massive rock of Quebec. Michel and René were excited by the arrival, but Claude grew pensive. The rock rose suddenly from the narrow channel, a natural fortification. Indeed, a century and a half of hardy French explorers and military men had settled on its brow, the wooden stockade even now like a sort of fur cap. Yet sheer size of the stone gray cliff, a bulwark against the flowing river and the advancing tide, made him shiver with a deep and sudden awareness of the elemental savagery of the place. Like the fabled pillars of Hercules, this rock served as a gate, not to the sea at the middle of the earth, but to all the horrors and privations he had read about in the *Relations*.

Never stout or even remarkably healthy, the slight Claude Chauchetière was now emaciated. His cheeks were caved in, his chest bony and his spine hunched. His brown eyes were hollow and dulled by illness and he faltered walking down the ramp with his carpetbag, nearly empty since he had long ago thrown his stinking blankets overboard.

While the captain supervised the unloading of his cargo and the *habitants* breathed and stretched in the clean new air of the lower town, Claude Chauchetière climbed with his two fellows to the Jesuit provincial house on the top of the rock. They were welcomed warmly and given a mutton stew with potatoes and carrots that Claude strove to keep down, and a goblet of wine that made his head swim. A middle-aged *donne* who managed the place gave Claude a new cassock and showed him to a cot with a straw tick in a cell up under the eaves. Claude slept the remainder of that day and the next, awakening at last at the matins bell, surprised that the earth was not rocking back and forth.

He rose, knelt and recited the *lectio divina* in his cell, then he crept down the stairs and out into the yard. The air was crisp and clean. The green leaves of trees and, in the garden, the fragrant herbs and blooming roses and lilies lent his soul the color it had hungered to see for six weeks on the gray ocean. For the first time since he left Poitiers he had a desire to paint.

After a silent breakfast, Father Gabriel Bernier, the superior of the house, met with the new missionaries in his office.

"We welcome you," the ascetic old priest tried so hard to smile it appeared his face was cracking. "We are in great need of you just now as we have recently founded a mission for the displaced Hurons about three leagues upriver. Are you familiar with the fate of the Huron nation?"

"That is where Father Jogues spent his missionary years," René said.

"Yes," the priest nodded. "Nearly forty years ago he went there. He spent six years administering to the Hurons who grew in faith under his care. He was returning to them from here when he was captured by the Mohawks." The priest sadly shook his head. "I arrived in Quebec five years after Father Jogues was martyred." He bowed his head and made the sign of the cross. "Shortly afterward, the Iroquois massacred the Hurons, wiping their villages from face of the earth, sending any survivors forth like birds of the air." He shook his head sadly.

"Our missionaries gathered a band of fugitives on the shores of St. Joseph Island in Nottawasaga Bay. Starved and fearful of more depredations of Iroquois, about three hundred Hurons and sixty of our priests and their assistants came down river here to Quebec where we quartered them on property we held by royal grant. Still, the Mohawks do not let up."

"What impels the Mohawks to act so demonically?" René asked.

"They are unique among all the native peoples," Father Bernier said. "They are the most ferocious warriors by far. Pridefully they never forget a slight and, once roused, they fight to the death without any concern for survival. But on the other side of the coin, I have heard from Fathers Bruyas and de Lamberville that once converted, their piety knows no equal in France or in New France. Their singleness of purpose, the depth of their character and natural propensity to be loyal and true does not brook any backsliding. But back to the Hurons. After de Tracy's raid and the treaty, the Hurons again ventured outside these walls of Quebec. Father Chaumonot established a new mission, Notre-Dame de Foye, about two leagues west of our walls seven years ago. With the influx of some Christian Iroquois the mission found itself cramped for both land and timber, and so it removed three years ago to a new site about three leagues west. Here Father Chaumonot built a chapel modeled after the Holy House of Loretto. We call the village 'Notre-Dame de Vielle Lorette' or simply 'Lorette.' This is where you will be assigned, Father Claude."

Father Claude bowed in obedience.

"We have need of Father René in our chapel at Troies-Rivières, and you, Father Michel, we have assigned you to a mission farther upriver, near Montreal, that is relocating this year."

Father Michel bowed his head submissively.

"This mission will illustrate what I have said about Iroquois converts and in particular one who is known even among his people as the Great Mohawk. Our order possessed a seigneury, La Prairie, on the south bank of this mighty river, opposite Ville Marie on the island of Montreal. Given that the land is flat and not well fortified and that it is along the river and so open to attack, it was worthless so long as the Iroquois were raiding. But after de Tracy brought peace by burning the Mohawk villages, Father Rafeix built a house on this land. His initial idea was to surround himself with *habitants* who would farm and raise livestock and so increase the value of our lands, but soon another use, by the grace of God, announced itself.

"Father Bruyas had journeyed among the Oneida, the second

nation of the Iroquois, with only a smattering of the Huron language. This language bears a resemblance to the Iroquois language about as close as Portuguese bears to French. Only by laborious effort could he make himself understood. An Oneida woman, though, Gandeacteua, tutored him in the Iroquoian tongue until she and her husband Tonsanhoten left Oneida to accompany a fur trader to Montreal. It was winter when Gandeacteua, Tonsanhoten and the fur trader arrived in Montreal, so they spent the winter of 1668-1669 there. They visited our church for the Christmas service. The woman Gandeacteua knew much about Christianity from helping Father Bruyas learn the language, and she and her husband decided to be baptized.

"The missionaries urged them to go to live at Notre-Dame de Foye, but they declined and started home. When they stopped at Father Rafeix's house at LaPrairie, though, they saw how close it was to their homeland and that year Gandeacteua tilled the ground as she was wont to do at home and her husband Tonsanhoten built a small long house which served as an inn of sorts to other travelers up and down the river. A new community of converts began to take root and it was called Kentake. Until this spring it thrived on the original location, but I have just received word it is moving a few miles upriver to a set of rapids where the travelers must leave the river and carry their canoes over the portage. This new place, where you will be assigned, Father Michel, is called 'Kanawaka,' which means 'At the Rapids' in the Iroquois language.

"Four years ago a Mohawk, perhaps the fiercest warrior of his nation, left his village alone in the dead of winter, and he happened into this settlement. Gandeacteua, whose husband was away, invited him to lodge with her, and she instructed him in the rudiments of our faith. He was baptized with the name 'Joseph.' He is known among his people as 'Joseph Kryn' or 'the Great Mohawk.' Immediately he returned to his village, likewise called Kanawaka for it had been built at rapids on his native river, and he enlisted many followers to come to Kentake."

Unfortunately, the good Gandeacteua died last summer, but the mission she helped to found thrives. Each summer since his conversion, Joseph Kryn has returned and brought more converts back, and he is credited with bringing about two hundred souls from the Iroquois villages to this mission. His devotion knows no bounds. He is possessed of great skill in all things, building houses, making canoes, negotiating peace, and has the highest degree of personal honor.

"You, Father Michel," Father Bernier said, "will be assigned to help my old friend Father Frémin who administers to our converts at Kanawaka, and is putting the mission on a solid footing. You can help these good people get settled this summer in their new location."

Father Bernier stood and reached for the hands of the young priests, and they knelt upon the floor.

"Let us pray. . . . Our Father, Who art in heaven, hallowed be Thy name. Thy kingdom come, Thy will and not mine be done on earth as it is in heaven. Give us this day our daily bread and forgive us our trespasses as we forgive those who trespass against us and lead us not into temptation but deliver us from evil, for Thine is the kingdom and the power and the glory forever and ever. Amen."

The Jesuit house hosted a dinner that night to fete the three new priests, and the next morning they parted, Michel and René up the St. Lawrence to Trois-Rivières and Kanawaka and Claude Chauchetière, kneeling uncomfortably in a bark canoe paddled by Brother Paul, up the St. Charles River to Lorette. The stirring accounts from Father Bernier and the heroism of the natives in resisting the Mohawk raids bucked him up on the short journey upriver in a flimsy, tipping birch bark canoe, but upon landing on a mud bank, and climbing a small rise he came upon a dismal, smoky, stinking collection of hovels and the filthy humans and skinny dogs they housed. This squalor far exceeded any filth and poverty he had encountered in France, and such was the mission of Lorette.

Four to five hundred natives, mostly Hurons, lived in thirty long houses, lazy smoke meandering out of the top like emanations of the squalor inside. Mangy dogs slunk around the yards, barking at him as he walked up the path and onto a mud flat where a little naked child welcomed him by squatting and defecating in his path.

Brother Paul, a leathery faced Huron who sang baritone in the choir, led him to the rectory, a low log cabin with a thatched roof beside another small cabin that had a crucifix on top—the chapel. Father Claude met Father Pierre-Joseph-Marie Chaumonot, founder of Lorette, with whom he would now share the hut they called a rectory.

Claude emerged from the rectory soon after accompanied by Father Chaumonot. They went together into the chapel, they came back out, they walked through the village where naked children ran and dogs looked at him suspiciously and bare-chested native women pounded corn in mortars made of tree stumps. Every move of his was watched by these small, swarthy people and Claude felt accusation in their eyes, perhaps because the squalid reality of the mission did not measure the grandiose, romantic image he had invented.

"Unimaginable barbarity!" he wrote his younger brother Jacques. He wrote about the primitive hunting, planting, cooking and eating, but he did not write about the lack of privacy which suddenly confronted him with natives, both men and women, urinating in his sight and now and then the sight of a couple in the throes of passion.

"Are there no taboos?" he asked Father Chaumonot.

"Young people of one clan must look outside that clan in order to marry," the priest replied.

"I meant about copulating where others can see."

"The Hurons consider copulation a normal function. We have done our best to ask converts to engage in that privately."

"It cannot be good for the children," Claude observed, when in truth his sensibilities were affronted.

He tried to feel tolerance, but the squalor and ignorance and filth shocked and dismayed him and so a familiar depression lengthened like a shadow over him. Each morning he said the mass in Latin, and the communicants seemed to know what transpired—at least they knew when to stand, when to sit and when to kneel—but the language barrier made him dependent upon Father Chaumonot whom he regarded as a happy ignoramus. Unkindly, Claude tried to fathom whether the priest was that way before he arrived, or if this place removed whatever spark of intelligence he might have possessed. Each morning Claude visited parishioners in their long houses. The poorest of the poor in the slums of Paris lived like royalty compared to the filth and privation of these Hurons.

He wrote to his brother:

They live communally in a long bark hut through which the wind and rain, and in the winter, snow, readily penetrate. Each bark huts, it seems, belongs to a separate family ruled over by a matriarch and forms part of a larger clan. Five, six and seven open fire pits run down the middle of the houses. In clusters loosely aligned with family ties they cook and eat and sleep and copulate. In summer the men walk about in breechclouts that cover their genitals. Since the advent of the whites, they make these of cotton or wool, fastened with a leather strap about their waists. Prior to the white man's appearance, these were no doubt made of buckskin. The women wear fabric skirts, and many of them work and pound the corn with a wooden mortar or plant in the fields wearing no garment on top, but their dugs readily observable. In summer the children all run about naked and get into all manner of mischief.

His observations soured in subsequent letters:

I considered at first that I would grow used to this, or that I at least would cease being shocked, but the smell of these people is such that I find myself standing upwind when there is a wind, and when there isn't I must gulp to hold down my gorge. They never bathe and at the latrine they do not wash, but simply wipe their hands on leaves. Mothers cleanse their infants with sawdust from rotten stumps. They eat their corn porridge they call sagamite with their fingers and they bite into meat and then saw off the piece they wish to chew with their knives so that it looks as they are eating they might amputate their noses. Everywhere is the stench of burnt meat and excrement. I do not see how I might lead them to God when the proximity of Europeans for more than a generation has had no effect whatsoever on their sanitation.

Oh, my brother, I despair of the graces I sought by this assignment. I have been banished from my home, my books, my studies, my fellows, from my chores instructing the youngsters in mathematics which I so hated. On this foreign shore I have been cast up among heathens and savages who cannot read, will not learn, and though they are fervent in their worship, I suspect they have merely supplanted their notion of a sun god with a notion of ours. The mystical presence of the Eucharist interests them, but I doubt whether in any way they can understand its deep meaning. I keep asking myself, 'What have I done? Why has God deserted me?'

In his next letter to his older brother Jean, he observed:

From the time I first read of Father Jogues's suffering and death at the hands of these natives, I admired how he forgave them, loved them and tried to save them. My admiration for his Christ-like patience and tolerance has increased tenfold since I have been here. Not only do I not suffer at their hands, but in truth these simple natives do me honor and give me their respect as the minister of the rites of our faith, and yet I cannot summon one-hundredth of the love Father Jogues felt for them since I cannot see children of God, but only creatures bowed by ignorance and superstition, chained to rites and sorceries and dream rituals that seem to the western mind haphazard and inexplicable.

The responses from his brothers were diametrically opposed. His older brother, Jean, worried about his well-being and wrote back that Claude should examine his conscience to discover there what the Lord expected of him, that this assignment had been his election and certainly now was not the time to reconsider every logical underpinning of the process that got him there. Jacques, the younger, told him to cease the unedifying correspondence. In the usual manner of sharing letters from New France with the provincial house, his peers had demanded to read what Claude wrote, and Claude's doubts and concerns and failings caused him untold consternation and embarrassment.

Winter howled down the river. Wrapped in infinite darkness, pelted by relentless snows, frozen bitter, Claude utterly despaired. The simple ignorance of the natives allowed them survival. They ignored the insult of frostbitten toes and fingertips. They laughed and sang as they chopped wood for the fire. With magnanimous hearts they invited the priests to their communal feasts of bear stew and now he saw the children in their leggings and hoods of fur as small and joyful embodiments of that survival urge that he, with all his theology, lacked. No longer did he pour it out in letters to his brothers, but he strove during his prayers, both his private prayers and those in the chapel attended by the furred and feathered Hurons, to find quiet and peace in his heart. His most ardent desire, to find in these people the worthy vessels of divine faith and love, had been dashed, and he fully believed that anyone who considered that they might rise up and embrace the faith were only deluding themselves.

His ignorance of the Huron language, beyond a few prayers and some elemental words, underscored this. Drinking in this new world of bark huts and fur robes and braided corn husks and butchered meat, the smoky, greasy cooking fires that backed down the escape hole when the wind rose or the snow flew, this foreign shore populated by a squat, swarthy people who grunt and nodded to communicate, who might strip a birch or an elm to built a watertight canoe in an afternoon but couldn't spell a word and had little capacity for abstract thought, he lacked the language skills to make himself understood and so his heart beat impatiently and he considered his sojourn into this land a futile gesture, a vain romantic impulse.

Nor was Father Chaumonot much help. While surely possessed of a kind heart, the ancient priest, weakened and desiccated by three celibate decades in the wild, seemed disengaged from the denizens of Lorette. He appeared to Claude haughty and disdaining, comfortable in his superior knowledge of what to the natives must have appeared an elaborate charade of hocus-pocus babble and awkward, if solemn and measured, hand signals.

"Keep your distance," he advised Claude even as he taught him the cognate languages of Huron and Iroquois, "familiarity breeds contempt."

The priest best embodied his own advice. One day near the equinox as the ice on the river was groaning and breaking into floes as big as Parisian city blocks, the senior priest announced, "Father Superior has asked whether I can spare you, Father Claude. I sent back word that I could."

The news stung Claude. Try as he might to conceal his

unhappiness, to vent it only in letters home, somehow it had leaked out and his unhappiness, his weakness, he suspected and feared, was universally known.

"Why would he make such a request?" Claude despised the reedy pitch to his voice.

"He seeks to deploy you upriver at Kanawaka."

"But Michel Cocteau was sent there, was he not?"

"Michel has petitioned to be reassigned."

"Has he given any reason?"

Father Chaumonot shrugged. "Jacques Frémin? Isn't that reason enough?"

"I don't follow your thinking."

The sense of great unseen forces moving behind the veils unsettled Claude.

"Father Frémin is a headstrong man, nearly fifty, I'd wager. He's a most effective manager and Kanawaka grows each year. Do you need to know more than that?"

"Is there more to know?"

"There is always more to know, my son. Nothing ever reveals its deepest secrets."

"What is it, then?"

"Father Michel, it seems, caused some concern with how well he might be keeping his vow of chastity."

"That's absurd!" Claude said. "I knew Michel in the novitiate, and though I don't know him well since I went as an instructor to Tulle, I cannot believe that sin could ever cause a concern with him."

"Well," Father Chaumonot smiled with a smile that lent some justification to the opinion that he was a cynic, "perhaps it's only in the eye of the beholder. Frémin's eye might be keen enough to see what truthfully is not there."

"And he will now be my superior?"

"Although you have not settled your heart in this place, you will grow to miss me."

"Where can one ever find peace in this world?" Claude asked, but the priest did not understand his expectation that it be a rhetorical question.

"Not in the missions," Father Chaumonot answered.

Claude regarded him critically. He realized that he despised the smug superiority Chaumonot believed his white hair conferred upon him. Father Jogues, too, had exchanged the Hurons for the Mohawks, though under far different circumstances.

A month later, when ice floes no longer threatened the delicate bark canoes, Claude knelt in the bow of a canoe while in the stern knelt the brawny Marcel, a scarred Huron warrior with an enviable collection of scalps. In the center sat Gaçon, a youth of fourteen summers. They were one of nine canoes making the journey in a flotilla, paddling through the blistering sun and the chilling rain, fourteen and sixteen hours a day, camping at night along the river where the ferocious Mohawks used to prowl.

The journey upriver worked an odd change in Father Claude. Behind him smoldered his despair in embracing this raw country, seeking a benign Eden but finding instead a brutal wasteland of impossible cold, depthless ignorance and superstition. He saw how, in his failed first effort to acclimate himself, the readings of the *Relations* merged into the physical world and he, a humble denizen of Poitiers and son of a jurist, was now fully immersed in this place where titles and lineage and rank held no privileges and survival was the only skill. Beyond the elitism of his status to conduct rites and administer sacraments, he was nothing more than a man, a set of arms and shoulders, a spine bending into the paddling to carry himself into the future of his next assignment or an ambush, whatever lay ahead.

Upriver, against the current they went day by day, with a stop at Trois-Rivières, then past the palisade of Fort Richelieu where water flowed down from Mohawk country where Jogues had been dragged, then to Montreal and the rapids of La Chine. The journey took seven days with a stop at the parish in Trois-Rivières to meet the Jesuits there. When they approached the mission of St. Francis Xavier at the Sault, plump old Marcel grunted excitedly, "Kanawaka! Kanawaka!" and slapped his paddle on the side of the canoe between strokes.

The sun broke free of the clouds and radiated down upon the small stockade and the cluster of small cabins and long houses, one peaked building with a crucifix upon it in the center. Two dozen or so canoes were inverted on the bank, and a grass swale let up from the river to the flat land. A large man on the shore spied them and raised his arms in greeting. He was lashing a bark panel to the ash framework to make a new canoe. Chauchetière reached behind himself and located his wide-brimmed hat to identify himself as a priest, and as they drew closer he observed the large man leave his work and walk easily along the bank to welcome them.

"Kwe! Kwe!" the man called with his right hand upraised. He was at least six-feet tall and light-skinned. He wore no paint or tattoos. His hair rose above his scalp about three inches in the Mohawk rooster comb. Down his back was a long braid tied up with a red eel skin ribbon. He had a massive jaw and great shoulders and arms. He was working bare-chested, and he wore fringed buckskin trousers and moccasins. Around his right wrist was a rawhide bracelet. "Welcome, Marcel! And our new Father! Who is the young man you have doing all the work?"

"He is Gascon," Marcel called. "My sister's son. A most skilled navigator."

"Who is that man?" the boy asked his uncle.

"It is Joseph Kryn, the greatest of all the Mohawks."

Claude shuddered as he looked upon the man. Whether from

his presence or the legend, Claude immediately felt his charm and his air of command.

Joseph Kryn waded into the water and took the bow of the canoe in his left hand and gave Father Claude his arm in a firm salutation. Father Claude felt the bulging muscles of his forearm as the chief squeezed his own. Looking directly into his eye the priest felt his strong, stamping masculinity held in check by a stronger will, and an even stronger intelligence. Joseph Kryn beached the canoe and helped him out. Marcel came up out of the river, his leggings and moccasins sloshing, and he picked up his wiry nephew and tossed him to the war chief.

"I'll wager you're a skilled hunter!" Kryn said holding the boy high in the air. He flipped the young man so he landed miraculously on his feet but, looking around, could not figure out exactly how. Marcel then ran at Kryn and nearly knocked him over. Kryn lifted him up in a great bear hug and the two were as foolish as boys together.

"Come, Marcel, you shall share my long house. Things are growing a bit crowded here, but that is good!"

"They say in Lorette that you built a house of timbers and planks with a pitched roof."

Joseph Kryn laughed. "I built it for myself and my family, but the Lord had other plans." He pointed to a large frame building with a crucifix on top. "The fathers needed a larger chapel so I donated it to the mission, and I am now working to build myself another. We shall make you comfortable, and you," he threw a brawny arm over the slender priest, "shall put your bag in the rectory. I will introduce you to everyone."

Father Claude paused a minute to turn and look out over the river. The rapids boiled and thrashed over rocks and a well-worn path showed where the portage trail ran. Across the river were a cluster of thatched huts, the village of La Chine, and far beyond, just visible in front of the pale blue of the distant mountains, another village, Ville Marie, behind a low stockade. To his right was a large headland, Montreal, the Royal Mountain, where it was rumored, but he could not see, a cross had been planted twenty-five years ago by Sieur de Maissonneuve.

"Come along, Father!" Joseph Kryn urged him. "It's time to rest and eat."

"Thank you," Father Claude said, and then he noticed something quite shocking. He was speaking the Iroquois tongue without effort. Father Chaumonot's instruction had taken hold.

With Kryn carrying Gasçon on his back, the three men walked together through the swale, past the broad fields along the plain where women were planting and away from the blue river that flowed so purely and boiled white over the broken rocks.

Chapter 21

❧

Tekakwitha Is Baptized "Kateri"

THREE WINTERS FROZE THE LAND with blizzards and ice since Kryn's departure; three springs bloomed with wild flowers and strawberries; three summers of corn ripened in the drone of lazy bees. Still she lived with her uncle and her aunt, an empty life of duty and drudgery in thrall to Iowerano's power and his desire to return to the old ways before the coming of the whites. He made one concession. Given the exodus of his people, he finally agreed to let a blackrobe settle at Kanawaka. In 1674, Father James de Lamberville, came to the mission of St. Peter there replacing the aged Father Boniface who had opened it. Occasionally Tekakwitha saw the blackrobe in the lanes of the village, but her uncle and aunt forbade her to speak to him.

As she walked through the cornfield with her hoe one morning, the shawl shielding her eyes from the bright sun, Tekakwitha stepped into a gopher hole and badly sprained her ankle. Not wanting to draw attention to herself, she stood up and worked all day, but by evening the ankle had swollen so badly, she needed to be carried from the field on a stretcher. She lay by the fire that night, in such pain that she broke into a sweat, and after a fitful rest, Karitha looked at her ankle, swollen to twice its usual size, and told the girl she must remain on her pallet the following day to recover.

Next morning, Father de Lamberville was making his rounds from long house to long house seeking out the old and feeble to bless and counsel, as well as the infants to baptize. Iowerano had paddled down to Albany and Rainbow and Spotted Fawn were visiting the invalid. As Father de Lamberville entered the long house, he spoke:

"Hail, sisters. What have we here?"

"She's hurt her ankle," Rainbow said.

"Let's see," the priest drew closer.

"We have to be off," the other girl said, and they excused themselves and left for the fields.

"Is it painful?" The priest knelt down beside her pallet.

"No, Father. The swelling just needs to go down and I'll be fine."

She looked into the priest's kind face. He had eyes of pale blue and a warm smile from his years of meditation and prayer.

"I hope you feel better," he said and he touched her hand.

"Father?" she asked. "Do you think . . . would it be possible for me to learn the Prayer?"

He smiled and looked deeply into her eyes. Her eyes, so impaired from the smallpox, were unfocused and they were encrusted with a white discharge. He looked from eye to eye to divine which might be seeing him.

"Everyone can learn the Prayer."

"I've wanted to for ever so long."

"Did you ever meet with Father Boniface?"

"No," she looked away. "My uncle, chief of the Turtle Clan, hates the blackrobes. My aunt heaps ridicule on the customs and the ceremonies; yet I long to become Christian."

"Well, then," de Lamberville said, "shall we begin?"

"Yes, oh, yes!" she said, a deep sob welling up within her. "I would like that so very much."

"Can you come with me?"

"Of course."

"I will carry you."

He lifted her up and carried her out of the dim long house. She was quite small and very light and she put her arm around his neck and rested her head upon his chest. As they emerged into the light, she adjusted her shawl. He carried her out of the village to a stone on the hill in the middle of the waving corn. They looked down upon the flowing river and the clouds that swept over the low hills. He sat her on the large rock.

"In the beginning," he began, "God created the heaven and the earth."

"Our elders teach that a woman created the world on the back of a great turtle."

"It will help you learn the Prayer if you put aside such legends. There was nothing before God spoke the word, not a heaven, nor the earth, nor the water, and certainly no turtle. The earth was without form and void and as God created the earth, there was darkness upon the face of the deep, and He moved upon the face of the waters. And God said, 'Let there be light,' and there was light, and God saw that it was good."

She groaned as he said this, so he asked: "Does the light hurt your eyes?"

"Sometimes it is too bright and I must shield them."

"Such is the majesty of God in heaven, my daughter. How are you called?"

"Tekakwitha. She who gropes her way along."

"And yet you see what is hidden from many others. We're created not to see only the world, nor what is of the world or in the world. We're created to see what is within ourselves, the light that shines from within."

"Yes," she sighed, "oh, yes."

"It is a light God has placed within each of us, and it is good."

"I have seen it," she said, "even at night."

"God created the firmament and called it 'Heaven' and he collected the water below heaven in one place and the dry land appeared, and He called it 'Earth.' He called the gathering waters 'the Sea,' and He saw that it was good. And God spoke, 'Let the earth bring forth grass, and the corn-yielding seed and the sweet berry bushes,' and the earth did as He commanded and it was good. And He created two great lights and put them in the sky, one to light the day, which he called 'Sun,' and the other to light the night, which he called 'Moon,' and these lights were to rule the darkness, and He saw that it was good."

The young woman leaned back and closed her eyes and lifted her veil so that the sun kissed her face. She sighed deeply.

"And God brought forth life from the seas, fish of every sort, the great whales, and winged fowl, and God blessed them and said, 'Be fruitful and multiply,' and the fish filled the water and the birds filled the air. And then God created the beasts of the earth, the deer and the elk and the bear and the moose and the wolf and the bobcat, and He saw that it was good, but still it was insufficient. So He created man in His image and likeness, walking upright. And he gave man dominion over all the earth, the fish and fowl and beasts and every creeping thing. He formed man from the dust of the earth and breathed into his nostrils the breath of life, and man became a living soul."

Tekakwitha groaned.

"Then God planted a garden to the east, in Eden, and from the ground He caused to grow every tree that is pleasant to the sight, and in the middle of the garden He planted the Tree of the Knowledge of Good and Evil. And a river went out of Eden to water the garden, and God put the man into the garden to keep it, and He told the man, 'You may freely eat of every tree in the garden, but of the Tree of the Knowledge of Good and Evil you may not eat, for if you do, you will surely die.' Then God said, 'It is not good that man should be alone. I shall make a helpmate for him.'"

"Was Adam a white man or Houdesaunee?" she asked.

"Adam was the first man, father to all of us, no matter what color our skin, white or red or black or yellow."

"There are black and yellow men?"

"In the far corners of the earth there are people who are black and people who are yellow and even now our fathers, the followers of St. Ignatius, seek them out to teach them about God."

"But it is the white man's God, is it not?"

"God is the God of all. He created us all and once we learn of Him, to Him we all will turn. After this man, Adam, named all the creatures, God caused a deep sleep to come over him, and God took out one of his ribs, and from the rib He made woman, and He brought her to Adam and Adam awoke and said, 'Bone of my bones, flesh of my flesh. She shall be called "Woman" for she was taken out of a Man,' and therefore shall a man leave his father and his mother and cleave unto his wife, and they shall be one flesh. They were both naked, but they were not ashamed."

Tekakwitha sat up and pulled her shawl more tightly about her.

"And then evil entered the world," Father de Lamberville said. "The serpent was more subtle than any of the beasts of the field. He crawled into the garden and spoke to the woman . . ."

"Snakes could talk?"

"All the animals and birds spoke in that magical time before sin, and the man and the woman understood their languages. So the snake asked, 'Can you not eat of every tree in the garden?' and the woman answered, 'We may eat the fruit of every tree but one, for God said if we do we shall die.' And the crafty serpent said, 'You certainly will not die, but you will be gods when you know good and evil.' So the woman picked the fruit of the beautiful tree for she thought that she would be wise and that wisdom would be good. And she ate and gave it to her husband. He ate, too, and their eyes were opened and they saw for the first time they were naked."

Tekakwitha sat up, pulled down the shawl against the bright sunlight and opened her eyes to look at the priest. She looked steadily, unflinchingly at him, as if he were the first person in her life who could lead her from the smoky fires of the long house out into sun. He looked into her eyes. He saw her horror and her shame, and also the struggle within her between courage and fear. He saw there a fleeting glimpse of hope until her eyes squinted with customary doubt and she looked away.

"What did they do, knowing they were naked?"

The priest heard in her voice how vulnerable she was and his voice was ever so gentle. He resisted touching her on the shoulder, but he placed his hand above her shoulder.

"They picked fig leaves," he said softly, "and sewed them together and they made aprons to cover themselves, and when they heard the voice of God walking in the garden, they hid from him. The Lord God called to them, and Adam answered, 'I am here, Lord.' And God asked him why he was hiding. 'I am afraid,' the man said, 'for I know I am naked.'

"'Who told you that you were naked?' God asked.

"'No one.'

"'Have you eaten of the fruit of the tree that I forbade you to eat?'

"And the man answered, 'The woman you gave me told me to eat of the fruit, and I did.'

"So the Lord said to the woman, 'What have you done?' and the woman answered, 'The serpent tricked me.' And the Lord said to the serpent, who then had arms and legs: 'Because you have done this, you are cursed to live below the cattle and the beasts of the fields. Upon your belly you shall crawl, and you shall eat dust all the days of your life. I will make the woman your enemy, and she shall bruise your head with her heel.'

"Then God turned to the woman and said, 'In sorrow shall you bring forth children, and your husband shall rule over you.' Then to the man he said, 'Because you listened to the woman and disobeyed me, thorns and thistles will spring up in your garden, and you will make your living by the sweat of your brow until you return to the earth for out of it were you taken. Dust you are and unto dust you shall return.'

"And then the Lord made coats of skins for the man and the woman to clothe them, then expelled them from the garden to till the earth by the sweat of their brow, and he placed an angel with a flaming sword at the gate of Eden to guard the Tree of Life forever."

They sat upon the stone together, this slender, ascetic in his black soutane, his weathered face and long bony fingers, and the small scarred, half-blind Mohawk girl, shrouded from the sunlight by her shawl.

"Were they ever allowed to go back?"

"No. They lost Eden forever. These were the parents of the whole human race, yours and mine and everyone's, condemned to work and bear children and suffer from disease and pestilence because of their sin."

"And God punished them and us and never relented?"

"You are wise, little one, far beyond your years. He did relent. He did forgive. That is the message I bring to you. God sent his only son down upon the earth. God gave Him human form, and His son is Jesus Christ, our Savior, born to lead us to the eternal kingdom of heaven."

She was nodding.

"You know of Jesus?"

"I have seen Father Boniface place the wooden baby Jesus in the manger in the chapel in the winter." She turned to look at him and her eyes, again, were unfocused. She spoke softly. "I have longed to learn of Jesus, but my uncle threatens to banish me from the long house, if I learn the Prayer." She looked up and tried to focus her eyes against the bright sun. "Is this Prayer you teach, the knowledge of good and evil?"

Father de Lamberville smiled at her quick logic. "Yes, the Prayer is the knowledge of good and evil."

"Then it brings only death and banishment?"

"You tie my words into knots."

"I want to understand." She looked curiously at him. "I have witnessed the death of prisoners, only through my ears, for it is wrong to attend such events. If the Prayer brings death, as it did to the first father and the first mother, why do we learn it?"

The priest plucked long stem of the grass and snapped off seeds at the top. "Do you go to the fields to plant the seeds of corn and squash and beans in the mounds?"

"Yes. I have a planting stick, and we do that after the snow leaves and the earth softens."

"Are the seeds alive like this?"

"No, the corn is dried from hanging in the rafters of the long house all winter, the beans and squash from being stored in bark bins."

"Before it can be reborn in the soil, the seed must die. In such a way, we must die in order to be reborn and to grow."

"But I do not wish to die."

"This is the heart of my message. Because Jesus Christ died on the cross for us, we need not die to be redeemed. He has done it for us. Instead of burning prisoners to gain strength, we celebrate Christ's sacrifice during the mass. We transform the bread and wine into his body and blood, and we eat the bread of life and drink his life-giving blood, and with the knowledge of good and evil, we are redeemed. Our life of banishment and sorrow has a purpose, then, the destination of heaven."

"Joseph Kryn led Anastasia and many others to La Prairie. He returns each summer to lead others there as well."

"The Great Mohawk is an able leader and a good man."

"He believes that the mission is a place of redemption."

"You progress very rapidly," the priest said.

"I have longed to know the Prayer my whole life. My mother was Christian and I see now why that was so."

"Why?" the priest asked

"Because my mother was full of love. I remember her from time to time, how she possessed me. Unlike my aunt now, my mother held no envy or criticism or anger or frustration." She sighed. "If I might only regain that . . ."

"You shall," the priest said, and he stood and gathered her. "I will show you the path."

From this initial talk, Father de Lamberville sensed the deep spiritual gifts of this young woman. He inquired about her among the villagers. Reports of her virtue were universal. Although she embroidered designs upon the skins and made the wampum belts for the councils and treaty ceremonies, she was plain in her dress and simple in her habits, retiring, shy and docile. No whisper of criticism did he hear.

In the ensuing weeks he saw that her compliant behavior disguised a firm willpower, and strong opinions, such as her opinion on marriage. On the issue of chastity she never wavered. The scars of her face and the faulty eyesight caused lusty hunters and young, untested warriors to pass her by, to attend the Green Corn Moon festival and the Harvest Home with the coquettes who braided beads and feathers in their hair. She had lived apart all of her nineteen years, asking only a subsistence for herself, serving her aunt and uncle and the rest of the long house by fetching water and firewood, by pounding corn into meal with mortar and pestle, by embroidering the festival garments and the ceremonial robes with her strikingly original patterns and emblems.

Father de Lamberville followed up the meeting with another. He gave her a rosary and he taught her the *Pater Noster* and the

Ave Maria and the *Gloriam*, showing her how to tick off the beads as she prayed. She carried the rosary everywhere, a symbol of her studying to enter the new faith. He instructed her in doctrines of the church: the holy trinity, the virgin birth, transubstantiation. He showed her from his picture book the golden bliss of heaven, the fiery tortures of hell. He read to her from his hagiography on the saints, and she was transported hearing how so many suffered so much on account of their faith.

The priest was honestly surprised at how quickly and how deeply she learned the lessons of faith. Her mind grasped abstract concepts with a preternatural skill, placing them immediately into her growing matrix of beliefs and giving herself over immediately to the new idea. His instruction intensified the flame of her faith and her zeal so that her whole being resonated with new spiritual energy.

Witnessing her swift progress, Father de Lamberville soon offered to baptize her. She accepted immediately. Yet sensing his own well-being and that of his mission might be in jeopardy for converting the "daughter" of the chief, he conditioned her baptism on her informing her uncle. Never sneaky or duplicitous, Tekakwitha soon approached her uncle to tell him of her choice to receive the priest's teachings. She waited until he was content after a good meal of grilled trout and venison and he was sitting back smoking his pipe.

"Have you had enough to eat, Uncle?" she asked.

"Our hunters and fishermen please me," he said, "and you are skilled in preparing the meat and the fish upon the fire. This peace has many benefits."

"I am happy that I please you," she said. "Can I have your ear for a moment to inform you of a decision I have made?"

"You have chosen a husband?"

"No, Uncle." She bowed her head, astonished yet again by his insensitivity. "I have spoken with the blackrobe."

"Oh?" He opened his eyes and she saw his anger. "The one who encourages women to be upstarts and our villagers to leave for the north? That same blackrobe?"

"It is not like that, Uncle. He is a good man."

"He brings the double-tongued words of the whites to un-man us in battle and turn the other cheek even as they steal our lands. Is that a truthful man? Is that a good man?"

"He reveals a world beyond our land, a place of peace and beauty and radiant sunshine where there is no hunger or sickness or suffering, and he shows how we might get there by following the path of righteousness."

"Daydreams!" Iowerano spat into the fire pit. "He tells fables and the gullible believe him until one day we will be cleared from our lands and the whites will plant our fields and dig their metals from our hills and sweep along our rivers in their sailed vessels. All their lies about a better place are intended to lull us into passivity so we won't resist them. There is only here and there is only now and when we die, we're dead."

"I do not seek to persuade you, Uncle, I only tell you so you know what I am doing and it will be no surprise."

"You are seeking my approval?"

"No. I make my own choice in this as in all things. I simply don't want you hearing it from anyone else."

"Well, you are honorable to inform me yourself and not go behind my back." He smoked his pipe and considered. "Perhaps it is not so foolish as some of the girls who chase after the young men and soon must wear the papoose board with no hunter to bring in fresh meat."

"I will be going to the chapel each morning," she said, "and on Sundays, one day in seven, I will not work, yet I will make up for it by accomplishing more during the other six days."

"Very well," he said. "See that you do."

She left him smoking his pipe. She pulled up her shawl to form a hood and went out into the bright afternoon and hastened along the lanes to the chapel. The chapel had a door of split logs, fashioned after the manner of the French, on leather hinges. She opened the door and drew in the smell of sanctity—pine from the boughs decorating the altar, beeswax candles, a faint suggestion of incense. She knelt and blessed herself as the priest had instructed her, and she gave herself over to joyful prayer, in complete thanksgiving that a great obstacle had been removed.

Father de Lamberville wasted no time in bringing this young woman into his congregation. On Ash Wednesday he told her that if she wished, he would baptize her Easter Sunday.

"Oh, yes, Father!" she wept for joy. "Oh, thank you!"

As her training proceeded, she chose the name 'Kateri', the Mohawk form for the name Catherine of Siena, a mystic virgin who, despite her aristocratic birth, served the Lord by bringing the papacy back to Italy from its interregnum exile at Avignon, France. Possibly, too, she recalled the holy Catherine who converted Kryn.

It was too early for wild flowers, but the women decorated the rustic chapel with pine boughs and feathers and furs. Father de Lamberville rehearsed the choir—all shapes and sizes and ages of natives—to sing the harmonious mass of Christ's triumph over death.

The morning of April 5, 1676, was sunny and cloudless in the valley of the Mohawks and the new and old converts sat on the log benches at St. Peter's chapel in Kanawaka as Tekakwitha walked up the aisle in a simple tunic of white doe skin, her hair braided and tied with a red eel skin ribbon, her leggings tied with leather thongs, her eyes downcast with humility, but her heart soaring with joy. She knelt and Father de Lamberville asked her the questions:

"Do you renounce Satan?"

"I do."

"And all his works and wiles?"

"I do."

And when she answered his questions, he dribbled holy water upon her forehead and as the choir sang about the risen Lord, he made a sign of the cross with chrism:

"I baptize thee 'Kateri' in the name of the Father, and of the Son, and of the Holy Spirit."

"Amen," she said and tears of joy flowed from her bedimmed eyes.

Chapter 22

Kateri's Life As A Christian
In The Valley Of The Mohawks

KATERI'S JOY AT BEING BAPTIZED a Christian knew no limit. It was not the label or the association with others of like mind. Rather, it was a deep shift within her where her yearning for transcendence had now found its path. All her confusions and difficulties vanished before the two great commandments of Jesus—love the Lord your God and love your neighbor as yourself. The crucified savior over the altar where the priest consecrated the bread and wine, and where she prayed each day, reminded her constantly of Christ's blood sacrifice, freely given to end all blood sacrifices.

She attended mass each morning at four and remained in the chapel afterward praying. Once or twice during the day she broke away from her work and hastened to the chapel to kneel in the dim quiet and tick off the prayers on the beads of her rosary. Always retiring and shy, she retreated even further from life in her long house and the village, hardly speaking to the others, never gossiping or maligning others, even as she joined more enthusiastically in the life of the mission chapel. The priest guided her impulse with wisdom and with care and was astonished as she progressed in the knowledge and love of Jesus Christ. He surmised that faith and hope and charity, slumbering in her soul as it slumbered in every soul, was now awakening. He noted that all within the Christian community felt touched by her grace, her humility, her kindness and inner peace.

At first Moneta and Iowerano gave her complete license to practice her faith. Viewing it as a silly indulgence, they ignored her comings and goings. Such an outcast had she always been among them, they rarely noticed her absence. As reports of her good works reached their ears, though, how sweet and kind she was to a child, how she attended at a rather difficult delivery of a baby, how she brought food to an elderly man, envy crept into their hearts for she thought more of others than she thought of her own family. The persecution began about a month after her baptism.

Moneta found chores in the fields surrounding the village to keep Tekakwitha from returning to the chapel in the afternoon to pray. She assigned her the farthest section of the fields to plant and gave her the largest bag of seed corn and then she followed up by ridiculing the young woman for not properly weeding the mounds where they planted beans and squash and corn.

One day, Kateri did not appear for the noon meal. All the other women and girls assembled under a spreading oak and they reclined and ate dried fish and strips of venison jerky and corn porridge, and they drank out of a gourd cup from a nearby spring, but Kateri never came. As the women went back to the fields, Moneta went searching for her. Kateri was not in the field where Moneta had assigned her. Rather than call and alert her, Moneta wanted to surprise her. She found Kateri's planting stick and doeskin bag at the edge of the forest near a path into the trees. Into the shade Moneta went, stealthily, her bare feet on the cool earth of the path. Fifty, a hundred steps, two hundred she went until she found the thicket where Kateri knelt, her arms spread, her head back and her mouth moving in prayer. On the great pine tree before her Kateri had placed a small cross.

"So, this is how you waste your time when the rest of us are working?"

Kateri turned, an otherworldly smile upon her face. "I did not realize so much time had passed." She stood.

"You missed your meal and all the food has been eaten."

"I was not hungry for food," Kateri said. Seeing such happiness and joy in her face, Moneta exploded in rage.

"I will see that you give up this madness! Get back to work!"

"I will work, Aunt. I always do. You need not be concerned about that."

Moneta reached out and tilted the young woman's face up. "The disease has left your face pitted and scarred. What sort of man would have you?"

"We've resolved all that, Aunt. We need not discuss it anymore. I will work. You need not fear."

With submission and respect, Kateri walked past her and picked up her planting stick and her bag of seed and returned to her work while Moneta watched her suspiciously and wondered how she could be so content by herself as the others relaxing in the dale nearby chatted and gossiped and giggled.

From that day forward, Moneta carried her resentments closer to the surface. Whether she knew and envied and hated Kateri's mother, or whether it was that Kateri's great virtues cast a stark light on her duplicities, Moneta actively persecuted the young women. When on Sundays Kateri remained home from the fields, Moneta deprived her of food for the whole day:

"If you're not going to work as a Mohawk, you won't eat with the Mohawks," she said, and Kateri quietly retreated to her corner and fasted, offering up her hunger to her Lord Jesus Christ. After four or five Sundays, she told Father de Lamberville, and he responded.

"Their persecution shows they hold you in a high regard."

"A high regard by depriving me of food?"

"They want to break you. This signifies they are testing you to see if your faith is strong. Although it seems to be punishment, it is really a measure of their admiration for if they were indifferent they would do nothing. Can you bear it?"

"I am Mohawk. I have lived through famines and on the hunt when there is no game. This is not so difficult for the body. It is difficult only for the heart, because it seems so needless."

"Go on about your life with cheer and hope. They will soon see their punishments do not affect you, and they will stop."

And yet, rather than abate, the criticism and ostracism grew more severe. Young children threw stones at her as she returned from mass in the chapel and called her "Christian" in derision. Her peers, never close or sympathetic to the scarred and orphaned half-breed, ignored her now completely as they decorated themselves with dyed eel skin and necklaces of wolf teeth and quartz. Her uncle hardly noticed her, and when he did, he merely grunted as if she were a dog who needed to be trained.

One rainy morning, as she embroidered in her cabin, a young warrior rushed in and waved a war hatchet high above his head: "Christian! Renounce your faith or I will kill you!"

Kateri showed no sign of fear. She kept up her embroidery and never looked at him, and seeing he could not penetrate her equanimity, he fled from the cabin. It was agreed by this incident, that she always kept herself ready to die.

The worst test of her faith, though, came again from Moneta. As the trees mellowed in the fall, Kateri accompanied her uncle in a trading party to Albany so that she might hear what the whites wanted by way of embroidery. They were gone ten days. Soon after their return, Kateri referred to Iowerano by his name, which was a familiar and intimate method of address, and not with the customary "uncle" that showed respect. Moneta, in a sour mood, hastened off to Father de Lamberville.

"I have a bit of news about your precious little Christian," she said. "She traveled with my husband, her uncle of the blood, and near the trading post she seduced him."

"What causes this belief in you?" the priest asked. He skepticism caused Moneta to become aggressive.

"All along I have suspected her clandestine relationship with my husband, and now I have it confirmed. She called him 'Iowerano.'" And Moneta nodded all-knowingly.

"She did that?" Father de Lamberville found it difficult to take this woman seriously. He smiled. "Then that is surely proof of her mortal sin."

"You have said it, not I." She folded her arm in a huff. "Now what do you think of your precious little Christian?"

"I will speak with her," he said. As he escorted the woman from the dim chapel out into the sunshine, he mused how the rare purity Kateri possessed could engender such envy among the defiled. "Send her to me."

Later that afternoon Kateri appeared at the chapel. "Father, my aunt said you wished to speak with me."

He observed her expression and her posture—not a hint of guilt or defensiveness.

"She told me you addressed your uncle by his given name."

"I did."

"Why did you do that?"

"He put our relationship upon a different footing."

"How do you mean?"

"My name, since I have received the holy water, is 'Kateri,' and as 'Kateri' I wish to be known. He called me 'Tekakwitha,' my former name which means 'she who gropes her way along.' I am no longer blind, Father. I do not grope, as if in the darkness. I see more clearly now than ever before. His name, 'Iowerano,' and means 'Cold Wind.' When he called me by my old name, I called him by his. Was this a sin?"

"Your aunt says it signifies you have been intimate with him."

The young woman looked at him directly. Her eyes, usually bedimmed or clouded with a film, were clear now, deep and direct.

"She knows that is not so," the young woman said quietly. "Why does she feel it necessary to lie in order to discredit me?"

"The world cannot abide purity." He waved toward the crucifix. "Look at what they did to our Savior."

"I am no threat to her, or anyone else," the young woman said. "They behave the same when I refuse to marry. I live as I wish. It should be nothing to them. How can I respond to their hatred and their criticism and their gossip?"

"Does it make you angry?"

"No," she bowed her head. "I think of what Jesus suffered for my sake. I keep His goodness always before me in order to remain pure. What business is my conduct to anyone? Their lies are harsh and waste much time and energy."

"Come with me," the priest said, and he led her to the chapel. Together they knelt at the split-log communion rail. Before them hung Jesus Christ crucified. They prayed together for Him to give Kateri strength in her trials.

Emerging into the sunshine once more, the priest spoke:

"You must get away from all of this. It is not healthy for you to suffer from their calumny."

She inclined her head toward the priest. "Tell me."

"You should live where people love and respect each other as Jesus taught us to do. You will not prosper here with the envy of these villagers always singling you out for ridicule. They try to pull you back into the old ways even as you move forward into the new."

"Where can I live, then?"

"The mission in the north."

"With Joseph Kryn and Karitha and little Martin?"

"Yes," he said.

"Even Rainbow, my sister, has moved there!" Kateri began to sob and she buried her face in her hands. "Oh, yes, Father! How often have I wished for that!" She dried her tears, and an uncharacteristic fear shone forth. "Rainbow's mother divorced my uncle and moved her to the mission. I am still under his sway and Moneta is terribly opposed. My uncle will never consent."

"Perhaps," the priest said gently, watching for her reaction, "you don't require it anymore."

The notion that she might make her own decision of where to live, as she had about her faith, caused her to brighten. She dried her eyes and said nothing, but Father de Lamberville realized she was even then making up her mind to depart.

The following day the priest visited Moneta as she was pounding corn in front of her long house.

"I have spoken to Kateri," he said. "I am satisfied that she committed no sin."

"I knew you would clear her. Such are her wiles that she is able even to deceive you."

"Your hatred and your suspicion are directed at her to ruin her peace of mind," he said. "I understand this. What you should understand is how you are losing her."

"Humph!" Moneta grunted. "Where would the likes of her go?"

"The mission."

"Let her go! Let her go! Garahonto and Rainbow have deserted us, too! What does it matter anymore? She doesn't want to embrace our ways. It took outright bribery for me to get a young man to consider marrying her. Who will have her other than her family? Let someone take her in. She is nothing but a burden to us. Another mouth to feed."

"Be careful," the priest said. "Sometimes we get what we wish for."

"The blackrobe speaks in riddles. Let her leave our family if she must. It will be no loss to us."

"As you say," he nodded, tipped his wide-brimmed hat and moved away from her.

Chapter 23

Kateri Escapes To The Mission

Each spring, men from the missions stopped in Kanawaka on their way to invite other Iroquois to travel north and settle on the banks of the St. Lawrence. Joseph Kryn came each year to encourage his relatives and friends to join him, but this year, before he arrived, another great warrior, Hot Cinders, the Oneida chief, came to Kanawaka shortly after ice left the river.

Hot Cinders, like Kryn, was respected for his valor in war. His name reflected his smoldering personality, able with the flimsiest of kindling to burst into flame. Hearing that his brother was killed in the north years before, he concluded the murderer must be French and set off in a rage toward Ville Marie vowing to kill the first Frenchman he found. He camped for the night at the mission of St. Francis Xavier, and there heard that an Algonquin, not a Frenchman, killed his brother. Rather than return to Oneida and arouse the sympathies of his nation against the Algonquins, he remained at the mission and received instruction in the Christian faith. After a few weeks, he summoned his wife, and she brought their children. In due course they were baptized together and Hot Cinders built a house for them. The two warriors, Hot Cinders and Joseph Kryn, who had built another large house at the mission, became dear friends.

With his fiery oratory, Hot Cinders preached the gospel to the Iroquois. He railed about the horrors of the infernal pit of hell that awaited sinners, and in happy, glowing terms he described the rewards awaiting the just and the virtuous in heaven. Soon he was chosen as a chief for the mission, but during the ceremony a mistake was made. Customarily when a chief was chosen, he was given an antlered bonnet, a reed mat for sitting in the council and a calumet pipe. During his investiture, Hot Cinders received the bonnet and the pipe, but there was no mat to sit upon. Immediately afterward he stormed into Father Frémin, the superior of the mission:

"They treat me like a child! By giving me no mat, do they expect me to hold council out of doors?"

Amused, Father Frémin assured Hot Cinders this was simply an oversight. He reconvened the elders to rectify the mistake.

When the Oneidas realized their great chief was lost to them, they sent an emissary to the mission to inform him they would welcome him home and allow him to live as a Christian among them. At first he sent back the message, "I care for nothing but my faith and so I will remain here," but considering how they had reached out for his leadership, he saw his opportunity to convert many of them, and so he journeyed to Oneida to recruit new converts. To accompany him he chose a young Huron and a young Algonquin from Trois-Rivières. The Algonquin, Jean-Baptiste, had just married Kateri's adopted sister Rainbow who was baptized Camille. In a long canoe of elm bark Hot Cinders and his two companions paddled up the Richelieu and across the long lakes. They beached and hid the canoe and trekked overland to Kanawaka.

As news of the arrival of Hot Cinders spread, the villagers came out to meet him. He paraded up from the landing place like a conquering hero, and in through the gate to the central yard he went.

"My people!" he cried with his arms raised, for he was an accomplished orator, "I have come from the mission where your good Joseph Kryn now makes his home. He wishes you well and encourages all of you to join us at the Sault. In the midst of the mission we have built a chapel. The bell in the chapel regulates our days, calling us to prayer or sending us into the field. There is no idleness. There is no drunkenness. We live in peace and tranquility, working and praying together."

The crowd numbered three hundred who had turned out for the speech, and in the front, able to reach out and touch Hot Cinders, stood Kateri Tekakwitha, listening and forming her vow. "Here, in this land, you have constant war. The English and the Dutch soak your villages with brandy and gin to cheat you of a fair price for the furs, serving the interest of kings across the sea. We can no longer ignore the whites in our land. If we were to wage war for a generation they would still keep arriving in their great ships. If we cannot rid this land of whites, then we must choose and give our loyalty to those whites who best serve our interest. The French treat us with respect. Father Frémin has rid us of the whiskey traders. The blackrobes teach us how to live in peace and harmony together, not always fighting for what we do not possess. If you want to live in peace, you must leave this place and journey to the mission."

Hot Cinders spoke for three hours, and the villagers listened in rapt attention. At the end of his speech, Kateri approached him.

"I wish to accompany you to the mission," she said.

"How are you called?"

"Kateri Tekakwitha."

A great smile spread across Hot Cinders's face. "Joseph Kryn told me to seek you out and bring you to the mission if you are willing."

"I long for nothing else."

Hot Cinders called over the Algonquin lad. "This is Jean-Baptiste," he said. "He has married your sister, who is now called Camille."

Jean-Baptiste bowed respectfully. "Camille, whom you knew as 'Rainbow,' asked me to locate you and bring you back with me."

Kateri nodded, closed her eyes and knew that God was opening this path for her escape.

"I am not immediately returning to the mission," Hot Cinders continued. "I am journeying to Oneida to speak with my countrymen and I hope to lead another party to the mission. These young men, though, will be going back tomorrow, and you are welcome to take my place in the canoe."

"I left Camille at Fort St. Louis," Jean-Baptiste explained. "We must go to Trois-Rivières, but I can take you as far as Fort St. Louis and we can send word to the mission."

"I will leave with you," she said with determination.

Kateri's uncle and aunt happened to be away, gone to Albany to negotiate a treaty with the English. Kateri went to see Father de Lamberville.

"I listened to Hot Cinders speak, Father, and it has stirred me to action."

"Will you now journey to the mission?"

"Yes, never to return."

"I understand. I shall write you a letter of introduction. I know Father Frémin well. He will make you feel welcome."

"Anastasia is there, and Joseph Kryn and Karitha and Rainbow who is now called Camille, and many others of our village. I am certain to find a home."

She returned to her long house and put her few belongings in a pack. After a fitful night of sleep, she met Jean-Baptiste and the Huron youth at the eastern gate. The autumn sun was rising over the mist of the river and the trees were beginning to change color. They set out on foot together toward the Dutch settlement of Corlaer. There they would buy bread with wampum beads and then turn northward.

Although she told no one but the priest of her plan, White Adder, the shaman, observed their departure. He sent a boy to summon Iowerano with the news. Indeed, Iowerano had just portaged the Cohoes Falls on his way home when the boy reached him. Breathlessly he related that Kateri was fleeing.

"This is what comes of the blackrobe's meddling!" Iowerano exploded. He put his back into the paddling. When he reached Corlaer, he disembarked, loaded his musket and set off across the pine barrens to intercept them on the trail.

Meanwhile, the three were just west of Corlaer. Jean-Baptiste told Kateri and the Huron to hide in a clump of pine while he went into the village. As he approached riverbank across from the stockade, Jean-Baptiste saw Iowerano lumbering across the shallows.

"Hiro!" the chief called in greeting. Jean-Baptiste answered. "Have you seen a girl on the trail? She is small, this high, and wears a shawl to cover her eyes. Her face is marked with scars and she walks slowly because her eyes are poor. I am her uncle and she is my kin."

"I have seen no one like this," Jean-Baptiste said.

The chief expressed his frustration. "She is in the company of two young men!"

"I have not seen them," Jean-Baptiste said.

"If you do, tell her to return to the village at once. If I catch them fleeing, they will pay with their lives."

"Who would ever think to flee such a household?"

Iowerano paused, narrowed his eyes suspiciously, and Jean-Baptiste bowed and moved past him. After buying bread, Jean-Baptiste returned to Kateri and the Huron lad and they set out.

When they reached the bank of the great lake three days later, Jean-Baptiste and the Huron brought Hot Cinders's canoe out from the brush where they had hidden it. They helped Kateri step into the middle and they began the long journey up the lake.

Beneath the rickety wooden stockade of Fort St. Louis, at the point of land where the Richelieu pours into the St. Lawrence, a cluster of huts had been thrown up to house the itinerant natives going up and down river with their pelts and wampum and, occasionally, tin or iron goods to trade. Camille met Jean-Baptiste's canoe at the docking place, and cried out in joy seeing Kateri. First Camille hugged her husband, and then she held Kateri tightly.

"It is good you have come," she said. "You will be so happy at the mission."

Kateri held Camille more tightly. "I have prayed and prayed for this day."

"We live with Anastasia. I'm sure she will welcome you to join us."

"Anastasia!" The joy in her heart knew no limit. Tears streamed down her face. Hand in hand the four of them went to a low hut and shared a meal of sagamite. A canoe, unfortunately filled, was departing for the Mission of St. Francis Xavier, but they sent word along that Kateri was at the fort. The following morning, Camille and Jean-Baptiste and the Huron started down river to Trois-Rivières, and Kateri stood upon the bank of the broad river, the broadest she had ever seen, waving farewell.

Chapter 24

❧

Kateri Arrives At The Mission

AFTER SHOWING FATHER CLAUDE the new chapel, Kryn deposited him at the rectory, promising to collect him in a short time for a meal in the long house of his old friend Anastasia.

Father Claude knocked gently on the lintel and entered. After living with Father Chaumonot, he felt apprehensive about sharing close quarters with two other men who had far more experience than he among these people. Also, Father Frémin and Father Cholenec had just ejected Michel Cocteau on a suspicion of impurity.

"Is that the new father?" he heard.

"Father Frémin?"

A white face loomed out of the shadows. It had thin, abstemious lips, a lean jaw with a pointed chin and small brown eyes.

"Welcome, my son." Frémin was in his fifties and many winters had aged his complexion. "You may put your bag upon that bunk. You will share a room with Father Cholenec. He is across the river in Ville Marie at present, but shall return in a few days."

"I have met Joseph Kryn and he has invited me to supper. Would you care to join us?"

The priest tightened his thin, bloodless lips and worked his neck up out of the Roman collar. "I don't believe undue fraternizing helps us with the natives," he said. "They hold us in such reverence we should insulate ourselves from their perceptions of our more human natures."

"Are you saying I should not attend the supper?"

The priest's eyes bored into his. "Now, now, let's not put words in my mouth. I said nothing of the sort, nor was I hinting at that. I merely suggested that fraternizing with these savages has its perils."

"I met Joseph Kryn," Chauchetière said, "and I was most impressed."

"Kryn is one of our hardiest warrior chiefs."

"There are others?"

"Yes," Father Frémin said proudly. "We have an Oneida chief, too, named Hot Cinders. This man is mercurial and explodes anytime he's challenged or senses others are hemming him in. He and Joseph Kryn are our chiefs now, and have become great friends. Hot Cinders is away just now, returned to the land of the Iroquois recruiting more converts. The mission grows and grows." A smile played at Father Frémin's lips for he took credit for the great expansion.

"Soon you will have all of the Iroquois nations walking these streets."

"Our mission is God's special place," Father Frémin said to address the note of irony he heard in Claude's retort. "Here natives from all nations assemble to free themselves from the violence and superstition, and together, like voices in a choir—under my guidance they have developed into two quite accomplished choral groups, men and women—we plow the earth and grow the corn and live our simple lives. They cut the timber and build the houses. They journey into the forests and hunt game for meat, and they dress the skins for clothing."

Claude looked about with appreciation. This place surely had a more beneficent feel than Lorette. "St. Francis seems a very holy place," he said.

"Consider, Father. We do not enslave the natives as do the

Spaniards in Mexico; nor do we corrupt them as do the English with their liquor and their wars. So quickly does our mission grow, that we require a new chapel which is under construction by French carpenters."

"Joseph Kryn took me there," the younger priest said.

"You will see that the spiritual gifts of these natives are second to none. They have proven to me that God is universal to all races, Father, not dependent upon language or place. Opening their hearts to the message of Christ is our gift to them, and their gift to us is the affirmation of our highest ideals."

"I look forward to experiencing this," Father Claude said. "I was a year at Lorette, and the ignorance and squalor were overwhelming. Here the ground is fertile indeed."

"One caveat, though, Father."

"Yes?"

"The devil lurks everywhere. The temptations of liquor appear each time a trader beaches his canoe and enters the mission. The temptations of the flesh follow the natives from their homes and spring up when they get lax or fall away from our regimen. The temptation to backslide into dream ceremonies, or shaman cures occur during times of personal stress. We must be ever vigilant against the wiles of Satan. So, as I say, be careful, Father, of fraternizing too closely."

"Well spoken, Father."

Father Frémin raised his index finger. "Caution and vigilance. We have a duty to them, yes, but we have a duty to ourselves and our order and our God."

"I told Joseph Kryn I would sup with him," Father Claude said.

"Then go along. The generous fellow has given us the house he built for himself to use as our chapel until our new one is completed. He lives in the next row of long houses directly behind here. Stow your bag in your room and I will show you."

Father Claude sighed as he regarded the room to which he had been assigned. It was small, five-by-six and seven feet high. A window, its vertical shutter propped open with a stick, looked down to the river. In the corner was a pile of skins and three makeshift shelves served as storage. On the wall hung a wooden crucifix, carved in France from walnut. Gazing upon this familiar object, he was comforted. Fifty leagues he had paddled and portaged to reach this outpost. He took from his bag his paintbox and his box of chalks. Father Frémin's reservations aside, he felt at home here already.

"Shall we go, Father?" Frémin adjusted his wide-brimmed hat and led Father Claude out into the evening.

The sky was resplendent with sunset, long reaches of pink cloud deepening in hue. As they walked, the sun shone from behind the clouds, casting a bright orange light upon the river and the fields and the houses of the mission, gleaming from the crucifix atop the chapel in the center. Gulls were flying in wide circles above the river bank.

"It is peaceful here," Father Claude observed.

"It is a place God has blessed," Father Frémin agreed.

Children playing in the lanes called greetings to the pastor who occasionally paused and introduced the new priest. When they arrived at the long house, Father Claude held open the bearskin curtain and they entered the long, dim, smoky room. At the center, three fires in, a large group of natives was sitting and squatting on the ground. The house was bigger than the ones at Lorette and the ceiling seemed like a barrel arch over a church aisle. Father Claude saw, as they picked their way along the sleeping shelves, corn with braided husks hanging from the ceiling, and the antlers hung as trophies and the animal skins hanging here and there as a shield for probing eyes. "Hello, Father!" Joseph Kryn called to him and all eyes turned.

"May the Lord be with you," Father Frémin said. "Let me introduce Father Claude to you. He will be helping me and Father Cholenec here and I know you will extend to him every kindness."

Father Claude bowed and those at the feast bowed in response.
"I will leave you now. Feed him well for he looks as though he
could use a good meal."

"Sit down, Father," Kryn said, springing up. "This is my wife
Karitha, this is my son Martin, and this is our kinswoman Anastasia."

Father Claude nodded and greeted each of them. Anastasia stood
up to make room for him. She was a large, commanding woman
with penetrating eyes that, Father Claude observed, possessed a
mesmerizing light. He sat upon the mat they cleared for him and
he accepted a bowl of sagamite sweetened with strawberries. He ate
with his fingers as he listened to the men discuss a fishing expedition.

He understood much of what they said, and as he listened, he
observed them. These were the very Mohawks he had read about.
Physically they seemed larger as a rule than the Hurons of Lorette
and their skin not as swarthy. They seemed vigorous and quick,
gifted speakers and natural story tellers with a wit and a sense of
humor that caused them often to burst into laughter. Father Claude
observed that their ferocity had been focused. Even with violence
channeled, they displayed an unyielding attitude, a presence in the
moment that was strong and firm and commanding. Surely they
approached learning and practicing the tenets of Christianity with
the same fervor.

After dinner Father Claude walked alone on the mud flats. He
gazed up at the moon and murmured a prayer for allowing him to
journey here and to feel the great virtue and magnetism of Joseph Kryn
that, despite the caution of Father Frémin, seemed to be an emanation
of this new place. After so much traveling and doubt, Father Claude
knew that he had arrived where good work might be done.

When he returned to the rectory, Father Frémin was asleep.
Quietly he unpacked his paintbox in the moonlight. He counted
the sheets of paper he had brought and found there to be seventy-
three. He had a used set of chalks and a set of six drawing pens

and ink. He had four paint brushes and a case of pigments. With these he might sketch and even paint people and objects about him. In the moonlight, leaning his back against the log wall of the hut, he began a sketch of the Oneida woman, Gandeacteua, and her husband Tonsanhoten, trudging into Montreal on snowshoes nine years before to found this mission.

In the coming days Father Claude considered the very air of the place charmed. He said daily mass in the chapel. On Sundays the men's and the women's choirs sang the high mass—*Kyrie, Sanctus, Agnus Dei* as well as entrance and communion and recessional hymns—and the joy that pervaded the square where the children played, the fields where the women planted, the new chapel where native men helped French carpenters, lifted his spirit with hope as he felt the bonds of these people being knit into a community.

Father Pierre Cholenec returned from Ville Marie. A few years older than Claude, he seemed agreeable, if a bit distant. He volunteered to answer whatever questions Father Claude might have. Father Claude kept mostly to himself. In the ensuing weeks, Father Claude, the youngest of the three, drew the most menial of duties. All the fathers celebrated mass and administered the sacraments. Father Frémin, the superior, set policy, approved or disapproved building projects, policed the river bank to keep traders with their liquor away, and heard whatever complaints the villagers had with each other. Father Cholenec, next in seniority, administered many of the spiritual needs, confessions, counseling, instruction in the faith and visiting the sick and dying. Father Frémin assigned Father Claude to instruct the children and to fill in as necessary with the other duties.

A messenger had arrived as Father Claude was beginning his second month. He announced that Hot Powder, on his way back to the Oneida nation, had sent a young convert north to the mission.

Her companions were headed for Trois-Rivières, though, and so had deposited her at Fort St. Louis. Father Claude heard Kryn and Anastasia discussing the arrival of this young woman.

"She has received the Prayer then," Anastasia said. "I doubt that Iowerano approved."

"No," Kryn said. "He feels the bite of an insult whenever anyone acts in a manner different from what he would do. He cannot see that we all have free will."

"Tekakwitha always displayed a strong will," Anastasia said.

"Yes, and she showed exceptional talent with embroidery."

"Who is this woman?" Father Claude asked.

"She is my kinswoman," Anastasia said with pride. "Her mother was a Christian Algonquin from Trois-Rivières. The family was stricken with the pox, and the girl escaped with only scars and diminished sight. She has refused to take a husband and is therefore considered poor and destitute. She is the adopted sister of Camille who lives with me, and so I will lodge her at my fire."

"She is a favorite of Karitha and little Martin," Kryn said. "I would be happy to house her, when the chapel is completed and I return to my home."

"Let us see what she will say of the matter," Anastasia said.

"I will go and bring her back," Kryn said, and he set out, alone in his canoe, that very night.

Father Claude thought little of the matter—another communicant boded well for the mission—but it did not seem extraordinary in any way.

He was saying his office one evening, walking along the broad river. Sunset colored the water a deep red, a blood red. He walked slowly, a lone figure, slender, stooped beneath the black, wide-brimmed hat. Gulls cried and circled in the flaming sky and the river poured like lava out of the troubled heart of the continent. The priest was reading his daily office.

"Father?"

It was the voice of Joseph Kryn and it seemed quite close. Father Claude stopped, turned, noticed then the fiery evening and the hush. He folded his book.

"Out here, Father."

Father Claude looked over the water. The voice had come to him easily from a canoe gliding toward him. He saw the bulging arms and shoulders of Joseph Kryn in the stern, his strong, silent paddle scarcely breaking the surface.

"Look who I bring!"

In the bow of the canoe knelt a small figure, a woman, stiff and bolt upright. A blue shawl covered her head. Joseph Kryn's face beamed in the rose light of the sunset. With two more strokes he beached the canoe. It scraped upon the pebbles. Joseph Kryn vaulted easily from the rear of the canoe, his moccasins and leggings splashing in the water. He pulled the canoe high up the shore, then gently helped the small woman stand and step over the gunwale.

The priest approached curiously. Joseph Kryn beamed with joy. He had his big arm about her shoulders, her face still covered. "It is Kateri, Father. From my village. Kateri Tekakwitha."

Father Claude leaned forward to see her face. She was quite small and slender, and painfully shy. She wore a white tunic and leggings and moccasins and she did not look at him. He took all this in waiting to see her face, but she simply stood there, within the shawl.

"Kateri has a letter for you," Joseph Kryn said.

At Kryn's urging the small woman produced a folded paper. Father Claude read it. Father de Lamberville's ornate hand greeted him from the creased and darkened paper. "To Father Frémin: I send you the treasure of my mission," de Lamberville wrote. "Care for her as I have."

The priest, curious, bent and looked into the shadow of the woman's veil.

"It's Father Claude," Joseph explained to her, urging her to reveal herself. Slowly, she lifted her veil. Father Claude gasped for, expecting to see the comely features of a young native woman, he saw instead a squinting face disfigured by pockmarks. Her hair was oiled and braided and done up with a red eel skin band. Despite her scars and half-closed eyes, she held herself with dignity. When she opened her eyes sufficiently to take in light, they were filmy.

"Welcome to La Prairie," Father Claude said, knowing of nothing else to say at the shock of her scars and the film of her eyes.

"I have dreamed of joining you," she said. Mysteriously she pulled her shawl back to hide her face.

"Greet our father in the manner of the whites!" Joseph Kryn said and took her hand and offered it to the priest. When Father Claude touched her hand, he felt an extraordinary surge of energy. Sensing this, she looked up at him imploringly, up out of the shadows of her shawl in the gathering darkness. Pity for her flooded his heart. Her hand was small but strong, and she had callouses from hard work. She put her hand back beneath her shawl.

"Anastasia and her mother were friends," Joseph explained.

"Is your mother back in the land of the Agnies?" Father Claude asked.

"My mother lives now in heaven," Kateri said. "She was Christian."

"I am sorry," the priest said.

"No. She is happy, as you blackrobes teach," the young woman said. "She died long ago, and she is with my father and my baby brother."

The sun had set. Its fading purple light gleamed upon the flowing dark water.

"Let us make you comfortable," the priest said. The touch of her hand, interrupting his prayer, awakened something within him.

Joseph Kryn set his strong jaw and with his arm around the woman, he reached for the priest and they moved off together.

"Come, Father, we will bring her to Anastasia's hut."

Anastasia sat outside the door to her hut pounding corn in a wooden mortar. She saw the three walking toward her up the lane. As she recognized the small woman between them, she dropped the pestle, brushed her hands on her apron and rushed forward.

"Can it be? My little bird!"

Kateri, still within the shawl, curled into the older woman's embrace.

"I've known this child since her birth," Anastasia boasted. "My precious, precious one! Her mother was my dear friend, who died, and now Tekakwitha joins us!" Radiant with joy, Anastasia pulled back the blue shawl and held the young woman's head in her hands, kissing her scarred face all over. "My beautiful, beautiful child!" she said. Kateri opened her eyes as wide as she could, and she spoke. Her voice was soft, a whisper:

"It is well we are reunited, Mother. I have been baptized. I am Kateri now."

"Kateri! Yes. We recently lost our Catherine here, and now the Lord sends you to replace her. Come inside! You must be hungry and tired." Anastasia nodded at Joseph Kryn and at Father Chauchetière, and led the young women into her hut.

Chapter 25

Kateri Makes Her First Communion

LIKE A WHITE DOVE RELEASED FROM A CAGE, the soul of Kateri Tekakwitha rose up on new wings and flew strongly and surely into the purest clouds and sunlight. Nature itself sparkled more brightly, breathed more deeply, spread out in the hush of moonlight with more soft mystery than ever in her life because her soul, at last, had found peace. Gone were the grinding quarrels and the constant gossip and eruptions of drunkenness and lechery and unpredictable passions of dream festivals at the narrow old Kanawaka. Now, day and night, in the rising and falling light, the warming and cooling seasons, ever-present here was prayer.

In the morning she stood near a large cross upon the riverbank at this new Kanawaka, her shaded, half-blind eyes drinking in light from the shimmering waters of Lac St. Paul and the foaming rapids of Sault St. Louis and, far to the north in the distance, the slumbering mass of Montreal. The tendrils of smoke in the morning from the chimneys of Ville-Marie cheered her. She stood upon a rise at the foot of the elevated cross, awestruck at the magnificent sweep of this vista, the green of St. Paul Island, and at the base of the rapids, Heron Island. Thrilled with the certainty she had been delivered, her heart, her soul, her very life had been saved, she wept when Father Cholenec read from the Book of Isaiah for she now knew the place where—

"The wolf also shall dwell with the lamb, and the leopard shall lie down with the kid; and the calf and the young lion and the fatling together; and a little child shall lead them. He will judge between the nations and will settle disputes for many peoples. They will beat their swords into plowshares and their spears into pruning hooks. Nation will not take up sword against nation, nor will they train for war anymore."

Father Frémin assigned Father Cholenec to be her confessor, and Father Cholenec observed immediately the spiritual gifts of de Lamberville's note, as he later described:

"The child could scarcely find words to express her happiness. She possessed a true and noble heart; a strong spirit and a courageous character, and as far as myself and Father Chauchetière were able to discover, an insatiable thirst for spiritual knowledge and a great zeal to put into practice all that she understood.

"Her soul was well disposed toward perfection; and throwing herself into her new life with singular devotion, she adopted all the practices which she saw were good in the older converts. In a matter of a few weeks she stood out among all the other women and girls of the village. Here we see Kateri Tekakwitha, having preserved her innocence and holiness through twenty years among the evildoers and unbelievers, become at our mission in such a short time, a saint among the just and the faithful."

Immediately she adapted to the rigors of her new life. In her shawl she hastened through the lanes between the long houses and through the rickety gate of the stockade into the chapel at four each morning. She knelt and prayed until Father Cholenec or Father Chauchetière celebrated the first mass at daybreak. She might return to Anastasia's cabin for breakfast, but then she came back with the entire village to attend mass before going to work. She remained behind in the village while the others went to work outside, the women to the fields and the men to building houses for new immigrants. Kateri worked at her embroidery and beadwork by the cabin fire. Whenever the flood of her feelings for Jesus and Mary overflowed its banks, she quietly left her work, pulled her shawl over her face and hurried to the chapel to kneel and shudder as strong emotions passed through her. Later, in the evening, with the villagers returning—often singing—from their work, she accompanied them again to the chapel for vespers.

If the weather beckoned her to work outside, she sometimes accompanied Anastasia into the forest to gather wood or to the spring for water. Hating gossip and small talk, she avoided the society of others, preferring to remain private about her past and her devotions; yet to Anastasia she opened up, for Anastasia had been her mother's bosom friend.

"Ah, your mother," Anastasia said. "It is no accident you are given to the Prayer. After her baptism in the chapel at Trois-Rivières, she dedicated her life to Holy Mother Mary and had nothing to do with men. We were smoking fish along the river one day when the Mohawks fell upon us. They slew the men and hauled us off to Ossernenon where they made us slaves. Because of her beauty, she escaped torture and death. They spared me as well, though I was far less comely than she. So impressed was the chief of the Turtle Clan by her modesty and her constancy and her lack of any idle vanity, that he took her as his wife. While she wished to remain chaste and apart from men, when she was compelled, she became his dutiful wife, bearing him yourself and your little brother."

"Tell me once more about my family," the young woman asked.

"Your mama's joy at your birth was unbound. She confided in me that her capture and forced marriage, as horrible as that had been, were happy events when you and your brother blessed her life. For four years she was completely devoted to your father and to you, but then the dark cloud of the white man's pox swept through the village. How can I relate those horrors? Most of the village was infected, red sores erupting from the skin of people, and so sudden! In a few days they lay groaning on their pallets; the village was like hell. I was away on a fishing expedition, but when I returned I nursed many who suffered, yourself most of all, and for some reason I was spared.

"Twice the Lord has saved me," Kateri murmured. "Once when my body was threatened by disease, and recently when my soul was threatened by the corruption of our homeland. If the wonders of this mission are mere worldly deliverance, Mother, imagine what heaven will be!"

Sundays and feast days were special to Kateri. She spent the entire day in the chapel on such days. Father Cholenec wrote of the devotion of the entire mission, how the men on one side of the chapel, the women on the other, sang in Iroquois the *Kyrie* and the *Gloria* and the *Credo* and the *Sanctus* and the *Agnus Dei*. So greatly did both priests respect the natural eloquence and the spiritual progress of the Iroquois, they often allowed one of the chiefs to deliver the sermon.

Father Frémin, an accomplished linguist and musician, adapted Iroquois prayers to the eight psalm tones from medieval Christian services. He trained the men and the women's choirs to sing their morning prayers, the liturgy of the mass, the ten commandments, Iroquois hymns, the *Ave Maria* and the benediction of the Blessed Sacrament according to the ancient chants. As Father Cholenec observed later, Kateri soon learned these chants and joyfully participated in them:

"Her devout love for the church services was wholeheartedly sincere. In attaching herself to God, she pursued all avenues to remain in communion with him and to preserve throughout her entire day the good sentiments she experienced early in the morning at the foot of the altar."

So inspiring to all were this neophyte's spiritual gifts that the two priests often discussed her as possessing saintly qualities.

"The moment I met her," Chauchetière told Cholenec one day in autumn, "I felt the spirit of holiness within her. Almighty God chooses special vessels to carry His divine grace among us, and I must submit and bear witness, Father. I have never met anyone who possesses her spiritual gifts."

Father Cholenec nodded, but advised caution. "We must not question His choice, Father. We must bow to God's will which has made us not only witnesses, but ministers to this young woman."

"True beauty and purity shine forth from her," Chauchetière said. "She is the fairest flower of all, so meek, so humble, so retiring, that I worry about the fate of such purity and virtue in this world."

"You don't think her faith could be corrupted?"

"So often has my own faith faltered, I hope beyond all hope hers will be sustained."

Father Cholenec thought for a moment, his finger to his chin. They were sitting together on a bench enjoying the slanting rays of the autumn sun just prior to ringing the mission bell for vespers.

"One recalls the lives of the saints, their hearts so filled with divine love they cannot hide the sacred fire. I believe, Father, such holiness is different in quality, not just in degree, from what ordinary mortals possess. The divine fire within her shines forth like light from a hearth through the windows of a cabin in winter. She is a daughter of these people. Yet so endowed is she with the spirit of God, that despite the shawl and her humble posture, her words shine with divine rapture, and she cannot hide these manifestations from our view."

Again Father Cholenec lapsed into silence. He was considering deeply some great matter. Then he spoke:

"When she appears for the service, could you bring her to me?"

"Of course, of course."

As the mission bell rang for vespers and the workers in their humble clothing filled the lanes of the village, Father Chauchetière waited until she was passing and then he went to her.

"Kateri?"

"Yes, Father?" She had been in deep meditation, preparing herself for the service, but she smiled and her eyes strove to focus on his face.

"Father Cholenec has asked that I bring you to him in the sacristy."

"I have not displeased him, have I?"

"No, of course not."

He touched her elbow to guide her toward a back door in the chapel, and he felt once more her extraordinary energy. Father Cholenec was dressed in his alb and stole and cincture as he welcomed them, "Come in, come in."

"Shall I leave you two?" Father Claude asked.

"No, please sit." Father Cholenec motioned them to two chairs, and he continued to pray silently as he donned his green chasuble. When he was in his vestments, he spoke: "Father Claude and I have observed you, Kateri, and your progress is exemplary."

"Oh, Father!" she sighed. "It is heaven on earth for me to be here with nothing in the way of my devotions."

"Yes." He went to her and reached down and cradled her chin in his hand. "Many have been the backsliders we have baptized and so we have become cautious . . ."

"I am not one of them, Father."

"No, you are not." He smiled kindly. Father Claude looked from one to the other wondering what this all portended. "I have decided that you are ready . . . or rather that you will be ready upon receiving instruction from Father Claude from now until Christmas Day, to receive the Eucharist."

Kateri emitted a cry, fell to her knees and embraced the

priest's legs, sobbing: "I so want to share in the Eucharist, Father, but I am unworthy!"

"You are a ready tabernacle, Kateri, for receiving Our Lord." Father Cholenec turned to Father Claude and Father Claude observed a smile of deep beneficence and even joy upon his pale lips.

"Oh, Father!" she sobbed. "To welcome Our Savior into this body I so detest! To think that He will abide within me! It is more than I have ever hoped. I am humbled beyond words, but ever so grateful!"

The nights lengthened and cold winds blew. Snow came, hesitantly at first, like feathers from a bird in flight, and then more steadily, and then in howling blizzards. From the lazy cornfields of summer and the fishing grounds of autumn, the natives usually packed up their kettles and their bows and arrows, spears and muskets and trudged into the forest on snowshoes for the winter hunt. This year, though, the villagers at the mission remained behind in order to celebrate Christmas Mass and witness the first holy communion of their sister Kateri Tekakwitha.

How they decorated the chapel for the great event! With evergreen and soft furs and embroidered robes for the altar and the communion rail, with candles and rush lamps they lit the interior so that its light shone forth upon the snow. Father Claude and Father Cholenec coached the choir to sing the four-part harmonies of the Shepherd's Mass.

Anastasia insisted on dressing her young kinswoman in white, and she stitched a fringed tunic from a white doeskin. Anastasia braided white beads and feathers in her hair, and used remnants of the doeskin to fashion white leggings. Over her head Kateri pulled her blue tunic, and she and Anastasia labored through the deep snow to the chapel where the choir was already singing carols.

As she entered, the congregation rose and sang *Adeste Fidelis*. Kateri bowed humbly and walked to the front bench where they insisted she hear the mass. As the congregation remained on its feet, Fathers Frémin, Cholenec and Chauchetière came out of the sacristy in white chasubles, the celebrant and two deacons.

The mass proceeded with great happiness and joy, a festival of lights near the longest, darkest night of the year. During the procession at the offertory, Father Frémin lay a wooden carving of the infant Jesus in the *creche* that they had fashioned from branches and evergreen. The congregation was in a state of ecstasy, welcoming the infant Jesus into the world as He had been born to the Virgin so many centuries before. Then at communion, before any of the other communicants received, Father Frémin turned from the crucifix, and he held a host above the ciborium and waited for the maiden to advance.

Bowing her head as the men's and the women's choirs sang *The First Nöel*, Kateri walked slowly up to the communion rail and knelt. Father Frémin with the ciborium and Father Chauchetière with the patten advanced to her. Kateri slowly pulled back her veil so, uncharacteristically, her face might be seen. Making the sign of the cross with the host, Father Frémin held it aloft. As Kateri leaned back her head, opened her mouth and extended her tongue, the priest placed the host upon it. As the host touched her tongue, she shuddered and closed her mouth and bowed her head and made the sign of the cross. As the choir lifted the melody in the flickering candlelight, she stood and found the way back to her pew and knelt and bowed her head in deepest communion with her savior.

Chapter 26

Kateri Leaves The Mission
For The Winter Hunt

THE DAY AFTER CHRISTMAS, villagers packed their kettles and weapons, bedrolls and tents, fastened their snow shoes and trudged off into the foothills and forests. Joseph Kryn's party departed before sunrise. Knowing of Kateri's skills with handiwork, Camille and Jean-Baptiste asked if Kateri would join their party. Kateri took the matter to Anastasia for advice.

"Karitha asked me to join the party of Joseph Kryn, and I declined. I prefer not to go on the hunt," Kateri stated flatly. "Here I have found my heart's delight, and I never want to be away from the chapel and daily mass."

"The mission will be deserted, though," Anastasia told her. "Food stores are running low. You should go on the hunt for there will be fresh meat and much idle time which you might turn to good effect by praying."

Kateri mulled over the idea. She visited Father Cholenec and asked him for guidance.

"True it is that the hunt is a time away from mass and the sacraments, but Anastasia is correct when she says that food will be scarce this winter."

He arose and went into the next room to summon Father Chauchetière who brought a folded paper with him.

"I asked Father Chauchetière to draw calendars for each hunting party. We give them to an advisor in each party to keep track of Sundays and holy days, and to calculate when Easter will fall so that you may return on Palm Sunday." He handed her the folded paper. She looked up at Father Chauchetière and he looked kindly at her. Although he was the quietest of the three priests, he surely was the most sensitive, and she felt he understood more than the others. Father Cholenec continued: "Take this calendar with you, observe it, and all will be fine."

"You're going off with a hunting party?" Chauchetière asked.

"I'd rather remain at the mission with the services and the sacraments."

Father Claude turned to Father Cholenec and spoke in French words she did not understand: "Why don't we employ Kateri in some small way? We could keep her at the mission."

"No," Father Cholenec said, "the hunt is a time of relaxation for these natives. It removes them from the discipline of this life and they return renewed and rededicated."

"But she is so fervent in her practices."

"She should not be singled out for special favors, Father. It would not serve her spiritual progress." Father Cholenec turned to her and spoke in her language. "Your sister desires that you keep her company, Kateri. We desire that you keep her party to the schedule and return them home for Easter."

"As you wish," she said, and she bowed and left them. She returned to Anastasia's cabin to ready herself for the trek to the hunting grounds. Camille was packing the kettle and Jean-Baptiste his musket, his spear, his bow and arrows, his hatchet, hunting knife and fire bow-drill. Upon a square of canvas Kateri folded her doeskin blanket, a tunic of wool, her bone and metal needles of various sizes, her array of dyed porcupine quills for embroidery, a two-pronged iron fork, a knife and a bowl and plate of bark. In her coat she placed her rosary and her small wooden crucifix. They rendezvoused in front of the chapel. They went in and knelt and prayed for good hunting, then they fastened their snowshoes by leather thongs and set off south into the hills.

The wide, bright vistas hurt her eyes and so she pulled the shawl down. She walked in the path behind Jean-Baptiste and Camille. Down her back the heavy pack hung, attached to an eel skin band looped about her forehead. The snow shoes made the walking slow and laborious. So long used to sitting by the fire, she found the exercise tiring and painful, but she did not complain. She bowed her head and leaned into the path and kept up while three dogs fanned out as their scouts.

For five days they walked, a party of twelve—four men, five women, a youth and two little girls. They slept two nights in the shelter of bushes on the plain, and reaching the hills on the third, they slept in a thicket of pine. From the darkness of the cold morning, awakening wrapped in her sleeping robe under a dusting of snow, she rose and knelt on the snow and offered up her prayers to the cold, gray, unanswering sky—sorely missing the small chapel with its railing and altar and tabernacle and crucifix—and then she packed and fastened the band across her forehead and started off once more. As the hills rose into low mountains, Jean-Baptiste looked for a suitable camp. Water was essential, and when he came upon a level tableland sheltered by a forest of pine next to a frozen brook, he signaled they would stop there. In a matter of hours they erected their hut, and while the women set about finding firewood and water, the men went immediately off to hunt.

"Bring some water from upstream," Camille gave Kateri a kettle to be used as a bucket, and the young woman took up a hatchet to cut through the ice, and went outside. The evening was dark and still and the stars glittered like crystals. She fastened on her snowshoes and walked upstream to where the stream gurgled beneath the ice. She chopped a suitable hole in the ice and cleared away the snow, and dipped the kettle into the cold, clean running water. As she pulled the kettle up from the water, she recalled the story of Jesus and the woman by the well, and her heart ached to be in the mission chapel where she might kneel and listen to the priest recite in broken Iroquois those stories of Jesus and his apostles from the New Testament, and from the Old Testament the stories of the nations and kings of Israel and the long exiles into Babylon and Egypt.

A stone's throw upstream Kateri saw a thicket of pine. She left the kettle in the snow, and walked a few steps and bowed and entered the thicket. As sheltered as a chapel it was, boughs above her forming an arch and boughs on all sides enclosing her in a snug little praying cell. She knelt in the snow and wept bitterly. She did not know the cause of the tears, but she missed the quiet chapel and the singing and the regularity of the mission and the daily liturgy. It would be three long dark months before she returned. Until then she would mind the children and hear the gossip and petty complaints of the women, the stories of their lives before coming to the mission, while the men hunted for meat.

"Help me, O Lord, be patient. Help me show love for these people who have welcomed me among them," she prayed, yet her heart ached for she felt very much a stranger in their midst. "I will ask them to recite the lives of the saints or sing the hymns as we work," she murmured, "and that will pass the time without their pointless chatter, and I will come here as often as possible to pray."

Back she went then, her heart lighter with her vow and her strategy, and she picked up the kettle and carried it down the hill to the hut where no one noticed how long she'd been gone.

The following day, fetching water for camp, Kateri brought a hunting knife, and in the thicket she carved a large cross in the bark of the largest tree. She cut boughs, too, and spread them as a carpet upon the snow for her to kneel and she prayed in thanksgiving for this place of solitude and her knowledge of the prayers and the stories of the lives of the saints and the hymns that opened in her imagination and in her heart such comforting meditations.

On the fourth day in camp, living until then on the dried meat and fish that Camille and Jean-Baptiste had packed, young Eugene killed a caribou. Home came the men, Jean-Baptiste proudly carrying a forequarter, Eugene and his brother Daniel each with a hindquarter, and Jean-Baptiste's brother Pierre carrying the head on one shoulder and a forequarter on the other. The youth, Lucien, who had remained behind with the woman to chop wood, pestered Jean-Baptiste to take him along hunting now that they'd found game.

The women stoked up the fire. Jean-Baptiste skillfully butchered the meat and they hung it by ropes in four hide bags from the branches so racoons and the dogs and wild dogs could not reach it. Kateri took charge of the hide which she would scrape and fashion into a robe or blanket with her needle. Later Jean-Baptiste spoke as he sat cross-legged in front of the fire where rib-eye slabs of the caribou were cooking:

"Before we eat of this gift, let us thank the Lord for sending the caribou to us. Let us also thank Eugene for being vigilant in tracking him, and courageous in running him down and killing him." He looked about the small gathering. "I am mindful that in our former lives, we'd be praying to Aireskou and then eating until we grew sick, until all the meat was gone so we did not draw scavengers. Let moderation regulate our lives, now, so we may be happy and serene. Let us say, then, the Our Father," and the small group recited the prayer, their voices rising at "Give us this day our daily bread." Jean-Baptiste dished the meat to them on bark plates and hungrily they ate until they were full. Collecting the scraps from the meal, Camille tied those into a bag as well and placed it in a corner of the hut where the head and the hide were stored, opposite the door and beyond the fire and the human smell to discourage the prying snouts of the badger and racoon.

In late January the deep cold set in. All day the skies were cloudy and often it snowed for twenty or thirty hours straight, piling up snow at the entrance of the hut, requiring the hunting party to dig itself out. By now life in the camp had settled into a routine. Kateri kept the calendar, marking off the days, reminding Jean-Baptiste to observe Sundays with an hour of prayer before they set about their chores. Her strategy to initiate discussions about the saints or to sing hymns worked and few were the tittering discussions about men or courtship, and the constant praying eliminated the usual backbiting and gossip.

Two or three times a day Kateri left the cabin for water and she went to her chapel in the pines to pray. Here in the cold, deep, white heart of the forest, she emptied herself of memory and fear and dreams about the future, and she opened her heart to feel the presence of God. Here there were no candles, no decorations, no vestments, no golden props—chalice and ciborium and monstrance—of the mission chapel. Here there was no priest to deliver parables and sermons. Here there was no choir to help her in her quest to feel God's presence. Yet it was at last, as lonely as she felt, away from Anastasia and Joseph Kryn, alone in the forest that she allowed her heart and soul to open and she meditated –

– *upon wisdom* in the Holy Ghost, a white dove! If she closed her eyes she heard the fluttering of pure white wings, and she sensed the wisdom of her solitude and the reward of her chastity.;

– *upon sacrifice* in the offering of Christ crucified looking down from his cross, his face streaming with blood from the crown of thorns, his hands and his feet pierced with iron nails, hanging upon the cross much as torture victims hung upon the pole on the platforms of Ossernenon when she was a child, "Father, Father, why have you forsaken me?" She felt his despair, how alone and betrayed and slowly murdered, with humiliation, an object of derision and revilement until the moment of death. What agony! "And you did this for me!" she sobbed, beating her breast. "You suffered and you died for my sins!"

– *upon order and reason and peace* of God the Father, a white-bearded old man, older than Deganawida and Hiawatha. He was the all-powerful God, possessor of winds and thunder and the lightning bolt, the looser of blizzards and frosts. He held the sun like a fiery ball in his hand that he sent up from the east each morning and hurled through the sky, even behind the darkest clouds, in and out of the occasional eclipse. He cast the moon into its phases like the shaman juggler tossing bones after the feast, brightening and then darkening the land and then brightening it again, and lastly, her favorite

– *upon purity* in the blessed virgin Mary. How Kateri wept when she considered the perfection of this woman, able to keep her virginity and to bear the savior at the same time. She was the purest vessel of all mankind. She responded instantly to Gabriel's call and received in the secret recesses of her womb the will of God. She bore the infant Jesus and placed him in a manger while the shepherds came and the magi followed the star. She nursed the savior at her breasts, and soothed him and comforted him, helped him learn to walk and speak. And then she was rewarded for all this with the seven sorrows, *mater dolorosa*, which she bore until He sent for her and then opened the clouds to assume her bodily into heaven.

And as she finished her meditations each day, she felt complete. The Holy Trinity together with the Blessed Virgin Mary formed a perfect union. All lay within the circle and only chaos and darkness and violence lay outside. It was as timeless as the sun and as solid as the earth, and the seasons would pass in and then pass out and the days would lengthen or shorten and the weather grow cold and then hot, the crops and fruit rise up and give forth their harvest and then die, but the Holy Trinity and the Blessed Virgin Mary would always remain.

Indeed, the days were lengthening and soon she noticed from the shelter of her chapel the songs of birds. The Lord had blessed their camp with much success and the hunters had brought back deer and elk and caribou as well as hares and possum and racoon that she and Camille and the other women had butchered and skinned. A great pile of hides was stacked in the corner facing the door of the hut, and this would purchase for them hatchets and scissors and knives and bolts of cloth when the traders came upriver from Quebec. In that season the priests feared the liquor the traders brought to addle the minds of the natives in order to cheat them, but Jean-Baptiste was clear-headed and above such idleness.

Still they hunted during the day, and Jean-Baptiste and Daniel and Eugene and Pierre were also building four canoes in the forest so that when the season came and the ice began to melt, they might journey down the stream to the lowlands and the river. Far easier would it be to return to the mission than it had been trudging over the wide acres from the river into the hills.

The young men, Daniel and Eugene, and little Lucien returned at sunset one evening and announced that Pierre and Jean-Baptiste had continued on the trail of a moose. The boys concluded that they had enough meat and skins, but the men, brothers who hunted together when they were young, wanted to demonstrate their perseverance. The others ate their evening meal and then settled down to sleep.

Deep in the night, the hide curtain of a door opened. Kateri awakened briefly to see the stars through the door, and then she fell back asleep. The men jostled the sleepers and found themselves places on the ground where they might curl themselves into their robes and sleep. In the morning Camille was up first. Kateri awoke to see her looking down, arms fold, scowling above her. Kateri did not understand the ferocity of her expression, but needing to get water she arose and went out with her kettle and escaped to her shrine and her morning prayers.

According to the calendar Kateri kept, Palm Sunday was two weeks away. The sun was spiraling upward in the sky each day and clumps of snow cascaded through the branches of pine. Birds brightened the wood with their singing.

"Help me," Jean-Baptiste asked her one morning. "The boys are gone and I need to slide the last canoe from where we have constructed it."

Kateri and Camille were sweeping up the cabin. Kateri put her broom aside and followed him out the door, leaving Camille to finish cleaning.

Down from the hunting grounds they soon were paddling. The creek was high with meltwater and they rushed past the standing waves of whitewater and pools swirling with the strong currents, to the lowlands below. What had taken five days to walk, took only two to traverse by watercourse, and soon they entered onto the broad St. Lawrence, filled with giant ice floes from the uplands. Carefully they paddled along until the mission appeared on the south shore. With a great sense of relief and joy and happiness, Kateri climbed out of the canoe and waded onto dry land.

Many villagers were on the riverbank unpacking. They shouted greetings. Joseph Kryn and Karitha and Martin called to her and Kateri went over and they embraced. Later that afternoon the mission bell rang and all of the villagers assembled in the old chapel—the men on the left and the women on the right—and they intoned the hymns and listened to the gospel of the Prodigal Son returning and the homily welcoming them home delivered by Father Cholenec. At the consecration, with the host held high and the words, *Hoc est enim corpus meam*, spoken as Father Chauchetière, serving the mass, rang the bells, Kateri felt her emotions give way and she wept in adoration of the blessed sacrament and with joy at being safely home.

Father Cholenec was surprised two days later when Camille

came to see him. Her manner was subdued, a gravity he knew did not portend anything good.

"One of our most revered members, Father, may not be what she pretends to be."

The priest cocked his head. "Who?"

"My sister. Kateri."

The priest hid any surprise he felt. "How so? I've heard nothing but testaments to her faith, her purity, her virtue. Are you saying these are . . . *false* . . . ?"

Camille nodded. "We all know what men are like, Father, you more than myself for you listen their confessions."

"You mean, their behavior toward women?"

"Absolutely." Camille folded her arms and set her jaw and nodded. "I caught Jean-Baptiste in a tryst with an Abenaki woman four years ago."

"But that occurred before you arrived here at the Sault. Before you were married."

"Exactly," she nodded. "So now we are married and he and my adopted sister have been carrying on."

"You must be mistaken."

"No, I am sure of it."

"What makes you believe this?" the priest asked.

"As we were preparing to leave the hut where we had wintered, Jean-Baptiste came in very late one night. In the morning he was sleeping not next to me but next to her."

"Were they under the same sleeping robe?"

"No," she scoffed. "That would have given away their game! They wouldn't do that. But they were close enough to show me what had happened."

"But the hunting camps are cramped generally, are they not?"

"He knew where I was. He always found me in the night before this. No," she shook her head sadly, "but that's not all."

"What else?"

"When we were about to leave, he asked her to accompany him into the woods to get a canoe he had built."

"And she went with him?"

"Yes."

"And was there a canoe?"

"There was. They slid it out on the snow. And they were laughing like children!"

"Well, what's the suspicion there?"

"It was the way they carried on, laughing and joking and she referred to him by his name, with familiarity."

"What is it you think I should do?"

"It is your task, to confront her with her behavior and see how she responds."

"But the confessional is secret. I can't reveal what others confess."

She tossed her head with a haughty disdain. "I care only about her soul, not about my husband. I already know I cannot trust him when there is a woman younger than myself around."

"I will speak with her."

That evening, the priest related this to Father Chauchetière.

"Impossible!" Father Claude said. "Camille has the problem, not Kateri. Camille envies the purity of her sister. I have never known Kateri in any respect to stray from the path of purity. She is incapable of such a thing."

"Father Frémin always warns us that we must be vigilant to the snares of the devil. We know how relaxed morals get on the hunt."

"I would stake my life on it, Father. Forget what you have heard. To confront her with this calumny would be to credit it and demean yourself as a carrier of rumor."

"No one is above temptation, Father. I shall get to the bottom of this."

The following day, after he had slept on the issue, Father

Cholenec summoned Kateri to him and he invited her into the rectory.

"Yes, Father?"

"Do you know why I asked to see you?"

"No."

"You were on the winter hunt with Jean-Baptiste and his wife Camille?"

"Yes." Her eyes were unfocused and cloudy.

"How well did you know them before the winter hunt?"

"Jean-Baptiste brought me here from the land of the Mohawks."

"And are you grateful to him for that?"

"More than I can ever tell him or show him."

"How well do you know Jean-Baptiste now?"

"Much, much better than before. He is a good man."

"There has been an allegation that you have engaged in improper conduct with him."

She looked at the priest and her eyes cleared and focused on him. Her brown eyes penetrated into his. She was not defensive in any way. She looked evenly at him and slowly shook her head. "Whoever has spoken this, it is not true."

"Camille said she saw you one morning sleeping near him."

"He came in late, after we were asleep, and he lay down near me. Her suspicion is unfounded." A look of sorrow passed across her face. It was pity for Camille and for her envy. "Why, Father, do people need to suspect evil in each other? Don't they see that they are only seeing the evil they carry within themselves?"

"She also said," the priest tried to demonstrate to her the reasonableness of his doubt, "that you helped him slide his canoe out of the forest where he built it and into the water."

"I did. He asked for my help and I helped him." She looked at the priest with perfect frankness. "You are my confessor, Father. You don't believe her suspicions, do you?"

She raised her voice at this last word. Father Cholenec bowed his head for he had harbored a suspicion that in her presence now seemed cowardly and mean-spirited.

"No, of course not, Kateri, but it is my duty to inquire as to your spiritual well-being."

"I am grateful for your attention," she said evenly and she rose from the chair and started for the door.

"Kateri," he said, his voice catching in his throat.

She paused on the threshold and turned about. "Yes, Father?"

"I should not have said anything."

"It is, as you say, your duty." She looked at him with beneficence and love. "I will pray for Camille, that she may trust her husband more. I have already made a vow, Father, which you now confirm."

"Yes?"

"Nevermore will I go on the hunt. Next winter, I will remain at the mission. The hunt is a custom from the former time, and I am no longer interested in honoring it. You need not fear this allegation will be repeated, for I will keep company with women exclusively and stay away from men." She pulled the shawl down over her eyes and she went into the bright spring sunshine.

Father Cholenec sat in his room before the hearth where the ashes were wet and gray, and he was depleted of energy. Now he had the unenviable task of telling Camille

Before he could, though, Father Claude returned:

"Have you spoken with Kateri?"

"I have. She was not defensive or upset in the least."

"She is God's chosen one."

"I wish I had your faith," Father Cholenec said.

"I wish you did as well," Father Claude answered him and walked away.

Chapter 27

✣

Kateri's Band

KATERI TEKAKWITHA WAS WATCHING the men work upon the new church. A framework of hewn timbers rose thirty feet in the air with a peaked roof like the massive church across the river in Ville Marie. The architect in his leather apron was at a table of planks on sawhorses and the men, half of them natives, were on the scaffolds of lashed tree branches, sawing and hammering the thick timbers. Kateri turned and saw a woman gazing as intently as she did.

"Which side will the men occupy, and which side will be the women's?" Kateri asked.

The woman was older than Kateri, in her mid-thirties. Lines upon her face and a quick lurch to her eye revealed that she had been through considerable darkness.

"I believe it will be as it is now. The women on the right and the men on the left."

They entered the roofless structure.

"This chapel of wood is not all God asks us to build," Kateri said in her low whisper. "Our souls, too, must be temples for Him to reside." She looked about. "I do not deserve to enter here when so often I have driven God from my heart. I should be ordered to remain outside with the dogs."

"I too," the woman said, bowing her head, making the sign of the cross, "am a great sinner."

"I have not met you before."

"I have been at the mission for three summers. I arrived when it was down river at Kenteka."

"I arrived last summer."

"Yes, Hot Cinders sent you. I know of you," Marie-Thérèse said. "You are Kateri."

"I am."

"I am called Tegaigenta, and was baptized Marie-Thérèse. I am Oneida like Hot Cinders. He has asked me about you, how well you have acclimated to life here at the mission."

Kateri bowed. "I can't control what others say."

"No, but it is from concern. He is a good man, if a bit explosive. My husband grew up with him in the same *ohwahchira*."

"You are married?"

"I was," she said, and she looked up at the church wistfully. "My husband died on the hunt."

The noise of the hammers was distracting them. Kateri spoke: "Each morning I walk down to the tall cross that stands on the knoll above the river. Would you like to walk there with me?"

The two women walked together.

"I went on the hunt this winter," Kateri said as they walked. "I shall never go again. Being away from the mass and the sacraments grieves me so. Our people revert to the old ways outside the influence of the priest."

"Truer words have not been uttered." They reached the crucifix on a low mound overlooking a broad sweep of the river. They sat together on a large stone. "Since you know this, I will tell you my story," Marie-Thérèse said. She took a deep breath and expelled it with a shudder. "Three winters ago, we went into the woods, eleven of us, my husband, myself, my sister's son, three other men, three other women and two children. We journeyed north to the river of the Ottawa to hunt, yet the snows came so heavily the deer and caribou and moose could not migrate. After some days we only killed one animal and it was quickly eaten. Famine threatened us. We boiled and drank hot water to ease the agony in our stomachs. We boiled and ate leather we'd packed to stitch into moccasins. We dug for roots and boiled the bark of trees to eat. At last we gave up the hunting camp and fled down river to reach the valley and find meat.

"One of our number, a Mohawk, indicated he wanted to split off from the group and go hunting. He took the other man, a Seneca. In three days the Mohawk returned and no longer did his eyes shine with the glow of the hungry. We all knew he had slain and eaten the Seneca.

"At this time my husband became sick, delirious. Because he was ill, the others eyed him to slay and butcher and eat him, but myself and my sister's son guarded him day and night. Seeing we would not agree to sacrifice him, they proceeded along without us, and soon after the three of us were alone, he died. My nephew and I buried him and then we hastened to catch the others. Now there were nine of us. The Mohawk eyed the woman who slept alone with her boys, thinking to kill and eat her, for she was the most vulnerable. He asked me, as the Christian of the group, whether Jesus Christ excused murder because of the necessity of eating."

"He needed to ask?"

"Yes! Perhaps it was just for formality, or maybe he was joking!" Marie-Theresa clasped Kateri's arm. She was sobbing. "But I did not reply! The Mohawk asked me a question about the teachings I had studied. I was struck dumb with fear as to what he would do with me and my nephew if my answer displeased him. So, he went ahead and killed her and her two boys. And we," she was sobbing inconsolably, gripping Kateri's arm, "we . . . ate . . . them!"

The bright spring sun shone over the river where white cakes of ice floated breezily along. Kateri put her arm around the other and held her. "The winter hunt puts all our souls in peril."

"I feared that if I tried to stop them they would turn on me and kill my nephew and me. I promised the Lord, our God and Savior," Marie-Thérèse was imploring her to understand, "that if ever I was delivered from that ordeal, if God rescued me, I would confess my sins and change my life forever."

"Let us vow then, you and I, that when the winter comes will shall remain at the mission, two women without men, and get along as best we can."

"It shall be so," the other said and she embraced Kateri. Sitting on a bench, they looked out over the river.

In the ensuing weeks the two women established a deep friendship. Their conversations ranged far into spiritual realms. They examined their past lives for incidents of shortcomings and they devised plans to avoid the gossip and quarrels of other villagers. Marie-Thérèse initiated Kateri into the practice of mortification. She led her into the forest and cut a handful of willow shoots. In a secluded place, she exposed her back and instructed Kateri to whip her. She did this for penance, to chastize her flesh for its weakness and failures.

Silently Marie-Thérèse accepted the pain and soon her shoulders were a deep red and blood was showing through the skin of the abrasions. As she pulled up her tunic to cover the marks, she answered Kateri's quizzical expression thus:

"The pain takes away my guilt and sorrow and replaces it with joy, for the Lord knows I am truly sorry and I accept this penance for my sins."

"May I try?"

"Of course."

Kateri loosened tie of her tunic and pulled it down, exposing her back to Marie-Thérèse. The elder, more experienced woman stood to the side and firmly holding the willow shoots, whistled them through the air and applied them to the pockmarked skin. Kateri emitted a small groan, but at the second blow she closed her eyes and pressed her lips together and internalized the pain. A dozen blows Marie-Thérèse administered, and then she stopped and tossed the shoots aside and went to Kateri, gently pulled up her tunic and held her as the younger woman shuddered from this new experience.

"Are you in pain?" Marie-Thérèse asked.

"It has cleared my mind and soothed my heart," Kateri said. "I meditated upon Jesus as the Romans scourged Him at the pillar."

"Let us return to the chapel and pray," Marie-Thérèse said, embracing her, speaking into her ear. "May this help us both to receive the Lord more deeply and more often."

Daily they met and walked to the small rise above the river where the large log cross stood to mark the mission. One day, looking across the rapids of Lachine, the rising sun caught the buildings of Ville-Marie and made them shine.

"I have long wanted to journey over to Ville-Marie," Kateri said. "Anastasia, whom I call my mother, grows old and set in her ways and does not wish to make the journey."

"I will go with you," Marie-Thérèse said. "Let us borrow a canoe and go tomorrow."

"Yes," Kateri said. "I will ask Father Claude for a letter to take so we may visit the chapel there."

Marie-Thérèse agreed to borrow the canoe, and Kateri approached Father Claude after evening benediction for a letter of introduction.

"What is it you wish to see?"

"We wish to see how the French live in their community."

"I think it will be an edifying journey," the priest said, and he went to the rectory and composed a letter of introduction to the Sisters of the Hôtel-Dieu and the Sisters of the Congregation.

The next morning, the two native women sallied forth upon the water, paddling to the new French settlement on the Isle of Montreal. Around the island they paddled, and along the riverbank where it faced the east, past wooden docks and warehouses built on piles driven into the mud. They landed and climbed up the hill from the water into a wondrous village of French soldiers and clerics, log cabins, natives and women in religious habits.

With a smattering of French, Marie-Thérèse asked her way and soon they were received at the convent of the Sisters of the Congregation. They were shown into the small room Mother Bourgeoys used as her office. As the good nun entered, they stood and were pleased to find that the mother superior knew their language and was happy they were visiting. Many were the questions they had.

Mother Bourgeoys gave them to a sister, and she took them on a tour of the school. The two young women marveled at the white habits and the cleanliness of the place, the order to the classrooms where the young Canadian girls were taught. At midday they were welcomed into the mess hall where they ate with the nuns. They watching in awe as the nuns wielded slender iron knives and forks to cut and spear their meat and boiled squash and the fluffy white potatoes.

Later in the afternoon, they visited the Hôtel-Dieu, a hospital operated by the Hospitallers of St. Joseph where the ill and wounded and dying were brought to be nursed and cured or kept comfortable until the end. Again, the two Iroquois women were charmed by the order and cleanliness of the halls and the wards, the spotless white habits of the nuns and the calm manner in which they administered to the invalids.

Toward evening they walked back to the riverbank, got into their canoe and paddled home.

When they met the next morning to sit by the great cross, Kateri had formulated an idea:

"I should like to live as those women live," Kateri said. "Do you know how one comes to join that house?"

"I have a friend who lived for many years in Quebec," said Marie-Thérèse. "She also spent much time at the Huron mission of Lorette. I suggest we ask her."

They walked together through the village to a long house at the eastern end. A native woman in her fifties greeted Marie-Thérèse warmly, and when she met Kateri, she embraced her. Her name was Marie, too. Marie-Thérèse put the question to her:

"We visited the nuns in Ville-Marie yesterday, both at the hospital and at the school for girls. How does one become a woman to serve in that way?"

The older Marie shook her head and said with a sad smile, "The blackrobes share with us the mysteries of their faith, and they counsel us to receive the sacraments and lead lives of virtue and prayer. But they keep such a secret knowledge away from us. I don't know if a native can become a nun or a priest, but I was told once how it is done."

"Well, tell us what it involves, and we will ask Father Frémin."

"Come, let us walk," Marie said, and the other two led her back down to the cross overlooking the river. At the foot of the boiling rapids there was a small island named for the herons who frequently flapped their wide gray-blue wings to land there and fish with their long bills.

"The biggest rule they enforce is that women and men, when they enter the order, renounce associating with each other. They don't marry, they don't cohabit, they don't have children."

"That poses no difficulty," Kateri said.

"The priests retreat from the world and study for ten or twelve years. Only after they have read many, many books and proved themselves to be honest and dedicated can they submit to the bishop and be accepted into the priestly class. However, only men can aspire to be priests."

"Why?" Kateri asked. "Among our people it is the women

who rule the *ohwachiras* and appoint and remove the chiefs, and thereby control events. Why is it only men can become priests among the French?"

"They view women as unclean," Marie said. "That is why they worship the virgin."

Kateri looked in wonderment a both of the others. "They believe women are unclean?"

"Yes," the older woman said.

"Unclean and weak and changeable," Marie-Thérèse added. "Don't you know?"

"No," Kateri said. "That is nonsense. Men are unclean until they receive the Prayer. Men are crude and insensitive. They insist on more than one wife, and change wives at will. While women till the fields and bear the children, creating life, men kill. They hunt and they wage war. I have kept myself from men not because I was unclean, but because they were. Not until I met the blackrobes did I understand that men could be so gentle and meek."

"Well," Marie explained, "the religious take vows, both the men and the women. They vow three things, poverty, chastity and obedience."

"We have not done it formally," Kateri said, "but those vows might equally apply to us."

"Yes," Marie-Thérèse agreed.

"Why don't we ask the priest if we might begin to dress alike and take those vows and devote our lives to such a great purpose?" Kateri asked.

"Who will ask him?" Marie asked.

"I will," Kateri said.

"And where shall we remove ourselves to? Surely we cannot remain in the village!"

Kateri looked across the boiling water. "We shall go to Heron Island."

"Yes," Marie-Thérèse said.

Kateri vacillated on whom to ask for permission. While Father Claude was agreeable and pleasant and never declined any favor, Father Cholenec was more austere and her confessor. He would be preferable. Father Frémin, though, was superior of the mission. If she asked either of the other two, they would need to ask Father Frémin, and so that afternoon she went to the rectory.

"Yes, my daughter," Father Frémin said cordially, escorting her into the sitting area, "what can I do for you?"

Kateri took the chair that was offered and pulled back her shawl and looked at the priest with blank, unfocused eyes.

"I need guidance, Father," she said.

The priest rubbed his chin and mused to himself it was no wonder she never married. The smallpox scars marred the skin of her face and, no doubt, the skin of her body, and may have, as with others who contracted the disease, rendered her barren. The reputation of this young woman was known to him. She was a child still, an exemplary and worthy child of these forests and rivers who worshiped with such fervor that hers, as everyone said, was a special grace, for a native.

"I am happy you came to me."

"Marie-Thérèse and I visited the convents, attached to the hospital and the school in Ville-Marie."

"It is good you have seen that. These are holy women who dedicate their lives to others. They display the highest of aspirations of our French culture."

"Yes," Kateri said, "and we wish to live as such women do."

The priest put up his hands and shook his head. "That is quite impossible. The rules forbid any orders taking natives in as novices without regard to their virtue or progress or other merit."

"We understand that. We have spoke with Marie, too, a woman

of much experience who lived for a time in Quebec and at Lorette. We have a proposal for you and hope you will agree."

Father Frémin's eyes were alight with mirth. He admired how composed she was, and undaunted. The childish thinking of the natives amused him, and their response to the pictures Father Claude drew of heaven and hell and a whole line of saints and sinners demonstrated for him that their spiritual gifts, instructed in the mysteries and the doctrines of the faith, remained rather primitive.

"Tell me."

"We want you or the great Onontio or else your king across the salt sea to grant us Heron Island so we can found an order of native sisters there."

"You what?" Father Frémin began to laugh. "You want to found your own order?" The thought tickled him. She nodded in earnest, which only made him laugh harder.

Kateri leaned back in her chair and watched this grown man, this holy man, clap his hands and laugh. "Oh, that is good!" he said. "Wonderful! You three want to start your own order of sisters!" And he laughed and laughed and laughed as she stoically observed him.

"Why should we not?"

"Why, you're . . . you're too . . . too young in the faith! Where would you live?"

"Heron Isle."

"Young people go there to . . . to frolic . . . and hunters camp on that island. You wouldn't have a day's privacy. You wouldn't be safe. The idea is foolish and completely out of the question."

Kateri, her fierce Mohawk pride offended, narrowed her eyes and whispered, "I'm sorry, Father, to have taken up your time."

She rose slowly and walked with her head held high out of the rectory as the priest enjoyed his good laugh.

Chapter 28

*Kateri And Marie-Thérèse
Make A Vow*

KATERI TOLD THE OTHERS the priest disapproved of their idea to found an order of sisters. She did not tell them he laughed at the notion. His laughter made her feel foolish and shamed, quite the opposite of how ennobled and connected she felt when praying in church. Kateri and Marie-Thérèse went to a cabin in the mission graveyard where they might be alone. They whipped each other's backs in punishment for their vanity in thinking they might aspire to the spiritual height of a Frenchwoman. Clearly, they saw now, they were of a lesser rank and order in this religion. Still, that did not nullify the message of Jesus Christ.

Anastasia, feeling she was losing Kateri's love, nominated her—and not either of her new companions—to be a member of the Holy Family Society. Father Frémin, realizing his mistake in laughing at her notion, approved. This exclusive praying society, in the manner of the medicine societies of their former village, accepted Kateri into its rites and ceremonies, and she began to attend with devotion.

Anastasia welcomed the opportunity twice a week to pray with her young protégé, and Kateri showed her the utmost of respect and affection. But Anastasia had noticed a change, and she went to Father Cholenec with her concern.

"The girl went to Father Frémin," the priest said, "with the idea that she and two others could start a convent on Heron Island."

"Marie-Thérèse has alienated her affections from me, her mother's best friend, the one who saved her from certain death and now her sponsor and guide here at St. Francis Xavier."

"She is still young," the priest observed. "How old?"

"Twenty-two," Anastasia said.

"She might still marry," the priest observed. "There are many young men who could benefit from a union with one so blessed with spiritual gifts. She need not have children. If she chooses not to know her husband carnally, many of our married couple have taken a vow to live as brother and sister."

"She will never agree," Anastasia said.

"Propose it to her," the priest urged. "It hurts nothing to ask."

"I will put her sister Camille up to this," Anastasia said, not knowing of the episode on the winter hunt.

The following day, Camille caught up with Kateri on her way home from the chapel.

"We have not spent time together in a very long time, sister," Camille said. "I miss the discussions we used to have."

"I have been praying with Marie-Thérèse and, occasionally, her friend Marie. We keep to ourselves."

"That is true, but you still live, thanks be to God, with Anastasia and Jean-Baptiste and me. We miss your company. I have a request of you that would help all of the people you love, and most of all it would help you. If you would do this favor for us and for yourself, we all could be completely happy."

"What is it, sister?"

"Find a good Christian young man, someone perhaps like Joseph Kryn, and marry him."

Kateri adjusted her shawl downward, "There is no other like Joseph Kryn."

"It's not that Jean-Baptiste and I begrudge you the food you eat, but think about all of us. If you brought a hunter into our cabin, we would all benefit."

Kateri stopped and turned to her, pulled up her shawl to reveal her scarred face to show Camille how absurd the idea was. "I know you suggest this because you care for me."

"That is true. Above all we want you to be happy."

"It is a big step, so I pray you to give me some time."

"Oh, of course! Take as long as you need. It is not my intention to pry into your affairs. I know you will see the wisdom about what I ask when you think about it."

"Until I give you my answer, let us not speak of this again."

"As you wish." And Camille bowed and left her side.

The first thing the following morning Kateri sought out Father Cholenec and told him what Camille had proposed.

"You might keep an open mind," he said.

"My mind is made up. It is out of the question."

"Your conduct is so unusual among your people."

"Not at all. I saw two large houses filled with women who live so. I suggested to Father Frémin that we form such a society, and he laughed at us."

"But those were French nuns. I mean your conduct is highly unusual among your people."

"You teach that there is one God, Father, and we are all the same in His eyes. Why then are there different sets of rules depending on our race?"

"For one thing, you neither read nor write."

"Does God care about such things?"

"You can't possibly know all you need to know in order to take your vows."

"I know that my heart belongs to Jesus Christ. What else is there to know?"

"There are many doctrines . . ."

"Does Jesus care about these doctrines?"

"Yes. He does."

"Well, I do have control over myself."

"Absolutely," Father Cholenec said.

"Then I have decided I will not marry."

"Think it over carefully for Camille's idea has great merit."

"Father, I have thought about it in every possible way. Marriage is impossible for me."

"Why? Are you not concerned about providing for yourself in your later years."

"I do not fear my poverty. My work will furnish me with the necessities of life. I can find furs, rabbit skins even, to stitch together to make a covering for me in the winter. Didn't Christ say that his Father cares for the lowly sparrow?"

The priest did not laugh. He felt her resolve. "Do not close your mind, Kateri, but consider that Camille has your best interest at heart and perhaps, as a practical matter, it may confer more benefit to you than a spiritual one."

"How can you say that? Doesn't the virtue of chastity open our hearts to receive grace?"

"But there are other concerns, worldly concerns."

"Not for me."

"Give the matter more consideration."

Humbly she bowed and left the rectory. That afternoon her sister sought her out.

"Well?"

"The priest told me to consider it further, but my mind is made up."

"The way you carry on with your new friends! Don't you see you open yourself to the ridicule of men?"

"I care not what others say about me."

"But you expose yourself to temptation."

"I care not for the flattery of men or their gifts. Rarely do men give without expectation. Nor can any man give me anything I cannot get for myself. I'll never submit to a man, any man. Nor will I speak of this marrying business again."

As the days shortened and relentless pounding rain stripped the trees of their leaves and churned the village pathways into mud, talk of going on the winter hunt again filled the mission. Anastasia importuned Joseph Kryn to ask Kateri to accompany his family, and he did so.

"I am honored, Great Chief, that you would consider my presence in your hunting camp, but I made a vow to myself last spring that never more would I leave the mission to live in the wild."

"Such vows are not binding," Joseph Kryn said. "Karitha and Martin and my nephews Matthew and Luke were excited when I told them you might be with us this winter. Please reconsider."

"The use of a vow is that it settles things once and for all," she said. "My mind is made up, Great Chief. Thank you for inviting me, but I will remain behind in the mission."

Marie-Thérèse and Kateri continued to meet in the hut in the middle of the cemetery to chastize each other before confessing their sins. After one particularly severe session, where Marie-Thérèse begged her friend to whip her until she bled, she revealed her reason for wanting such punishment.

"I must go back on my word to you, Kateri," she announced. "I have been asked to join a hunting party, and I have no other means of supporting myself this the winter. I cannot remain at the mission. I hope you will forgive me." She brightened with a thought. "Perhaps you could come with us? We could be together."

"No," Kateri said. "I will remain here at the mission."

"What will you do for food?"

"I am more concerned about the food for my soul than food for my body."

Kateri encouraged her friend to whip her back and shoulders soundly for the resentment she felt at Marie-Thérèse's backsliding.

At the next meeting of the Holy Family Society, Kateri walked home with Anastasia.

"What have you decided about marrying?" the older woman asked.

"My decision has not changed."

"If you had listened to me, you would not be in this dilemma."

"If marriage is such a boon, Mother, why don't you try it again?"

"Ahhh. I see."

"Let there be no further talk about it then."

"There won't be."

The villagers left for the winter hunt and Kateri and Anastasia occupied the great long house alone. Through the cold, dark winter nights, they huddled by the fire and the winds howled down the frozen river and the snow whipped up into high drifts, and in the dark and the cold the idea of another vow took hold of Kateri. Without discussing this otherwise, Kateri sought out Father Cholenec in late February.

"I have survived the winter, Father, without a man in my life. I have proved to myself, and to you, that it is possible. I should like to take a vow of virginity in the manner of the French sisters."

"This would be unprecedented," he said. "Please take three days to weigh this matter, and after that time, if you still want to, I will consider it."

"There is no question of deliberation," Kateri said. "My resolution has been made for a very long time. I have been living according to it. I will never have any other spouse than Jesus Christ."

Father Cholenec rubbed his chin and thought. Finally he said, "This matter has been often discussed by you and by me and by those who care about you. I can see that it is sincere in you, and I believe now that it is not your ambition to emulate the good sisters, but rather it is a deep desire in you to follow in the ways of Jesus Christ."

"Yes, Father!" She closed her eyes and lay back in the chair.

"I will allow you to make such a vow before the congregation, then."

"Oh," she said, releasing her pent up breath in a long sigh, "thank you! Thank you, father."

She opened her eyes and looked at the priest. Indeed, with this deep personal struggle resolved, her appearance seemed to change. An inner quiet infused her. She was serene and deeply happy.

On March 25, the feast of the Archangel Gabriel's announcement to the virgin that she would be the mother of the savior, with the men's choir and the women's choir singing the offertory hymn during the giving of gifts, Kateri walked up the aisle of the chapel. She wore a tunic of white borrowed from Marie Thérèse. Anastasia had braided white ribbons in her hair. Unlike the last two solemn occasions where she had approached the altar to receive baptism and the Eucharist, this time she brought her gift to the altar. It was all she had to give, the purity of her body and her soul, which she gave freely to Jesus Christ. She knelt at the altar rail and renounced marriage and vowed perpetual virginity.

"I pray you, Blessed Lady, to present my soul to your Divine Son for I shall be espoused only to Him until the day of my death. I pray also that you will allow me to consecrate myself to you, my only mother."

She rose from her prayer as the chorus swelled *Immaculate Mary*—

"Ave, ave, ave, Maria,
Ave, ave, Maria!"

Chapter 29

❧

Healing The Sick

FATHER CLAUDE HAD WATCHED KATERI from afar. On occasion he'd discussed her progress with Father Frémin and Father Cholenec. Cholenec as her confessor and Frémin as superior of the mission answered to most of her needs and by nature she was so reserved, Father Claude had little opportunity even to speak with the shy, retiring Mohawk woman. He had seen her praying in the chapel and often he had placed the Eucharist upon her tongue. They had nodded to each other in the village lanes. He had often seen Kateri and Marie-Thérèse at the great crucifix, but except for half a dozen short conversations he knew her only from afar.

Shortly after Kateri's vow of chastity, when the river was free of ice, Father Frémin went down to Quebec in order to return to France for the summer. He left Father Cholenec in charge of the mission. Father Cholenec put Father Claude in charge of visiting the sick.

Kateri's austerities continued. Confirmed in her vow of celibacy, the young woman fasted two days a week, often sprinkling ashes in her food to make it less appealing. With Marie-Thérèse she found new ways to mortify her flesh: they walked barefoot on the snow; they immersed themselves in the freezing currents of the river. One night in the throes of her devotion, Kateri branded her legs with live coals as her people branded their slaves to show she was the slave of

319

God. Another night she put a live coal between her toes and burned a hole in her flesh. She wore a belt with iron points around her middle when she went into the forest to cut wood and even when she fell one day and lay on the ground gasping for breath, she refused to let Marie-Thérèse remove it. Upon learning from the priest that a saint in the Old World had slept on thorns, she cut thorn branches and put them in her bed to remind herself of the suffering Lord.

The mortifications did not come to the attention of the priests for a long time, and when Marie-Thérèse finally confessed as to the severity of the whippings, Father Cholenec told the women to stop immediately. Still the fasting, the exposure to the elements, the constant prayer wore at her constitution, and as spring arrived once more, Kateri Tekakwitha was quite weak.

The first time Father Claude administered to her, she had been chopping wood and a branch fell on her leg so she was confined to her pallet. He went into Anastasia's cabin and that good woman was stirring the kettle. She nodded and pointed her ladle at the sleeping shelf where the young woman lay. Father Claude went quietly over and squat down beside her pallet.

"Kateri?" Father Claude whispered.

She lay upon her back, her eyes closed, her palms upward. Only after he spoke did he understand she was praying, not sleeping, and he felt as though he were intruding. Slowly she opened her eyes as if from a sweet dream. She looked up at him, and his heart stopped.

"Father," she said softly. The light from her eyes bathed him in an other-worldly radiance. He suddenly felt enveloped by beauty and love. The energy, the force he felt in the light of her eyes came from an inner place, and now the communion she held with this grace momentarily included him. The sounds of the long house abated. His soul awakened and he felt she was ministering to him. He dared not breathe for he sensed Kateri had found a pathway for direct contact with God. At that moment he realized she was in the mystical state he had reached on Christmas Eve eleven years ago, and he did not want to disturb her.

Kateri held up her crucifix in both hands, inviting him to touch it, and when he touched her hands, the energy filled him completely and he looked down into her eyes. Her eyes were struggling to focus. She was in another place, and up from the depth of feeling which was beyond all understanding, she looked at him. Her look was welcoming, beckoning even, as if to say, "Approach! Approach!" So he knelt, overwhelmed and he hung his head.

"Oh, Father," she murmured, "I love Jesus so!" Her eyes rolled back and she closed them and swallowed. "Jesus loves us all," she whispered, "and in Him and only in Him can we love each other." She slowly opened her eyes and reached up and touched the priest on the back of the hand. "Release all your doubts, Father," she said as if she could hear his thoughts, and she smiled so beautifully that he began to sob. "Surrender," she whispered, "surrender."

Tears flowed down his face and his heart was bursting for he saw that all the weakness, all the illness and the injury was in him, not in her. She was healing him! She was opening his doubt, his humility, his self-abasement as if opening doors to greater awareness and she was shining her brilliant light into all the dark corners. She felt it too, how different was this man, how receptive. The other priests were closed off by their theology, their narrow thinking, their smug certainty about the order of the universe. Father Claude's yearning and doubt, what he considered his weakness, allowed him to be receptive, and her spiritual energy, sensing all those empty interstitial places in his heart and in his soul, flooded in and filled him up and nearly lifted him off the ground.

"You should rest," he said, and then the noise and the presence of others in the long house was upon him.

"Thank you, Father," she murmured, and she lapsed back into repose. He placed the sign of the cross upon her forehead.

All the rest of that day as he went about his work he wondered if he hadn't dreamed or perhaps manufactured this epiphany, yet each time he revisited those moments he felt the great flood of light and love from deep within her. Clearly she held the healing powers that his sick heart needed. Before sleeping that night, he knelt in his small cell and he prayed for a revelation about her holy presence in the mission and in his life. As he prayed, Father Claude found himself praying to the powerful light within her that he had seen and felt, and then he realized he was praying *to* her! His doubtful nature whispered the word "idolatry" in the face of such heavenly rapture, but he put aside those doubts for once, as he had on Christmas Eve so long ago, and he opened himself to the radiance.

The next morning and the next he returned to her cabin. Rather than abate or become depleted by familiarity, the holy energy grew in strength and brilliance even as her body wasted away.

Spring was slow in arriving. Frost steamed from the earth and birds were singing in the naked trees as ice groaned and cracked and squealed in the warming river. Father Claude murmured a prayer as he lifted the bearskin curtain and entered the dim, smoky cabin. A shaft of daylight penetrated the murk, then died as the flap fell closed. He coughed at the smoke from the low fire.

"Why, Father!" Anastasia rose from her seat, surprised. She was grinding corn for the day's meals. There was a stirring on a pallet to the other side of the fire.

"She is weaker today," Anastasia said, "and I keep her company."

The priest stepped around the fire pit and squatted down at the side of Kateri's pallet. She lay upon her back. Her long black hair was unbraided, fanned out upon the pillow. Slowly she turned her head and opened her eyes. In the dim light of the cabin she could open her eyes fully.

"Hello, Father," she whispered. Her lips were dry. Gently Anastasia lifted her head and held a dipper of water for her to sip. Kateri smiled faintly. "Thank you for visiting. I am not dressed to welcome you."

"You must strive to get back your strength." Gently he touched her cheek. "We need you among us."

"If it is God's will." She sighed and lay back upon the deerskin.

"We prayed for you in chapel this morning."

"I miss mass, too, Father, and communion. Communion most of all."

He took up her hand and squeezed it. "We shall nurse you back to strength."

"She hardly eats," Anastasia said.

"You must eat," the priest said.

"I try, Father, yet I do not hunger after bodily food."

The priest bowed his head and said nothing. He made the sign of the cross upon her forehead. "I will return at midday."

"Thank you, Father."

Father Chauchetière conferred briefly with Anastasia, and then he pulled aside the bearskin curtain and again daylight briefly illuminated the two women in the smoke.

"He was weeping," Anastasia said. "He is afraid of losing you."

"I'm so tired," she whispered.

"Sleep, little one." Anastasia went back to grinding her corn.

As he left the long house, Father Claude felt starkly once again the utter desperation he had felt on his crossing from France, at loose upon the open sea. As massive rolling waves churned and broke, lifting him up and plunging him down, the wind howling annihilation in its every gust, the possibility of losing this young woman blew a gale into his soul. He felt he was aloft now in the winds with those skinny sailors, high in the rigging and the crows' nests, feeling the full force of the wind that brought death. Not since attending at his father's deathbed had he felt the possibility of such a loss. Now he knew. She was leaving the world behind. The effulgence of her light would soon be extinguished. He had thrown himself into the arms of God as a boy when he lost his father, and his life, all the seeming wrong turns, had brought him to this moment. She was the opposite of his father. Lacking ambition or vanity or worldly aims, her passivity, her docility, surely her unyielding Mohawk will showed him his path. His faith had vacillated between certainty and doubt for decades and now he must throw himself into God's arms again, and he felt she would show him the way.

He had to do something. His duties included teaching the children, and when he went to the class that morning and they greeted him with such innocence and cheer, he knew what to do for Kateri. He taught the children their lessons, then he asked if they would visit her with him. They became excited and happy. Leading half a dozen children along the lane, he entered the long house and instantly the quiet, smoky place was filled with children's laughter. Anastasia propped Kateri up on her pallet and Father Claude arranged the children three on each side. He showed them his drawings from a picture book, drawings of the nativity scene, Jesus as a lad among the elders, John the Baptist baptizing Jesus in the River Jordan with the Holy Spirit hovering in the rays of the sun, Jesus healing the blind, raising Lazarus from the dead, the entry into Jerusalem, the Last Supper, the agony in the garden, the crucifixion, Jesus rising from the dead.

As he showed the pictures, the little boys and girls happily recited what each represented. Father Claude called them, "my little magpies," as they strove to win Kateri's favor, and when they finished they took her hands and recited at Father Claude's direction: "Get well, Kateri. Soon it will be spring and we can play outside."

"Thank you for coming to see me," she whispered. A smile flickered at her lips. "Listen to Father and learn your lessons well."

"We will!" they promised, and they were skipping from the cabin out into the clear, chilly sunlight.

"Thank you, Father," Kateri said. She looked up at him. "You are so very kind to me." In the dim light her eyes were fully opened, though unfocused, as if she were looking beyond him.

Tears pressed at his eyes again and he struggled to keep from sobbing.

"She's so tired," Anastasia said, and gently she helped the priest up and urged him on his way. He was slow to stand. One of the little girls stuck her face through the crack of light in the doorway.

"Are you coming, Father?"

"I am." He was weeping now, peering down upon Kateri's small wasted form recumbent on the skins in the smoky cabin. "Do not leave us, Kateri," he said and he began to sob once more. "These . . . these little ones have so much to learn . . . from you." He fought back his emotion before it broke.

"We must do what is willed," she whispered. Her eyes fluttered and she nodded her head and folded her hands and sank in repose.

"Come, Father," Anastasia put her hand beneath the priest's elbow. "She sleeps." He hid his face in a handkerchief. The woman led him from her fire pit to the door and then out into the sunlight. The sun upon the brown mud of the fields and the sparkling blue water with massive white cakes of ice floating startled him after the smoky confines of the sick chamber.

"Bring her back to us," Father Chauchetière said, pressing her hand in both of his. "Please, Anastasia, bring her back."

"I am praying, Father."

Kateri On Her Deathbed

JOSEPH KRYN, ON SNOWSHOES, carried the haunches of a caribou upon his back. Behind him, the twins, Peter and Paul, each carried a forequarter, and Martin, his son, proudly carried with his good hand the head, antlers up. The hunting was favorable this year, deer and elk plentiful, and now the caribou were migrating south for the sweet grass. In a blind Kryn waited while the boys chased a large male into a defile and he killed it with his spear and field-dressed the carcass with his hatchet and knife. In former days, he cut the heart, still warm and pulsing, and held it to the sun god before cutting it into strips and feeding it to his fellow hunters. Today he offered the heart to his Lord who watched over him and sent plentiful game so he might provide for his family.

Out of the forest they came to the hunting camp by the river. Facing south and east, the camp saw sunlight all day and was sheltered from the stiff west wind and the blizzards that pounded the western side of the mountain. A long, blue panorama of the lowlands and rivers opened before him.

"Again you return with meat!" Karitha said. She was outside scraping an elk hide stretched upon a frame. "God be praised!"

Joseph Kryn deposited the haunches on the snow and went to his wife. His shoulders and arms bulged from the recent exercise. He embraced her, brushed his nose against her cheek with affection.

"Good wife," he said. "The time of the sun now exceeds the time darkness. We should break camp and return to the mission."

"The hunting is good and we have ease here," she protested. "The skins we have cured will bring us cloth and the knives-that-meet and hatchets and saws for cutting wood to build Father's new church. The earth will not be ready for grubbing and planting until the moon grows full once more. There is no hurry."

"There is, though," Joseph nodded solemnly.

"Tell me, husband."

"I have held brave warriors as they died. I have sat by the pallets of the sick as the death rattle sounds in their throats. I have returned from the hunt and military campaigns to find loved ones gone, and in sorrow I have lamented not being with them at the last moment."

"What has this to do with returning?"

"Kateri."

Karitha narrowed her eyes. "You believe Kateri has died?"

"She was so weak when we left. She was in my thoughts today."

Karitha scowled. "You always think of her."

"I sensed she was with me at the moment when I slew the caribou. She told me she is being called, but wanted to give to us one last benediction before she leaves."

"What was she wearing?" Karitha asked.

"You trifle with me. What does that matter?"

"I wish to judge if it was truly Kateri."

"She wore moccasins and leggings and a white tunic. She wore her blue shawl like a veil pulled down over her face."

"Did you see her eyes?"

"What is the meaning of your questions, wife? Do you doubt me?"

"It is comfortable and easy here," Karitha said. "Look how the sun shines all day upon us and how we have been blessed with good hunting. The journey will be difficult now when ice is in the river and the rocks so slippery on the portage trails. If we capsize in the rapids we can't climb out and we will perish. Let the Sugar Moon die and the Fishing Moon rise before we leave and our journey will be far less perilous."

"Kateri has called me and we must go," Joseph Kryn said.

"We gave up the dream feast when we embraced the Prayer," Karitha pointed to the cross upon the door to the hut of bark and skins.

"We will leave in two days," Kryn said. "This caribou will provide the meat for our journey. Tomorrow you may dress the skin and ready the packs for departure."

"As you say." Karitha turned away. Kryn, though, moved toward her and turned her toward him.

"Please understand, wife. Kateri wishes to bless us before she leaves. This was her message to me. Let us go down to the valley and receive her graces."

"But what if she is gone by the time we arrive?"

"Have faith, wife. Faith brought you our son and faith brought us back together and faith will bring you peace and understanding. I wish to bid adieu to Kateri."

"As you say."

The following day, Karitha dressed the caribou hide, scraping off the fat, and she collected the bundles of fur from the winter's kill and stowed them in the canoes. They packed their cooking utensils, the knives, the spoons, the kettle, and on the morning of the second day, a dark, lowering day that threatened snow, they struck camp and set off.

Joseph Kryn manned the lead canoe, his bulging shoulders and arms skilled in navigating the white water. His nephew Peter steered the second canoe, following him closely. The current was high and strong with meltwater. Ice floes rattled along with them through the churning water and tumbled down the rapids they shot. A blizzard blinded them the second day, forced them to camp until it spent its fury, and then on they went, the water drawing them down beneath the solemn gray sky and the dull white of the snow.

Late on the fourth day they reached the broad St. Lawrence. So swollen with ice was the river that Kryn decided to camp rather than chance the remaining hours paddling in the dark. As the sun rose over the river on the fifth day, a warm blue sky greeted them and a gentle wind bristled the water where ice in fantastic shapes moved swiftly along.

Joseph Kryn walked out upon the flat beach where they had camped and he spread his arms and sang to awaken the young ones.

"Up rise the birds from their perch in the trees
Up burns the sun in the crimson sky
Up stands my spirit to walk in the world
Get up, take my hand, and walk bravely with me."

The boys came running from the tent and they joined him at the river. He lifted his son Martin to the rising sun, and the twins danced and sang. Karitha awakened the fire and grilled loin cuts of the caribou. They ate and then struck camp and soon were on the river among the ice floes that gulls and pigeons rode complaining and squawking.

Ahead, the island of Montreal hove into view. The rapids at La Chine forced them to shore to disembark and portage, and finally they were on the river near the mission to the southeast, the gray stockade, the small cabins with smoke curling and in their midst a chapel and its cross and simple belfry.

Joseph Kryn and Peter steered their canoes to shore. Ten or twelve canoes were inverted on the beach but the lanes of the mission were deserted.

"We returned too soon," Karitha said. "We are the first ones back."

"Let us hope we are not too late," Kryn said. He climbed from his canoe into the water and hauled the canoe up on the bank. He spread his arms in thanksgiving for a safe transport. He left the twins and Karitha and the girls to unpack and with Martin he climbed up the bank and crossed the flood plain. Anastasia was hastening from the chapel toward her cabin.

"Anastasia!" he called. "Have all the souls followed the priest to heaven?"

"You would do well not to joke, Joseph Kryn!" She turned abruptly and hurried on.

"Wait! Why do you hurry so?"

She stopped and turned. Tears were flowing down the lines of her weathered face. "We are losing her! Kateri!"

Kryn and Martin joined Anastasia and they hastened to the cabin. A line of the parishioners led up to the doorway, waiting to go inside.

"Father brought the sacrament to her," Anastasia explained. "She was too weak to attend mass, and everyone marvels that he would do this, bring the Holy Eucharist out of the tabernacle, out of the chapel and into a cabin. She is so weak, he sent me for the holy chrism to anoint her."

They wended through the crowd and into the dim cabin. The poles and beams of the ceiling were depleted of dried corn. The fire had been built up and cast a flickering light upon six or seven forms that surrounded Kateri's pallet as many more stood in the shadows looking on. Muffled sobs filled the cabin. The priest, Father Chauchetière, was kneeling at the head of her pallet, speaking with her in mumbled tones and about to give her communion.

"Wait!" she whispered hoarsely, raising her hand in the air. "I sense . . . Father, I sense Joseph Kryn has arrived."

Chauchetière turned from the pallet and saw Kryn's large buck-skinned form approaching in the firelight.

"Hello, Father!"

"She has been asking for you all morning," the priest said. His face was contorted with grief and tears flowed freely down his cheeks. He was holding a host between his right thumb and forefinger.

"Come nearer," Kateri whispered. She was dressed in a white chemise Marie-Thérèse had lent her. "It is good you have come, Joseph Kryn, for I am about to leave you now."

Anastasia wailed as she said this and many of the women sent up the cries customary for the death of a child. The priest quieted them. "Please, please, she wishes to speak to us. Listen to her."

She lay silently for a long moment, her lustrous eyes roaming about, looking at the smoke hole in the ceiling where the smoke was curling into the open air.

"I must go, my dear friends, Jesus is calling me . . ." Kateri closed her eyes and exhaled as if she were viewing a magnificent sunrise. She opened her eyes, surprised to find herself still in the dim cabin lit by flickering firelight. She reached for Kryn's hand.

"Good Joseph Kryn."

He knelt by the pallet and held her hand. This strengthened her. Faintly she smiled.

"Do not be sad, you whom I love." She turned to the priest and nodded. Her eyes were unfocused. She opened her mouth, extended her tongue to receive the host. Father Chauchetière trembled as he placed the host upon her tongue. She closed her eyes, took the host, savored it and then slowly swallowed. Opening her eyes once more, a look of deep contentment passed over her features. She shuddered and held out her other hand to the priest.

"Protect our people," she whispered.

The sobbing grew louder.

"Please stop weeping," she whispered. "Where is Marie-Thérèse?"

"Here, my sister."

"I know what you did today to purchase me an easier passage. Cease in that custom, sister. Promise me you will."

Marie-Thérèse was weeping inconsolably. "I will. As you say."

Kateri tried to lift her head off the pillow. Her eyes were unfocused as she looked about. "Do not be sad, people I love. I go now to a place of glory. I will be present at the death of each of you, and I will pray to God the Father and to Jesus and Mary on your behalf. I will be with you always."

The priest bowed, anointed her head with chrism. She gasped and let her head rest back upon the pillow.

"If only you could see all that is here," she murmured. "Take comfort. At the moment of your death, you too will see why you have lived."

The priest was weeping openly. This unnerved the villagers who had not seen such emotion from a blackrobe before. Joseph Kryn placed a hand upon the priest's shoulder. "Do not grieve, Father."

"I will be with you always," Kateri whispered hoarsely, "but I must go now."

She fell back upon the robe and gasped with exhaustion.

"Oh, my friends, pray always to Jesus and to Mary . . . to Jesus and . . . to Mary . . ." A deep sigh broke from her lips and she shivered imperceptibly, "Jesus and Mary," she whispered and she closed her eyes and breathed her last.

"She is gone!" Father Chauchetière cried. "Gone!" He dropped her hand and looked away, "Gone," he said, his fist at his lips. Anastasia and Marie Thérèse began again to wail. The priest wrung his hands, then held them up in prayer and he looked up to where the smoke from the fire curled along the ceiling poles and passed out into the light of the afternoon.

It was then a baritone lifted their hearts as Joseph Kryn intoned the *Te Deum*. One by one the natives took each other's hands and they swayed back and forth singing. The priest, too, who had taught them the hymn, stood and he held their hands and he sang over the sunken, ravished flesh of the young Mohawk maid. The voices of the assembled floated out upon the fresh spring air, out over the untilled fields, over the cross atop the chapel belfry and farther out over the sweep of the broad blue river.

A quarter of an hour passed. The villagers had threaded out into the sun, leaving him alone in his vigil. Father Chauchetière knelt by Kateri's pallet murmuring prayers. He looked up from his prayers and shook his head as if to awaken from a dream. His mouth fell open and his eyes opened wide. He bent closely over Kateri's reclining form, then he stood and he turned and ran out into the lanes of the village.

"Anastasia! Joseph Kryn! Marie Thérèse! Come everyone! Come back!"

The villagers heard him and they hurried to him in the lane. "She is with us! Kateri! You must see!" He held wide the bearskin curtain and led them back into the death chamber.

"What does it mean, Father?"

"It is a sign."

"She is so beautiful!" Marie Thérèse said.

"Never have I seen anything like this," Anastasia said. Joseph Kryn simply folded his brawny arms and looked down.

In the dim firelight, with an unearthly radiance, the face of the dear departed girl glowed with a heavenly light. Gone were all the scars and pockmarks that had marred her complexion. Smooth was her skin now, and her features lit with a heavenly glow.

"She is entering heaven!" Anastasia whispered.

"Praise be to God," Marie Thérèse said.

The curious eyes of other villagers peered over their shoulders to see the miracle. Father Chauchetière was on his knees praying before the small, starved, reclining form of the Mohawk maid that lay transfigured with celestial light.

The following morning two French *habitants* arrived at the mission for Holy Thursday services. By then Marie Thérèse and Anastasia had oiled and braided Kateri's hair, placed new moccasins on her feet and tenderly laid her out in the borrowed white chemise upon a robe of elk skin.

"Who is this beautiful girl who sleeps so peacefully?" one asked Father Chauchetière who entered behind them.

"The fairest of our mission," the priest said. "Today will be her funeral."

"She is dead?" they asked in astonishment, and they knelt and prayed at her side. After their prayers they asked if they might fashion a coffin for her remains in order to bury her in the European manner. Father Chauchetière gave them lumber and set them to work. He walked down to the riverbank in the bright spring morning.

"Hello, Father!" Joseph Kryn called. Father Chauchetière looked up and nodded. Though he walked in the bright spring sun, his thoughts were overcast. Skillfully Kryn was repairing his canoe with greased cord, elm bark and pine pitch. "After the Easter celebration I will take our skins from our winter hunt to trade at Trois-Rivières."

"That is as it should be. Life goes on."

"You seem troubled, Father."

"She is gone," the priest looked at the ground. "We had a saint among us . . ."

"She is with us still!" Kryn cried. "We carry her in our hearts." He beat his massive fist upon his breast.

"Yes, we do. So simple. So perfect. So free from every vanity. She returned to God as pure as he created her. Yes, Joseph, we do carry her in our hearts."

"Be of good cheer, Father. We helped her in her quest. I among our people and you in the paths of the faith. That was our purpose in her life, and her purpose in ours was to show us . . . perfection."

He slapped the priest on the shoulder. "We all have purposes in each other's lives. That is how you have instructed us. And then, when it is time, that purpose comes to an end."

"But I miss her," the priest said and turned away.

Kryn seized the priest in a strong embrace and lifted him so they were face to face. "I knew Kateri from the time of her birth. She urges us now to follow her where she has gone, to seek a perfect love, Father, selfless, eternal, all-powerful. Her memory unites us and we must go forward with this knowledge." He dropped the priest.

"Good Joseph Kryn."

"Sunday we will celebrate Easter, our risen Lord. Christ conquered death, and we have too."

"It is as you say, Joseph." He looked at the big man. "Thank you."

"Thank you, Father, for teaching us."

The priest passed along the river and heard Joseph Kryn singing at his work.

At sunset Father Claude Chauchetière in a purple stole and white surplice led a procession—natives from many tribes and nations, two acolytes, half a dozen French *habitants*, and Father Cholenec swinging the censer to sweeten the air with incense—through the village to the cemetery where Joseph Kryn and Peter and Paul had hewn a grave in the frozen ground.

They left open the cover of the coffin so all might see Kateri's face transfigured. When Joseph Kryn and the other pall bearers set down the coffin, Father Claude intoned the final prayers. With outstretched arms and a soaring voice, the priest commended Kateri's remains in the small wooden coffin to the earth, and as the farmers and the natives, refugees from many nations, bowed their heads, he closed the coffin lid. Some held hands and some were sobbing as Father Claude sprinkled the pine coffin with holy water and they lowered their beloved Kateri into the earth, and then, together, they all joined hands and sang.

on travaille aux champs

Springtime At The Mission Of St. Francis Xavier

Father Claude Chauchetiére's pen-and-ink drawing of spring shows a native
woman scraping soil into a hump in order to plant "the three sisters," maize
and squash and beans, and as birds fill the sky another woman climbs a tree to
gather eggs

Lightning Strikes

Father Claude Chauchetiére's drawing shows lightning striking the oak tree near the mission chapel in 1680. He credited Kateri Tekakwitha's protection for saving the chapel from destruction

Book III
Father Claude Chauchetière
(1680 - 1709)

She lived unknown, and few could know
When Lucy ceased to be;
But she is in her grave, and, oh,
The difference to me!

– William Wordsworth

Chapter 31

Light Of Kateri

The day after Kateri's burial, Father Chauchetière scribbled remembrances of her in his notebook. He had a vague notion of writing a biography. He was torn, though: the certainty that he had seen a saint walking the earth demanded he bear witness, but such an account would draw skepticism, even scorn. Who could imagine such piety among the Iroquois? It was a matter of faith, of course, and faith was a private concern. Better to say nothing, do nothing.

It was four in the morning on Easter Monday, the fifth day after her death, the quiet dark hour at which she would ordinarily enter the chapel and Father Claude was kneeling at prayer in his chamber. With folded hands he bowed over his *prie dieu* and murmured prayers to her. Suddenly a brightness flared up beyond his closed eyes as if someone had lit a torch. He opened his eyes, gasped and fell back upon his heels.

Hovering above him was his beloved Kateri, bathed in heavenly light. She held forth a kettle filled with maize. Her face was radiant, free of all blemish, and she was looking up to heaven in ecstasy. Her eyes, so dimmed and downcast in life, were open and bright and filled with joy.

"You return!" he whispered.

She said nothing. She lifted up the kettle of maize offering it to him and then in her circle of light two smaller visions appeared. In the first, at the right, the new mission church appeared overturned. In the second, at the left, a torture victim was being burned at the stake.

"These are prophesies?"

She said nothing. She continued to look upward toward heaven, her face unspeakably beautiful, her robes glorified in the purest white. Nothing distracted her from the rapture of looking heavenward.

Father Claude sat back in contemplation. He lingered upon her features, her long black braid and her deep brown eyes, her slender hands outstretched, her shining face of perfect innocence and purest love. He felt then a deep vibration—whether of light or of sound he could not say—calming him, comforting him, causing him to feel that this vision was eternal, never to fade. Light streamed from her as the light from the sunrise and a whispered voice said, "A vision even in daylight." Occasionally she looked down from her heavenly place. Once she looked directly into his eyes. Her look bespoke gratitude for his counsel while she had lived in the world, and as he felt her gratitude, he knew with uncharacteristic certainty and sublime joy that he had fulfilled the purpose of his life.

For two hours Kateri hovered in his cell, and then as the first rays of the sun blushed in the eastern sky and the birds in the trees began to sing, her image slowly dissolved. He was not saddened, though; rather, the vision filled him with joy and courage and a deep, quiet inner peace. He accepted her death and his life now without her since she had departed the physical world.

He told no one of the vision. Three days later, Anastasia sought him out.

"Father," she said excitedly, "Kateri came to me last night!"

Father Claude had never seen Anastasia so ecstatic.

"Everyone had gone to bed," Anastasia said, shivering with excitement. "I knelt praying by the fire until I was overcome with fatigue. I lay then upon my mat and hardly had I closed my eyes when I heard her say: 'Mother, arise.' It was her voice, no mistaking it! I wasn't afraid. I sat up and saw her, Father! She was like the sun, shooting out rays of holy light! And her face! Her face was clear and radiant, perfection itself. She looked at me with her eyes wide open, as if the pinched and darkened face she presented all those years had been a mask. It hid her true self that only now in death might be revealed. Up to the waist her body was pure light, and above, her face shone like the sun. She carried in her hand a cross and the cross was the most brilliant object I ever saw. From the cross came a light more intense and beautiful even than the sun.

"'Mother,' she said, 'look at this cross. How beautiful it is! This cross was my happiness during my life and now I live always within its light. I ask that you make it yours as well.' She held up the cross, Father. Light that came streaming from that cross slowly hid Kateri and the vision faded leaving me alone in my dark cabin." Anastasia looked inquisitively at the priest. "It was more real than anything I have ever seen! Are such things possible, Father?"

"Yes," he said quietly. "She has appeared to me as well."

"She is with us still!" Anastasia said, thrilled by his corroboration.

"And she always will be."

As the weeks and then months passed, Father Claude wrote more in his notebook. He tried to organize his thoughts and his memories. He did not tell Father Cholenec about the vision, nor when Father Frémin returned did he confide in him. Gone was any doubt that he'd been a witness to Kateri's mystical union with God. With his quill and paintbrush he might now reveal this saint to the world, yet he went about the task telling no one.

To obtain details of her life, Father Claude spoke to Anastasia and Joseph Kryn for they had known her since birth. He wrote about her life as an orphan in her uncle's home and her flight to the mission. He wrote what he observed of her at the mission. He found the work laborious and slow, yet it gave his life purpose and he enjoyed greatly making ink sketches of her portrait in the pages of his notebook.

Repeatedly Father Claude requested of Father Cholenec that Kateri's remains be exhumed and carried into the chapel. Father Cholenec declined this honor as, he felt, it would set a bad precedent with the other natives. Still Chauchetière advocated for her special recognition, praying for a sign from heaven that would convince the more skeptical priest.

The following winter a messenger summoned him to the home of a French farmer, Claude Caron, who could hardly breathe. A surgeon from Montreal told the family he would surely die, and that he should be given the last rites since no earthly medicine could save him. On the way to Caron's farm, Father Claude stopped at Kateri's grave, and he prayed:

"O Lord, confirm for me the holiness of your virgin handmaiden. In her name, cure this man of his affliction. A cure will prove my faith in her sanctity and will call others to pray to her as well."

Father Claude traveled to the Caron farm and found the forty-year-old *habitant* in his bed gasping for breath.

"I started here to anoint you," Father Claude told him, "and to hear your last confession, but instead I ask you to pray with me for the intercession of Kateri, the young Mohawk woman, who died in our mission last spring. She may heal you."

Caron nodded assent, and holding his hand, Father Claude lifted up his eyes and prayed: "Most beloved Kateri, this good man who is about to die asks for your intercession with the Lord. Help him recover and restore him to his family." He turned to the man, unshaven and unkempt. "Do you renounce your sins and invoke the intercession of Kateri Tekakwitha in order to be healed?"

The man nodded, his brown eyes lurching, his black hair and beard mussed. "I do."

Father Claude then made the sign of the cross in front of him. "May you be restored to health, then, by the intercession of Kateri Tekakwitha."

The anxious wife and two elder daughters stood by wringing their hands, biting their lips.

"Can you perform the last rites as well," the wife asked, "just in case the cure does not work?"

"We must have faith," Father Claude said, and he returned to the mission.

Shortly after he left, the wife and daughters sought to make Caron more comfortable. As they raised him from the bed, he collapsed and fell on the floor. Alarmed, they sent again for the priest and lifted him onto the bed. Caron lapsed into a deep sleep, and within the hour Father Claude was back. Caron awoke, sat up and looked about him in surprise.

"How do you feel?" Father Claude asked.

"As if a great stone has been lifted from my chest." Caron turned to his wife. "I am hungry, woman." She was flustered by this sudden development, and she busied herself fetching a bowl of stew and a piece of bread.

"May Kateri be praised!" one of the daughters exclaimed.

On his way back to the mission, Father Claude stopped at Kateri's grave to pray in thanksgiving.

News of Caron's cure spread. Others sought Kateri's favor. Things she had touched became relics, swatches of her clothes, dirt from her gravesite effected cures of pneumonia and rheumatism, gout and hearing loss. Soon the virgin's intercession was regularly sought by women in childbirth. René Cuillerier, a *habitant* whose wife had difficulty in delivering their first child, prayed to Kateri so that his wife might survive the ordeal. Together they promised to visit Kateri's grave and when the delivery was successful, they made a pilgrimage in thanksgiving.

When a stable door fell upon Margueritte Picart, thirty-three and pregnant, the infant was displaced in her womb. She prayed to Kateri, promising to have a mass said and make a novena, and she drank water into which earth from the grave and ashes from the clothing had been dipped. Two days later the babe returned to the upper portion of her womb and was delivered without a problem when at last she came to term.

As Marie-Magdeleine Fortin struggled in labor, no skill of a midwife could deliver her, and it was feared she would perish. A neighbor brought a bag of earth from the grave and ashes from Kateri's garment, dipped it in water and after the young mother drank the water and promised to make a pilgrimage to Kateri's grave, the babe was born without difficulty.

News of these cures was accepted in Lachine and among the French more readily than among the Iroquois at La Prairie. Originally a skeptic who considered Kateri a creation of the Jesuits to draw attention to their conversion effort, Father Pierre Rémy of the Sulpician order, at last prayed to her and was cured of an ear infection. Now convinced of her healing powers, he applied to the Jesuits of Kanawaka for a supply of earth from her grave and ashes from her clothing. With this he made a sort of tea bag to dip into water, and also an unguent to apply to the skin. When the ill came to him for relief, he gave them a tea made from the earth and ashes, or else applied the ointment. He counseled the sick to make a novena of nine *Ave Marias* each day for nine days, and bolstered by a mass he said, cures ensued.

Kateri appeared twice more to Father Claude, on September 1, 1681 and then on April 21, 1682. Instead of appearing as the sunrise, though, her light now streamed from above, much as the light of the noonday sun. She gave him a mandate: "Behold, and paint a favorable likeness." By now Father Claude had made several drawings of Kateri as he remembered her. He used these drawings to instruct the children. He longed to paint her on canvas with oil paint, but when the materials arrived from France in the fall he still hesitated from doubt as to his ability to capture her essence. He did, however, write about her in a long letter to his superior detailing events at the mission:

Iroquois mission of Sault St. François Xavier,
this 14th of October, 1682.

My Reverend Father,
Pax Christi.

In answer to Your Reverence's letter respecting what you have asked me, I will say that we are in a part of the country where the climate is not as good as in France, although, thanks be to God, I am in very good health. We are in a very high and beautiful location, with a fine view, 60 leagues Distant from Quebec,— which is called "the Iroquois mission." It is the finest mission in Canada, and, as regards piety and devotion, resembles one of the best churches in France.

The river St. Lawrence here forms a lake two leagues wide; and the place where we are is so high that the waters of this great river fall here with a loud roar, and roll over many cascades, which frighten one to look at. The water foams as you see it do under a mill-wheel. We nevertheless readily pass over it every day in our Bark Canoes; and I cannot help saying that one must be crazy to run the rapids as we do, without any fear of being drowned. . . . In truth, one must always be prepared for death in this country. You may Judge by this how much I need your prayers, for I am obliged to be continually on the water, going and coming alone in a canoe. . . .

Our village grows larger every year, while the Lorette mission, where Father Chaumont is, steadily diminishes. That of the mountain does not decrease, neither does it increase much; but ours grows continually. We think that in two or three years all the Agniez (Mohawks) will be in this place. More than eighty have settled here recently, We have a chapel 25 feet Wide, and nearly 60 feet Long. We have three bells, with which we produce a very agreeable Carillon; and the savages will soon have another bell, weighing two hundred livres, to complete the harmony.

The usual exercises of our mission are as follows: In the early morning, the bell is rung at 4 o'clock, which is the hour at which we rise, as in our houses in France. Many of our savages, through a spirit of devotion, come at once to the church, to adore the Blessed Sacrament; and they remain there until the first mass, which is said in winter at a quarter to 7, and in mid-Summer at 5 o'clock. While they are saying their prayers, I withdraw to my chamber, which is 6 feet Long and 5 feet wide, to say my orison; after this, I say the first mass, at which many are present although the bell is not rung for it. The 2nd, which is the mass for the savages, is said at half past 5. I am present at it; the whole village also attends it every day, without a single person being absent; and the prayers are said aloud. Afterward the 3rd mass, which is for the children, begins, at which also I am present. We make them pray all together, after which I give them a short instruction on the Catechism. Such is my daily occupation.

In addition to this, the savages come frequently during the day to visit the Blessed Sacrament, when they go to the fields and when they return from them. From eight o'clock until eleven, which is the hour for our repast, my occupation consists in visiting the savages, or in working to make books for them (because, as their nature is very fickle—of which They themselves complain—they must be often visited, either to give them suitable encouragement, or to prevent and appease their disputes, or to prepare the new-comers for receiving the sacraments). There are sixty Cabins—that is to say, from one hundred and twenty to 150 families, as there are at least two in each Cabin. To perform these visits with profit demands all the time of one missionary; another would be required for the children, and one for those who are more advanced, who need to be instructed in virtue.

My work is made easier in this way: I sketch upon paper the truths of the Gospel and the practices of virtue invented by Monsieur de Nobletz. Another Book contains colored pictures of the ceremonies of the mass applied to the passion of our Lord; another contains pictures showing the torments of hell; another the creation of the world. The savages read these with pleasure and profit, and these Books are their mute teachers. One of our catechists, with the assistance of these books, preaches long sermons; and I experienced much pleasure yesterday when I found a band of savages at the door of a cabin, learning to read in books of this kind.

To return to the manner in which our time is employed, and to our usual occupations: at eleven o'clock the bell rings for our examination of conscience, and, at the same time, the Angelus is rung, which the savages recite with great devotion. Our afternoon is spent in teaching in the cabins. For my part, I visit the sick who would keep one man occupied. I have also charge of a Curé, consisting of a hundred French houses. With regard to Father Bruyas—who is the superior of the entire mission, and with whom I remained alone here during the whole of last year—he attends to the temporal and spiritual wants of the savages, and he is a father to them for both their bodies and their souls.

You will be pleased to hear from me respecting the austerities practiced by certain savage women—although there may be some indiscretion in their doing so; but it will show you their fervor. More than 5 years ago some of them learned, I know not how, of the pious practices followed by the nuns in Montreal who are hospital sisters. They heard of disciplines, of iron girdles, and of hair shirts, this religious life began to please them very much, and three of them formed an association, in order to commence a sort of convent; but we stopped them, because we did not think that the time had yet come for this. However, even if they were not cloistered, they at least observed Chastity; and one of them died with the reputation of sanctity, 3 years ago next spring. They, and some others who imitated them, would be admired in France, if what they do were known there.

The first who began made her first attempt about Christmas in the year 1676, when she divested herself of her clothing, and exposed herself to the air at the foot of a large cross that stands beside our Cemetery. She did so at a time when the snow was falling, although she was pregnant; and the snow that fell upon her back caused her so much suffering that she nearly died from it—as well as her child, whom the cold chilled in its mother's womb. It was her own idea to do this—to do penance for her sins, she said. She has had four companions in her fervor, who have since imitated her. Two of them made a hole in the ice, in the depth of winter, and threw themselves into the water, where they remained during the time that it would take to say a Rosary slowly and sedately.

One of the two who feared that she would be found out, did not venture to warm herself when she returned to her cabin, but lay down on her mat with lumps of ice adhering to her shoulders. There have been several other inventions of similar mortifications, which men and women have discovered for the purpose of tormenting themselves, and which constitute their usual exercises of penance. But we have made them give up whatever was excessive.

During the past two years, their fervor has greatly increased since God has removed from this world one of these devout savage women who live like Nuns, and she died with the reputation of sanctity. We cease not to say masses to thank God for the graces that we believe we receive, every day, through her Intercession. Journeys are continually made to her tomb; and the savages, following her example, have become better Christians than they were. We daily see wonders worked through her Intercession. Her name was Kateri Tegaskouita. During her lifetime, she had made an agreement with a friend to make each other suffer, because she was too weak to do so by herself, owing to her continual illness. She had begged her companion to do her the charity of severely chastising her with blows from a whip. This they did for a year, without any one knowing it, and for that purpose they withdrew, every Sunday, into a cabin in the middle of the cemetery; and there, taking in their hands willow shoots, they mingled prayers with penance.

Finally, when one of the two saw that her companion had fallen sick at the end of the year, she was pressed by scruples to reveal the matter, and to ask whether she had not sinned in what she had done. At that time, people here used only willow shoots, or thorns, which here are very long; but since they have heard of disciplines, of iron girdles, and of similar instruments of penance, the use of this daily becomes more general. And, as the men have found that the women use them, they will not let themselves be outdone, and ask us to permit them to use these every day; but we will not do it. The women, to the number of 8 or 10, began the practice; and the wife of the dogique—that is to say, of him who leads the singing and says the prayers—is among the number. She it is who, in her husband's absence, also causes the prayers to be said aloud, and leads the singing; and in this capacity she assembles the devout women of whom we have spoken, who call themselves sisters. They tell one another their faults, and deliberate together upon what must be done for the relief of the poor in the village—whose number is so great that there are almost as many poor as there are savages.

The sort of monastery that they maintain here has its rules. They have promised God never to put on their gala-dress (for the savage women have some taste, and take pride in adorning themselves with porcelain beads; with vermilion, which they apply to their cheeks; and with earrings and bracelets). They assist one another in the fields; they meet together to incite one another to virtue; and one of them has been received as a nun in the hospital of Montreal. . . .

When they pray or sing in the church, they do so with so much devotion that all the French settlers here who see them are impressed by it, and say that they are more devout than we allege. I was forgetting to tell you that, when they are in the woods, they have the Sundays and feast-days marked by small lines to the number of seven, one for each Day of the week; we mark crosses. upon the lines that indicate the feast-days and the Sundays, and they observe these very exactly. . . .

If you wish me to tell you something about the manner in which the savages dress—although, had I time, I would have preferred painting some for you—you must know that it is not wanting in taste, especially on feast-days. The women have no other head-dress than their hair, which they part over the middle of the head, and then tie behind with a sort of ribbon, which they make out of eel-skin painted a bright red. I myself have often been deceived, and have taken it for a real ribbon. They grease their hair, which thereby becomes as black as jet.

As for the men, they are ridiculous in dressing their hair, and there is not one who does not do it up in a special fashion. On Sundays and feast-days, the men and women wear fine white chemises; and the women take wonderful care to clothe themselves so modestly that there is nothing indecorous or uncovered about them—for they closely fasten the chemise. This falls over a petticoat, consisting of a blue or red blanket, a brasse or more square, which they fold in two, and simply gird around the waist; and the chemise, which falls over this sort of petticoat, reaches only to the knees. The savages have often asked us if there were any vanity in their dress. They are not accustomed to wear these except in going to church, on communion and feast-days. On the other days they are poorly but modestly clad.

I would like to give you a more exact description of their consciences, of which you may have a fair idea from what I have said. But, besides the fact that it would take too long, and that I shall send something about it to one of my brothers, I would fear that it might perhaps be thought somewhat exaggerated.

The savage women sometimes propound to us doubts in spiritual matters as difficult as those that might be advanced by the most cultured persons in France. The knowledge of the cases of conscience often renders us good service here; without it we would be in danger of making many mistakes respecting proximate occasions, the baptism of adults, and marriages. In truth, the working of the Holy Ghost seems admirable in these minds, which have been trained amid the forests and the woods.

When I read them your letter one Sunday, as I preached to them, they wept while listening to me; and the dogique then spoke to them in a very pathetic manner. They often ask me whether any prayers are said for them in France, and I assure Them that there are. From time to time, they deplore the misfortunes of their birth; and, after they become Christians, they live like angels, fearing to fall into the evil ways from which faith and Christianity have withdrawn them.

Father Claude's letter noted elsewhere that the healing cult dedicated to Kateri was growing particularly among the poor white *habitants.*

The prophecy of the overturned church from Kateri's first visitation to Father Claude came to pass in August, 1683 when a terrible thunderstorm struck the mission. Winds lifted the chapel and hurled it sixty feet from its foundation. All three priests were inside. Father Frémin was in the chancel and Father Cholenec in the sacristy. Father Claude was pulling the bell rope to sound the alarm. The two priests in the church were lifted and thrown aside along with sections of the building, and Father Claude had the bell rope pulled from his hand. None of the priests was hurt. By this Father Claude had a compelling argument for convincing Father Cholenec to move Kateri's remains into the church. The following year, Father Cholenec finally agreed. In a ceremony as solemn as Kateri's funeral, all of the burgeoning village attending, they disinterred her bones from the earth and enshrined them in a sarcophagus in the rebuilt mission chapel. Now the devout of the mission and pilgrims from far and wide might kneel and unburden their hearts and pray for miracles from the holy virgin.

Chapter 32

⚜

Marquis Denonville

In the much larger spheres of imperial politics, King Louis XIV grew alarmed at the incursions of the English who employed the Iroquois, particularly the Mohawks, as their war club. The English were monopolizing the fur trade, and this undermined the economic basis of the colony of New France. As in the days of de Tracy, the Iroquois needed to be chastised. The king appointed as governor an old veteran, Marquis Denonville, a pious colonel of dragoons who was as much at home in a battlefield tent as he was at Versailles.

Denonville landed in Quebec in the summer of 1685 with five hundred soldiers, half of whom climbed the rock of Quebec only to collapse from illness in the halls, the church, the granary and even the hen-house of the Hôtel-Dieu. While the nuns nursed his men back to health, the new governor journeyed upriver to assess the land and the fortifications and how best to proceed to win his undeclared war with England.

In October, 1685, Father de Saint-Vallier, Bishop Laval's vicar-general, escorted the governor and his wife to the Mission of St. Francis Xavier at the Sault. The governor was dressed in a long coat and breeches of golden brocade. On his head he wore a massive leonine periwig. His wife wore a well-cut gown of golden damask

357

and her hair was primped and curled into a high coiffure in which jewels had been braided. They had come upriver on a barge with thirty soldiers to assist them in camping for the night and portaging around the rapids. As they visited the mission, Fathers Chauchetière and Cholenec escorted them to the tomb of Kateri Tekakwitha in the wooden chapel. Father Claude explained:

"This Mohawk maiden died a virgin in the odor of sanctity, and since her death she has effected many cures. Natives and French alike come to pray at her tomb, and she answers many of their prayers."

"Indeed," the bishop's prelate said, "we consider her the Genevieve of Canada, our patroness in the court of the Almighty."

"Intriguing," the governor noted, and he passed a scented handkerchief before his nose. "Not a century old and Canada has its own saint. Quick work, Father."

Father Claude bowed, but the irony stung.

"Father Chauchetière is writing her biography," Father Cholenec said.

The governor nodded with approval. "You must publish news of this savage girl to all of Christendom. I'm sure she can teach us much about humility." There was a merry twinkle in his eye as he said this and his wife was snickering.

Again Father Claude bowed but he wanted only to escape from the governor's presence.

Nine months later, on August 1, 1686, Denonville returned to the mission, but this time he called for full military honors. Montreal sent its garrison of blue-coats. Joseph Kryn called out his native warriors in their war paint and regalia. As the governor disembarked from his barge, the soldiers fired canon and muskets to welcome him. Still arrayed in his golden robes and great periwig, Denonville left little doubt who was in command.

The soldiers marched beside him to the chapel where he knelt and prayed before the Blessed Sacrament on display. After kissing the monstrance, the general arose from the *prie dieu* and turned to Father Claude.

"I wish to meet the savage they call the Great Mohawk."

"We call him by his Christian name, Joseph Kryn," Father Claude noted.

"He has a reputation," the governor said.

"It is well-deserved. He and his warriors are waiting for you in a long house they have fitted out for your pleasure."

Chauchetière led the governor and his men through the village where men and women and children gaped at the fine raiment of the governor. The priest held the bearskin robe for the big man to stoop and enter the dim cabin. Natives had decorated the long house with foliage and skins and embroidered blankets. Father Claude served as interpreter.

"This is Joseph Kryn, your excellency, the one known as the Great Mohawk."

Kryn bowed in fealty. He wore a ceremonial breastplate and eagle feathers in his hair, but his face was clear of any war paint.

"Much is spoke about your bravery," the governor said. Denonville noted with approval Kryn's height and massive shoulders and arms. "It is told to me that you lead an exemplary life here at the mission. May I conclude from your fidelity to the one true God that you have a like fidelity to the king and to France?"

Kryn bowed. "My men and I are at your service."

"Would you say the same if it involved a campaign against your relatives, the nations of Iroquois?"

"My people have been corrupted by the English. Their thinking is clouded by greed and rum that the traders supply. Under the French king I have found the greatest of all treasures. If my countrymen choose not to open their hearts, I must protect myself and my people of the mission, even by warfare if necessary."

"Could you raise a force if we asked you to?"

"I could raise two hundred warriors within a week."

"Let it be done then," Denonville said. "I shall return next summer and we shall have a campaign. In return for your service, I shall act as your protector."

"Who do we need to be protected from?" Kryn asked.

"The Seneca nation. It has threatened to attack the mission. The Seneca are traitors and you must beware of them. Keep your fort here in good condition. I will send you *perriers* (small mortars) that will help you hold your bastions against their attack and will repel this cruel enemy. Send out scouts. Keep me informed. I will count on your vigilance and I will regard you as the guardians and defenders of New France."

Joseph Kryn bowed to his feudal lord. Father Chauchetière now led the assembled to the chapel for benediction. The governor celebrated it upon his knees, praying for guidance on his campaign against the Seneca.

True to his word, Denonville sent the mortars upriver and Kryn installed them in the bastions of the fort. The marquis also sent a letter to the Jesuit brothers in Iroquois country, Fathers James and Jacques de Lamberville—Kateri's first confessor who was still among the Mohawks, and his brother, a missionary at Onondaga— that he wished to hold peace talks about the continued fur trade at Fort Frontenac, at the mouth of Lake Ontario. He asked the priests to carry his invitation to the Iroquois chiefs. The chiefs deliberated at the Onondaga council fire. They sent the younger priest, James, to Denonville announcing they would attend the council, and they pledged to bring Jacques de Lamberville with them, not saying expressly what he was, a hostage.

While pretending his objectives were peaceful, Denonville landed a large force at Montreal in early June. In flat boats he'd transported eight hundred regulars, nine hundred and thirty militiamen and a hundred Canadians up from Quebec. He collected another hundred from Lachine and Ville-Marie. His army left Montreal June 13, 1687.

Fulfilling his promise, Joseph Kryn raised a force of more than three hundred native warriors—Iroquois, Algonquin, Huron, Abenaki—and they camped on the river bank awaiting departure in their battle dress and war paint. All through the night of June 14, the natives danced their war dance and ate grilled meat. Denonville's men rooted out four spies from among the natives, and hanged them summarily.

On the morning of June 16, the great force in three hundred flat boats with bellied sails swept across Lake St. Louis, the natives in canoes to the front and the rear of Denonville's army. Around rapids and across other swellings of the river they proceeded. Joseph Kryn's men were invaluable helping the soldiers scrape their boats up the portages.

On June 19, the army captured two Cayuga chiefs and two warriors, along with their wives and sons who were on a fishing expedition. Rather than allow them to escape and warn the Senecas, Denonville took them as prisoners. On June 24, Denonville ordered Joseph Kryn's Christian warriors to capture a large group of Iroquois fishing near Otoniata Island, but when Kryn's men reached the island, the Iroquois had fled. This taking of kinsmen troubled the Christian Iroquois warriors. Denonville's lieutenants accused them of warning the Iroquois to flee. A hundred of the Christian natives, then, abandoned the expedition. Joseph Kryn, however, remained firm.

Upon reaching Fort Frontenac, Denonville ordered his men to stake all his Iroquois captives in the yard of the fort. He had their arms severely pinioned with leather thongs so that they could not even swat the mosquitos and flies that tormented them. Some of the Christian Iroquois placed fingers of the captives in the bowls of their pipes to torture them. As Joseph Kryn entered the gate of the fort and saw this, he dashed to the first warrior and thrashed him. He then tried to meet with Denonville to obtain release the innocent prisoners, but the governor's man replied that he was in a council of war.

The deserting Iroquois spread word that Denonville was not honest in his quest for peace. One of the prisoners leapt the wall and ran to sound the alarm, racing overland to Onondaga, and the chiefs—till then planning on attending the council—balked and refused to go north. The Iroquois, though, did not kill Father de Lamberville for inviting them into an ambush. Ancient Garacontie called the priest into the council fire and explained:

"We know you too well, blackrobe, to think you would betray us. We believe you have been deceived as well. We will not punish you for the crimes of others, but we cannot afford to let you remain among us because of this treachery. Many of the younger warriors, whose blood is still hot for vengeance, will want to burn you, so we bid you depart."

Father Jacques de Lamberville wasted no time in closing his chapel and soon joined Denonville and his brother, reporting that the Onondaga council had been warned and would not attend. The invitation for the peace parley was still abroad, though, and when the appointed day arrived, forty minor chiefs from the Cayuga and Seneca nations arrived for the promised feast. Denonville sprang his trap. His soldiers seized the Iroquois as they entered the gate, bound them and threw them into the fort's dungeon. Immediately he made ready a small fleet of flat boats, and the following morning, he had these chiefs and the other prisoners, men, women and children, shipped down to Quebec in chains to be transported across the sea to serve as slaves in the king's galley ships.

Meanwhile, the plains about Fort Frontenac bristled with tents and wigwams. Denonville had assembled two thousand men. On his first day in the fort, a canoe arrived with news that a large body of allies were at Niagara. This force from Illinois and Michillimackinac (Michigan) had intercepted two parties of English traders and now waited along the river below the great cataract for a signal from Denonville. They had a hundred and eighty *coureurs de bois* and four hundred natives to join to his force. Soon they saw a canoe flying across the water, summoning them to attack the Seneca and they moved to join the main force.

Hundreds of sails of Denonville's fleet billowed westward from the shore of Fort Frontenac, the flotilla of La Durantaye, Tonty and Duluth and the Ottawas of Michillimackinac moved across the face of the water from the northwest, and three thousand men soon bivouacked on the sand bar separating Irondequoit Bay from Lake Ontario.

Fortune smiled kindly upon the marquis at this time, but his excesses troubled the native warriors, particularly seizing innocent chiefs and deporting them. Kryn, no stranger to the harsh realities of war, accepted this brutality as necessary and remained loyal to the cause. As sunset and a soft summer night breathed cool darkness up from the lake, the natives of many tribes and nations— streaked with war paint, naked or nearly so, iron earrings hanging below the headdresses made from the horns of bison, elk and deer— danced in the ruddy light of fires, miming attacks with their antler headdresses as the spitting pine knots sent up showers of sparks. When Seneca scouts hallooed from the bushes to ask why they were dancing the war dance, a reply came from a dozen throats: "To attack you!" Home ran the scouts to warn their people.

On July 12, Denonville gave his order to march. Flags with the *fleur-d'lis* were unfurled. The marquis left four hundred men behind to guard the *bateaux* and canoes, and the others shouldered their packs and followed the broad trail the Seneca had worn from their villages eight leagues to the lake. They hiked three leagues that first day, nine miles, and they camped for the night. In the morning, heat pulsed out of the sky, and they had to wade waist-deep through a swamp.

La Durantaye, Tonty and Duluth, the officers from the northwest, led the advance force of *coureurs de bois*, frontiersmen in buckskin who ranged through the shady, swampy forests without rank or file. To the left was Kryn and his Christian natives from the missions of St. Francis and Ville-Marie, marching against their own countrymen, and on the right were the natives from the upper lakes. Behind this force of eight or nine hundred marched Denonville's main body, four battalions of regulars in light armor and a battalion of Canadians in homespun cloth and buckskin. Leaving his brocade and his great periwig behind, the marquis struggled through the humidity in a shirt that hung, soaked with sweat, from his large frame.

Scouts reported they had reached the clearings about the first village and only a few women were in the field. Believing they could surprise the village, the vanguard left the main body behind and pushed quickly forward through the forest into a swampy defile. Dense woods hemmed them in on the left and in front, and to the right was a foul marsh. Suddenly the air exploded with war whoops. Muskets fired from alder thickets where the Seneca lay in ambush. One of the first volleys hit Hot Powder, and seriously wounded the chaplain Father Enjarlan.

Naked Senecas in war paint sprang screaming from the brush and attacked with hatchets and swords. Joseph Kryn drew up his men behind the fallen chief and priest.

"Stand your ground!" Kryn commanded and his Christian natives met the attack of their fellow Iroquois with muskets, hatchets and knives.

Thinking this was the entire invading force, the Seneca then closed the trap, hoping to massacre it slogged in the mire. Soon, though, Denonville marched upon the ambush from behind with his larger force of sixteen hundred. The din of muskets and the war whoops of the natives on both sides echoed among the trees. Many of the white soldiers, accustomed to fight in battle lines drawn up on a broad plain, fell to the ground in panic. Kryn rallied his men and they cut with hatchets and war clubs through the Seneca line into the marsh and then turned and hacked the row of them down to meet Denonville's advancing bluecoats. When it was clear the French army was swarming out of their ambush, the Seneca fled into the woods. Denonville did not press on, but gave the order, in view of the heat, to camp for the night.

Next morning, his troops advanced through the marsh and emerged into a clearing. On a hill above rose the black remnants of a great town of palisades and bark long houses. The Seneca had put it to the torch. A few large receptacles of the last year's corn harvest remained unburned, and hogs roamed about, which Denonville's men caught and butchered and cooked and ate as they paused again for the night.

The following morning the vast army marched half a league to the next Seneca village. Since it had not been burned, they fired it, as well as the surrounding corn fields. In the succeeding days, the army burned three more villages, but not a single Seneca was found. The French soldiers, feasting on green corn and fresh pork, became sick and the natives began to desert in droves.

On July 24, Denonville marched back to the lake and sailed to a post in Irondequoit Bay and then to Niagara. He built a fort on the site of a ruin used by LaSalle nine years before, and he left a garrison of a hundred men under Chevalier de Troyes. With the rest of the army, then, he descended in triumph to Montreal. Counting up the effect of his western campaign, Denonville noted he had captured and stopped two flotillas of the English, and he had burned all the villages of the Seneca, proving to them that reprisals would meet their consorting with the English. The Seneca had fled eastward to the Cayuga where they obtained shelter and food until they might build back their villages in their own land.

In a rare opportunity to speak with the governor, Joseph Kryn responded to Denonville's self-satisfied rhetorical question:

"Do you think, Great Chief, the Seneca have been sufficiently chastised?"

"There's an old saying among my people, Onontio, that if you knock over a wasps' nest, you must crush the wasps or they will sting you."

"What is that supposed to mean?"

"You have left the wasps alive."

Chapter 33

✣

Once More, Peace Talks

FATHER CLAUDE CHAUCHETIÈRE had requested to serve as chaplain to the expedition, but Denonville selected instead a priest from Montreal, leaving Father Claude to tend to the souls of his mission. In his leisure he turned to his writing and his painting, and he was in his cabin, quill in hand when the shout went up that the expedition was returning. He walked to the riverbank in time to see the canoe of Joseph Kryn bravely shooting the rapids. Others followed. Kryn back-paddled and drew his canoe onto the bank where all the villagers were now greeting him like a conquering hero.

Taciturn by nature, the Great Mohawk rose out of his canoe, waded ashore and walked among the villagers, clasping their hands and embracing them warmly. When he came to Father Claude, he genuflected to receive a blessing. The priest made the sign of the cross over the warrior, and he rose again and held up his hands for silence.

"I must report to all that our great chief Hot Powder died heroically in a Seneca ambush."

The assembled groaned and bowed their heads and crossed themselves as Father Claude uttered a blessing.

"I witnessed his death. He was hit by a musket ball in the first volley. He dragged himself to our chaplain and calmly told him, 'Father, I am dying. God wills it so, and I praise Him with all my heart. I do not regret losing my life because Jesus Christ gave up his life for me.' And Hot Powder fell at the feet of the priest, and with names of Jesus and Mary on his lips, he breathed his last."

"Lord have mercy on his soul," Father Claude said.

The villagers were deeply affected by this report, and Joseph Kryn then drew a lesson from it. "War serves no one. We must work to end these disputes between ourselves and the English so that everyone in this land will live in peace and harmony."

Joseph Kryn went to Karitha and Martin and embraced them, and together they went home. After settling into his commodious new lodge, he walked down the lane to visit Father Chauchetière.

"I am greatly troubled, Father," he said when they were seated.

"Tell me, Joseph."

"When I pledged to lead a company of warriors from the mission, I understood that the governor would wage an honorable war. I am no stranger to campaigns and I have felled and scalped many an enemy before I embraced the faith. I know of the English infidels and how they use rum to destroy my people and cheat them of the furs, and I know the importance of the great Sun King to rule in this land in order to keep the missions thriving and the faith strong. Still, the governor showed no restraint.

"He captured innocent Iroquois who were fishing among the islands and he tormented them in the fort. By trickery he invited the chiefs convened at Onondaga to a feast. He communicated this ruse through Father de Lamberville, the brother of our dear friend who sent Kateri to us, and thereby exposed that good priest to torture and burning. When the chiefs declined to attend and others appeared for the parley, he threw them in chains and has transported them now across the sea, laughing that they will row the king's ships until they die. So blinded is he by his vanity, he does not see these cruelties will be revenged."

"Do you know when or how?"

"I no longer send or receive messages from the Mohawk villages, but I know my people. These are not the days of de Tracy. The Seneca will not allow this depredation to go unrevenged. I fear, since I drew a large force from the mission, that they may fall upon us here and obliterate our mission from the face of the earth."

The priest rose out of his chair and reached for the hand of Joseph Kryn. "Pray with me, Joseph. Let us pray to Kateri that she may help us achieve peace in this land."

They knelt together on the floor. Father Claude spread out his arms: "Beloved Kateri, we who knew you and loved you in life, now ask for your intercession with our Lord Jesus Christ and his mother the Holy Virgin Mary. Petition God the Father for us that he will cause all men to see the foolishness of war and sit down and negotiate a lasting peace. You loved this mission above all. Protect us in our vulnerable location on this riverbank, and allow the Mohawks and the other Iroquois nations to see at last the advantages flowing from peace and prayer."

"Amen," the Great Mohawk said, and as they stood he added, "but I believe we must do more than pray."

"What would you do?"

"Travel among my people, down to the river where I was born, and sit in council with them to urge them not to seek revenge."

"That would be noble, Great Chief, but you should seek permission from the governor for what you propose to do."

"Onontio does not understand my people and shows little desire to do so. I need no permission to act on behalf of the mission."

"And yet the governor calls you to Montreal," Father Claude held up a letter. "He asks that I bring you to him."

Across the river the next day Joseph Kryn, Father Claude and five other Christian natives paddled and they met with Marquis Denonville within the fort at Ville-Marie. A change had come over the great man. For thirty years he had fought in Europe and Asia and he displayed his vigor before his men. This campaign, however, with the difficulties of diplomacy among warring tribes and the insolence of English governor Thomas Dongan had slowed Denonville, aged him. He'd cast aside his great periwig permanently, and he dressed no longer in brocade, but in a white cotton blouse.

"Your service on the late campaign was exemplary, Chief," the governor began. "Your loyalty and skill have been tested like gold in the fire."

Kryn bowed, though Father Claude knew now the feelings were not mutual.

"I need to learn the temper of your people, the Mohawks, and also the people of our unfortunate Hot Powder, the Oneidas, and the Onondaga, too. I would like you to serve as an ambassador on our behalf."

Kryn bowed again.

"Go to your countrymen. Ask that they come to see us and seek a lasting peace. You may tell them that if they pledge to remain neutral, I will release two Onondaga and one Oneida captive."

Kryn accepted the task, and left immediately. Time was of the essence while opinions were still forming about Denonville's raid on the Senecas and how to respond. As he paddled down Lake Champlain, he met a party of sixty warriors encamped on the shore, heading north to attack.

"Who goes there?" Joseph Kryn called.

"Mohawks," answered Bluestocking, chief of the war party.

"Are there any Senecas with you?"

"No."

Kryn and his two ambassadors of peace paddled into the cove. "I am Joseph Kryn and I wish to parley."

"Come to shore."

Bluestocking welcomed him to the camp where they were

roasting a small deer on a spit over a fire of hissing coals. They traded greetings. Kryn was invited to eat with them and share their camp for the night. In the morning, Joseph Kryn acquainted Bluestocking with the governor's invitation. Bluestocking's companion, a hot-headed young man named Jannitie, asked why the Great Mohawk did not return to live in his former village.

"I am not interested in being caressed as a prisoner," Kryn replied. "I have embraced the Prayer and I will not return to the lands of the People of Flint so long as they drink the English rum. Perhaps someday, if a blackrobe were welcomed at Saratoga where the sacred waters flow, many of our people who have accepted the Prayer would settle there."

After the meeting, Joseph Kryn went among the sixty warriors, greeting old friends and relatives. He then gave a speech, exhorting them to abandon their raid upon Canada, hoping they would see, in the manner of the humble maiden Tekakwitha, whom many had known, that each man and woman should work for peace and forgiveness instead of vengeance. Joseph Kryn then sent his nephew and one of his friends as emissaries to the Mohawks, and to the Oneidas and the Onondagas, telling them to relate that Onontio was not angry with them, only with the Seneca. His mission accomplished, Kryn turned homeward. So powerful were his words that four of the party followed him to the mission in order to convert.

In gratitude for Kryn's great service to the French crown, Denonville gave him and his native soldiers clothes and food stores to compensate them for their time away from the fields and the hunt. "I cannot praise too highly the assistance we receive from the Great Mohawk," the governor-general wrote, "and from his warriors in the Iroquois village of Sault Saint Louis." The gifts, however, seemed to the natives guilt offerings in view of how dishonorably the campaign was conducted against their relatives.

With his many missteps, Denonville now sought to make peace. His reputation in this land hinged upon neutralizing the Iroquois. Scurvy and other diseases reduced the garrison at Fort Niagara from a hundred to twelve men so Denonville dismantled it. Shamed also by his precipitous act in abducting the chiefs, Denonville agreed to return the prisoners if any still lived. Thirteen survivors of the fifty-one seized only a year before were returned, and Denonville sent them back to their villages and families. Finally, his plaintive request for additional troops fell on deaf ears in Paris. Still smarting from Denonville's attack on the Seneca, an Iroquois chief aptly named Big Mouth raised an army twelve hundred strong and in October he presented himself to be escorted from Fort Frontenac down the St. Lawrence to Montreal. Justifiably worried with the army poised to attack, the French officers presented Big Mouth to the governor.

"We come to Onotoio as a free and independent people," Big Mouth began. "We are subjects of neither the French nor the English king. We wish to be friends to both. We hold our lands by a right descended from the Great Spirit and we have never been conquered in war. Just now I have at my beck and call twelve hundred warriors who could burn all the houses and barns of Canada, kill all your cattle and burn your grain as you have done to our Mohawks and our Senecas. Our people want to put this plan into motion but I alone have halted them from it. I have been deputized to offer peace and given four days within which to return. Give me a favorable answer, let us sign a neutrality agreement and a larger delegation from the confederacy will travel here to you and conclude a general peace."

With his back to the wall, Denonville accepted Big Mouth's offer. They set out the terms on a large parchment, and Big Mouth and his ambassadors drew pictographs of birds and beasts to serve as their signatures.

Indeed, Big Mouth returned to the council fire at Onondaga and the terms were accepted and a deputation named and sent north to Montreal to finalize the terms of peace, but they never arrived. On the way they were ambushed by a wily Huron called "the Rat."

From his quiet post at the mission Father Claude Chauchetière watched the war and diplomatic disasters with a sinking heart. Marquis Denonville, having begun with such a stirring campaign to bring all peoples under the reign of his glorious Sun King, had been caught in a web of tangled alliances, fueled by liquor and greed for the lucrative pelt trade. Back and forth, west and east, north and south, armies and envoys had proceeded on dire missions to defend and rescue and attack, but still the snow howled out of the sky and the great swollen breast of the river carried away canoes and sheds in the spring thaw. The only real treasure anyone had attained, incapable of being stolen or bartered, diminished or destroyed, was the innocence and saintliness of his Kateri. This quiet, docile little woman with a retiring way, a will of iron and a love of God that radiated from her like the sun, opened and lit for Claude Chauchetière the path to salvation.

Locally, he promoted her cause, urged priests and medical people to turn to her for cures and signs. As the war clouds rolled in and then rolled out, he kept her image deeply imbedded in his heart, a distillation of feminine purity, more sacred to him because of its origin among the rivers and forests of this wild continent. The turning point of his life, as he reviewed it in his self-reflection and on his retreats, was the day of her death, April 17, 1680. From that date he measured his new life free from grave doubts and comforted in faith that he might be saved. Though he still shied from publishing his sacred tract to the world, he continued to work upon it.

Chapter 34

The Massacre At Lachine

"The Rat" was aptly named. Like Atotarho, his head a mass of writhing snakes, the Rat was a master of intrigue. He possessed subtle political skills and a unique ability to lie. He also had the strength of will to seize an advantage out of a loss, to turn chief upon chief and reap a worthy destruction in the winds of change. The Rat was a Huron chief from Michillimackinac, the sworn enemy of all Iroquois who continually attacked and massacred his people. The French admired him, courted him and employed him, and he pledged that so long as they fought the Iroquois, he would fight with them. But now the French were making peace!

The Rat raised a raiding party of forty warriors during the summer of 1688 and he traveled down the rivers and lakes to attack the Iroquois. Stopping at Fort Frontenac, he heard that the deputies from Onondaga promised by Big Mouth would soon travel to Montreal to meet with the Onontio in a parley.

"That is well," he said with a nod, but instead of proceeding home to enjoy the fruits of this peace, he led his band to a camping place where he knew the Onondaga deputies would soon land. There he hid in ambush until, as expected, the Onondaga deputation came paddling across the lake. As they landed, the Rat ordered his men to fire, killing one of the chiefs, wounding the rest. The Rat took all of them prisoner except one who escaped with a broken arm.

"I am in the service of Onontio, the great Denonville," he lied to the shocked Iroquois chiefs. "You are my prisoners."

"But that is not possible," one of their number said. "We are journeying to Montreal as envoys of peace to sit in council with him."

The Rat exploded and gave a show of great rage and indignation: "Did Onontio not summon your brothers to a feast last summer only to cast them into chains and ship them to be slaves to his king?" The Rat trembled so with rage that he was soon dancing a war dance. "Why do you believe him? Why did I? Too often has he made me the instrument of his lies and his plots to attack my brothers. These French will never stop until they destroy our people and seize from us all of our land! No longer will I be an agent of his plots. I was told you were a raiding party and that I should kill you and not take any prisoners. I will disobey my orders, then, my brothers. I will not take prisoners, save one. Go! Even though there is war between us, you are free. Our common enemy, Onontio, enlisted me to violate every trust of our people, and so I send you home to rouse your five nations and take a just vengeance on the French."

The Rat kept one warrior as a hostage, ostensibly for his own safe passage, and returning to Michillimackinak he handed the hostage over to the French garrison there. The soldiers had heard nothing of the peace, and when the young Oneida warrior began to rail that he was a brother to the French on his way to finalize a peace treaty, the Rat commented, "How shamelessly he lies to save his miserable life!" The French soldiers marched the hostage before a firing squad and shot him. The Rat then sent for an old Iroquois, a prisoner for years among the Hurons.

"Look at how these French treat your people! I gave them a young Oneida warrior to hold as you have been held these long years among us, and they killed him. In response to this, you shall have your freedom. Go back to your people and tell them the cruelty of these French."

Meanwhile, the Iroquois with the broken arm who had escaped reached Fort Frontenac and told the garrison of the treachery of the Rat. The commander sent the Iroquois down river to Denonville who flattered him and pampered him and gave him gifts, then released him to return to Onondaga with an explanation and apologies.

"The perfidious Huron known as the Rat has interfered between us," the great Onontio insisted, "but neither the French nor the Iroquois should allow this meddler to undermine our solid peace."

On the surface the chiefs seemed satisfied with his explanation, yet as another year passed, the Iroquois decided it was time to teach the French a lesson.

On the stormy night of August 4-5, 1689, as hailstones pelted the seventy-seven small structures clustered along the rapids of La Chine, a vast and silent horde of Iroquois, fifteen hundred strong, landed upriver and crept quietly upon the village. They surrounding each and every house. Suddenly a war whoop sounded and the Iroquois unleashed the fury of hell upon the sleeping French families. The Iroquois burst through the doors and windows with their hatchets and they seized men, women and children out of their beds, tomahawking them in the skulls, slicing off scalps, collecting prisoners to be tortured and burned and eaten. In two hours the Iroquois killed twenty-four and hauled seventy prisoners away.

One of the villagers escaped and ran the three miles to the garrison of Fort Rémy. The captain of the garrison, Daniel d'Auger de Subercase, sent word immediately to Forts Rolland and La Présentation, and soon two hundred soldiers and a hundred civilians were in hot pursuit, seeking in a pitched battle to free the prisoners the Iroquois held.

Although Denonville and his force of seven hundred were

bivouacked in the fort of Ville-Marie only two leagues from the massacre, he declined to respond since, he reasoned, punishing the Iroquois would succeed only in rousing them to new furies. Not only did he remain with his seven hundred men safely behind the stockade, but he issued an order that Captain Subercase must cease and desist from following the Iroquois and return immediately to his garrison.

With seventy prisoners, the Iroquois paddled across Lake St. Louis, just above the rapids and the mission where Father Claude and Joseph Kryn were watching the black smoke from the burning settlement billow against the rainy sky. Immediately upon reaching the shore, the Iroquois planted poles in the ground and built huge fires and tortured and burned and ate many of the prisoners, holding the rest as hostages, and adopting three of the parentless children into their families. Some of the survivors, traded later in peace parleys, told how the Iroquois had forced parents to throw their own children into the fires.

As Denonville cowered behind the walls of Ville-Marie, the Iroquois massacred a small detachment that issued from Fort Rémy on its way to Fort Rolland and they roamed unmolested over the island of Montreal. They then took to their canoes and paddled back upriver, attacking the village of La Chesnaye on the way and slaughtering its forty-two inhabitants.

As the mission of St. Francis Xavier at Sault St. Louis lined the river bank to watch the smoke roll up against the swollen gray sky, Joseph Kryn spoke to Father Claude:

"Let us paddle over there and see if we can be of service. I will protect you since I know some of the warriors. You might be able to administer confession or the last rites to some of the injured."

"Good Joseph Kryn," the priest said. He went to the rectory for his stole and his holy chrism, and soon the two were paddling across the river while the villagers watched them.

They landed just below the rapids at La Chine and climbed up the boulder-strewn shore and onto the grassy plain. Nearby, the barns and houses were still smoldering. Cows and pigs had been hacked apart by war hatchets. As they entered the lanes of the village, corpses of farmers and their wives and children were strewn upon the ground, hanging in and out of windows, slumped from stakes in the village green where they had been tied and tortured, staring vacant-eyed at the sky. Skulls were crushed from the blows of tomahawks. A low acrid smoke hung over the village. Crows and dogs and vultures were feasting.

In one of the cabins Kryn located a young woman whose left arm and scalp had been hacked off. Her skin was still warm, but nothing registered in her vacant eyes. Father Claude knelt beside her, kissed his stole and put it around his neck and then anointed her forehead and lips with the chrism, saying the last rites in Latin. When he was finished, the priest closed her eyes with his thumb and his forefinger and pulled a blanket over her face.

"She is about Kateri's age when she entered heaven," Father Claude said, and he bowed and wept.

The two walked about the charred ruins, unconcerned about roving bands of Iroquois who even then were drunk on the settlers' brandy, torturing and burning their prisoners across the river. As they paddled back to the mission, Father Claude said: "Kateri protected our mission. That is why we were spared."

"Yes, I am sure."

"What other explanation can there be? Your reputation for attacking the Seneca is well-known, Great Chief. Your attempt to negotiate a lasting peace, your rejection of the old ways and your embracing the Prayer, all these make you and all our Christian natives ideal prey for their rampages. Yet so near at hand, they spared us. Imagine the lanes of our mission smoldering like La Chine, all our good people dead or dying."

"Kateri cared nothing for war," Joseph Kryn observed. "I find it a necessity in protecting one's nation and one's family, and so I will wage it."

"And yet, you didn't protect us this time, Joseph, she did. Far greater is the self-sacrifice and the love and the forgiveness that she exhibited than all the prowess with muskets and war hatchets. There will be no lasting peace until men follow her example and learn to live in harmony."

"There will be no lasting peace until the English are gone."

Father Claude mused upon their different interpretations of the same events, yet Kryn, always the man of action, tried to anticipate the next campaign.

Chapter 35

⚜

Death Of A Warrior

IMMEDIATELY AFTER his cowardly response to the massacre at Lachine, the great, vain, grandiose Marquis Denonville was recalled to France. Reports circulated that recall had nothing to do with his rash attack upon the Seneca, his brutal kidnaping of the fifty-one Iroquois or his bungling of peace negotiations, not to mention his cowardice during the attack on Lachine. The king then re-appointed the blustery old Count Frontenac to return to New France and establish a lasting peace with musket and sword.

Frontenac formed a bold plan of falling upon the British in New York and Albany and thereby seizing that colony, yet the lack of a navy and land troops substantially reduced his capacity. He outlined three campaigns, one into Maine, one into Massachusetts and one into New York, and he sent his first raiding party down through the lakes into New York in January, 1690. The army was ill-prepared, scantily provisioned and deployed upon a sneak attack of unknown destination. The body included native soldiers under Joseph Kryn. As the food supply ran low, Kryn demanded to know the strategic object of the attack in order to gauge whether they could reach it and also whether his men were being asked to attack their relatives still residing at Kanawaka..

"We are going to Albany," the French commander told him.

"Since when are the French so ambitious?" Kryn asked.

"We must regain the honor we have lost, and this requires a bold stroke."

"Bold? It is impossible."

Albany's garrison would put them to flight!

A thaw had melted the ice and they had to struggle through the muddy swamps. The men were hungry, cold and tired. When they approached the fork in the road, one leading to Albany, the other to Schenectady, they took the shorter route toward Schenectady to obtain food and shelter. They came upon a cabin where four native women offered them their fireside and a kettle of food. The men crammed into the little space to get warm, and while they were within, Joseph Kryn spoke:

"I urge you, my comrades in arms, to cleanse in blood all the wrongs done to us on behalf of the English who are the authors of all the warfare and bloodshed in this land. Let us fall upon this fort and leave no building standing and no inhabitant alive! May divine Providence guide and protect us!"

Cheers and battle lust met his exhortation. They departed from the cabin and, guided by the women, they crossed the river against a dark, howling wind. In a heavy blizzard they assembled at the east and west gates, left carelessly ajar, and then they stealthily entered the stockade and surrounded each dwelling. At a signal, the French and Joseph Kryn's men screamed and smashed doors and windows with their tomahawks and war clubs. They knifed and shot and tomahawked the unsuspecting civilians as they rose from their beds.

For two hours the massacre proceeded. Thirty-eight men and boys were killed, ten women and twelve children died, and nearly ninety prisoners were taken. After the violence abated, Joseph Kryn stationed lookouts in all of the lanes. He located rum in two taverns, and he stove in the barrels so the men could not drink it. Thirty

Mohawks who had been visiting Schenectady were allowed to return home. Frontenac wanted to assure the Iroquois he harbored no ill-will toward them. He was only punishing the English.

The French army set fire to all the buildings and the stockade, and captured forty horses. They departed with twenty-seven men and boys, leaving about sixty old men, women and children behind. Back through the north country they fled. Swelled by victory, the army traveled more slowly and when they required meat they killed and roasted a horse. They returned to Montreal, having lost only nineteen men.

Frontenac again called Joseph Kryn and his Christian natives into service against the English in May. Reports came to him that the English were ranging in the territory around the Salmon River, stirring up the Mohicans. Leaving the mission by canoe, they paddled to Sorel and on May 18 they marched though the swamps. On the fifth day of the expedition, Joseph Kryn's scouts heard gunshots. They came upon two temporary huts with fourteen Iroquois inside who, upon questioning, revealed that the English had roused the Mohicans to attack New France, and a body of seven hundred was only a day and a half away.

Badly outnumbered, Kryn thought it would be prudent to retreat to Montreal. He paused with his men to build new canoes on the shores of Lake Champlain and the Salmon River, and that night, as they slept, a band of Algonquins from Trois-Rivières, loyal French allies, mistook them for non-Christian Iroquois. The Algonquins surrounded the camp and before dawn, charged the sleeping Christian Iroquois. Joseph Kryn, the first to rise to defend his men, was also the first to fall. So long invincible to his enemies, Joseph Kryn was killed by friendly fire.

News of Kryn's death deeply disturbed Father Claude who held a funeral service at the mission chapel and delivered a eulogy about his courage, his loyalty, his unswerving faith.

"We have lost our protector, a giant among his own people, among all peoples of the earth. He fell defending our king and defending his faith and now Joseph Kryn is happy for he is in heaven with our beloved Kateri."

Sobbing filled the chapel. Father Claude struggled to maintain his composure as he turned back to the mass, and held the host high above them, "*Hoc est enim corpus meam.*"

Chapter 36

❧

Retirement At Ville-Marie

THE LOSS OF JOSEPH KRYN was incalculable to Father Claude. Since his happy years at the mission he'd witnessed the departure of saintly Kateri, and now, a decade later, the noble Kryn. They died as they had lived, she at peace in the odor of sanctity, and he by force of arms. What end did this portend for him?

Still Father Claude worked upon Kateri's biography and, with oils and canvas, he painted her full-length portrait. From the stark and lonely pinnacle of his faith he now looked down upon the affairs of men and their states—the rise to power, the greed that impelled them, the constant violence to protect advantages gained, or acquire more, and then the inevitable fall—and he accepted now the inevitability of war. Didn't Michael the Archangel's constant battle with the forces of darkness prove evil will never be vanquished? Loyola was a soldier, of course, before he gave his life to Jesus Christ and his followers, too, waged war against the evil one. Wars were like storm clouds passing, they swelled into dark, monstrous shapes and shook the world with their thunder and lightning, and then they dissipated into vapor.

Yet it tired him now as he aged, all this deep-thinking. Worldly pursuits, the hunger for power, the storing up of riches for moth and rust to eat seemed so base and trivial and nonsensical. He counted a single memory, the vision of a dying maiden, transfigured and radiant upon her sleeping pallet, as the attainment of his life. She had been tested like gold in the fire and found worthy. He saw that seeking wisdom beyond this would be like trying to catch the wind.

Father Claude's health began to slip. In 1692 he suffered from severe headaches and also from St. Anthony's fire, a red skin eruption upon his face. He contracted dysentery at Montreal and scurvy while visiting Fort Frontenac. His eyes weakened, as he read and wrote and painted, but he refused to wear spectacles and so he squinted to see, which made him look annoyed and irritable. To his fellow priests and to the communicants he grew a bit fussy.

When his sixteen-year assignment as a missionary ended in 1692, he went into semi-retirement. He wrote his surviving brother from his new post, as a lecturer in mathematics and a parish priest on the island of Montreal:

To my Reverend Father, Father Jean Chauchetière,
of the society of Jesus, at Limoges.

Villemarie, this 7th of August, 1694.

My Reverend Father,
Pax Christi.

I have admirable things to tell of the Sault mission. As regards our Savages, they have continued this year as fervent as they are accustomed to be. Kateri's band (I wrote you her life last year. I know not whether you have received it because one of our ships was lost while returning to France, and those papers were perhaps on it, and you do not speak of it. I had placed her portrait therein.) continue in the practice of the most Christian virtues, and in the heroic exercises that they have undertaken. Last winter the most hardened were touched by God, and performed an act that deserves to be written down. It was called hotouongannandi, that is to say, "public penance," because it was done in the name of all. The men, gathered together according to the savage custom—that is, at a feast—expressed their detestation of drunkenness, which mastered them.

This was done as follows: after agreeing together as to what they could do to give satisfaction to God, they came to the conclusion that each should speak for himself in full meeting; and that they who on account of illness, or for any other reason, were unable to do so, should have some one speak in their names. This was done to prepare for the festival of Christmas. Each spoke as the spirit of penance moved him; and some did so more eloquently by the tears that flowed in abundance from their eyes, than by their voices broken by sobs.

Words were followed by results; the women, whose demons were gaming, vanity, and voluptuousness, completely abandoned the first of these; for a year, we have heard no more about it. Confraternities are being founded among them, and especially among the young girls, with the object of mutually assisting one another to live as Christians, and to prepare themselves for the most heroic actions. . . .

We see in these savages the fine remains of human nature which are entirely corrupted in civilized nations. Of all the 11 passions they experience two only; anger is the chief one, but they are not carried away to excess by it, even in war. Living in common, without disputes, content with little, guiltless of avarice, and assiduous at work, it is impossible to find a people more patient, more hospitable, more affable, more liberal, more moderate in their language. In fine, all our fathers and the French who have lived with the savages consider that life flows on more gently among them than with us. The faith, finding all these predispositions, makes astonishing progress with them. They wish that they had never seen any but the black gowns; and they repeat this to the confusion of our French Christians!

My occupation this year will be the same as during the last— namely, that of proto-regent of Villemarie, with 12 or 15 pupils; and I teach mathematics to some young men who are officers in the troops. On Sundays we have our confessions, which keep us busy; and on the first Sunday of the month it is most often I who preach. And although the gentlemen of St. Sulpice observe only certain outward relations with us, nevertheless on the principal feasts we go with them into the choir to hear the office, and chant vespers, and even in the processions. There is an agreement between them and us that we shall each say a mass for them, and they say one for us once a year—we on the feast of the presentation of the blessed Virgin, and they during the octave of St. Ignatius; and when any one dies on either side, we say the usual Prayers for the dead. Nevertheless, they are very hierarchical. . . .

You inform us of the misery that prevails in France; but it is otherwise in this country. Grain is common; cider is made, instead of wine; and trees are successfully raised, becoming continually more numerous. Last year we had excellent melons; but this country is very unreliable for plants that require heat. However, it is asserted that wine will be made this year; for close by is a vineyard belonging to the Gentlemen, which yields French grapes. What the country can produce is not yet known, because we try to grow only wheat and hay. The wild apple-trees, and those that are raised from seeds, bear very fine apples, and the branches are easily grafted. The peach-trees produce abundantly, but like the vine—that is, the fruit is all on the ground, because the tree has to be covered with straw or other protection until the month of April, lest it freeze. The pear-trees are more delicate; I saw one that blossomed twice last year—once in the spring, and once during the course of the summer.

This year we saw an apple tree loaded with large apples in June, which had one branch all in blossom. The cherry-trees bear hardly any fruit; they do nothing but blossom and shoot out branches and roots—in such numbers that a forest of trees grows up at their feet, but the people do not know how to keep them down. There are black plums resembling black damsons, which remain on the trees during the winter, and are excellent eating in the spring. I have eaten some at the foot of the tree, on Ascension Day, which had been borne in the previous year. The cold cooks them as does fire, and they become like those that have gone through the oven; the sun softens them. There are quinces that are fairly good, but the tree grows like the peach-tree, and has to be covered during winter. This year we have had a rare flower in our garden, a white lily . . .

Farewell, my dear Father and dear brother; I never cease to remember you at the altar and elsewhere.

Claude Chauchetière,

of the Society of Jesus.

Post Scriptum: I must preach, but I have no sermons.

* * *

He must preach, Father Claude wrote his brother, but he had no sermons. He had seen and done wondrous things, but he saw little use in drawing lessons to share with the faithful. His ambivalence triumphed once more. But maybe not. He had learned a truth that few ever will, yet in his wisdom he saw that men and women rarely listen and learn only from their experience, and so sermons were a waste of his time. He knew in his heart that he had glimpsed eternity. In Kateri's eyes he had seen shining the infinite love of God. Upon her deathbed he had witnessed the miracle of her transfiguration. How could mere words communicate that?

It was at last a matter of faith, Father Claude saw in his maturity. Those who believed accepted these things on faith; those who didn't

believe let doubt and skepticism rule. It was not his responsibility
anymore to convince. He did feel duty-bound to communicate the
marvels he had seen so others might make up their minds, and so
he called upon Kateri to guide him in his effort. She returned to
him, too, not in heavenly visions but in memories, as he composed
her biography in labored prose, as he painted her portrait as an
untutored folk artist. He felt again her sanctity, he reflected upon it,
and he believed it to be so profound and universal that if imitated
and carried forward person-to-person into the world, it would heal
all the violence and ignorance and superstitions. He prayed to her
nightly, and when he felt challenged in his faith—a feud with the
new bishop, for example, nearly got him interdicted—he simply
brought to mind her transfiguration and he was calmed. In this
spirit he completed in the same year, 1695, his oil painting of the
full-size portrait of Kateri Tekakwitha, and also her biography. In
his introduction, he apologized for having taken so long:

> *The pressing reason for keeping silent so long on this matter
> was the reluctance I observed in the mind of the French to believe
> in such great miracles, that perhaps I measured too much by myself
> who had such difficulty in believing the things I saw every day, or
> perhaps for having believed the French who doubt there is faith
> among the Savages. The main reason was certain difficulties that
> the Reverend Father superior of Quebec made for believing things
> when he saw them set forth in a little notebook I kept during 1680
> so I might give an exact account, and in order to discover what was
> of God and what could not be of God.*
>
> *The reason I had to speak was a powerful summons to speak
> out and no longer hold back in the shadows and silence a truth
> worth of being published all over the world, that God was first to
> put forth by ordinary signs that he uses to make known to the living
> the merit and glory of the dead, and not deprive the missionaries
> of the recompense that God has given for their labors in showing*

in extraordinary ways the virtue and faith of the Christian savages
who are so often attacked by slandering tongues.

The finished portrait was displayed in the chapel where it has hung now for three centuries. The biography was circulated to mixed reviews. Father Cholenec felt obliged to set some of Father Claude's observations in perspective, and so wrote his own biography of Kateri the following year. His work was less effusive and more direct. It focused less upon her humanity and pleasant attitude and influence over others in their praying than it did upon her chastity. Unavoidable, surely, is the tendency to record the world outside as it is felt by the heart and soul within, this account being no exception to that rule.

Kateri's influence was felt in wider and wider circles, from the humble mission, thence to Montreal and Quebec, and even to France, and as her circles widened, Father Claude's narrowed. Never gregarious, he became a recluse. He alone had escaped to tell the tale. He retired to the Jesuit rectory in Ville-Marie where the holy Jogues had lived and prayed, and in his meditation Father Claude often went back in memory to find Kateri at her prayers in the chapel, or in the long house working at her handicrafts, or ambling through the lanes of the village huddled in her shawl. He enjoyed these sojourns and they sent smiles flickering across his features as he napped in the afternoon sun. So retiring and shy was Kateri, so sweet yet so firm in her resolve, and so certain God possessed her completely, that Father Claude enthroned her as his spiritual treasure, the end of his long and painful quest. Let others think and feel and speak as they wished about her or about him. Again, it was a matter of faith.

One vision of Kateri, though, has never made it into the accounts, not Chauchetière's nor Cholenec's nor Rémy's, or any other letter or history extant in the musty archives in Montreal or

Paris, simply because there was no one to record it. This appearance occurred in Claude Chauchetière's humble chamber of hewn logs and thatched ceiling in the Jesuit rectory on April 17, 1709. By then he had been retired from the missions nearly two decades, and was lapsing into old age.

As he prepared to go to the chapel to commemorate the twenty-ninth anniversary of Kateri's death, he was startled to see, as he turned, Kateri standing in his doorway. She seemed unchanged, exactly as she had been thirty years before, not floating in rays of heavenly light nor looking up at the radiance of the Almighty, just a slight, frail presence standing apart, not looking at him. The familiarity of her being there brought a smile to his face. How had she come to be in his chamber? She was dressed simply, the shawl obscuring her face, the tunic and moccasins as he first saw her when Joseph Kryn introduced her on the river bank.

"Kateri?" Father Claude asked.

She lifted her veil and her face was as radiant as the day she died. From her eyes shone the heavenly light he had seen that day she lay upon her sickbed. She reached out her hand to him.

"Come with me, Father," she said softly.

"Where are we going?" he asked, reaching for her hand, nearly touching it.

"You answered that question many years ago."

Their fingers touched. Father Claude felt a surge of energy flood into his body, and he closed his eyes and surrendered to it.

"Come," she whispered, "the others are waiting. Can you hear them?"

Father Claude listened. Faintly he could hear a choir singing and thought he heard the voices of Joseph Kryn and Anastasia among the others.

"Have they returned too?" he asked, looking about his humble cell. "Where are they? In the chapel?"

"No," she said, and she smiled and inclined her head. Radiance shone more brightly from her eyes. "It is time for you to join us." She clasped his hand ever so gently, and looking deeply into his eyes, into his heart, into his very soul, she led him to the holy stream that flows into the river of light.

The End